Shadowborn

Alison Sinclair

A ROC BOOK

ROC
Published by New American Library, a division of
Penguin Group (USA) Inc., 375 Hudson Street,
New York, New York 10014, USA
Penguin Group (Canada), 90 Eglinton Avenue East, Suite 700, Toronto,
Ontario M4P 2Y3, Canada (a division of Pearson Penguin Canada Inc.)
Penguin Books Ltd., 80 Strand, London WC2R 0RL, England
Penguin Ireland, 25 St. Stephen's Green, Dublin 2,
Ireland (a division of Penguin Books Ltd.)
Penguin Group (Australia), 250 Camberwell Road, Camberwell, Victoria 3124,
Australia (a division of Pearson Australia Group Pty. Ltd.)
Penguin Books India Pvt. Ltd., 11 Community Centre, Panchsheel Park,
New Delhi - 110 017, India
Penguin Group (NZ), 67 Apollo Drive, Rosedale, Auckland 0632,
New Zealand (a division of Pearson New Zealand Ltd.)
Penguin Books (South Africa) (Pty.) Ltd., 24 Sturdee Avenue,
Rosebank, Johannesburg 2196, South Africa

Penguin Books Ltd., Registered Offices:
80 Strand, London WC2R 0RL, England

Published by Roc, an imprint of New American Library, a division of Penguin
Group (USA) Inc. Previously published in a Roc trade paperback edition.

First Roc Mass Market Printing, May 2012
10   9   8   7   6   5   4   3   2   1

PUBLISHER'S NOTE
This is a work of fiction. Names, characters, places, and incidents either are the
product of the author's imagination or are used fictitiously, and any resemblance
to actual persons, living or dead, business establishments, events, or locales is
entirely coincidental.
    The publisher does not have any control over and does not assume any
responsibility for author or third-party Web sites or their content.

of Alison Sinclair

"Brilliantly contrived and fascinating."
—Romance ...

Shadowborn

"Readers will relish the paths to the final battle . . . a delightful finish. . . . Fans will enjoy the latest entry in the Sinclair mythos." —Genre Go Round Reviews

"A stunning story . . . never-ending action and political intrigue will keep the reader interested until the last page."
—Fresh Fiction

Lightborn

"[An] engaging mix of chaos, angst, and manners . . . including genuine surprises." —*Locus*

"This story world is highly complex and certainly unique. . . . Readers should find the plot and players fascinating. . . . What will the imaginative Alison Sinclair come up with next?" —Romance Reviews Today

Darkborn

"Alison Sinclair's *Darkborn* plays like a sweeping historical novel in a teeming preindustrial city whose residents are divided into those who can only tolerate light and those who can only exist in darkness. A sprawling cast of characters argues and schemes and practices magic in secret— until a calamitous chain of events reveals the whole city to be under siege from a mysterious and ruthless enemy. Despite swift action, broad conspiracies, and monumental life-and-death stakes, the heart of the book is a delicately rendered love triangle that tracks the human cost of any grand adventure. I can't wait to read the next book about these complex and engaging characters."
—National bestselling author Sharon Shinn

continued . . .

Author's Note

Darkborn concluded with Telmaine, Balthasar, and Ishmael beginning separate journeys. *Lightborn* tells the story of Telmaine's return to Minhorne to face further Shadowborn intrigue and the consequences of her own and others' secrets. *Shadowborn* begins with Balthasar and Ishmael on their mission to the Borders to avert a Shadowborn invasion, and continues the story past the end of *Lightborn*, to its conclusion.

One

Ishmael

These riders are good, Ishmael di Studier thought, ruefully. Otherwise he would have heard them before they were almost on him, even on the pleated and twisting old post road. And then he would have been behind the wall on the far side of the field, well out of range of sonn, rather than crouched in a dip behind a boundary marker a mere twenty yards from the road, impersonating a rock. The riders—however many there were—were traveling with muffled hooves and carefully wrapped metalwork, on horses trained to be silent and easy in darkness. They had crept up on him. His inability to tell their numbers—six? eight?—was testament to their quality.

If they were friends, he knew how they would be riding: in two staggered lines, spacing precisely maintained, each one listening and casting sonn to his or her own side. It was an order and discipline he had developed with them. They might well be friends, since the ducal order to raise the Borders for possible invasion should have the entire Stranhorne troop turned out on alert for Shadowborn. Perhaps even with instructions to find him as well.

But they might also be enemies, search parties ordered out on the archduke's warrant for his arrest. Worst of all, they could be soldiers from Minhorne, sent to the Borders on that same warrant. Ish had no doubt that the warrant had included instructions that he was to be brought back unharmed; equally, he had no certainty that those instructions would be followed, not for a fugitive charged with a lady's murder and sorcery.

He sensed diffused sonn, scattered back from the tall grass and tares around him, and thought rocklike thoughts. Midnight damp seeped through his steadying knee and a painful cramp settled in his calf muscles. He dared not shift his weight. The riders would have hearing as acute as his own, and some of the veteran border troopers had intuition that seemed akin to magic. And if his profile broke that of the marker, a bowed spine did not echo like stone.

A horse stamped and blew, and despite himself, he twitched. He could have sworn that he made no sound, but a woman's voice carried clearly through the night. "Ishmael, is that you there?"

He knew the voice; a held breath went out of him in a sigh. "Yes," he said. "I'm here."

Gloved hand on the boundary marker, he pushed himself up. He had hiked and jogged upwards of thirty-five miles in the latter part of the previous night and the earlier part of this one, carrying a pack and weapons, and he was no longer twenty, as his knees were informing him. A little stiffly, he made his way back to the party on the road.

The woman on one of the two lead horses grinned triumphantly down at him. "I *thought* I caught a movement. You're slipping, Ishmael." She was not that much past twenty herself, a leggy young woman, long hair braided and wound around a broad brow, features too marked and mouth too wide and mobile for conventional beauty. She wore a practical jacket and a divided riding skirt, had a rifle slung over her shoulder, a revolver and a knife at her hip, and another knife in a boot sheath. Hers was hardly the typical attire of an heiress, even in the Borders, but she was a delight to sonn, nonetheless. He returned her grin with one of his own. "You're good, Lavender—you're all of you good— and y'well know it."

Smiles widened around him. He did not recognize any of the six men and one woman with her, but they'd all know him by reputation as Ishmael di Studier, Baron Strumheller, hunter of Shadowborn, and mage. For all he was no longer most of these things.

"Nicholas," Lavender di Gautier said, "give him your horse, and mount up with Thalia. The two of you will be easier on a horse than the baron and I." The youngest and lightest of the troop swung down and dutifully handed over the reins. Ishmael took a moment to free his rifle from his pack and strap his pack behind the trooper's provisions. The horse tried to sidle; he cuffed it, growling at it for taking him for a novice.

As he climbed into the saddle, she said over her shoulder, "You want we should head back, or finish the loop round the Pot?"

Back would be to Stranhorne Manor, her family seat, and his destination since he had jumped off the southbound coastal train just before Stranhorne Crosstracks. The Pot was a small, perfectly round lake at the bottom of a steep-sided pit, immediately recognizable on any relief model. Almost certainly it had been made by magic.

"Back," he said, though not without thought. But after spending yesterday in the open, in a day-blind pitched in shadows, he would feel much happier with stout walls around him.

"Come up by me."

His lips quirked with amusement at the confident command in her voice, even toward him. The others smoothly rearranged themselves as he eased his horse forward. They were good; neither the baron, her father, nor her twin sister would have allowed her out with anything else.

"Are you all right?" she said in a low voice.

"Aye," he said. "I am now."

"We heard"—there was a slight tremor in her voice, despite herself—"we heard you were dead."

"Came closer to't than I like, I'll admit," he said. He tried for an easy tone, but that near miss had probably cost him one of the most precious things he had. Two lives—especially those of Lady Telmaine and her daughter—should be a fair exchange for his lost magic, but if someone were to ask him outright, he could not honestly swear that he would not rather have died.

She would never ask him, but she knew him well enough to hear something of it in his voice. "I suppose," she said, "I'll have to wait until Stranhorne to hear all of it. I presume that is where you were bound."

"Aye."

"Well, you're safe now."

"That's more your promise than th'truth," he chided her. "For all it's welcome."

"This warrant for your arrest—"

Had her father told her both of the charges, or just the one? With the city broadsheets being delivered every night by train, she could not have remained ignorant for long. "False, both of them."

"I *know* they're false," she said with spirit. "I know *you*. Surely the archduke—surely Lord Vladimer—"

The less said about the archduke's attitude, the better. "Until Lady Tercelle's true murderer is produced, suspicion will remain on me. And as to th'other"—he weighed what to say, given that he was not supposed to talk about this at all with her—"it's for Lord Vladimer t'do the convincing of my innocence, since he was the one I supposedly ensorcelled. He's a wily man, and it no doubt suits his purposes to have me leading this chase."

She made a disgusted noise but expressed no further opinion. "Then what about this ducal order? All it tells us is that the ducal order of six twenty-nine was suspended, allowing us to mobilize troops beyond our allotment to guard the Borders against threats. Who are we supposed t'be guarding against? We've not seen claw nor hair of Shadowborn all this summer."

She showed her youth there, Ishmael thought, believing that quiet was good. He'd spent the summer in Strumheller as fidgety as a man in burlap britches. The Borders took their name because they abutted the boundary of several thousand square miles of uninhabited land, the Shadowlands. The mages who had laid the Curse that made the Darkborn had lived near the center of what was now the Shadowlands. Some residue of that, or other, terrible magic, had given rise to the Shadowborn, marauding monsters that were the Borders' constant hazard.

Ishmael had passed the better—or worse—part of twenty-five years fighting Shadowborn, first as a trooper for hire, then as a professional Shadowhunter, and ultimately as Baron Strumheller, organizing an integrated system of warning and defense that had about halved the casualties from Shadowborn incursions. In twenty-five years, he had never experienced a summer so ominously quiet.

He had fretted and roamed and listened, but it had been Lord Vladimer Plantageter, the archduke's brother and spymaster, who had raised the possibility that this might be a prelude to Shadowborn activity more organized and extensive than any they'd encountered before.

"Here's the short of it," Ishmael said. "Th'archduke sent the ducal order on th'urging of Lord Vladimer. There's been Shadowborn at work in th'city, Shadowborn with seemingly the wits of men, the gift of taking on the likeness of others, and an appetite for chaos."

He heard her catch her breath, though with admirable discipline, she did not turn her attention from the road ahead.

"I'll tell th'whole of it in Stranhorne, but these Shadowborn were nearly the death of Lord Vladimer—which was the second charge laid against me"—sorcery, the mere suspicion of which had landed him in prison—"and were th'death of upwards of a hundred and fifty Darkborn in the Rivermarch, when they set it alight during the day." He had nearly been one of those, too, having escaped by a combination of experience, knowledge of the history of that old and none-too-salubrious district, and luck. He had been spending his luck prodigiously of late. "It's likely"—indeed, he was certain of it—"that the Shadowborn had the doing of the murder that's been laid at my feet, since Lady Tercelle herself had dealings with them." Intimate dealings, which he would explain to all of them once they reached the manor. "Seems," he said with grim amusement, "that I'm in no great favor with them."

"Ishmael—," she said, and fell silent. He could almost hear the hum of her thought. He had first met Lavender and her sister riding with the Stranhorne border troop in boys' disguises. The disguises had been done quite well, and the rest poorly, so he had torn strips off both their hides for being more of a hazard to themselves and their fellows than the Shadowborn, sent them home under escort, and assumed that was that.

"What about Strumheller?" she said.

Ishmael shrugged slightly. "The order of succession was sent and signed, and the barony has passed to Reynard. My brother has no great love for me, but he's got too much sense t'meddle with the arrangements and men I put in place—not with the Borders on alert. You'll have no weakness on your flank."

"Reynard *can't* hold on to it, not with you still alive."

Having disinherited Ishmael, their father had spent years grooming Reynard to succeed to the barony. His brother had never forgiven Ish for being reinstated, or for the two or three times he had turned up since, alive after long absences. Best to change the subject. "How's your sister? Is she keeping well?"

Unlike Strumheller Manor, which had been reduced to smoldering rubble in the border uprising and civil war of two hundred years ago, and rebuilt as a whole, Stranhorne was a seven-hundred-year-old architectural accretion. There were rumored to be ruins three times its age buried underneath its foundations, but Xavier Stranhorne had dryly observed that even he would not knock down his manor to confirm, historian though he was. Inspired by the fate of Strumheller Manor, the Stranhornes had turned their minds to fortification. South- and west-facing walls were doubled and as sheer an ascent as stonemasonry could make them. The top three stories had sniper windows overlooking an open killing ground strewn with noisemakers, and on the roof were three mounted cannon, a detail that appalled Ishmael, who had fought a shipboard action beside cannon. His ears had rung for hours after. The gardens on the east and the courtyard on the north were protected by a fifteen-foot-high wall with enclosed guard posts. There were two gates, the main one into the courtyard, and a smaller, seldom-used one into the gardens on the east of the manor. The massive courtyard gate was now opened and closed by a steam winch, one of the few concessions to modern technology that Stranhorne allowed.

Even if the features had been added with a mind to repel Darkborn attackers, they should do very well against Shadowborn.

The headquarters for the Borders troop had originally been a ballroom on the northeast side of the manor. It was a late addition, conceived last century as a stage for the high social ambitions of one of the baronelles. But after her triumphs, the tiered balconies, the elevated orchestral platforms, and the lush reliefs and scrollwork had grown shabby with decades of neglect. Tradition held that sometimes the ghost of the baronelle could be heard weeping for its ruin, though from what Ish knew of the lady, weeping with rage was more likely.

The courtyard and ballroom were bustling. The courtyard was full of horses, mules, and carts; the ballroom was full of men and a number of women, milling around the entrance to the armory off in one intimate gallery, the mustering station for departing and returning troops, and the entrance to the kitchen. Troops were generally young and inevitably hungry. A final group was gathered around a huge relief model in an open side gallery. A woman was stretching over it to place a marker, her reach slightly impeded by the swell of her abdomen: Lavender's identical twin, Laurel, married a year, and five months' pregnant.

At her shoulder, to Ishmael's not unmixed relief, was her father. Most Darkborn were relentlessly modern in outlook; Baron Xavier Stranhorne was an exception, having personally taken an ax to the first telegraph pole raised on his land. He was a relatively young man, only a few years older than Ishmael, and well educated, with a degree in history from the university in Minhorne and a lifelong interest in scholarship. His opposition to "progress" had equal parts Borders obduracy and considered decision.

His opposition to magic was equally uncompromising. The first time Ishmael had called on him as Baron Strumheller, Stranhorne had taken him into his private library and delivered an ultimatum: "I have opened my doors to you, sir, as a peer and a neighbor. But should you exercise or even discuss your unnatural practice within my halls, my doors will be closed to you forever. Do you wish to dispute this?"

"These are your halls, sir. I do not." Stranhorne nodded—he had the refreshing trait of not needing to beat down an adversary who'd submitted—and the matter was settled. Ishmael had scrupulously respected Stranhorne's prohibition, and Stranhorne had scrupulously extended to him the courtesies of a peer and host. Were it not for Stranhorne's daughters, their relationship would have remained that of cooperative but distant neighbors. Ishmael would have regretted that.

Lavender hailed her father and sister cheerfully. "Told you we'd find him." Turned her head, sonning the gathered troops. "Pay up!"

He might have known there'd be a pool as to who might retrieve him.

Xavier Stranhorne's face was unreadable, which was not reassuring; the scholarly baron was not particularly demonstrative, but he did not hide what he felt. He said, "Welcome, Strumheller"—which title was no accident, undeserved though it was. "I'm afraid I'm greeting you with awkward tidings. Your sister sent a telegram from Strumheller this evening. Ferdenzil Mycene's been charged with the warrant for your arrest. He's on his way with a dozen mounted men."

Lavender caught her breath, her expression horrified. "Mycene! What was the archduke *thinking*?"

There was no love lost between Stranhorne and the Duke of Mycene and his heir. Mycene's territorial ambitions included the extensive archipelagos off the Stranhorne coast, including the island home of the late Baronelle Stranhorne. And the warrant was for the murder of Ferdenzil's betrothed, Lady Tercelle Amberley. For the sake of his peace of mind, Ishmael was glad he had not known Mycene was hunting him.

"Mycene's also got a prisoner: the physician who was traveling with you."

Ishmael had been afraid of that. When Ishmael had decided to leave the train, his ally, Dr. Balthasar Hearne, had gone on to Strumheller to carry word to Ishmael's brother and sister that he was still alive. Ish hoped the physician had not suffered for his willingness to act as messenger and decoy.

Laurel stepped forward and hugged him firmly. He returned the hug, gladdened to feel her girth. The last time he had passed through, she had been worrisomely thin and sick with early pregnancy. He was not surprised to hear her murmur against his ear, "Library—we'll join you." Laurel had always been the cunning one of the pair.

"We can give you provisions," Lavender said urgently. "Get you away on a fast horse."

"No," said Ishmael and Stranhorne together. Ishmael continued. "I was coming to Stranhorne, whatever befell. You need t'hear my report. You need to know what's behind the ducal order."

"That can't be more important than your freedom, surely," Lavender said.

"I think it is."

"Then let me intercept Mycene," urged Lavender. "Misdirect him." Her father got a pained expression on his face; Lavender was a notoriously poor liar. Laurel just said, "Lavender, *think.*"

This was best not discussed in an open hall. With this many men and women around, there were bound to be those who, for the best or worst of reasons, might reveal information to a man carrying the archduke's warrant. Ishmael nodded to Stranhorne and worked his way through the group, returning handclasps and greetings as he went, but not stopping. Alone, he made his way to the baron's study. Which seemed to have had several more shelves added, though he would have sworn there was no room. In a bunker built of books alone, Stranhorne *could* hold off a

Shadowborn army—but that whimsy was rapidly followed by the sobering awareness of possibility.

Stranhorne, Laurel, and his younger son, Boris, arrived promptly enough to prevent Ish from nodding off in a soft armchair. Lavender was downstairs, organizing sweeps, knowing that if her father did not tell her everything, her sister or brother would. Stranhorne served Ishmael brandy from a bottle sequestered behind a particularly forbidding tome, and rang for lemonade for his daughter and son.

"If you hoped," Stranhorne said, sitting down with his own brandy glass, "I'd shield you, I'm likely to disappoint."

Ishmael *had* hoped that; he could not deny it, at least to himself—hoped for shelter, for time, for help. "I know," he said, without rancor. "Would have been one matter to have city agents arriving hours or days behind me, but here's Ferdenzil Mycene hard on my heels. The last you want is t'give him time to take the measure of Stranhorne's full assets when y'think you might come to need them against him, someday that might be soon."

Stranhorne sonned him crisply, but it was no secret that, should the Duke of Mycene and his son act on their ambitions to annex the islands, Stranhorne would support his late wife's people, in arms, if need be. With the men and women that Ishmael himself had helped train to fight Shadowborn. Ishmael added, "His knowing that you know he's taken me is some security that he'll return me to Minhorne for trial, and not just stake me out for th'sunrise."

"I think I can make sure of that."

"I didn't murder Tercelle Amberley," Ishmael said. "Th'appearance was cursed compromising, I'll admit, but I'd been lured to be discovered with the body still warm. I'd hoped to prevent harm to her, if she'd been blameless, and get some answers if she hadn't."

Stranhorne's nod said that he accepted that. "We've been stockpiling munitions," he admitted. "And rotating our reserves in for training. We know that Mycene has been building up a presence in the isles. We weren't sure that this business about the Shadowborn wasn't a distraction. The city has never taken much interest in Shadowborn before now."

"Lord Vladimer has," Ishmael dissented.

There was a silence. "Vladimer," said Stranhorne. "Yes."

His opinions of the archduke's brother and spymaster had to be mixed, Ishmael thought. Vladimer was the best of allies to those whose interests aligned with his brother's policy. And the worst of enemies to those whose interests did not. The former Baron Strumheller well knew where the archduke's policies did not entirely serve the Borders. "In this, at least," Ishmael said, "Vladimer's our ally."

"Ah, and what would 'this' be?"

"You'll have t'know first that this touches on the matter that you asked me never t'discuss within your halls. There's no getting away from it."

"I somehow thought it might. Go on," said Stranhorne, no promise of forgiveness in his tone.

Ishmael waited until the servant had delivered the lemonade. Then he laid out the story: Vladimer's suspicions that the lack of Shadowborn activity indicated that the Shadowborn might be organizing their forces for the first time in history. The apparently unrelated scandal of bastard twins born to Lady Tercelle Amberley, Ferdenzil's betrothed, by a father the lady claimed, impossibly, to have been Lightborn, or at least to have been able to move through the day. Attending physician Balthasar Hearne's suspicion that the twins might be sighted, as no Darkborn had been since the Curse was laid. The murder of Tercelle Amberley, and the attempt to frame Ish for that murder. Lord Vladimer's sudden, uncanny coma, attributed to sorcery. Ishmael's arrest on suspicion of murder and sorcery, his imprisonment and escape. Rescue, rather—he skated lightly over his condition at that escape. The reappearance of Lysander Hearne, Balthasar's long-missing brother, claiming Tercelle Amberley's children as his own. And Ishmael's confrontation with a Shadowborn at Lord Vladimer's bedside, in a ducal summerhouse full of people unconscious under its influence. Alive, the Shadowborn had resembled Lysander Hearne. Dead, it had not.

He did not tell them about Lady Telmaine, Balthasar Hearne's wife and Ishmael's unexpected ally, a lady of courage and spirit and a mage of considerable strength. The lady had hidden her magic all her life, terrified of social ruin. And who was he to condemn her, he whose father had summarily disinherited him? His feelings for Lady Telmaine were nobody's business but his own—and hers, admittedly, since they were both mages. And he did not tell the Stranhornes about the price he had paid to save her life. A mage drew upon his own vitality to power his magic, the efficiency of that drawing determining the strength of the mage. Ishmael had been born as weak as mages came, but he had still succeeded in holding back an inferno around Telmaine and her daughter when her magic failed. In doing so, he had permanently damaged the connection between his vitality and his magic. The least use of magic now risked killing him.

"These Shadowborn have strength," he said to Stranhorne. "To change one's form—it's what underlies magical healing, only we regard it as a perversion of th'use and won't try it—but to fully change one's form argues considerable strength. Th'one we met was able to hold an entire household under ensorcellment—though it may be that it was at its limits, which made it vulnerable t'me." A lie, but he could not tell them that Lady Telmaine had valiantly set her untrained magic against it, distracting it enough to let him in range. "They seem t'like fire as a weapon: the burning of the Rivermarch, the firing of the warehouse where Lady Telmaine found her daughter."

"Mmph," said Stranhorne. Laurel was listening intently, while Boris was sitting very still, obviously thinking rock-like thoughts, to Ishmael's well-hidden amusement. Boris was seventeen and only lately admitted to his elders' councils. "You'll understand," Stranhorne said at length, "how much I'd like to disbelieve you, but Max sent me an account by courier of Lord Vladimer's report to the dukes and barons, and it tallies with what you say. The ducal order has been extended to the dukes—they're allowed to mobilize their own reserves."

Ishmael, mindful of tender young ears, did not swear. The Dukes of Mycene had held the archducal seat until two hundred years ago, and that Sachevar Mycene still coveted the seat was common knowledge. Sejanus Plantageter was secure—after forty years as archduke he ought to be so—but still . . . giving his rival leave to bring forces into the city . . . Vladimer would surely have argued with him vigorously, if he were able.

"Lord Vladimer?" he said. "Was he there? How'd he appear t'Max?"

Max Stranhorne would never have been able to tell if Vladimer were suffering any ill effects of the ensorcellment, aside from the effects of the experience itself—which could not be discounted. Ish himself had sensed nothing, and Lady Telmaine would surely have said . . .

"Lord Vladimer gave the report. Max thinks he may have been hurt—possibly ill, but Max thinks hurt. What prompted the extension of the archducal order," Stranhorne said, distinctly enough that Ishmael knew he was aware of Ishmael's distraction, "was the death of the Lightborn prince."

On the other side of sunrise lived the Lightborn, as utterly dependent on light as the Darkborn were on darkness. Both races had been created together by an eight-hundred-year-old act of magical vengeance. For eight hundred years, Lightborn and Darkborn had shared the land, trading, negotiating through paper walls, but never able to meet face-to-face. For much of the land, Darkborn and Lightborn cities, towns, and villages were separate—the Borders themselves were almost empty of Lightborn, for reasons no one among the Darkborn understood—but Minhorne, the largest city, was held in common, and the seats of Darkborn and Lightborn rule were separated by fewer than five miles.

The death of a Lightborn prince was not in itself an unusual event: Lightborn custom allowed the ruthless culling of faltering, incompetent, or corrupt leaders. But Isidore was a seasoned, steady statesman of no more than Ishmael's age, who had for twenty years survived the machinations of his wife's relations—she was the daughter of one of the potentates of the southwest desert—not to mention the ambitions of his own.

"How?" Ish said.

"Magic," Stranhorne said. "The lights in his rooms failed."

Darkness was as rapidly fatal to Lightborn as sun- or mage light to Darkborn. It left a tacky residue that smelled, distinctively and repugnantly, of old blood.

Even as a student, Stranhorne would never have lived in the areas that Ishmael had; he would never have smelled that odor for himself.

"I understand that the lights are magical talismans enspelled to absorb and reradiate sunlight," Stranhorne said.

He understood correctly, as Ishmael would expect. Though they had never discussed it, he knew from other directions that Stranhorne had as much theoretical knowledge of magic as any man who was not a mage. "The prince is protected—layers deep—by mages," Ishmael said. "Anyone tried t'annul the magic on the lights, they'd know; they'd warn th'prince and they'd stop it."

In the aftermath of the laying of the Curse, the last remaining Lightborn mages had begged protection from the most powerful of the emerging warlords; out of that had come the compact ruling magic on the other side of sunrise. A mage could not use magic against a nonmage except by publicly declared contract with another nonmage. Mages were indemnified against all harm done by law of contract.

"It doesn't make sense," Ishmael said slowly, "that the mages—the Mages' Temple—would have lifted its protection from Isidore."

"Yes, but—" Running footsteps outside, the snap of a floorboard, and Lavender threw open the door. She shut it hard and stood with her back to it, as though pursued. "He's here," she said in breathless anger.

"Mycene?" said her father, calmly.

"Ishmael has to get away now. He can leave by the east gate, through Mother's garden."

"And go where?" said Stranhorne, but to Ishmael, not his daughter.

Ishmael said nothing. Vladimer had sent him south to make sure the Borders were prepared to defend themselves, and then if no invasion materialized, to scout the Shadowlands personally. And *he* had come south to make sure that the Borders—Stranhorne and his own barony of Strumheller—knew what they might be facing. He had done that.

And now ... Stranhorne had it right. Ishmael could keep running and be nothing but a trouble and a distraction to men and women who needed to keep their minds on the true enemy—and possibly get himself mistakenly shot by one of Stranhorne's own patrols, in this time of high tension. He could demand sanctuary, and divide Stranhorne's family, setting the twins against their father. Or he could surrender, let Mycene take him north, and trust to the law and events proving his innocence. He had no doubt Vladimer had turned his own formidable resources to the task, though Vladimer would have troubles of his own—Sejanus extending that ducal order, for one. *And,* Ish thought ruefully, *Vladimer has perhaps a little too much confidence in my ability to survive.*

At least if Mycene took him back to Minhorne, he would be near Vladimer and Lady Telmaine. He was worried about them both; Vladimer because he had already been ensorcelled once, and Telmaine because he and her husband had left her to guard Lord Vladimer's back. Her strength, coupled with her inexperience, had its hazards.

"Laurel," Stranhorne said, after a moment. "Go downstairs; greet Lord Mycene. Settle him down if he needs settling—tell him ten minutes."

"Ishmael," Lavender appealed to him.

"There's no point t'it," Ishmael said, projecting calm. "I could go pelting about the countryside, but he'd likely find me within two or three days—the man's a good soldier, a good leader, whatever else we may think of him—and I'd be two or three days more weary. This way's safer for me." *And all of you,* he thought. "It's not as though I think I'll get left out of th'fight somehow."

. Laurel, passing, rested her hand on her sister's arm and said something to her, too quietly for even Ishmael to hear. Lavender's shoulders slumped. Laurel slipped out and closed the door behind her.

"Did you get it all moved?" Lavender said to her father, her tone flat.

"I think so, but I'd like you and Boris to go down and make sure that it is—and that it's well concealed, or at least well disguised. There's no reason for Mycene or his men to go into the cellars, and we'll keep people on them, but I'd not put it past them to try."

"Nor I," Lavender growled. She opened the door and stalked out, her younger brother trailing her.

They listened for a moment as the footsteps receded. Stranhorne rose, took Ishmael's glass from him, and refilled it. "I wish it didn't have to be this way," he said, passing it into Ishmael's gloved hand. *Hospitality or anesthesia,* Ishmael wondered.

"Y'can't afford to give Mycene reason to demand a search of the manor under th'archduke's warrant," Ishmael said, stoically. "Not with a cellar full of munitions bound for the Isles. I'm grateful you took my report in full. My sense is that whatever's coming is coming soon, now they've broken into th'open in the city."

Stranhorne balanced his glass on his fingers, shoulder against a crammed shelf. "But what's coming? That is the question." He sonned Ishmael. "You know I have material collected from the period of the Curse and after."

"Aye," Ishmael said. "I'd heard that. But asking after it would have been treading too close t'matters you'd asked me not to speak of."

"True," Stranhorne said, soberly. "A dictate I hope not to live to regret."

Surprising himself as well as Stranhorne, Ishmael laughed. "In all truth, it never occurred to me t'ask. Even before m'father sent me on my road, my tutors had to nail my breeches to the chair. Heresy, in this household, but there 'tis." He set down the glass, still half full, and said more seriously, "But I'd be glad of the dunce's version. First of all, who might be in th'Shadowlands?"

"I know nothing for certain," said Stranhorne. "In the second and third century after the Curse, multiple expeditions went into the Shadowlands. Those that returned re-

ported a barren land—previously, magic had been used to
alter the weather patterns to bring rain—that was otherwise uninhabited. Those that passed beyond a certain line
some two hundred miles in never returned; we do not
know why. Shadowborn entered the written record late in
the third century, and became an increasing nuisance through
the fourth, leading the archduke eventually to withdraw
support for campaigns into the Shadowlands." Which led
to the establishment of the Borders baronies, and eventually to the Borders uprising and the war of Borders' inde-
pendence, and the order of six twenty-nine that limited the
Borders' standing forces. That history Ishmael had not only
had hammered into his thick, juvenile skull, but had personally contended with these past twenty-five years. Stranhorne
continued. "But *if* there are men in the Shadowlands—and I
remind you I have no support for this—I might speculate
that they are descended of the mages who were involved in
the laying of the Curse, though why they should have
waited eight hundred years to make themselves known, I
can't say."

"Known other than by the Shadowborn and th'Call," Ish
noted. The Call—the Call to the Shadowlands—was Ishmael's personal curse, a bizarre ensorcellment that was a
legacy of his years roaming around the Shadowlands. Nobody knew what made it take hold, but every year, dozens
of bordersmen and -women followed the Call, and none
was ever heard from again. Stubbornness, distance, trusted
guards, and, on occasion, chains had kept Ishmael on the
right side of the border. "Lord Vladimer had it in mind for
me t'go and find out. He was concerned that there was mischief behind the unnatural quiet of this summer."

"He was right, but that was risky for you," Stranhorne
said, which amounted to gushing concern. "You are assuming that the Shadowborn—as we know them—are related
to this. Suppose they are not. Suppose they are an entirely
separate problem."

"From where I sit, th'separation seems academic."

The corner of Stranhorne's mouth quirked at the slight
truculence of tone. "Though *if* there are such mages, their

quiescence is still unexpected, given the type of . . . powers attributed to the mages prior to the Curse."

"There's fair magical strength on the Lightborn side," Ishmael noted. "Maybe the Shadowborn hesitated to tangle with the Lightborn, and we've been the beneficiaries."

"Which raises two more questions in my mind: first, how much do the *Lightborn* already know about these occupants of the Shadowlands, assuming they exist?"

Ishmael spread his gloved hands. Minhorne, as well as being the seats of both governments, was also the headquarters of the Mages' Temple, which ruled magic on the other side of sunrise, and, effectively, among the Darkborn as well. There were few Darkborn mages whom the Lightborn recognized as strong, the Lightborn having carefully cultivated strength among their lineages while the Darkborn left mages to arise by chance and scrabble for survival when they did. The Temple was not given to advising Darkborn of their doings, much less allowing them a say.

"You realize," Stranhorne said, "that that might make sense of the prince's death, if the Lightborn have formed an alliance with the Shadowborn. Second," he continued, while Ishmael was still taking that in, "tradition says that the magic that laid the Curse killed all those involved. But am I mistaken that all our experience of present-day magic is that any persistent magical effect—talismanic magic or ensorcellment—depends on the survival of the mage responsible? As the saying goes, magic dies with the mage."

"Aye," growled Ishmael. It was an adage entrenched in law—the legal penalty for sorcery being execution—and the one sure way to free the victim of all influence. Ishmael's growl was less at the reminder of his own jeopardy than at what Stranhorne implied. Magic, rooted as it was in the vitality of the mage who worked it, never outlived the mage—with the one great exception. After all these centuries, nobody gave thought to the possibility that the Curse was *not* the exception, even with the example of the long-lived Lightborn archmages before them. "You're saying that you think one of the mages who laid the Curse *survived*?"

If *they*, whose Curse the Lightborn lineages had for centuries tried to break, were the Shadowborn, then even he must despair.

"It is entirely speculative, you realize," Stranhorne reminded him judiciously. "I think it highly unlikely that those involved in the laying of a malevolent curse eight centuries ago would have waited all this time to make themselves known to us—not when it has been evident for centuries that we would prosper. But it *is* the simplest explanation for the anomaly."

"Curse it, Stranhorne," Ishmael said, with deep feeling, "not even Vladimer had that notion." He had to remember, though, the first time he and Vladimer had spoken about this, Vladimer had no more to go on than the extraordinarily quiet summer in the Borders. And the second time, Vladimer was newly awakened from ensorcellment and very shaken.

"Vladimer's a man of the modern age," Stranhorne said. "I am a historian. . . . There are ruins in the south desert that date back thousands of years, and outside the Sundered Lands I'm told there are other ruins, other deserts, oral traditions of other magical catastrophes. Perhaps this is merely a cycle that repeats itself."

Ishmael drained his brandy glass, wishing it were three times the size.

"When you first called on me," Stranhorne said, "I considered forbidding you my halls. To this day, however, I have not regretted my decision to receive you. Although," he remarked in a lighter tone, "some of my peers—and particularly their wives—were appalled at how you have corrupted my daughters."

"I had th'inborn proclivity to work with," Ishmael said, shakily.

"I'm quite sure it came entirely from their mother." There was a silence of weighing and sorting of words. "My prejudices obscured my recognition that that domination was not the only seduction magic offered. You were born with as much secular power as any man could wish, and yet at the age of sixteen, you rejected that for magic."

"M'father had more t'do with that than me."

"You need not have brought your magic to his, or any-one else's, attention," Stranhorne pointed out.

As Telmaine had, gifted with far greater power—and greater sense, perhaps—than he. Facing back across the years, he considered the stew of conviction and rebellion that had led him to compel his father to recognize the magic in him.

"When your father disowned you, I spoke up in support of it. When he reinstated you, I knew he had been forced to it. When you inherited, I wrote the archduke, urging him to refuse to sign the order of succession."

"I knew that at the time," Ishmael said. "I fully expected y'to run me off your lands that first time."

"I gave it some thought," Stranhorne said. "Even though everything I had heard of you was to the good. It is the virtues of mages, the good they do, that persuades people to discount the evidence of history—and so the cycle repeats. . . . How soon will you be back?"

The unexpected question took him by surprise. "I'll be—" He cleared his throat. "I'll be working t'get loose the moment we clear your gates—you can count on that. If I'm brought to th'city, I'll have Vladimer's backing, and his testimony that I meant him no ill." Though with a charge of sorcery and a suspicion of influence, that might be less an advantage than otherwise. "But if th'situation changes here, you can be sure mine will."

Stranhorne set his glass down and relieved Ishmael of his own. "Our ten minutes are up, I think. I've sent for Jeremiah Coulter from the Crosstracks, to test that warrant. If there's any crack to be found in it, he'll find it."

Ishmael

The Stranhornes had managed to pen Mycene in the ballroom, even if Laurel's smooth delivery was sounding rather strained as they came through the door. Ishmael's pursuer was almost toe-to-toe with the lady, though he was at a disadvantage thereby, being a good six inches shorter than she. His face was distinguished from commonplace by its asymmetry; one cheekbone noticeably higher and narrower than the other, one eye slightly offset relative to the other, nose slightly displaced by an old break. His hair was fine, straight, and pulled back from a high forehead into a braid or a queue, which had been tucked into his collar. He wore a greatcoat split for riding, heavy weight and of highest quality, and well-rubbed breeches. A holster rode on one hip, and the sheath of a long knife on the other.

Half a dozen of his men were lounging or sitting about, seasoned troopers conserving energy. The remainder must have been delegated to tend the horses. Dr. Balthasar Hearne was standing slightly to one side, haggard and road worn and, except for a too-large jacket of Borders style, still dressed as Ish had left him, but alive and apparently uninjured.

"Ishmael di Studier," Mycene challenged him. "I have here a warrant for your arrest for the murder of my betrothed, Lady Tercelle Amberley, and for suspicion of sorcery against Lord Vladimer Plantageter." His head twitched toward a man leaning against the wall with folded arms and a cynical expression on his face. If he'd never met the man, Ish would have taken him for a smuggler. Which he was said to have been in his youth; nothing teaches a clever man the law like the evasion of it. Sensing their sonn, Jeremiah Coulter shook his head slightly; the warrant was sound.

As Stranhorne had said, and Ishmael had expected. The brandy or Stranhorne's conversation, or the combination, had stunned him sufficiently that "I surrender myself to your hands" came out evenly. But he was glad that Lavender was in the cellar. Laurel merely chewed on her lower lip.

Mycene seemed perplexed, as a man is who pushes hard at a supposed obstruction, only to find it yield. "Right," he said. "Hand over your weapons. We're going north."

"There isn't a train until tomorrow," Stranhorne said. "The northbound express will have gone by the time you reach the station."

"Then we'll ride," Mycene said.

With a quiet sigh, Balthasar Hearne swayed and slid to

the floor in a dead faint. There was a slightly embarrassed silence at such unmanly behavior, and then Laurel settled carefully to her knees beside him, feeling his pulse. Before her pregnancy, the Strumheller surgeon had frequently drafted her as his assistant, for her cool head, steady hand, and ready understanding of terse orders.

"This man's exhausted," she reported. "He won't be traveling any farther today, unless it's in a coach."

Mycene shook his head in curt disgust. "Then we'll take a coach."

Stranhorne said, "You have maybe four hours to sunrise, which will put you in the inner Borders. I daresay you will be able to find lodgings from one of the households, but then you have—what?—another ten hours the next night, at best. A coach would slow you down even further. And given the ducal order, I think I would be fully within my rights to refuse you the use of fourteen or fifteen horses from my stables until this crisis is over, despite your warrant."

His lawyer gave a buccaneer's grin.

"I offer you the hospitality of my household until tomorrow night," the baron continued, reasonably. "We will deliver you and your prisoners to the station, where you will be able to catch the train up to the Summerhouse Terminus, and the first day train to Minhorne."

Boris was failing to conceal his dismay—no wonder his sisters always cleaned him out at cards. Ishmael was impressed by Stranhorne's nerve, and alarmed at the risk he was willing to run—on Ishmael's behalf? With a cellar full of munitions and an active plot to support the Isles, Ish would have punted his enemies out the door as fast as possible, never mind decent. Or perhaps Stranhorne hoped to continue that intensely disturbing conversation.

Ish would rather be carried off north in chains.

"I accept your invitation," Mycene conceded, sourly. "But I'm setting a guard on both those men. Di Studier's under arrest for murder and suspicion of sorcery, and Hearne for aiding and abetting. I'll have *you* up for aiding and abetting if they're not both on the train north tomorrow."

"Less risk having him here than rousing his suspicions as to what we had to hide," Stranhorne murmured to Ish a few minutes later, on the stairs. By the fourth flight, they had opened up a little distance between themselves and Mycene's guard, who had had a hard ride in his train. "We'll keep him and his men well fed and wined, and make sure they don't go wandering and meeting locked doors. We know who to keep away from them, too."

"And y'blame Lavender on your wife."

Stranhorne cocked a half smile at him. "Of course. It's Laurel who's all mine. . . . We'll dine just after the sunrise bell."

Balthasar Hearne was sitting up in bed when Ishmael came in, Stranhorne having persuaded Mycene to leave the guards outside the rooms his prisoners were to share. Balthasar was still fully dressed, except for jacket and boots, with a quilt thrown over him. He seemed tired but quite alert. He waited until Ishmael had closed the door, and said, abashed, "It was all I could think of to delay them. I'd already exhausted every other argument."

"It was convincing," Ishmael allowed, relieved and privately amused. *Curse it.* A man yearning after a married woman had no business liking the woman's husband.

"Not bad," Laurel allowed, judiciously. "For a man." To Ishmael she said, "Father managed to stall them? Then I'd better go and find something to occupy Lavender—it's too late to send her out again—and check with the housekeeper about dinner." She swept out.

Ishmael clasped hands with Balthasar. "Good t'find you again," he said, and sat down. "Did you make it to the manor?" Since the age of sixteen, he never had been able to refer to Strumheller Manor as "home," for all his sister's chiding.

"After a delay. Mycene was waiting at the station," Balthasar said, the tightness around his mouth betraying what his stoic face tried to conceal. "They questioned me." No small ordeal for a man beaten nearly to death under questioning less than a week ago. "They affected not to believe me and they took me up to the manor, claiming you might somehow have got past them. It was close to sunrise, anyway." So Reynard and Noellene had had the dubious pleasure of entertaining Mycene and his arresting party over a day. "Your sister was gracious and most relieved to learn that the reports of your death were mistaken. Your brother could not be faulted as a host, but he ... gave me a message for you. He said that this time he would settle the inheritance in court."

"Ah, well, that's no surprise," Ishmael said. "He's not a bad man, m'brother, just too often disappointed." Even Reynard's marriage, arranged by their father, had been a disappointment. After ten years of childlessness and increasing estrangement, his wife had insisted on a divorce. "I'm like one of those alley cats, always turning up when y'think you've sonned the last of it."

"Your sister expressed her disappointment that you did not send your brother a personal letter."

That made him grin: Noellene had been born when Ishmael was sixteen, and had inherited their city-born mother's beauty and refinement—but she was enough their father's daughter to strip hide with her tongue when truly riled. She was probably right about the letter, but what was done was done. "Y'could explain as well as I could ... And then you came on tonight. Hard ride, was it?"

"I cannot say I remember the last half," Balthasar admitted. "I just concentrated on staying with the horse."

"No mean feat, in that company. Now, I've some news t'give you, and it's not good. I think Stranhorne and I both need to hear your take on it—given you've served terms on th'Intercalatory Council, and live shoulder to shoulder with a Lightborn."

"Floria, yes."

"This does concern your—" He wasn't sure how he could, or should, characterize Balthasar's relationship with his neighbor. They were as intimate as a man and woman could be who would never meet in the flesh; that he knew. And he knew how Balthasar's wife felt about it. "Mistress Floria," he said, sidestepping awkwardness. "Since she's vigilant to the Lightborn prince. Isidore's dead."

"*Dead?* How?"

"Lights failed in his rooms during the night."

"That's—not possible," Balthasar said. "The prince's lights would be enspelled by multiple mages. They could not fail unless all those mages died at the same time."

"Or unless the magic was released or annulled."

"Not . . . possible," Balthasar insisted.

"Unless the Temple lifted its protection from Prince Isidore."

"In the whole of the history of the compact, the Mages' Temple has only once canceled contracts with a prince, with ample warning, and only after that prince had abused magic and mages egregiously. Isidore had no such history—and no such warning. Floria would have told me if there had been any hint of it." He paused. "Shadowborn?"

"That's my thought," Ishmael said grimly. "Which means strength enough t'overwhelm Lightborn high masters. Or collusion."

He waited, sonn playing over the other man's face as he thought that through.

"That we haven't already met that kind of strength doesn't necessarily mean it's not there," Balthasar said, slowly. "It may simply not have been needed. But as for collusion . . . No, I think that if the Lightborn were involved, even the Lightborn mages, they would make their demands directly. They have survived by the compact between earthborn and mageborn. Lightborn magic," he said, an appeal audible in his voice, "is not *chaotic*."

"I hope you've the right of that, Hearne."

"Have you heard again from Telmaine since she contacted you on the train?"

"No," Ishmael said. He caught his hand's unconscious movement to his chest and laid it casually down, hoping Balthasar had not noticed. "I know th'turn I had frightened her. She didn't understand before what it meant, the damage I had taken."

"You should have made that plain to her and to Vladimer," Balthasar said, levelly. "We made our plans assuming that you and Telmaine would be able to use magic as a line of communication."

"Curse it, Hearne—" He checked his defensive reaction. "You're right. I should've. I'd not let myself think how bad it could be. Now let it be."

Balthasar Hearne let it be. "The prince should not have died by magic. The Lightborn police abuse magic. *They* should have dealt with the Shadowborn we fought, not us. Are you certain that what we are dealing with is Shadowborn, and not factionalism within the upper echelons of the mages, both Darkborn and Lightborn?"

"A mage war," Ishmael said. *Sweet Imogene—Vladimer, Stranhorne, and now Balthasar.* He should have begged the whole bottle from Stranhorne.

"Yes," said the physician, simply, and waited.

"Some Shadowborn—glazen, for instance"—he indicated where the scars ridged the corner of his mouth, since he knew Hearne already knew that story—"use magic in their hunting. They're animal and it's instinctive, but I know the sense of it, and I sensed the same magic in the one at Vladimer's bedside. It's unique—Telmaine sensed it, too—and you doubt the Lightborn would collude."

"I think," Balthasar said, slowly, "knowing what I know of the Mages' Temple, the Lightborn would either dominate or be forced into submission. And if the Lightborn dominated, then it would be a lawful domination, not a chaotic one."

As a bottom-ranked mage, Ish had almost negligible dealings with the Temple, but listening to the Broomes—the leaders of the commune of mages within Minhorne—he, too, had formed an opinion of lawfulness to a fault. "The last possibility Stranhorne put to me was that th'Curse is not an exception to the way of magic after all, that one of Imogene's conclave, or even Imogene herself, survived to hold it."

"That's . . . always been a possibility," Balthasar said, sounding more thoughtful than rightfully terrified. "Although given the attention that the mages have paid to the Shadowlands over the years, if there were that much magical strength anywhere in them, they should have found it."

"I'm told that if a mage has good control or isn't making use of his strength as magic, then it's near impossible to know that a given vitality is his—unless you know that person. And there's nobody on either side of sunrise of an age t'know Imogene."

"Eight hundred years," Balthasar said a little faintly. "If Imogene had the viciousness to do this to us in the first place, then she would not wait eight hundred years to finish it. And if she were experiencing a belated remorse—"

Ishmael snorted. "Like no remorse I've ever met."

Balthasar took a deep breath; Ishmael could hear the waver in his diaphragm. He held it, then steadily released it. "There are a number of these scenarios that you and I simply cannot do anything about. You are a first-rank mage suffering from severe overuse." At least he had been kind enough not to say "disabled." "I have a very rudimentary sense of magic, I'm told, which lets me sense magic on the scale of a weather-working, but nothing else. So"—his voice was strained but firm—"our obligation remains unchanged. Find out what is going on, and get the information to the people who can do something about it."

Ishmael set a hand on his shoulder and stood up. "Which we have done, for the moment. The next thing is dinner and a wash for both of us. The ladies won't thank us for coming in reeking to the rafters of sweat, mud, and horse."

Balthasar

Dinner was served just after the sunrise bell, in an intimate dining room in one of the newer parts of the manor. To Balthasar, the occasion had the unreality of a parlor drama, as though comfort and security were already more novel to him than pain and danger. A few hours ago, he had been pounding along the roads in Ferdenzil's train. Now, in borrowed formal clothing, he was dining on snails imported from the Scallon Isles in the company of Ishmael di Studier, Ferdenzil Mycene, Baron Stranhorne and his son, and the ladies of the house.

"We were sixteen, you understand," Baronette Lavender said, extracting a snail from its shell with an economical twist of her two-tined fork.

"T'be presented the following year," Baronette Laurel said. "That was, if Lady Calliope di Reuther had any say in it. She'd chosen to take an interest in us poor, motherless things." Wisely suspicious of exotic foods, she signaled for another serving of smoked chicken.

"Find out if either of us could be polished up sufficiently for her darling boy," Lavender said, maliciously. "As if we'd be fool enough t'place ourselves within her reach."

Balthasar decided not to mention that said darling boy was married to his wife's close friend, Sylvide. He could not, however, dispute their assessment of Lady Calliope. The twins' father listened with an expression of benign amusement; he, no doubt, had heard it all before.

"And," Laurel said, returning to their joint tale, "we'd been reading all the wrong kind of literature."

"Aye," Ishmael rumbled. "That you had."

"In those stories," Lavender explained cheerfully to Bal, "all a girl needed to pass as a boy was to have boys' clothing and a cap. It was always the cap falling off at some untimely moment that gave them away. *We* made sure that *our* caps were proof against a gale."

"We'd ridden short, local circuits with the Stranhorne troop," Laurel said. "We'd heard *all* about Baron Strumheller, who'd Shadowhunted for more than twenty years, and we were all afire to meet him." She gave Bal a rueful smile. "We'd no idea the female walk was different from the male."

"Well," Lavender said with a sly grin, "that's what he *claimed*. But we'd also no idea what kinds of entertainments there are up in the city that'd teach a man to know a woman in man's garb." Ishmael opened his mouth and, wisely, Bal felt, closed it again. "Have you visited the burlesques, Dr. Hearne?"

Bal remembered one of the early lectures in his training concerning the difference between male and female anatomy. Even then he had recognized the lecturer's considerable achievement in managing to bore sixty young men with the intimate details of the female body. He decided against attempting to reprise the feat, though he tried to emulate the tone. "I'm doubtful that theater would have given you any better source material for your impersonation than your adventure stories. . . . I take it, then, that Ishmael recognized you were young women."

"The moment he met us," Lavender said. "Though he did not take us aside until later, after he'd judged our competence. Then he tore bleeding strips off both our hides and sent us straight home, under escort. We were too shocked even to cry."

"It wasn't that he shouted or insulted us," Laurel explained. "But he told us in explicit terms just how unprepared we were for the style of fighting he expected, and how we were putting at risk our lives and the lives of the men who'd be with us."

"We were in disgrace for *weeks*," Lavender said. "Admittedly, there were compensations. Lady Calliope quite lost interest in us as prospective daughters-in-law. And"—she settled her chin on her sinewy hand and cast a teasing burst of sonn over Ishmael—"once we recovered from the shock, we were in *love*. Sixteen, remember."

Ishmael found diversion in his plate. Ferdenzil Mycene's expression was somewhere between intrigued and appalled. Bal understood it, for all he thought himself progressive in his attitudes. Everything about them was outrageous, from their first-name address to a man so many years their elder, to their ease in discussing things that city society would have found mortifyingly improper, to their readiness to take to the road with the troop. Yet he could not but hope that in fifteen years he would share a meal in such comfort and informality with his own grown daughters.

"We spent the entire winter and spring and half the summer trying to make up the deficiencies Ishmael had so mercilessly pointed out. And then we took the train to Strumheller, all escorted and proper, to prove that we were fit to be troopers."

"He allowed as we'd improved," Laurel said. "And, miracle of miracles, he got Father to agree that we could ride escort on visitors and such on the near Borders."

"I am surprised," Ferdenzil said, though his tone implied something stronger, "that your father permitted it."

There was a brief, disconcerted silence; perhaps the ladies were not used to hearing city prejudice manifest at their own table. Stranhorne merely murmured, "I'm at times surprised, too."

"It's th'glazen," Ishmael said. "One of the most dangerous Shadowborn. About the size of a large dog, most of them, but they can ensorcell a man so he'll let himself be eaten alive. Only men; we do not know why. A woman with a steady hand and nerve can save a dozen lives, if not more."

This silence had a different texture to it. Bal remembered Ishmael's lawyer telling him that the scars on Ishmael's face, scars no mage of any strength should carry, had been made by a glazen. If these young ladies knew him as well as they seemed to, they might know that story.

Ish himself broke the silence. "Though it wasn't as troopers I wanted them."

"Indeed, no," said Lavender with a laugh, and waved a hand, inviting him to elaborate.

"Two baronettes, raised t'be chatelaines of a manor, able to manage a staff of a hundred or more and oversee th'organization for events involving hundreds. They'd won the help of the men of their troop, so I knew they'd the leadership. I'd give them two or three summers' seasoning, then set them on the logistics. Took some doing for their father t'agree, but I think he's judged the merit of it long since."

Stranhorne, his smile dry, raised his glass toward Ishmael.

"And that," Lavender said, "is what we've been doing for the past three years—managing the planning, provisioning, and tracking of the Stranhorne Borders defenses." She smiled sweetly at Ferdenzil. "Shocking, isn't it?"

Ishmael softly cleared his throat. A warning, Bal thought.

"And does your husband approve?" Mycene said to Laurel. She was married, Balthasar understood, to the Stranhornes' envoy to the court of the Dukes of Myerling, in the Isles.

"Not at the moment, of course," she said, demurely. "But I met him riding escort."

"Do many of your women ride with the troop?" Ferdenzil said.

Ishmael's face, alert and unsmiling, turned toward Lavender. That he nudged her foot under the table, Bal could not know for certain, but he suspected it from her twitch. She said, coolly, "Are you one of those who believes where the language says 'men,' that only men need apply, Lord Ferdenzil? Our standing troop numbers are within the ducal order of six twenty-seven, men and women both."

"I fail to see how women can be an asset to a troop, then. Women lack the strength and the will to fight."

"Raw strength, maybe, but a gun in a woman's hand is as deadly as in a man's," Ishmael said, "and they've often the sharper ears and the better judgment as to when t'shoot."

"But none better than you," Lavender said, staunchly. "I was there when he dropped a scavvern at six hundred yards, by ear. He was ahead of us on the road, and the first thing we knew was when he shouted the warning and shot. Could you shoot a Shadowborn at six hundred yards, Lord Ferdenzil?"

"I would not try," Ferdenzil said. "Sonn is sure; anything beyond, and you're a danger to your own people."

"A different kind of warfare," Ishmael said, setting down his spoon and addressing Mycene straight, one man sharing his experience with another. "Once a scavvern's near enough t'sonn, you've got two shots, maybe. Our people know our routes, know t'respond to our challenges, so we can challenge and shoot t'sound, as long as th'fighting formation holds. Once it's gone, then yes, we have t'shoot to sonn, rather than risk harming our own."

Lavender Stranhorne folded her hands before her plate and shifted in her chair, as though she were tucking her feet beneath her. "Then if you don't care to shoot beyond sonn, you cannot care much to sail the Islands, Lord Ferdenzil," she said in a silken tone.

"On the contrary, Baronette," Mycene said, carelessly, "I find the islanders' methods of addressing the problem of navigation most ingenious."

"But, alas, controversial," Bal murmured, drawing the

attention of both parties. He took a well-timed sip of wine. "I have served several terms on the Intercalatory Council that mediates where the common affairs of one race impinge upon the other. The choice of shore sites for the signal bells and message drums can be contentious; after all, the Lightborn *sleep* at night."

"It's always seemed t'me to be a brave thing t'do," Ish remarked. "To sail in these waters, trusting knowledge of the seas, skill in reckoning speed and direction, and the sound of the bells. A man's sometimes glad to be too preoccupied with his belly t'worry about the rocks."

"And what," Lavender said, "would you say of a man who goes Shadowhunting at sea?"

"I am well aware," Ferdenzil Mycene said, coldly, "that di Studier is a folk hero in the Borders. But I am here with a warrant for his arrest for the murder of my betrothed, Lady Tercelle Amberley, so you will forgive me if I do not share your admiration."

"Lord Mycene," Lavender said, "*Baron* Strumheller is more than a folk hero. He's the man who organized the baronies to *stop* this scourge of generations from preying on our towns and villages, when all your fine northern dukes and lords gave us were distrust and suspicion and threats to rule us in rebellion if we raised the force we need."

"Lavender," said Ishmael, "the warrant for my arrest is signed by the archduke, with the law of the land behind it. As is the ducal order enabling the raising of the Borders."

"Yes," said the baronette bitterly, "now the Shadowborn have come to the city." She stood up. "Excuse me, Father, Lord Mycene. If I stay, I will say something I will regret. Though not nearly as much as I should." She left, skirts swinging with her long stride.

On their way back to his shared suite with Balthasar, Ishmael continued the twins' account. He had done his utmost, as he promised their father, to keep them to less-risky duty, escorting noble visitors on the inner Borders roads. Their single encounter with a Shadowborn had occurred on an illicit jaunt into the highlands while Ishmael himself was far down in the interior, helping organize the Odon's Barrow troop and reserve. "Never came quite so close t'fainting on my feet as when I read that letter," he admitted. "I was glad t'leave the hide stripping to their father." Who had, Laurel had assured him, done a superb job of it, one quite worthy of Ishmael. "It was Laurel's shots took it down. Lavender's better on the range, but Laurel's got the cooler head."

Once they were in the suite and the door closed, he said more soberly, "The way the ladies are pleased t'tell it, the troop's an adventure. I didn't know the rest until months after.... The year before my father died and I was still Shadowhunting for hire, I'd been hired on by a lady in a little manor on the boundary between Stranhorne and Strumheller. Her son, fifteen years old, the lord of the manor, had vanished off the road. We were nearly four weeks in the Shadowlands but we found no trace.... The boy and Lavender had known each other from childhood, and were set on marrying when they came of age."

"And the young ladies didn't tell you."

"No. It was from their father I learned it."

Two

Ishmael

For the second night in a row, Ishmael awakened to the sound of dripping and running water, though this time the sound was coming from high overhead, and not from rain drumming on a day hide stretched above his face. He could not hear birdsong, only the voices of a manor very much awake. He had overslept. He started to sit up and abruptly became aware of another presence. He snatched for a revolver that was not there—Mycene having thoroughly disarmed him—before his sonn resolved the form of the man reading in the chair across the room. "Hearne," he noted, drawing his arm down. "What's th'hour? I'd have thought Mycene would have had us on the road as soon as the sun was down."

"He would have," the physician said, laying his book aside, seemingly oblivious to the meaning of Ishmael's abortive movement. "But there's nearly two feet of snow outside."

If Balthasar had snatched off his warm quilt, it wouldn't have brought him upright as effectively. "Two feet?" He had had no sense of magical weather-working whatsoever. Sweet Imogene, he must have slept like the dead. Balthasar, too.

"It stopped snowing just after sunset, I'm told. Baronette Lavender has sent some parties out on skis and snowshoes, to determine how wide the effect is."

"But none of the regular sweeps," Ishmael said. "Is that

what you're telling me?" He threw back his covers. Balthasar started to lever himself stiffly out of his chair, intending to return to his own room. Ish waved a casual hand at him. "Stay," he ordered. "I've nothing y'haven't sonned a hundred times before. You understand what power's needed t'influence th'weather."

"Yes," Balthasar said. "That kind of working would take several Lightborn high masters, and is probably beyond the reach of living Darkborn mages."

"Stranhorne will understand that," Ishmael said.

"Will he have shared that understanding?" Balthasar said, in sober assessment.

"That is likely, considering. The man's no fool."

Ishmael lifted clothes laundered of the odors and grime of the road, and went into the adjacent dressing room to wash and dress. Clad, he padded past Balthasar to the outer wall and lifted the bar and opened the shutter of the narrow, light-sealed window. It was unglazed, since its purpose was defensive. He propped a foot on the low bench on which a rifleman would kneel, and pushed his head through the gap—it would not pass his chest or shoulders—then inhaled deeply and listened. The doubled walls were wide, but the gap widened to the outside, allowing a sniper a better-than-sixty-degree arc. Snow: there was no mistaking the scent of it, but the air was warming and he could smell the grass and scrub of the Borders rising on the wind. The thaw would not be long in coming. Could he console himself that the mages who had called the storm down on them lacked the strength or commitment to keep the cold? Or had it already achieved its purpose, pinning them down, preventing the Stranhornes' sweeps?

He could hear voices from his left—children, screeching delight at this novelty, and two or three adults—and swung his head to better place them. They would be within the enclosed garden to the east, since there was nowhere else for children to play in time of high alert. It had been the baronelle's garden before she died. He was fully oriented now, and unnerved by more than the snow. He jerked his head back in, closed and tested the shutter automatically, and turned to face his traveling companion. "Hearne," he said, "I need your help."

"Anything," the physician said.

He would rather, he admitted to himself, be facing down a scavvern with a butter knife. "Y'know the reason we were t'meet in the first place."

"Lord Vladimer thought my skills might be useful to you," Balthasar said. "In dealing with the Call." Balthasar Hearne had a growing reputation in the treatment of addictions and other irrationality; his success with one of Vladimer's other irregular agents, Gil di Maurier, had attracted Vladimer's attention.

"Aye. You've an interest in the treatment of compulsions." He passed a hand down his face. "I've th'strongest urge to go straight downstairs, out the door, and start walking southwest as fast and far as my feet will take me."

"That is all?" Balthasar said.

Of course he would miss the significance of the direction, not knowing that for as long as it had ridden Ishmael, the Call had pulled him due south, not southwest. "Yes," Ishmael said, fighting impatience. "That's all th'Call is—an urge t'go into the Shadowlands and not come back, even knowing it would be the death of me."

"Is there any basis to this compulsion—a sense that someone important is waiting for you there, or that you have something to do?"

"No," Ishmael said. "It's just th'urge t'go. Southwest." He almost felt as though he had lurched in that direction, but sonned no reaction in Balthasar's intent face.

Balthasar said, "Sit down, if you would, Baron."

He waited until Ishmael had sat down and then said, "Have you ever lost control to the extent that you started to move in that direction without intending to?"

"Not waking," Ishmael said through a tight jaw. "I'd sleepwalk when it was at its worst. Wanted a guard, sometimes chains."

Balthasar's lips compressed, whether at the implications of someone sleepwalking during daylight or at Ishmael's measures. "And are you close to losing control now?"

"No, but it's strong, and th'direction's changed. All these years, it has pulled south. Now it's pulling southwest."

"Southwest, but still into the Shadowlands." He paused. "How do you interpret that?"

"That whatever or whoever is holding th'Call on me is moving. Likely moving north." *Toward Strumheller.* He sank his fingertips into the arm of the chair.

"And what have you tried to break the compulsion?" the physician said.

"What haven't I tried, Hearne? Magic, of course; overspent myself often enough to drive th'futility through my thick skull. Phoebe Broome tried. She'd have asked her father, but her brother Phineas tried t'send me off the first months I was in their commune, and wound up taking a mild case of it himself. She was afraid her father'd get in too deep and suffer worse. The mage who'd had me as student tried. I downed various potions and medicines, too, though it was as well I'm hard t'poison, or some of your colleagues would have done for me."

"Did you ever approach a Lightborn mage?" Bal said.

"Had some correspondence with one, but we'd never th'intimacy for me to raise the question with him. Darkborn mages tend not to want t'attract their attention that way— they've the greater power and they think to rule magic on both sides of sunrise. I've always wondered if they weren't the more vulnerable to th'Call, though if Lightborn were lost in numbers in the past, we've no record of it."

"Floria never seemed to have any difficulty talking about Shadowborn."

"Mistress Floria's not a mage," Ishmael said flatly.

A thoughtful pause. "What do you know about therapeutic hypnosis?"

Ish shrugged. "Not so much."

"Most important, in this instance, is that it has nothing to do with ensorcellment or subordination of the will. I am not a mage—as you well know—not a fairground magician, and definitely *not* the hypnotist in a sixpenny melodrama." That emphasis suggested past trying experiences. "I could not induce you to do anything that you might not wish to do."

He paused. "If you wish to touch-read me to know the truth of that, you may."

Ishmael did not move. It was a generous offer, given that Ishmael's presence, as well as Telmaine's confession of magic, for which Ishmael was also responsible, had perturbed Balthasar's happy marriage. Ishmael and Telmaine had at no point acted improperly, but there was a warm, mutual attraction between them. "I've got many wishes best not acted on," Ishmael said, truthfully.

"I've never known anyone who didn't. But I'm not talking about impulses, although hypnotism can be very useful in subduing impulses, even quite compelling ones. Will you let me attempt to hypnotize you, Baron? It may be that I can augment your resistance to the Call."

"Aye," Ishmael said. "Have at it."

But now, as years ago, when he was trying to elicit the fullest strength from his magic, Ishmael was hampered by his hyperacute senses and keen, worldly awareness, the consequences of years of vagabondage and Shadowhunting. He knew there was danger outside; he knew danger had to be attended to. Every voice or closing door, familiar or otherwise, snapped him from his trance.

"Hold," he said at last, and leaned forward, rubbing his temples to coax away an incipient headache. Balthasar sat silent, his expression a professional mask.

"Maybe I should have said t'you that I was not that good at th'exercises that mages use. The mage who took me on when I couldn't stick in the Broomes' commune had th'idea t'overwhelm my vigilance. He had me down at the fish market when the barges docked." Balthasar's grimace proved that he, too, had visited the fish market at that time—probably as a cash-strapped young student after cheap, fresh fish. Ishmael grinned. "It seemed t'work, Hearne. So maybe—"

Telmaine's silent scream, the sear of magic across his awareness, caught him completely unguarded. He felt his body spasm with the shock of it, and then he lost all sense of himself as the reverberations shuddered along his nerves. Their passing left him in a state of desperate uncertainty.

He willed a silent voice to speak, longed for a whisper or even a wisp of vitality that would tell him if she prevailed, whether that was a shriek of mortal injury or a battle cry. He could not endure— He must— He must not try to— The crushing pain in his chest nearly caused him to black out, and left him sweating and shaking and afraid he had groaned aloud. His teeth were locked, hard enough for his jaw muscles to spasm, and he felt chilled and nauseated. Balthasar's fingers probed his pulses, felt for his stuttering heart; through his touch, he felt the physician's recognition and concern at this second episode. He lifted his head groggily, finding himself propped half in, half out of the armchair. "Cursed . . . habits," he managed, and, struggling to think, let his head fall back.

He had sensed Shadowborn—he could not mistake them. Sweet Imogene, had another Shadowborn found her? They knew there were at least two in the city. If so, had Vladimer been there? Judging by what she said of her encounter with the first Shadowborn, her best chance— perhaps even her only chance—of survival was to have someone present with a ready hand and a revolver, and Vladimer was as good as Ishmael at close quarters. But there had been Lightborn magic in that sear, too. Had she run afoul of the Lightborn mages, despite his best hopes that his warnings and her own aversion would restrain her from contravening their laws on the use of magic? Or were the *Lightborn* in league with the *Shadowborn*, as Stranhorne had suggested? It would explain the magical taints, and why she fell under attack.

Sweet Imogene, what was happening in the city?

He roused himself at the rattle of small bottles as Balthasar unrolled his medicine pouch. "No need to dose me," he said. "It's just th'effects of overreach again."

Balthasar paused and said, firmly, "You have to stop trying to use your magic."

"Th'head knows; it's just slow t'reach the reflexes." He pushed himself up too soon; he had to lean forward, head in his hands, until his heart rate steadied and the pain in his chest eased.

When he raised his head, Balthasar was waiting for him. "Was it Telmaine?"

The man was no mage, but he had witnessed Ishmael's previous spasm while talking to Telmaine, and she would be foremost in his mind. In a few words, not sparing either of them, Ishmael sketched what he had sensed.

Balthasar's shoulders bowed with guilt. "How could we do this to her?" he whispered. "How could we put her in such danger?"

"Th'job needed done, and she's the best we have." His choice of tense was deliberate.

"I'm her husband, Strumheller," Balthasar said. "I promised when I married her to cherish and protect her, and I sent her into danger."

There was not much Ishmael could say; Balthasar knew what they faced, knew what it had already cost them. And Ishmael knew how he felt—indeed, he envied the other man his right to express it. "We'll be bound north before sunrise," he said, half prayerfully. "If Mycene has his way."

They ate breakfast in near silence, having exhausted speculation as to what might be happening in the city or outside in the snow. Mycene would not release either of them, though they heard Lavender arguing with him in the hall. Nor would Mycene permit the twins to visit them. He was convinced that the young women were plotting Ishmael's escape, whatever their father said. He was quite right, if Ishmael knew his baronettes. And who was to say Lavender had not been right when she had urged him to ride out before Mycene arrived? If he had, he would have been out in the snow—or beyond the snow, with whatever might be out there.

He persuaded Balthasar to dose himself out of his medical bag to relieve the aches of the previous night's ride. The dose, breakfast, and lingering fatigue made him drowsy, sparing Ishmael his too-sharp attention and his too-imaginative worrying about Telmaine and what had happened in Minhorne. Like Vladimer and Stranhorne, Balthasar could imagine disasters that might never have occurred to Ishmael. That left Ishmael to listen to the snowmelt running in the gutters and feel the Call dragging on him.

Stranhorne himself arrived while they were eating lunch. His face told them the news was bad. "Roads have cleared enough that a post rider made it through. I've had a telegram from my elder son in Minhorne. The archduke and several others were injured this morning in a magical attack. The archduke suffered severe burns; he may not live. A regency council will be instituted for the emergency, and the heir will be recalled from their summer estate. At present, the main suspicion falls on the Lightborn."

That was what I felt from Telmaine, Ishmael thought in horror. The Shadowborn's cursed fire raising again. Were Lightborn involved as allies or agents of the Shadowborn? Or had they, too, opposed the Shadowborn attack, finally involving themselves against these rogue mages? It would be a bitter irony if the Lightborn had been trying to protect the archduke and now were blamed—but that was the way the world worked. And Telmaine—was she alive or dead? If the archduke had been attacked, she would have done what she could to stop it; he could not imagine her doing otherwise. . . . She had abundant power but precious little experience, and what he had sensed suggested her situation had been desperate. All that beauty, refinement, and strength of personality and magic, burned, perhaps dead—because he was not there. . . . "Vladimer?" Ishmael asked, because he could not ask first about Telmaine—he had no reason to ask about Telmaine—and she should have been close to Vladimer.

"Lord Vladimer appears to have suffered a mental collapse, having shot and killed a lady guest."

"Who?" whispered Balthasar, and then in a near shout, *"Who was she?"* He controlled his voice; it shook with the effort. "My wife . . . was a guest at the palace." His thoughts would have followed the same course Ishmael's had, likely more swiftly.

"It was not your wife," said Stranhorne with compassion. "The lady's name was Lady Sylvide di Reuther. My son made no mention of Lady Telmaine."

Ishmael remembered the lady, a sweet-faced feather-head, gossiping with Telmaine at the archducal ball—about Ishmael's reputation, as he recalled. Why Vladimer would have had cause to shoot *her*, he could not imagine. Was this some residual effect of the ensorcellment? Had the Shadowborn ensnared him anew? Balthasar had surmised that Vladimer had not told them everything about his encounter with the Shadowborn, and Ishmael was certain he was correct.

"Did your son say anything about whether . . . Lady Sylvide's form changed in death?" Balthasar said.

"He did not," Stranhorne said, slowly. "Is that possible?"

"Aye," Ishmael said, grimly.

"It has to be Shadowborn," Balthasar said. "If the archduke dies—"

The archduke's heir, being his youngest child, was only twelve, little older than Sejanus Plantageter himself had been when he succeeded his own father. "The regency council'll be Imbré, Rohan, Mycene, and Kalamay," Ish said slowly, thinking aloud. The three other major dukes, and Claudius Rohan, who had sat on the regency council for Sejanus's own long-ago minority and was Sejanus's closest friend; no one would deny him that service for Sejanus's son. Imbré was the only other one of that long-ago council still alive.

Balthasar Hearne understood the political implications as well as either baron, perhaps better, for he had served several terms on the council mediating Lightborn-Darkborn affairs and understood the stress points intimately. Neither Mycene nor Kalamay had any tolerance for Lightborn. Sachevar Mycene—Ferdenzil's father—coveted the land they held, and Xerxes Kalamay found them and their magic to be an offense to the Sole God.

If their neighbors had turned against them, the Darkborn were terribly vulnerable. As they had been a hundred years back, when the genocidal Lightborn Odon, styled Odon the Breaker, set out to rid his lands of Darkborn.

Stranhorne said, "I've commissioned a special train to take Lord Mycene and his men to Strumheller, now the thaw is well advanced. It'll be faster than the coastal express, but you'll likely have an overday stay in Strumheller or some point north—with Lightborn unrest, the railways won't want to risk day trains."

Ishmael agreed. Balthasar's face was grim. Likely recalling the abortive attack on the day train taking Telmaine and him to the coast to save Lord Vladimer. Lightborn, Telmaine had said. "We need to go north as soon as we can now," Bal said.

"Father," Lavender's voice came from outside. "Get *out* of my way, you knucklehead. This is an emergency. *Father!*"

Stranhorne himself crossed over and opened the door. "Let my daughter pass," he told the guard. "If she says it is an emergency, it is."

Lavender half fell through the door, muttering not entirely under her breath about the guard's habits and antecedents. "The inbound post coach just arrived," she said, anticipating her father's reproach at her language. "The post riders from Upper Eastbridge and the Heights didn't make their rendezvous. Several carts of wool were due into Lower Eastbridge from the Heights; they didn't arrive. A midwife who went out in that direction last night to attend a childbed hasn't been heard from, and no one who lives in that direction has made it to work or market. Dyan's mustering and mounting a double squad to take the road to Lower Eastbridge, to scout. Post coach is going on to the Crosstracks—"

"Under escort," Stranhorne said.

"Yes, a squad—Carlann's taking them. Laurel's writing the telegrams to send t'Strumheller and points south along the wires."

"Strumheller Manor and Crosstracks, both," Ishmael said. His brother had to get the word, with no dithering. If Stranhorne weren't so obdurate, they'd be able to send the telegrams from here. Ishmael had had Strumheller Manor wired the month he inherited, although nine years later, his engineers were still working against skeptical villagers, distance, gales, rain, and frost in their efforts to string and maintain a working network along the hill roads. "The rail-

way head office, too: they'll need to decide on th'trains."
Which likely meant that he would not be heading north
under guard tonight, if the trains were stopped and Stranhorne could not spare fifteen horses. "And Lord Vladimer
in Minhorne. Plain text; no cipher." If Vladimer were incapacitated and couldn't read it, others would; it might push
them into action.

Though, given the regency council, that action might not
be what he wished. Mycene, for one, might take advantage
of the archduke's incapacity and the pressure on the Borders to make his move on the island territories. Unless the
archdukedom itself proved the greater plum.

The Plantageters would have to look to their own interests. Ishmael had all he could manage in the Borders.

"I need a telegram sent to my wife," Balthasar slipped in.
"She was staying at the home of her sister, Lady Erskane.
Ask her to wire that she is all right."

Lavender nodded and said to her father, "We're sending
a squad south toward Stonebridge and Hartman's Barrow.
They'll meet up with the squad quartered in Stonebridge
and swing out by the Barrow."

"Double squads," Ishmael said. "Even from here. Same
orders as th'ones to Eastbridge. And pass the word to
th'post coach to hold their outbound runs."

"Already done," Lavender said. Then she said, "Will you
lead the squad to Upper Eastbridge? You're one of the best
we have still."

Lavender didn't know about the strengthened Call—
didn't know that his risk from it was any graver than at any
other time since he'd known her. Balthasar, subject to the
constraints of his profession, kept silent, though Ishmael
heard the breath he drew.

Stranhorne shook his head. "Mycene would never allow
it."

"Or he'd insist on a guard on me," Ishmael said. "And the
last thing we need is men in the squad who haven't been
trained in the way we fight—or have you forgotten th'hide-
stripping I gave you and your sister, all those years ago?"

She said with feeling, "Never."

"I'll be put to good use here, getting the manor ready."

"Do you think," Lavender said, sounding younger than her years, "it might come to fighting here?"

"Aye, I think it might. Those are ominous signs, as y'rightly understood. But we've got solid walls between us and them, and without the walls and the killing grounds, they'll rue the hour they crossed into our lands."

Except, he thought, *they have magic, and magic powerful enough to bring snow in late summer.* Her father knew that. But Lavender—it did not matter whether she knew or not. She could do no more than she was already doing, and would do it less well if she were frightened. "If y'can get me out of this room," he said, "I'll do what I can to take Lord Mycene and his men in hand. They'll be no danger t'anyone but the Shadowborn shooting from snipers' holes in th'upper stories." He gestured. "And they may take t'it."

"And this is good *how*?" Lavender muttered.

Ishmael grinned, despite the weight of his worries and the drag of the Call. "Th'enemy of your enemy, girl. It'll be all to the good, them knowing what we've been up against, all these years. Make them think twice about troubling your kin in th'Islands."

"Who is taking the squad south?" Stranhorne said, neutrally.

She set her lips, an answer in itself, and then said, half blurting, "Laurel and Boris will be here, and one of us—"

"Not necessarily," Stranhorne said. There was a silence. "Be careful."

"As a city lady guards her reputation." She kissed her father's cheek, clasped Ishmael's gloved hand, and made a strategic retreat before either Stranhorne or Ishmael could raise further objections.

"Stranhorne," said Ishmael. "I owe y'an apology. I promised to keep them out of danger." If he'd been born a sixth-rank mage, he'd be able to *lift* Laurel from here to safety in a moment—and he would have, even if her father banished him from his manor and she boxed his ears for it. But he couldn't even argue for sending her to relatives in the inner

Borders if the trains were stopping, and he could not pretend the roads were safe.

"Are you?" the baron said, tartly. "I had no idea you were responsible for the Shadowborn."

"Get me out of this room, please, before I start tearing through th'walls. Hearne, too. Is Linnea here?"

"Yes," Stranhorne said, the hint of weary amusement telling Ishmael a familiar story. Linneas Straus was physician and surgeon to the Stranhorne troop. As regularly as the turn of seasons, his daughter's husband was sacked from his latest job, the growing family descended on Linneas's home in need of shelter, and Linneas took refuge in the manor. "It's that," he'd said to Stranhorne, "or y'sit magistrate on my trial for killing th'wastrel."

Balthasar would no doubt learn all that and more once he met the physician. "Linneas Straus is the physician who takes care of the manor and the troops," he said to Balthasar. To Stranhorne: "Hearne's got city hospital training; be useful should things get busy. He might be able t'help us prepare for numbers of casualties. We've never dealt with a mass attack before." It would also keep the physician distracted from what might be happening in Minhorne. If his need was anything like Ishmael's, he should be grateful.

"And we can only hope we're not dealing with one now," Stranhorne said. To Balthasar: "Linneas doesn't have a city education—he was trained by apprenticeship, as were most of our surgeons—but he's been physician to the manor for thirty-odd years. Attended on all my children's births."

Balthasar took the caution as intended, though for him, at least, it was not needed; he had little city professional arrogance about him. Ishmael added, "And never mind his sense of humor."

"I'll have a word with Mycene," Stranhorne promised, and left them.

Balthasar sat down. "Oh, dear God," he breathed. "Vladimer was right."

"Seems t'have been," Ish said stoically.

"You think they'll need me?" Balthasar said.

"They might. But there's another reason I want us out

and about. If it comes to a siege, and it might, the manor's walls are strong, and its defenders skilled, but if there's an agent inside—if there's a Shadowborn inside—then that'll do them no good whatsoever. Remember what we found in th'archducal summerhouse: th'entire household ensorcelled into sleep. If that's done here, they'll have no chance."

"Have you sensed something in the manor?"

"Maybe. It comes; it goes. I've taken damage, I know, but I *daren't* let this pass."

Balthasar said, slowly, "If I were a Shadowborn shape-shifter, and I wished to sabotage the effort to defend Stranhorne, then I would try to replace you, Baron Stranhorne, or one of his children."

"Aye," Ishmael said. "That'd be my thought, too."

The physician's voice was oddly tense. "Perhaps *I* might sense it, if it is magé enough."

"Y'didn't sense th'one that wore your brother's form."

"I was flat on my back, weak and panicking with the threat to my daughter."

His probing sonn, his braced posture, revealed his purpose. Ishmael grunted. "You've more nerve than sense, thinking t'spook a Shadowborn when you're alone with it and unarmed."

Balthasar said, unsmiling, "You were out of contact for more than twenty-four hours."

"Well, I'm m'self. And this close t'you, I think I can be sure of you, too."

He waited, and was relieved to hear the change in the physician's voice. "A mage or mages strong enough to bring on snow in August would have the strength to breach even these walls."

"We can but hope they've a need t'preserve this manor. I wish I'd a sense of th'way they worked. It seems so erratic—oblique one moment, excessive th'next. Vladimer'd be able to get a sense of it. I can't." He pushed that worry aside; they had to deal with the dangers of the moment. "I want us t'try to smoke out any Shadowborn in the manor *before* their forces reach us."

"The Shadowborn who impersonated my brother, trying

to get me to tell him where Tercelle's twins were, did not attempt to touch-read me. It may be that Shadowborn do not have that ability. If they don't, we can check on each other, ask each other questions that superficial acquaintances would not be expected to know. But if they do—"

"In this flurry, we're likely safe enough. But you'd be best t'take care not t'be alone, or with one or two. That includes Mycene's men."

Balthasar's expression changed again. "What is't?" Ishmael said.

"Something I noticed during last night's ride . . . Something I—" His expression was frustrated. Plainly, Balthasar Hearne was not used to having his memory fail him. "You were about spent," Ish said. "It'll come t'you."

In the hall, an alarm bell clamored. "What—?" said Balthasar, as Ishmael moved.

"Call t'arms," Ishmael said, opening the door, and walking straight into the sonn of Mycene's guards.

Balthasar

To Balthasar's relief, they were all spared finding out whether Ishmael was prepared to stop, or how far Mycene's men were prepared to go in stopping him. Young Baronet Stranhorne arrived at a run. "My father's compliments," he gasped out. "You're all wanted in the ballroom immediately."

A diplomat in larval form, Balthasar thought, since he was sure that Ishmael was the one truly wanted. They arrived in the ballroom at the same time as did Mycene himself, who sonned them with a scowl and gestured, with a taut flick of the hand, for Balthasar and Ishmael to precede them. The ballroom, busy when they passed through it on arrival, was barely controlled mayhem now. Balthasar smelled blood, despite the dense overlay of gun oil, gunpowder, wet wools, leather, and sweat. By the turn of his head and the narrowing of his lips, Mycene smelled it, too. From the far side of the ballroom, a man shrieked through clenched teeth, and sonn resolved a bucking figure on a table, with others holding him down. Balthasar started in that direction, but a hard hand on his shoulder jerked him back. "Stay," the guard said.

"I'm needed—"

"*Stay*," growled Mycene. "I'm not having you take advantage—"

"Sweet Imogene, Mycene," Balthasar said, exasperated, "where would I *go*?"

A group of men and women wearing the uniform and livery of house staff thrust past them in disregard of Mycene's temper and rank. Most carried long-barreled guns, some more than one. Ishmael had explained that the south and west sides of the manor overlooked ground cleared, leveled, and strewn with gravel and the brittle shells of dried nuts, and cross-webbed with trip wires strung with rattles. Nothing could approach unheard. The narrow upstairs windows served as sniper posts. Mycene allowed the reservists to pass with no more than a grunt of sour approval. From within milling bodies and pulsing sonn, Balthasar could hear Laurel's clear voice issuing orders.

A man with one arm directed them to the side gallery, where they found Baronette Lavender, her father, and as grim, weary, and battered a group of men as Balthasar had ever managed after a brawling night in the Rivermarch, where he worked intermittently as a physician. They were gathered around a large relief model, which Balthasar recognized as being of the immediate area.

Mycene thrust forward. "What's happening?"

Stranhorne sonned him, nodded curtly, acknowledging him as a peer, but spoke as much to Ishmael as to Mycene. "Shadowborn, in force. Scavvern, balewolves, some kind of winged Shadowborn—no one's given a clear description. Ensorcelled animals—attacks by dog packs, horses, cattle, and goats, even mobbing by *sheep*. We've got envenomations, reports of beetles of some kind. . . ." He jerked his head toward the door, where the shrieks from the man on the table had diminished to a muffled keen, with an intermittent strangulation that Balthasar read as convulsions.

"Stonebridge"—Stranhorne pointed to a marker—"has

been overrun." The bell tolled, a slow, steady knell beneath his words. "We've got survivors pouring in the gate as we speak. Laurel is marshaling sweeps to bring in all those we can rescue, because we'll have to close the gate before the Shadowborn force reaches us. The squad quartered at Stonebridge was evacuating the town when last heard of. We've no word on Hartman's Barrow or the hill villages beyond. We've sent riders out to the Crosstracks, to raise the alarm, warn the railroad, and send telegrams to Strumheller and the inner Borders. Strumheller's our best hope of quick reinforcement, if we can hold the tracks and stop the wires from being cut. At least it's early in the night—we've got hours before we'll be completely unable to defend ourselves. If you want to take your chances on the road to the station, then we'll mount and supply you. But I'd not refuse a dozen good fighting men." He said that without a smile, without any play on the irony of his recruiting his enemies; the situation was too grim for that.

Mycene's grunt signaled neither assent nor refusal, but he leaned forward slightly, gathering himself for action. He was already committed to this fight, whether he knew it or not.

To Balthasar, Stranhorne said, "Are you up to helping Linneas? We've got casualties." He had noticed Balthasar's stiff movements. Balthasar simply nodded. "Good." To the one-armed man he said, "Erich, take him, introduce him."

In the ballroom, the reek of terrified, wounded, and sick people was even stronger, the noise louder. Somewhere, a woman was screaming wordlessly, a monotonous descant of horror, chopped by regular, wheezing breaths. To Bal's left, a small child's voice said, "Ma, Ma, Ma," with a dreadful persistence; worst of all, it went unanswered. He heard Erich say to someone, "We need t'get them calmed down and cleared somehow."

Erich slung Balthasar toward the narrow corridor into the former ballroom kitchen, now—for the sake of its stoves and drainage—turned surgery. The Stranhorne surgeon was already at work, hands digging into a man's belly. He barely acknowledged Erich's introduction: "Here's

th'city man, Linneas, t'help you. Name's Balthasar Hearne."
Bal noted that the man on the table still wore his boots, and
tallied that with the set to the surgeon's face and the viscous
strings trailing from the drapes onto the floor. Without a
word, he stripped off his jacket, rolled up his sleeves, and
went to the sink to scrub his hands and forearms with harsh
carbolic soap. Behind him, he heard an instrument fall, with
no sound of a fumble or missed catch, the tiny sound like
the last stroke of a distant sunrise bell to a man too far from
shelter. The sound of a body being lifted was always different after life was gone.

He let a few heartbeats elapse before he turned. Linneas
Straus was a heavyset man in his fifties. He swept his sonn
over Balthasar, approving his bared arms with a grunt.
"Y'know what t'do?" he said.

"If I don't, I'll ask."

Balthasar lost track of time. Smell, hearing, insight — all
narrowed to contain only the utterly necessary. He admin-
istered anesthesia. He helped pin down a slight boy while
Linneas amputated his ruined arm above the elbow, and
cleared vomit from the boy's mouth before he choked on it.
He set swift stitches into the lacerated back of a young
woman, knowing that for all his care, she would be scarred
for life, if she did not take a fatal infection. Worse than the
clawed ruin before him was the low, monotonous sobbing
that did not change, no matter how deeply the needle
pierced. One of the women acting as assistants whispered
to him that she was infant mistress in the Stonebridge
school, and that the school . . . She left the sentence unfin-
ished. Balthasar completed his suturing, the attendants carried her away, and he let the sound and the information slip
out of his mind. He knew to be grateful that it was not him
but Straus who must decide who to set aside as beyond all
help. Like the man with the crushed skull whose agonal
breathing had so often faded to silence and then rattled into
life again that when he finally died, nobody noticed at first.

Voices floated in from elsewhere. Lavender or Laurel
said, "Father, we may need your word to close the gate
soon."

"Oh, Mother of All," the other twin replied, "there hasn't been time for everyone—"

"We ran into what's left of the Stonebridge squad." This time it was Lavender. "The Shadowborn vanguard is three miles back. We've moved the armory into the second-floor gallery, and we've filled the ballroom and the lower floor with refugees, and set anyone whose nerves are up to it to reloading upstairs. Ishmael's handling that.... Curse Mycene, he should have been out on the roads."

"How many have come through the gate?" he heard Stranhorne say.

"Just over a thousand, by my count," Laurel said, her voice a half whisper.

Stranhorne said, perhaps to no one in particular, "At last census there were upwards of seven thousand between Stonebridge and the Barrow, and another three thousand in the hill villages between here and the border with the Shadowlands...."

Balthasar fumbled and dropped his scissors. "Curse it, city man," Linneas barked. "If you need a break, take one. This is likely just th'start."

Someone offered him a mug of tarry tea, sweetened and laced with brandy, and meat jerky and dried fruit, which he soaked in the tea with no regard for gentility. Then a man delirious with pain planted his foot in the center of his stomach, and he nearly lost everything. By the time he was done wheezing and retching, the man had slipped meekly under anesthetic, his last resistance spent. Balthasar braced himself against the table and, still bent over, set to work. Linneas Straus remarked, more cheerfully than before, "No need t'feel ashamed of yourself there; he's th'terror of tavern brawls from the Crosstracks to Stranhorne Port."

Three

Ishmael

*L*ife had taught Ishmael patience, and experience, priorities. So he wasted no spleen on his frustration at being mewed up in the manor and tripping over guards every time he turned around. He had nervous snipers to settle, reloaders to deploy, ammunition runners to direct. With so many of the regulars out on the roads, trying to bring in as many refugees as possible, the majority of the manor's defenders were reserves, trained only as far as would comply with the ducal order: manor servants, wives and sons and daughters of reservists, and young troops in training. And Ferdenzil Mycene and his men, who had listened when Stranhorne had refused to let them out on the roads because of their inexperience in fighting Shadowborn.

I might even start to respect the man, Ishmael thought wryly, *if Mycene keeps being reasonable.*

He wished he had had a chance to have Mycene and his men test shoot some rounds, to give them the feel of the weapons and distance. They weren't as used to handling rifles as they were shorter-range weapons, though several had trained and fought at sea—and Ish, no sailor, had to respect anyone who could master both his weapons and his stomach on a rolling ship. But he had no idea how close the enemy might be and would not risk losing any surprise there was to be had.

"So the idea is we shoot to sound," Mycene said, softly.

He knelt on a sniper's rest in a southern gallery in the fifth and topmost floor of the manor. Ishmael was propped against the wall to his right. Ishmael had half of Mycene's men in this gallery and half in the next, alternating with seasoned Stranhorne reservists. "Have you ever fought these kinds of actions before?"

"There's been th'odd incursion reach the manor before, but not in this force."

"If we'd had time to prepare, I would have suggested volley fire. With the range these have"—he gave a light, possessive caress to the barrel—"we could have started on them as soon as we knew they were within range. You don't appear to need to stint on ammunition."

Was that as innocuous an observation as it seemed? Ish thought, remembering the munitions stored in the locked cellars. In this stir, they hadn't been able to keep the wrong people away from Mycene. But coordinated fire would have been a cursed excellent idea to have had earlier. They were too used to fighting in the open, in small bands, against a haphazard enemy.

He sonned his captor, kneeling relaxed in the sniper's rest, his weapon resting ready on the ledge. Ishmael hadn't needed to correct his posture or settle him down; plainly he was one of those calmed by the approach of battle.

"How large is this force?" Mycene said, voice barely carrying.

"Unknown, except by measuring th'numbers they overwhelmed. Stonebridge was seven thousand people, a fifth of whom were weapons trained—" If Mycene didn't have an idea already of how large a reserve Stranhorne retained, he would before this night was fought out. "And a good squad."

"And what had Stonebridge in the way of defensible positions?"

"Only the terrain: it's built on a hill. Th'only reason the manor is walled and built for defense against force is that Strumheller was burnt to the ground during the civil war." By, as Ishmael recalled, an army led by one of the Mycenes.

Mycene turned his head and sonned him for the first time. "You think we can hold this manor?"

"Depends," said Ishmael, surprised to find himself inclined even toward that much truth.

Mycene returned his attention to the night. "And, of course, there is the question of magic. My father has a fixation with it; I never understood why. Always seemed unmanly to me."

"Nothing unmanly about th'strength needed to bring snow in late summer," Ishmael gritted.

"No. It slowed us detecting their approach very effectively. Have you given any thought to what a retreat from here would be like?"

"Aye," Ishmael said. "Bad."

A humorless smile turned Mycene's lip. "Worse if there's no planning for it, that I can tell you."

Mycene had suffered a dire defeat during his first campaign against an insurrection in his family's holdings on the south coast. He'd been young—twenty-two—and entirely too confident. His father had had to issue pardons and make galling concessions to ransom his son. Mycene had never let himself be caught out again.

Ishmael said, "Aye, nothing like one's own mistakes t'teach one. I'll put it to Stranhorne." He'd be surprised if one of the Stranhornes had not already thought of it. He shrugged off the wall. He wanted another circuit, to steady anyone who needed steadying and to take a last sense of anyone holding or loading a weapon. It might be futile. At this stage, he could not tell whether someone was nervous because of him or because of what might be moving in the night. And although he had intermittently had a transient sense of something that might be Shadowborn presence or magic, it was so faint that he was almost persuaded it was a phantom of his damaged mage sense. But surely—surely if he stood toe-to-toe with a Shadowborn shape-shifter or weather-worker, he must sense that strength.

The question as to what he would do then was one he had no answer for.

He moved away, the guards starting to follow. "Let him go," Mycene said, loudly enough for Ishmael to hear. "There's no hiding for him anywhere this side of sunrise.

Nor for anyone who helps him." Ishmael nodded over his shoulder by way of acknowledgment of the sentiment, if not the fact, and continued down the gallery. Behind him he heard Mycene say, "And where by the Sole God is di Banneret?" A murmur. Mycene snorted. "He was told not to eat the sausage."

Ishmael spared a moment of sympathy for the hapless di Banneret, who would have the insult of his fellows' mockery added to the wretchedness of his guts.

He moved from rest to rest, remembering to make a little sound to warn the taut-nerved snipers that he was coming. Speaking of mistakes teaching, he'd more than once nearly been shot by one of his own people before he'd learned not to pad noiselessly up behind them.

They seemed good, steady. Mycene's men, too, though most were wary of him, and a couple hostile. One of the hostile ones was a bordersman—by the accent, down toward Odon's Barrow—and one of those who handled a rifle with ease. Maybe later he would learn the story.

Boris caught him between rooms. "Father needs you," the youth said, breathlessly. He leaned closer. "The guards?"

"Called off."

"He needs you in the cellar," Boris whispered. "Take the east stair."

"Finish my circuit for me, would you? Make sure everyone has some food or drink with them, and preferably *in* them. You, too," he added, when Boris gulped. "Not a good idea t'start a fight on an empty gut; just makes y'shakier. Your sisters should have told you that."

"Yes. But," he blurted, "I'm not a fighter."

"Nor's your father, but there's a use for thinkers, too." He clapped the young man lightly on his arm, knowing not to press. He'd been too terrified to eat the first few times he had gone up against Shadowborn. And he had been even less a fighter than Boris when he had been cast out into the world. No village or town guard would take him, so it was Shadowhunting or banditry. "Go and check on your people."

"Ishmael," the young man said desperately, "the Shadowborn are less than three miles away. What do I say if someone asks?"

"Tell them the truth. Morale is one thing, trust another. What you do and say affects their trust in your family. So tell th'truth. That goes double if you've heard something about one of their families. Swap in one of the loaders if they're shaky; let them go with no reproaches." He paused. "You'll do well. Y'come of good stock, and you've solid people around you. They know what t'do. Your part is mostly to steady them."

The east stair, Stranhorne had said, which meant hurrying without appearing to hurry the length of the southern corridor, and down five flights into the cellar. It also meant that he encountered only two or three people on the stairs, since most of the movement was up and down the western and central staircases. Only the southeast portion of that wall had sniper cover; the northeast was walled, with a watchtower on that wall guarded by a squad of men. A squad because they had no means of retreat.

One of Stranhorne's men unlocked and opened the door at his knock, and led him through the cellars to where the baron and a knot of men stood around a pyramid of boxes of munitions. Stranhorne stepped quickly away from the pyramid, moving to block Ishmael's sonn—but not before Ishmael had recognized the detonators attached to one of the boxes.

Stranhorne took his arm and turned him toward a wall. "I'll trouble you to tell me," he said in a low voice, "what was the first thing I asked of you?"

Identity check, thought Ishmael: Stranhorne or Laurel, or both, had been thinking ahead. "That I never discuss or engage in my unnatural practice within your halls."

Stranhorne released Ish's arm with obvious relief and waited. Aside from the damp cold of the cellars, Ish sensed nothing foul or chill around him. He shook his head slightly. Interpreting the gesture, Stranhorne said, "We need to think about what happens if they force an entry."

"Y'already are," he noted.

Stranhorne gave a grim smile. "You tell me: how strong

would a mage have to be to survive this many tons of stone dropped on him?"

For a moment Ishmael felt like that queasy and terrified seventeen-year-old facing his first fight. "I don't know," he said. "If taken by surprise—" The Shadowborn that he and Lady Telmaine had faced together had been strong enough to ensorcell an entire household, and more than Telmaine could hold for more than a minute or so—but that minute or so had been long enough for him to put three bullets into it, and it had not been strong enough to survive those.

"That's the aim," said Stranhorne. "My engineers tell me there's a good chance we'll be able to drop the first and second stories into the cellar."

There is a reason, Ishmael thought, *why intellectuals make a plain working man nervous.* "And get out alive?"

"It's not a suicide plan," the baron said, though there was an edge in his voice that said even if it were, he would carry it through.

"The difficulty is," the baron said, "to work best, we need to be sure that if they do force entry, it's through the east gate. I don't know whether they're capable of punching holes in the walls, but if they come in through the north gate, we're going to have to leave to the east, which will put us behind their lines, or break out through that bricked-in entry to the west. I've got a couple of engineers up there preparing t'blow it."

"Y'ever heard Lord Vladimer on th'subject of plans that depend on enemy cooperation?"

"No," Stranhorne said. "But, then, I've not been in the habit of making them."

Except for the danger in which they all stood, Ishmael could have wished Vladimer were there. If anyone knew how to arrange enemy cooperation . . . "Whichever way we leave the manor could be encircled. We might have to fight our way through. Mycene was cautioning me about the difficulty of an unplanned retreat."

Stranhorne tipped his head back, listening and sensing the mass of stone buttressed above their heads. "I've read the histories of the civil war, and of the wars in the four and five hundreds. I knew there'd be some difference between sitting at leisure in my armchair and fighting a war, but this . . ."

This was not the time for Stranhorne to lose confidence in himself. "Every hour we buy gives time for the Crosstracks and th'inner Borders to prepare, and gives time for reinforcements to come."

"Did they tell you that only about a thousand people have made it in so far?"

He could not have told that from passing through the bedlam of the ballroom. "No," Ishmael said, "They didn't."

"I tell myself that if the Shadowborn were moving that fast, they may not have found or caught most of these people. But there is another explanation—that they may simply have slaughtered them."

Numbers or magic, Ishmael thought. *Either will do.* He could not simply exhort Stranhorne not to despair, or try to chide or shame him out of it. Nor could he leave him in this mood.

"If it's the manor they want, we can hold numbers," he said, at his most stolid. "If it's not the manor, if they roll past us, then we can muster and attack to their rear, though no leader of any sense would leave a force numbered and armed as we are"—not to mention vengeful—"at their back. So if they've any sense, they should make sure the manor has fallen first before they move on, and we should hold until reinforcements come from Strumheller." *Assuming by the direction of the Call that Strumheller has not been similarly besieged,* Ishmael thought. They should not count on timely aid from the north, not with Sejanus Plantageter down and the regency council in control.

"If it's magic," Ishmael said slowly, "and we're speaking of mistakes, those of us in the city should have put this before the Lightborn Temple as soon as we began t'wonder at it. If it's magic, and they force an entry, then your plan's as good as any. I'll be less than no help t'you against magic. I . . . held this back, thinking not to risk it reaching Shadowborn ears"—and because of his own cursed cowardice in speaking of it—"but I did something in Minhorne that likely finished me for magic. Bad overreach, means I try to tap my vitality and I drain it to th'dregs. Nearly done so twice already. I've still got th'touch-sense and maybe I'll still sniff out Shadowborn if they're close and strong enough; I've yet t'test it. But the rest—everything else—is gone."

He waited out the other man's silence. Stranhorne would be the last to acknowledge his grief. "In one respect," Stranhorne said, slowly, "I'm glad. It means I don't have to ask you to wait down here with us, in hopes that you might resist an ensorcellment long enough to throw a switch. I can trust that you'll do whatever it takes to get my son and daughters to safety, and as many of my people with them."

"Not something y'need t'ask, Stranhorne."

"Good. I'm not courting death; I've far too many books left to read. Or I will have," he amended wryly, "until we throw these switches."

"Think on it as having an excuse t'go shopping," Ishmael said.

"Now *that* is something your sister might have said."

Over their heads, eerie amongst the muffling, echoing stone, the alarm began to sound. "I need t'get up there," Ishmael said.

Stranhorne held out his hand; Ishmael clasped it.

Then he went up the stairs at a run, spilling onto the top floor to the sound of staccato firing, except for the far gallery, where he could hear crashes of massed fire; Mycene putting his notion of volley fire into effect. It was as good a use as any to make of him and his men. Ishmael ducked into the nearest room, a guest suite adjacent to the one he and Balthasar had occupied. The four slits were manned, all by Stranhorne reservists or retainers, one firing and one reloading, or at one of the slits, two snipers spelling each other. Those he recognized: a teenage brother and sister from the Crosstracks. Nobody reacted to his sonn.

In the next room he found what he wanted, a man he recognized as skilled and seasoned, who was interspersing his steady firing with brief instructions to his less experienced fellows. Ishmael set his back against the wall. "What's happening?"

"Noisemakers started cracking just before we sounded the bell. We shot some to sound, but the racket's too bad. At least they haven't brought th'cursed cannon into play upstairs." He tilted his head. "What're they doing down in th'gallery?"

"Mycene, trying coordinated fire."

A grunt from the bordersman.

"Are y'holding them?"

"Too soon t'tell." A sideways cast of sonn. "Y'shooting, or just idling?"

The corner of Ishmael's mouth tucked in, tugging at the scars. "Have no fear, I'll have m'turn. I—"

The man swore and jammed his shoulder into the slit, bracing himself with an outstretched leg as he strained to angle upward. He shot twice into the sky, grunting as the recoil pinned his shoulder against stone. Ishmael remembered then that Stranhorne had mentioned flying Shadowborn. Before the man spoke, he was running for the eastern stairs, one of four that opened onto the roof. In the stairwell he almost collided with Lavender di Gautier, bounding up the steps by twos and threes. She greeted him with gladness changing to shock. "You're not armed!"

Mycene's men had refused to let him carry even a knife, but it was an unforgivable oversight not to have rearmed as soon as Mycene loosed his jesses. Ruthlessly, she stripped the two troopers with her of their second revolvers—the ones she carried would never have suited his much broader hands—and thrust them and her own knife into his hands, and sent the junior of the two scrambling downstairs to rearm them. "You're not armored, either," she complained. She and her companions wore helmets and armor, hardened leather with metal breastplates and shoulder guards. The sound of shouts and shots from overhead forestalled any argument. She took off like a deer, leaving them scrambling in pursuit.

"Di Gautier," she yelled warning as she launched herself through the door to the roof, Ishmael's lunge for her belt falling short. His sonn caught her as she skidded to one knee in the open, revolver raised. He felt a surge of sickening Shadowborn magic, and then something dropped down at her back, wings spread. Shooting it risked shooting her. Ishmael converted his last stride into a dive, slamming into scaled knees and bringing the Shadowborn crashing down on him. He threw it clear with the strength of terror, fending off a raking foot with his left arm. Two shots sounded simultaneously, and its thrashing became uncoordinated.

Lavender gripped his uninjured arm, adding her hoist to his scramble up. "What *are* these things?"

Sonn confirmed that the creature was moribund, and he took a sense of its shape: winged, deep-keeled breastbone, manlike face, clawed hands and feet—claws that would have stripped her rib cage to bone, had they connected. He was shaking slightly and fighting to subdue his gorge; whatever subtler sense was lost to him, the magic around these Shadowborn was as foully potent as anything he had ever met. His left arm was achingly numb and he could feel the sticky warmth of blood between his fingers. He was glad the contact had been fleeting; he had no desire to touch-read that. "N-nothing I've met before."

"You all right?" she said, sharply.

"Overhead!" a man shouted, and reflexively they all three ducked as guns fired from three directions—Sweet Imogene, some idiot was shooting inboard with a rifle!—and with a screech, a Shadowborn fell splayed on the deck. Ishmael and Lavender bellowed simultaneously, "Sound positions and form up!" Lavender added, "Abandon rests. Form up on the stairwells!"

Ishmael's lips drew back in a seasick grin. *Brilliant girl.* They needed to defend the entrances to the manor now, not the periphery, and positioned around the stairwells they would have clearly defined quadrants to cover and would be less likely to shoot one another. And they also needed only one voice giving commands. "Troop's yours," he barked, and lunged for the stair housing. In the shelter of the eaves, he dropped to one knee with a jar that nearly made him heave, but held his revolver steady, angling above the head height of a crouching man, as figures scrambled across the rooftop toward them. Seven, eight, ten men — one supporting the other, who was stumbling and holding his thigh.

"Some cursed fool *shot* him," the first man accused.

Lavender shifted aside from the door to let him pass into the stairwell. "Everyone sound off!" she called, and was answered by ragged shouts from three directions and scattered yells from elsewhere. The nearest was a woman's voice, and Ishmael sonned her figure just starting to move toward them from one of the sniper's positions. Then sonn caught a plunging shape, and the woman shrieked and fell beneath it. Ishmael and the man next to him shot as one, and the Shadowborn reeled away and toppled from the edge of the roof, and did not rise again in the air. Nor did the woman rise, though she stirred a little, giving a bubbling sob that suggested a torn throat. Ishmael felt the other man start to move and blocked him with a rigid, bloodied arm. "No," he growled. "We need t'stay here."

The man clubbed his arm with the hilt of his revolver. But from his other side, an older man said, "He's right. Here they come."

Ishmael missed the first round, for the blow had awakened the pain in his clawed arm. Sweat running down his face, he balanced the revolver and fired upon anything that dropped from the air. He'd fallen into the easier task, he realized, having ducked for the outer stairwell; Lavender and others on the inside had to clear the area between the stairwells, without inflicting casualties on their own. With his arm screaming pain and the waxing and waning sense of Shadowborn making his head reel, he was less of a hazard here than there. *And, Mother of All, she is good,* he thought, listening to her shouted exchanges with the other groups, coordinating fire.

"How many of these cursed things are there?" muttered the man at his side, reloading. Ishmael's revolver clicked dry, and he jammed it into his waistband and drew the second. As he did so, vileness washed over him. Instinct wheeled him around, clear of the eaves. He sonned the Shadowborn even as it alighted on the stairwell roof above Lavender, folding gracefully on the crouch, claws extended to rake. Someone screamed warning at him, and he felt a gust of downdraft on his sweating neck. Knowing exactly the choice he was making, he braced the revolver with both hands and placed his bullet beneath his target's prominent breastbone. As he did so, he felt a metallic puff past his cheek and a hot burst of liquid on his neck. He smelled blood, sharp and rich, and grinned in crazed gratitude at his savior.

Then the dying Shadowborn toppled against him, the bare skin of its forehead brushing the bare skin of his neck, its thoughts invading touch-sense, the reek of its magic enveloping him. Under its weight, physical and psychic, he pitched forward onto hands and knees, aware of a roil of impressions that either body or mind or both must reject, so that he was either going to be thoroughly sick or simply pass out. Hands caught his jacket, hauling him into shelter by the collar and armpits, the urgent handling and brushed touches by his own a blessed antidote to the intimate sense of Shadowborn. Someone pushed his revolver back into his hand. "Thanks!" he croaked. "We need t'keep aware of the roof over our heads. And I need t'come through. . . ."

He switched his revolver to his injured hand, dropped to a crouch, and scuttled to Lavender's side. "Y'all right?" Lavender said, as he straightened up beside her.

"Been worse." He caught her sleeve, pulled her ear close. What he had to say had an even higher priority than having her undivided attention on the killing field. "I'd a touch-sense of that one. The mind's more man than animal. It wasn't chance that dropped th'other above you."

She gave an indelicate curse. He doubted she understood all the implications of the information, but knew she would understand what she needed to, here and now: these were cunning, mindful foes. "You've it in hand here," he said, with a private prayer to gods real and imagined that this would continue. "I need t'get down to th'north gate."

"Yes," she said. *"Go."*

He went, managing to be a turn of the stairs out of their hearing before the aura of Shadowborn, exertion, and injury overwhelmed him. The bout of vomiting was as short as will and self-control could make it; fortunately for his legend, it went unobserved. He'd owe the house staff a tip for the cleanup. He wiped his mouth on his sleeve and lurched down the stairs at a creditable run, already hearing shouts and shots from the direction of the ballroom. Sweet Imogene, if they forced the entrance, with the ballroom full of the weakest of refugees and the wounded—

He veered off on the third floor and ran for the door to the roof of the ballroom, which in the ballroom's glory days had held a rooftop dance floor. Now it held guard positions, but was usually only lightly manned—and if no one had thought to reinforce the guard, and they had been taken by surprise . . . It had a door to the third story wide enough to admit three in promenade, as well as a servant's side door. He wheeled around the final corner and sonned the door still closed, blessedly intact and barred. His sonn caught the figure of a slight man, hands to the bar, and for a heartbeat he thought it was Balthasar Hearne. "Hoi!" Ishmael bellowed. "Hold there." The figure whirled and plunged down the main stairs, moving far more spryly than he would have expected of the travel-worn physician. He would have pursued, but the servant's door opened and what stepped across the threshold was not Darkborn. He slammed against the wall and fired, two-handed, into the doorway. Curse it—he had neither the time nor the dexterity to reload, which left him with five bullets and a knife. "Stranhornes!" Ishmael roared at the top of his lungs. "To me! Ballroom roof!"

Balthasar

Trouble on the roof, Balthasar had registered someone saying outside some time ago. Straus had cocked his head, listening; he nodded grimly and went back to itemizing the many faults of his son by marriage. He and Balthasar were repairing the muscular back of a young drayman who had used his carriage to ferry the weak and wounded in the retreat from Stonebridge, and shielded his last passengers from attack with his own body. With fixed concentration, the Stonebridge apothecary dripped chloroform onto the mask over the patient's face. He had hardly spoken since he stumbled in the gate with the youngest of his brother's children in his arms. His own oldest daughter was upstairs with the defenders, but none of the rest of his or his brother's families had reached the manor, and no one could tell him whether they were alive or dead.

The drayman was carried from the table alive, though neither physician thought well of his chances. They had washed the wounds extensively and cleaned them of shreds of cloth, but the tissue damage was so extensive that they could not completely debride them, and Shadowborn lacerations infected easily, Straus muttered grimly as they stood side by side, scrubbing the blood off their hands. "Likely be dead in days, even if we're not overrun.... Y'any good with a firearm, city man?"

"No," Balthasar said.

"So I take it you've not got one?" Straus, Balthasar realized, was armed: his sonn outlined the shape of a revolver under the other man's surgical apron. Was the surgeon prepared to fight?

"No ... should I?"

"Not if it makes y'more hazard to th'wounded." Straus sonned him. "But there's some would like t'have a bullet for themselves."

Rather than die under Shadowborn teeth or claws. Bal understood. He knew there were some to whom the manner of death mattered, who believed that some deaths profaned body and soul. He was not one. Most deaths were ugly. He shook his head.

Straus said no more on the subject. "We'll take th'scalp wound next, if there's none worse next door."

Next door had been an intimate dining room for the baronelle and her circle. Bridal and naming-day cakes would have sagged under the weight of the decorative molding and piping. Rows of pallets held men and women waiting for surgery, recovering after surgery, or dying in the greatest possible comfort. Mostly now they were quiet, drugged or weak or resigned to pain, so that he could hear the sobs of the young woman rocking in a chair in the corner. Bal sighed. Her sister had gone into premature labor during the retreat. The child must have died. Perhaps the mother, too.

"Hearne." Stranhorne's one-armed aide wove between pallets to accost him. "The baron—Strumheller—wants a word with you. They've taken him over t'the briefing gallery. Not bad hurt," he added, as he registered Balthasar's reaction. "Baronette Laurel is stitching him. Get her off her feet for a while." Then he said, loudly enough to be heard by patients and helpers alike, "We've fought them off," and, quietly, to Balthasar, "though it was a near-run thing."

In the side gallery, Ishmael di Studier was leaning back in one of the chairs, arm extended along a narrow table. Laurel di Gautier was suturing two oblique lacerations on his forearm. Ishmael's teeth were set in a roll of leather and his sound hand was locked on the arm of the chair, but otherwise he endured without flinching.

She had obviously done this before, by the speed and deftness with which she set the sutures. Possibly even to Ishmael himself, given the ease with which she touched the mage. Balthasar waited as she tied off the last few. "I'm done," she said quietly, and began to clean the skin. Ishmael unclenched his teeth and removed the tooth-marked leather. He snagged a towel from the stack at her elbow and wiped his face and soaked hairline.

Balthasar cleared his throat, attracting their attention. "Hearne," said di Studier, hoarsely, before he could speak. "What did Lord Vladimer say first when he came to?"

"Ordered us not to move, or he would shoot to kill." That he would not forget, for his heart had nearly stopped as Telmaine had moved and Vladimer had shot into the floor just beside her head. He had not thought Vladimer would bluff.

Ishmael's shoulders did not relax. Deliberately, he held out his sound hand. "Touch me," he said. "Above th'glove. I've sound reason for asking," he added.

Balthasar hesitated, but could not persuade himself a Shadowborn would have willingly let Laurel inflict such pain on it as Laurel had just done on Ishmael. He pushed down the cuff of Ishmael's glove, fingers seeking his pulse and finding it, fast with pain and the aftermath of exertion, but full and regular.

The pulse jumped; Ishmael hissed out a breath. "Sorry," murmured Laurel.

Balthasar released Ishmael's wrist and stepped back. "Ask me," Ishmael said.

"I'd not have touched you if I had any doubts," Balthasar said, as the mage must know. "What was it you wanted to talk to me about?"

"First thing is, I just went skin t'skin with one of those Shadowborn." Laurel's head jerked before she caught herself; Ishmael, his head turned toward Balthasar, didn't notice. "Wasn't meant, believe me. The thing was dying, toppled against me." He stopped; Balthasar realized he was fighting nausea. "Foul with Shadowborn magic—"

Laurel paused in her cleaning to pass him a small towel that smelled strongly of mint, even at Balthasar's distance. Ishmael wiped his face, inhaling deeply of the scent. "*Cursed* unpleasant," he said with feeling.

"But informative," Balthasar said.

"You have that way ... of cutting to th'essence." He paused as Laurel propped up his hand and began to bandage his arm. Her head was cocked, listening. "It was a formed mind that touched mine. Not a sane man's, but no beast's, either. Th'thing had once been Darkborn—I'm sure of it."

"*Ishmael,*" said Laurel in horror. "You ... could sense that?"

"Aye, m'lady. I shouldn't be speaking of this in front of you—"

She shook her head crisply. "Father's prohibition might have made sense in the past, but it makes none now. We need to know what we're fighting." She split the bandage with a stroke of the scalpel and knotted the ties neatly around his wrist. "So, they're ... transforming Darkborn into Shadowborn." Her head came up; she sonned him. "Lavender knows?"

Thinking of her twin's lost love? Or her twin exposed on the rooftop?

"She knows. Can't be sure on that," Ishmael said. "Just that they've minds closer t'men than beasts. Though th'implications are ugly, for th'ones lost." He rolled his head on the back of the chair. "Second thing, Hearne, is I don't suppose y'were up on the third floor a little while ago?"

"No," said Balthasar, uneasily.

"Thought you mightn't have been. Trouble is, I sonned someone much like you trying t'open the door to the roof-top dance floor. He bolted just before th'servants' door opened and a whole scourge of Shadowborn tried t'pile through. I got reinforcements just as I shot myself dry."

"They've infiltrated us," Laurel said for him. "Come in with the refugees."

"You . . . didn't sense anything?" Balthasar said, cautiously.

Ishmael grimaced, scar jumping. "I sensed plenty," he said. "Was ready t'heave the whole time I was on the roof and fighting them in the hall. It wasn't false heroism kept me in place," he said to Laurel. "But no, I didn't sense anything from any particular one—but if they'd any sense, they'd have been keeping clear of me."

Stranhorne arrived with his one-armed lieutenant. The scholarly baron now had armor over his shirt and a hol-stered revolver at his waist. His hair was untidy and matted—with blood, by the smell. He shook his head as his daughter opened her mouth. "Not mine." She passed him a towel, pointed him in the direction of a washing basin and jug set on the side table. "Mother," she said, firmly, family shorthand, maybe, for *Mother would insist* or *Mother would be outraged* or *Mother would have hysterics.* Somehow, knowing the late baronelle's daughters, he couldn't believe it would be the last.

Laurel sketched in their conversation so far as her father scrubbed his arms and blotted the worst of the gore from his hair and leathers. Stranhorne said over his shoulder, "So, you've not lost it after all."

"Aye, it seems not. Though a man with a burned tongue might still taste spices, if they're strong enough."

"All right." Stranhorne turned. "We've fought off the first wave. And we need to take a moment to decide what else of our tactics we need to change—we obviously hadn't thought through the implications of having Shadowborn come in force from the air. We've still got about four hours to sunrise. Strumheller, what's your best guess on whether they're liable to be active after?"

"M'best guess, Stranhorne, depends on past experience, which has shown itself a poor guide in this."

"Take it nonetheless," the baron ordered.

"If they were once Darkborn, then they may be bound by th'Curse as we are." *We have the father of Tercelle's children to falsify that hope,* Balthasar thought, but did not say. "If they come by day, then they don't want us—don't want us to change or t'eat or any of th'other things they could do with our flesh. And if they come by day—it galls me t'say this—we can't fight them. We can only hope to burrow deep t'survive."

Something in Ishmael's face, something in Stranhorne's, disturbed Balthasar. "And how likely is that?" Stranhorne said in a still voice.

Ishmael hesitated. His voice sounded almost studiedly impersonal; unusual for him. "We might be able t'close some of us in your lower cellars, so that it'd be more trouble t'the Shadowborn t'dig them out than they'd care to take. Predators don't waste energy and don't put themselves at risk. They're in our territory, enemy territory. But we've never had them come at us in such force before."

"Should we evacuate now?" Stranhorne asked. "If the message reached the Crosstracks, and the telegraph is running and the tracks are clear, a relief force should be at the Crosstracks by nightfall. They might even be there already."

"We'd likely lose more doing that than waiting for the relief force," Ishmael said. "Unless we can be certain there's some they want more than others, and that they can tell us apart, if most of us went on the road, most of th'Shadowborn would follow."

There was a silence. Then Laurel said, quietly, "There is one other option."

Her father and mentor waited. "You know what it is," she said, "but you won't say it yourselves. Ishmael says they have minds like men, and we've certainly discovered that they will exploit our weaknesses and attack our commanders. If they're intelligent, we might be able to negotiate with them."

"Negotiate our surrender, you mean," her father said, though not harshly. "Nothing we've met suggests it would be otherwise. They need not speak to communicate their intentions most eloquently. If I thought we'd gain anything by it, I'd swallow my gorge and negotiate, but nothing they've done suggests they have aught else in mind but slaughter and domination."

"Father," she said, carefully, "would your answer be the same if they were not using magic?"

He frowned, not at her but at the thoughts her question inspired. "Truthfully, I can't know," he said. "But magical or nonmagical, we can judge them by their deeds. Strumheller, in my place, would you negotiate?"

"Never," Ishmael said, without a pause. "Maybe I'm influenced by the sense of the magic and the touch of the mind—but nothing in their deeds, as you say, suggests they recognize our right t'live in peace. Our best hope is t'bloody them; then they might listen." He rolled his head. "Hearne, what's your say?"

Balthasar, slightly startled at the question being referred to him, weighed it. His spirit rebelled against rejecting outright the possibility of negotiating and perhaps sparing lives on both sides. But years of torment by his brother, years of work amongst the oppressed and dispossessed of the city, and years of listening to and observing his social betters had all taught him that to many, negotiation was weakness, an invitation to further cruelties. He said, "Negotiation would only be productive if we had something they want—aside from our lives." *As food or slaves,* he did not say; it stood implied.

"I know," she said, quietly. "That's my thought, too.

But—" Her hand strayed to her rounded abdomen, and she did not voice what else she thought.

"As long as we can hold the manor, we stay," her father said. "But we should lay the groundwork for a retreat, as Mycene says. I'll get started on that. Laurel, I want you to rest. Hearne, you'd best get back to the surgery. I know we took casualties in the courtyard and on the roof. Strumheller, I've a request of you that will seem decidedly hypocritical, given the opinions I've expressed as late as last night. But we're fighting for our lives, here. I want you to find that infiltrator—or infiltrators. If they're Shadowborn or shape-changed or ensorcelled, you'll be able to tell, if you come close enough."

Close enough to touch, he meant. Close enough to read, unconsenting and perhaps unawares. Ishmael had told Telmaine that that was contrary to the code he lived by. His face stoic, Ishmael got to his feet. "I can do that."

Ishmael

Aside from the leadership and the vulnerable points, the points he would expect a Shadowborn to undermine were the roof, the entrances, the armory, and the munitions. Which had him roaming from rooftop to cellars like an unquiet ghost, three of Stranhorne's troop dogging his heels for his safekeeping. The sense of Shadowborn magic had dwindled since the attack, but not gone entirely, and when he reached the roof, he realized why—the damp night had turned to sleet and wind, making him shiver with more than cold. He found Lavender and Jeremiah Coulter at the southwest corner, supervising the lashing down of one of the three cannon underneath an improvised shelter. Coulter stroked its flank as covetously as a horse thief might a prime mare, his misspent past having included a stint as a pirate's gunner. Ishmael cautioned, "Y'realize that thing'll deafen everyone on the roof and below." That he knew from painful experience. He never wanted to be near cannon fire again.

Coulter grinned. Lavender frowned through the rain dripping from her hat. "We'll use it if we need it."

"Give me a head start at running first," he grumbled. "A word, if y'don't mind."

She let him draw her away. "This weather's not natural," he said, quietly.

"I don't need you t'tell me that," she said. "I know by the queasy expression on your face."

He'd thought he was concealing it better than that. She smirked, reading his mind.

"Boris said you gave him the talk," she said. "Are you about to give me the talk?"

"You don't need that talk. This is another one. If y'hear the retreat, retreat. Y'understand?"

"We'll have to disable the cannon. . . ."

Entirely sensible, with their enemies able to land on the roof and turn those cannon on the stairwell entrances. "If y'hear the retreat, y'won't have much time." Five stories down to the ground, and may the Mother of All Things—including of fiery young women with more courage than sense—guide her choice of a stair. He could imagine nothing worse than being down in the cellar with Stranhorne, knowing they must light the fuses, and knowing she was trapped above them. He still didn't know whether Stranhorne had told her what he planned—it was time he did, for the sake of the people with her—but it was not Ishmael's decision. "*Promise* me you'll get your people down and clear. Spike or throw the cursed cannon off th'edge of the roof if you must, but do it fast. We'll need you on th'ground to help with the breakout, and we don't want you cut off."

"I *promise*. Now you promise me, no more one-man stands."

"Not my choice—"

"No excuse," she said, sternly. "You told me that yourself: y'have to think ahead, leave yourself maneuvering space. Promise."

He promised, and he meant it as sincerely, he supposed, as she did. Time and circumstance would determine whether one or both of them would be forsworn.

She leaned forward as though to kiss his lips, and at the last instant faltered and brushed his cheek instead. He could not kiss her back—it would not have been proper, even if he had been willing to intrude further on her thoughts—but he brought up his gloved hand and cupped her cheek. "Please try to stay out of trouble."

He wanted to pull Coulter or one of the senior troopers aside and order them to make sure she did retreat, but knew she would be rightfully furious with him, instead of merely irritated, as her fleetingly sour expression attested. She wasn't a teenage enthusiast anymore, and she deserved the same respect he would give any fighting man or woman. Maybe it was as well that he'd never had a daughter. . . . He made his circuit of the men and women with her, trying as best he could to sense any additional aura of Shadowborn over the miasma rising with the rain. *Trying too hard,* the fierce pain in his chest warned him. He had no choice but to sit down on the wet gravel and pass off the spell as momentary dizziness from his injured arm. He went down the western stair, deliberately using the busier stair so that he met as many people as possible. Imogene's tits, he could only hope his movements were as unpredictable to any Shadowborn trying to evade him—assuming they'd even bother—as to himself.

Laurel was resting, on her father's orders, in a curtained corner of the ballroom. Neither her father nor she had wanted her to go back to her rooms, he because he wanted to be sure of her whereabouts in a crisis, and she because she had the opportunity here to listen. She whispered her suspicions of two groups who had passed her; he promised to check them.

The baron himself was in the side gallery with several of his troop, stooped over the relief, reviewing the route and deployment for a retreat. Ishmael circled, attentive to any recoil of the men and women he passed or any perturbation of his senses, but nobody shifted more than simply yielding him room. Stranhorne stopped him as he made to withdraw. "Raining again?" he said.

"Aye. Cursed near sleet."

By the tucked-in corner of Stranhorne's mouth, he understood the implication. He moved with Ishmael to the doorway. "Can we expect relief by sunrise?" he said, quietly.

A sensitive question, Ishmael admitted. If they didn't, he would not know whether the enemy had cut them off or Ishmael had failed in his duty to prepare for his own decease and the transition to his brother's rule. He had thought he planned well, but had never imagined the transition happening in the midst of such emergency, where a speck of grit in the mechanism could produce a fatal stall. And his marred relationship with Reynard was more than a speck. Noellene had been right: he had owed Reynard a full account, whether in person or in a letter—even though he might be certain that Reynard would believe not a word of it. But when events taught Reynard otherwise, then he would have that information.

Too late to regret that, either. He said, "Troops have been on th'alert or on the move all summer. Reynard's had the ducal order, and he's had Hearne's account. If the rider reached th'station, and the telegraph wires aren't cut, then they'll be moving as fast as they can. Reynard's no trooper, and he knows t'stay out of the way. And even if he doesn't, Noellene will set her hand to it."

Stranhorne smiled at the mention. "She will, that." He was fond of Ishmael's sister, and she of him, though not fond enough to marry, much to the vexation of Reynard's then wife. She had schemed for Noellene's respectable send-off from Strumheller. After Reynard's divorce, Noellene had settled in once more as chatelaine, and seemed likely to stay there. Notwithstanding her dainty beauty, citified airs, and expensive tastes worthy of Lady Telmaine herself, Noellene understood the Borders defense as well as her brothers. If Reynard needed spurring, she would apply the spurs.

"So, t'answer your question, I'm hopeful of it."

"But we should plan to hold out for the day," Stranhorne finished for him. "If we're not forced to retreat. Any hint of Shadowborn—inside?" he appended.

"Truthfully, be difficult for me t'tell, but I'm on it. Where's Mycene?"

Mycene and his men were in the courtyard, having reinforced the squad guarding the main gate during the worst of the attack. The Shadowborn had again made targets of the leaders, more successfully than on the roof. The defenders' mind-set had been too slow to shift from thinking of Shadowborn as unreasoning beasts capable of savagery but not tactics. Stranhorne probably owed the integrity of its north gate to Mycene and his men. *That is a less uncomfortable notion than hitherto,* Ish thought, slightly amused at how differently they greeted him, having now met Shadowborn for themselves. Mycene was no friendlier, since he still had every reason to suspect—or maintain the appearance of suspecting—Ishmael's involvement in his fiancée's death. However, Ishmael doubted he would ever again liken the profession of Shadowhunter to that of rat catcher, as his father had done more than once in Ishmael's hearing. Ish exchanged nods with Mycene's men and words with Mycene, noted they were down to eight, and accounted for three wounded—one seriously and two of whom they expected back shortly—and the hapless di Banneret, who knew no better than to eat sausage from a street vendor's cart.

Which made him think of the wounded, and wonder how Balthasar Hearne was holding up. He shied from entering the dining room, ward for the most seriously wounded. Arrant cowardice, he knew. He would have found it hard even when Stranhorne's prohibition against using his magic was on him, and now, now that he knew he was no longer able to help, he faltered at the door, at the sounds of murmurs and groans and of someone—a woman? a young boy?—sobbing brokenly.

As he stood there, a woman made to push past him, and he recognized one of Stranhorne's housekeepers, a sharp-tongued, sharp-witted woman who was an exacting manager for her portion of the staff. He could rely on her to know exactly who was doing what and where. He caught her arm. "Dr. Hearne, Dr. Balthasar Hearne—could y'please tell him that I'd like a word with him?"

"But, Baron," the woman said, startled, "he hasn't returned since he left with you."

Balthasar

Balthasar followed the orderlies carrying the stretcher for his last case into the ballroom to assess the next, and found Ishmael standing inside the dining room–turned-ward, hands pushed deep into pockets and shoulders hunched. "I need a quick word," the baron said, curtly.

"Is it your arm—"

"Nothing medical," said the baron, his expression strangely unreadable. "Nothing needing done here. I just need a word."

Balthasar's first thought was of Telmaine—that Ishmael had sensed more from Telmaine. That thought had him untying his apron even as he truthfully protested, "I don't have long. I shouldn't leave at all."

"A moment—that's all I ask."

Balthasar trailed Ishmael's hurrying heels across the ballroom, up the cast stairs. Ishmael brusquely deflected attempts to accost him with a "Later" or "Ask the baronettes."

Their room on the fifth floor was in use. Ishmael steered him to one on the second that was now largely cleared of furnishing and carpets, except for a dozen beds bare of mattresses. He recognized the packs propped against the near wall as belonging to members of Mycene's troop—this was where the troop had been billeted. The beds themselves would have been stripped of their mattresses to hold refugees and wounded.

"Have— Is it Telmaine?" Balthasar said as soon as the door closed.

"Telmaine?" said Ishmael, startled. "What about Telmaine?"

Not, then. "Have you found an infiltrator?"

Ishmael smiled. "In a manner of speaking."

Balthasar felt the heart within him chill, as though he had suddenly gained the sense of Shadowborn magic that Telmaine had described. That smile was no expression of the man he knew, for all the cast of face and the scars were the same. Sweet Imogene, he himself had warned Ishmael of just this eventuality. But, tired and caught up by the false

Ishmael's urgency, he had let down his guard, missed the clues of the lapses in accent and Ishmael's failure to show concern for Telmaine—indeed, now he thought of it, Ishmael's expression down in the ward had been wrong, oblivious to the suffering around him. Balthasar had been caught by the very ruse he had warned others against.

He swallowed and said, "This cannot possibly work. Ishmael himself is in the manor." He prayed this was still so, but surely the Shadowborn could not have caught Ishmael off guard.

"I *know* he's about, curse him," the Shadowborn said, hands fisted. "But it already *has* worked."

On him, for whichever reason the Shadowborn wanted him. "I'll be missed," Balthasar said, steadily. If the Shadowborn killed him and took his form, only Ishmael would be able to tell—until or unless the Shadowborn found himself faced with a chloroformed patient on a surgical table. The thought in itself was bleakly cheering; the prospect of how far the Shadowborn might go in his masquerade, sickening.

He kept such thoughts off his face and out of his voice. "You came with Mycene's men, didn't you? You were the young man—di Banneret—who lent me a coat. A coat that was too big for me—and for you." That was the inconsistency that had been nagging him, why a guardsman traveling light would carry a coat that did not fit him. Sweet Imogene, if he'd only remembered in time . . . "What is your name?"

"My *name*?" said the Shadowborn, taken aback at the unexpected civility.

Good; keep him off balance. "Do you not exchange names amongst your people?"

That smile again, a triumphant malice in it. "We *do*. Oh, we *do*, and you'll *like* learning mine. . . ." The Shadowborn abruptly moved with a crack of floorboards quite unlike Ishmael's near-noiseless tread. Balthasar recoiled, his sonn ringing off the bones in the other's skull as he pushed his face up to Balthasar's.

"Where are my sons, Balthasar Hearne?"

I should have shouted out, Bal thought, *while I still had a chance.* A claw balanced his carotid pulse on its tip, and his mind went blank with terror. "I don't know," he whispered. "Truly, I don't know."

"You sent them away," the Shadowborn breathed in his face. "Where to?"

"I thought they'd be safer if I didn't know," Bal whispered in turn. "Can you not read the truth from me?"

It was not a safe question, but an urgent one. He had thought the Shadowborn who had impersonated his brother, Lysander, claiming to be the father of the twins, had tormented him merely for the pleasure of it. But if not, if these Shadowborn could not touch-read, and if he survived to convey the information . . .

The claw tip stroked downward; he clutched at his throat, but his fingers found merely a stinging gash and a trickle, not a gush or even a spurt of blood.

"Truly," he gasped, "I meant them no harm. Or their mother, either."

"What did she tell you about me?"

"She said you had come to her in the daytime, traveling through the day. She was afraid the children would not be fully Darkborn. And they were—*are*—not. But they are also beautiful, healthy little boys, for whose safety I pray."

"But *she* was not safe," the Shadowborn said, in Bal's face. "She's *dead*. So why should *I* care about your stupid prayers?"

"I am deeply sorry about Tercelle," Bal said. "But my prayers are my own. I would not dare to ascribe their value to anyone else. Much less a member of a people about whom I know virtually nothing."

"You think you know nothing about us?" the Shadowborn said, grinning savagely. Then the grin tightened, as at some mental or physical effort, and the bones of it *shifted*. There was something intrinsically revolting about bone moving like muscle beneath the skin, but even if there were not, he had already met the phenomenon, lying pinned on Vladimer's bedroom floor as his brother's semblance warped to that of a stranger's and the nails of his poised hand elongated to shredding talons. Ishmael's face re-formed as a much younger but still familiar one. The young man—boy, no more than sixteen—smiled his older brother's mocking smile.

"Not such a stranger, am I, now? *Uncle* Balthasar."

The smile was there, the lips and narrow nose were there, but the cheekbones were more pronounced and the eyes more wide set. Lysander's features, mingled with another's. Mingled, as Balthasar's were with Telmaine's in their two small daughters.

Balthasar broke for the door. There was no planning in it, simply a raw impulse of flight. The Shadowborn caught him on his first stride, arm around his chest. A calloused palm slammed up underneath his jaw, pinning his mouth closed; fingers closed on his nose, blocking off all air. Bal bucked and thrashed, staggering with the Shadowborn, bringing them both to their knees. As they toppled, the Shadowborn twisted them both, throwing Bal down beneath him. Bal's injured cheek ground into the floor. His head pounded with air deprivation; he convulsed with the urgent need to breathe. His head struck the Shadowborn's jaw, and he frantically jerked it up again. The Shadowborn gasped out, "I am *not* letting you go. You *will* obey me."

And Balthasar *felt* the ensorcellment enwrap him, turn his muscles to meltwater and his will to . . . nothing at all. "Lie still," the Shadowborn said in the boy's voice, and he could not move, stripped of even the most primitive survival reflexes. He was all but unconscious when the Shadowborn released his mouth and nose and let him gasp in air.

"You are my father's brother," whispered the boy against his ear. "You are *family*, and so you should love me. Love me the way you love your own children. And *obey me*. The way you would obey your *God*."

With hopeless fascination, Balthasar observed the fragmentation of a mind from within. The ensorcellment would not extract from him a father's love or a believer's obedience, but it would crudely exact a slave's devotion. Even so, he recognized the plea in the demand, and some part of him responded to it with pity—this monster was little more than a child. A third portion of him weighed the experiences of Vladimer and Tercelle, the knowledge he had through his sister, Olivede, of magic abused, and knew that he was lost. And a fourth knew both reason and resistance, silently enumerating the ways the Stranhornes and Ishmael were equipped to deal with the enemy in the house. *Ishmael* must sense this ensorcellment. He choked on the slave's cry of warning and ground his aching cheek against the floor to stifle it.

"Get up," said the boy, in Ishmael's voice. Reason said, *Test his power*; the slave said, *Obey*. The conflict made him as clumsy as a partly strung puppet, but the slave brought him to his knees. The boy slapped him with sonn, jerking him to his feet. Reason said, *Ishmael's sonn was never so course.* "That's the way," the voice said, fully Ishmael's once more. "I want you"—a pause, to ensure the message was understood by Balthasar and the ensorcellment—"to go down to the ground floor, to the eastern gate, and *open it.* And don't try to warn anyone."

"I . . . will not," Balthasar said. Even as he did so, he felt himself take his first step toward the door.

"You will so." He smirked. "*She* didn't want me to learn how to do this, but I learned it all on my own. So go downstairs—don't worry; they won't eat you. They'll know you're mine."

"Guarded," Balthasar said, unable to stop himself.

"It won't be, by the time I'm done with"—the carpet in front of Balthasar burst into an arc of flame; he had barely enough time to register the heat before it was quenched—"my little diversion."

Four

Ishmael

*I*shmael turned at the sense of someone beside him. Laurel di Gautier was at his shoulder, blanket trailing from her shoulders. "I heard," she said in a low voice.

He bit his tongue on suggesting she go back to her rest. He needed another mind on this, one not distracted by a clawed arm, the Call, and the miasma of Shadowborn weather-working. "We need t'find Hearne and this Shadowborn. Any ideas?"

"You are quite certain," she said, "about Dr. Hearne? He met these Shadowborn earlier than any of us, didn't he? I was less worried about him because I didn't expect Shadowborn to have his skill." The corner of her mouth twitched. "Linneas Straus wouldn't have just anyone working in his surgery."

"Unless th'Shadowborn are subtler by far than I take them for, the man I touched not an hour ago was th'same man I met seven days past." Unless along with the shapes they stole, the Shadowborn were also capable of stealing memory and knowledge; if so, only their actions would reveal them. His heart started to race, making his left arm throb in tempo. His fingers found their way to his holstered revolver.

"I've had a late, unwelcome thought," he said. "Should have had it long since. There was one man of Mycene's I've not met, supposedly laid low by a sausage. We know a Shadowborn was in th'city: maybe he came down in Mycene's train."

She nodded. "I'll have someone—two someones—check," she said. "But what we need to know—"

From the east corridor an alarm began to ring, its rate frantic. Along the halls he heard a shout of "Fire!" His first thought was of the munitions, and the men waiting by them. He said to Laurel, "I'll go." Stranhorne was just emerging from the side gallery, his one-armed aide at his side. Striding by, Ishmael said, "Don't know; going t'find out."

The rhythm of the alarm told him it was on the third floor of the southwest corner of the manor; the Stranhornes had anticipated the difficulty of tracking sound through the ancestral pile. He had an unpleasant feeling he knew which room. Collecting seemed to go with the Stranhorne blood. In recent generations, it had expressed itself in bibliophilia, but several of the past barons had collected hunting trophies, including trophies of Shadowborn. Stranhorne's grandfather had offered the collection to the national history museum in the city. Given that Shadowborn defied orthodox taxonomies, the museum had declined most of those, so they were kept in a long gallery and storeroom off the south hallway.

Which made this arson what? Editorial comment? Revenge? Sick prank? Ish supposed he should be grateful the interloper's sense of humor or strength did not extend to animating them, setting the pack of false-toothed balewolves and mangy-pelted scavvern roaming the halls.

Smoke, harsh with burning straw and fur, and Shadowborn magic brought him to a halt just before he collided with the milling mob of manor staff, reservists, and ambulatory refugees summoned by the alarm. Boris Stranhorne was in the midst of the horde, valiantly trying to impose order and purpose. He didn't have the mass or the voice. Ishmael did. A lungful of air gave him the volume, and smoke in his throat gave him an ominous rasp. "We need th'hose run from the main water tank now!" he bellowed, making those nearest him bend away like wheat under a downdraft. "And a bucket chain from the main scullery."

They probably couldn't reach the former taxidermist's workroom, which was off the gallery, and furthermore he had no idea how long it had been since anyone had worked the taps in there; rust-locked taps or sludge-filled pipes would do them no use. "And all who's not got a clue how to drive a hose or pass a bucket need t'get yourselves out of this corridor. Now!"

Several staff members and reservists, wielding buckets, had already arrived. One reported, "We've gone for the hose, Baron. Where should we—"

Where indeed? It wasn't just his roaring that had cleared the bystanders: the smoke was thick enough to stir, and the heat, when he put his face around the open door, was ominous. The air roiled and twisted as his sonn reflected from the interfaces between ribbons of heated air. It was hideously reminiscent of the day he had been caught in the burning Rivermarch, having gone to ground after an encounter with the Shadowborn in a brothel incongruously called the Rainbow House. As far as he knew, he had been the sole survivor of all the ladies and clients. He closed the door on the blaze, hoping to contain the smoke and starve it of air. "We'll not quench this one without th'hose," he said. "Soak the walls. Soak the floor—and we need to soak the floor upstairs. We need t'make sure it doesn't spread." To Boris he said, "Tell th'ones who're running ammunition to keep their senses about them—we need to know if there are any others kindling—and get any of th'other youngsters who still have their wits about them t'help."

A bucket chain had formed, with buckets passed hand to hand down the line. At least they did not have a carpet to worry about; Stranhorne, like Strumheller, was furnished for the wear of a large household that was a center of government, industry, and defense. Overhead, Ishmael could hear running feet, furniture being dragged, and urgent voices, as the rooms overhead were cleared so that the floors could be soaked. He set his back against the wall, staying out of the way, keeping his chin down to mask his hard pulse. The reaction was a response to the bite of smoke in his throat and the memory of the Rivermarch. At least outside was still dark and not daylight—if a night full of Shadowborn could be said to be less murderous than the sun.

As a crew from the stables came dragging the fire hose—already spurting water over floor, wall, and people alike—the alarm began to peal again, signaling that the Shadowborn had renewed their attack.

Boris clutched at Ishmael's left arm. Ishmael winced, though he kept his voice light. "D'y'get the feeling that this is just not our night?"

He pulled Boris away as the fire-hose crew threw open the door into the gallery and turned the hose full on the interior, and a great belch of smoke and heat rolled over them all. He dropped to a crouch, bracing himself on his throbbing arm, alert to their coughing and ready to move in if any were overcome by smoke. Boris half fell down beside him. Ishmael said hoarsely, "Get down t'your father—tell him what's happening. Then spread word about a fire watch. Soon as they've control here, I'll move on. I need to find who's causing this."

Balthasar

The laminated outer door of the baronelle's study led into a vestibule between inner and outer wall, with an ironbound outer door as stout as the one into Strumheller. Balthasar wept silently as he wrestled down the two heavy bars bracing it, wept for his futile belief that he could evade this ensorcellment, and now for his remorse at what he was about to do. He could not stop himself: could not stop himself lifting the bars, turning the handle, setting his shoulder and then all his weight against the door, falling outward into the rain.

He tried to cling to the lintel, but even so, the ensorcellment was driving him forward. It came to him that this must be something akin to what Ishmael felt as he struggled against the Call. How could he ever have prided himself that his skills would be of any help, any help at all . . . ?

The ensorcellment harried him across a garden, turned wild in the storm. It punished him as he lost himself among the hedges. Beyond the wall he could hear wolves howling. Overhead, stone split and stone chips sprinkled over him; the snipers had tried to range on the sound. He scrambled along the base of the wall, almost on all fours, as bullets ricocheted. High in the air something screeched, drawing the snipers' fire.

And there . . . was the gate. His sonn caught the hard, rough profile of the arch, the smoother finish of the gate. It was a wide gate, but still not wide as a street. Yes, it might pass an army, but not all at once.

Two-handed, he forced the key to turn, felt a mechanism yield and the dead bolts draw in with a ragged thud. He felt the gate shudder as a body threw itself against the other side, and heard claws grind.

"Balthasar Hearne—stop!" cried a woman's voice.

The gate flew inward as something lunged at it from outside. He heard a tearing snarl, heard a shot. A bundle of fur and bristle skidded past his feet; he recoiled from its snapping jaws.

Twenty yards away stood Laurel di Gautier, alone and exposed, head bared, skirts bound to her legs by the wind, rifle to her shoulder, lips drawn back in a face stony with intent. Ishmael had praised her cool head, and Balthasar understood why as she shot and shot again into a gateway seething with Shadowborn with a calm precision he would not even have expected in his own capable wife. He crouched in the lashing rain, helplessly arguing with the ensorcellment that orders to *open* the gate did not preclude closing the gate, counting the shots, and wondering how long before she needed to reload, how long before the rain penetrated her rifle, how long before she missed, how long before one of those flying Shadowborn . . . Laurel slung the rifle on her shoulder, no time to reload, and in the same motion drew a revolver right-handed, and the next Shadowthing through the gate gained but one bound on her before she put it down. She took a pace forward. She meant, he realized, to clear the gate and close it if she could, before she shot her last. He willed her on, even if he could do nothing to help her.

Something dropped out of the sky to her left. She pivoted and fired, then managed to catch the next wolf with barely a beat. Another Shadowborn landed to her right, between Balthasar and her. He discovered then the limits of *open the gate and warn no one.* He surged out of his crouch with a rock in his hand, and with all his strength—and knowledge behind it—drove the pointed end of the rock through the fragile bone in the Shadowborn's temple.

She gasped, "What—" and shot and shot again into the gate.

There was no explaining, not in these circumstances, even if he could struggle sufficiently free of the ensorcellment to do so. He cast into the air, his sonn dissipating in seething rain and wind, but still catching at its limits something up there. He flung the rock at it. While evading the landings, she had lost all the distance she had gained. "Inside," he begged. *"Please."*

"No," she said.

He threw himself at her, intending to manhandle and drag her if he must—no planning, no timing. She swung her revolver; he did not hear the shot or feel it except as something like a punch in his side. He found himself half turned and down on one knee. More by reflex than by any urgent need, he put a hand to his side and felt the cold rain turn warm. There was strangely little pain. *Traumatic anesthesia,* the clinical part of his mind noted.

Behind him, the archway and wall blew in, as though struck by an immense fist, collapsing in a jumble of falling stones and blocks almost at his heels. The hem of a wet skirt flickered in his sonn, and he heard her take the first few running steps before rain and wind swallowed them. *She shouldn't be running,* he thought absurdly, *not in her condition,* and started to get to his feet. Stones ground behind him. Something huge and bristled set its paws on the dead thing beside him, and he froze, still as a rabbit. The wolf—larger than any wolf he'd ever heard of—sniffed speculatively at the belly of the dead one and then extended its head to nose Balthasar's bleeding side.

His sonn caught a small female shape, a hand reaching

out to cuff the wolf's muzzle. "Mayfly, leave that alone. You can eat it later."

Rubble crunched as a second person moved up beside him. A man's voice said, "Not him, Midora. Sense the ensorcellment."

"So he is here. Little *bastard.* Where's *Jon*? If he were in trouble and Sebastien ran—"

"Enough, Midora; Jonquil's dead," the man said, calmly. "We all felt him die. And without him, without his knowledge, what could Sebastien do alone in Minhorne?"

"Let's get this over with," the woman snarled.

Balthasar started to turn his head, to sonn the speakers, and felt a man's hand resist the motion. He flinched, trying to keep skin from contacting skin, opening him to the touch of what was surely a mage. "Best not draw attention," the man advised. To his companion: "Let me deal with Sebastien. He may be unpredictable, and he has obviously been learning."

"That little half-breed—"

"Ariadne's son," the man said flatly.

"Why bother? You won't keep him alive, after this. Emeya'll have him roasted—and with your blood for a sauce, if you're not careful."

A hand rested lightly on Balthasar's gripping fingers. "You're hurt," the Shadowborn noted, dispassionately. Then, startled, said, "That profile: *Hearne*. No. You must be another relation. The brother, perhaps. Well, well, well. I think we'll just—" Searing agony spread out from his wound, as though the Shadowborn had applied a cautery iron. Balthasar would have bucked or screamed, had he been able to move; instead, and this time in truth, he fainted.

Ishmael

Ishmael came headlong down the stairs, impelled beyond all caution by the nearby sense of Shadowborn magic. He reached the door to the baronelle's private study as Laurel burst through it into the hall, slamming it behind her, and caught woman and rifle as she stumbled, keeping them both upright. She was bareheaded, hair and dress soaked, revolver in hand, shaking as though fevered. She took a drowning sailor's grip on him. "Please be Ishmael," she gasped.

"Aye," he said. "I'm th'one y'told you loved Jeremiah Coulter." It had been a brief, intense, and fortunately one-sided infatuation when she was eighteen; he had never told anyone else what she confided.

She pressed her wet head against his chest and let him support her. "Something just destroyed the wall into Mother's garden," she gasped. "It doesn't make *sense*. Why'd he open the gate if they could destroy it that easily?"

Like her father, always thinking. "Why'd who open the gate?"

She lifted her head, taking her own weight again. "Dr. Hearne—or something in his shape. The corridor was unguarded." *Drawn off by the fire,* Ishmael thought, now understanding that mischief. "I got there too late to stop him. Things were coming through; I shot, trying to clear the window t'get the gate closed. Two of the flyers had a go at me. I killed one, Hearne got the other with a rock, but then he came at me. I shot him—pure reflex, and a wound only, I think—then the wall blew in and I ran. I just left him. I don't know what he was— But I— But why'd he open the gate if they could destroy it that easily?"

If it were Balthasar, then he had been ensorcelled or otherwise coerced, and might already be dead. Even if he were not, it would be death to open that outer door. "We'll get t'him as we can," he said. "But y'did the right thing. They could be through th'outer wall any moment, but at least they've chosen to force th'entrance best for us. Get the word t'your father. He'll want to sound the bell for the muster. Y'need to check the main way's clear." He eased her away and took the revolver from her hand. "I'll buy y'all the time I can."

She bit back appeal and thrust her ammunition pouch at him. Her face was full of the words she had too much sense to speak.

"If they've the minds of men, they've maybe the curios-

ity of men. I'll make of that what I can. And if not"—he
finished reloading and closed the firing chamber—"by then,
I'll know which one t'shoot first." Not to delude himself, he
reminded himself that he likely had only one shot. He felt
magic build on the other side of the door. *"Go,"* he said.

One shot, he thought. The question was whether to take
it—and likely bring magical retribution down on himself
and anyone within range—or risk not being able to take it
at all. Hand on the door, he felt the shudder of the assault
on the outer wall, and through the door heard stones grind
on one another. Sweet Imogene, how much of the wall were
they bringing down?

He threw open the door and set his back against the lintel, exposed as it was, so he could cover both inside and out.
His sonn delineated the gape in the wall and the rubble
heaped tidily to either side, swept clear of the breech by
the magic that had made it. Even the dust seemed to part.
Two figures were coming through the wall into the study,
the taller stooping slightly, and as near to side-by-side as
the breech allowed. He said, consciously deep and forceful, "You can hold where y'are, if you would. I want a few
words."

"And who might you be?" The voice was a light tenor, a
singer's voice with a careless delivery that suggested easy
power or studied manner.

This, Ishmael thought, *is where I ensure myself a conversation or a very quick death.* "Strumheller."

"Strumheller? As in Baron Strumheller?" Magic swirled
around him like a polluted river in winter, and he was glad
of his empty stomach and the bracing lintel. He concentrated on not letting his aim waver. "You're supposed to be
a mage. What have you done to yourself?"

His lips drew back from his teeth; he had just had the
welcome thought that the overreach spared him the need
to keep a bullet for himself. "Bad overreach, dealing with
one of your kind's ugly fire tricks. Your name, sir?"

"Do you expect that to mean anything to you? It's Neill."

He was correct; it did not mean anything. To sonn, Neill
was a rangy man in his twenties with a rawboned build that

Ish would have interpreted as late developer or idle skiver, depending on how charitable he felt. Perhaps this was Neill's usual form; perhaps not. He was dressed in a jacket made of irregular pieces of skins and leather, an embroidered shirt, and leather trousers. Even from where he stood, Ishmael could sense his magical strength. And sense, too, it was not entirely under control. Neill felt—allowing for the thoroughly repellant Shadowborn aura—like one of the stronger mages at the Broomes' commune, early in his learning and gaining capability faster than control. The difference was that the young man from the commune was fifth rank and conscientious. This man was far stronger. And Shadowborn.

"And the lady?" Whose shape was surely not her own, not with that aura of strength around her. She stood no more than four-and-a-half feet tall and had the diminutive, inhuman beauty of an expensive doll. Except for the curl of her lip. "Get on with it, Neill."

"We agreed we'd do this my way," Neill told her, without turning. And to Ishmael: "I'd like to talk, if I may, to Baron Stranhorne."

"Talk?" He'd met some smooth rogues in his time, including Rivermarch enforcers, but none of them had blasted in a man's wall before turning on the charm. Though he supposed Jeremiah Coulter might have, before he reformed. "If you'd wanted t'talk, y'could have knocked on the front door with a card. We're not couth by city standards, but that's still th'way it's done."

A sardonic smile. "You have me there. Call it . . . evolving strategy. For one thing, I believe you have something of ours." He raised his voice, and power rushed past Ishmael. "Sebastien," he said.

Ishmael had thought—no, he had hoped—that the Balthasar Hearne that Laurel had slammed the door on had been the Shadowborn. The falseness of that hope was confirmed by a blast of furnace heat at his back. He whirled—no resolution could have prevented him, whatever he put behind him—to face flame. He thudded back against the lintel, but by the time he turned his head again, he was completely ringed by fire. He could feel the skin on his face beginning to sear. His soaked clothing and hair would give him only seconds.

And then the blaze was quenched, gone as though the fire had never been—but for the heavy smell of wood smoke, scorched fabric and leather, and hot metal. He sonned the slight figure standing at the hall corner, swung his revolver, and just as his finger began to tighten, the smell of hot metal impinged itself on his wisdom. Cursed thing wasn't safe to fire. He removed his finger from the trigger, gasping slightly.

The newcomer—the very Shadowborn he had been searching for—was a youth of fourteen or fifteen, sixteen at the most, and surly and scrawny with it. He also had a disconcerting resemblance to Balthasar Hearne, though an incomplete one. He stood with fists clenched, arms almost vibrating with thwarted energy—his magic, though very strong, had not fully emerged.

"Why'd you do that?" he shouted past Ishmael. "That's the Shadowhunter."

"I'm interested in keeping him alive," said Neill, from closer.

Without turning his head, Ishmael passed the overheated revolver to his left hand, drew the other with his right, leveled it to where sound told him the man's chest would be. "I'm not likewise minded," he warned.

The woman said, "Sebastien, get in here."

Ishmael's sonn caught the boy as he started forward, jerking and palpably fighting every step. The woman's magic was the most mature of the three, deft and slick, and he had no doubt she could have crafted an ensorcellment that would have brought the boy running eagerly to her side, not this rough puppetry. Ishmael rolled his shoulder around the lintel as the boy drew near, not wanting to let him within striking distance or take his muzzle off the man's chest. Though there was no denying, with the power around him, that the revolver and even his presence were barely more than a gesture. Much as he wished to listen to the sounds around him, to know how the muster was proceeding, he concentrated on present and place. He did not know how much these three were capable of reading without touch. He trusted the Stranhornes to waste no time evacuating. In turn, he must give them all the time he could.

He wished he could be reassured that Neill seemed in no haste. Was he, as his countryman or kinsman—the one who had seduced Tercelle Amberley—had been, immune to daylight?

The boy, struggling still, lurched up to the woman. Deliberately, she raised a hand, transformed to the sinewy, scarred knuckles of a prizefighter, and hammered his cheek, sending him sprawling across a chaise longue and spilling half-hemmed baby clothes to the carpet. Neill, who had not intervened, said then, "Midora, enough."

"It is *not* enough," she said. "He killed Jonquil."

The boy snapped from dazed to accusing, arm outstretched toward Ishmael, ending in a quivering arrow of a finger. "*He* killed Jonquil! I wasn't even there."

Futile as it likely was for him to try to deflect attention from Telmaine, it was already established habit. "Bullets in heart, gut, and brain," Ishmael confirmed.

A gesture from the man, backed by a gush of his magic deflecting hers, spared Ishmael's life, if not his churning stomach. He'd be cursed if he'd vomit at their feet, but much more of this and he would. "Jonquil must have got careless," Neill said. "You may be good with these things"—a casual gesture toward the revolver—"but you're not up to his weight otherwise."

"Where were you," the woman said to the boy, "when he shot Jonquil?"

"More to the point," said Neill, "why are you here?"

The boy, sitting on the floor, drew his knees up to his chest and hugged them, rocking slightly, holding his bruised face. "I was in Minhorne. Jonquil had gone to the summerhouse. He was going to wake up Vladimer and . . . and then kill him." That hesitation suggested ugly things. "I felt Jonquil die. I went down to the station, waited for Vladimer to come back. That was the order, wasn't it? Kill Vladimer. Kill Vladimer. Kill Isidore. Kill *him*." He gestured to Ishmael, but Ishmael hardly registered his own name for the company it kept. "But Vladimer had a mage with him. She turned my magic back on me—*burned me*."

"In other words," she said scornfully, "she scared you, and you ran away. *She's* going to skin you, boyo."

"I thought it would help if . . . I sent someone to open the door."

"Which we hardly needed, now, did we?" Stones hopped from the two mounds of rubble and began to dance around him on the floor, jumping like vicious mice. He raised his hands to protect his face. "Neill!" he wailed.

Behind him, in the corridor, Ishmael heard a soft whistle. It penetrated his careful inattention as, he thought, it should have penetrated his sleep. His lips twitched in something that was almost amusement. *Fall back and join us, indeed.*

But if they were to execute Stranhorne's plan, they needed the Shadowborn to be committed, in the depths of the manor, before— *Don't think*.

He shot Neill. He did not try a second shot or wait to sonn his fall; he hurled himself away from the door, even as the boy screamed and a furnace blast of flame roared out from the lintels on either side. His wet clothing sizzled. Thank the Mother—or the drunken patron god he had invented for himself—his face had cleared the doorway. He threw himself to one side, rolling, as behind him the ceiling caved in—more than caved; was smashed in, the fragments of plaster and shattered beams hammering down and bouncing up to hammer down again. Someone fell screaming; a young boy, one of the ammunition runners. Ishmael lurched back toward him, even though he knew the boy was already beyond anyone's help—he could hear it in the sounds he was making. He was surprised that he himself was still alive—that Midora could not distinguish his vitality from the boy's. But the Shadowborn could bring down the manor themselves in trying to kill him. He let out a roar, putting into it all the fury and despair and revulsion at the child's hideous death, and then letting its authentic tones turn to a shriek, as though he himself had been caught by the falling roof. The stones' frenzy redoubled. *"Ishmael!"*

screamed Lavender. And, *"Let me go!"* He could not even answer her, else he'd undo his own ruse; he could only pray that they managed to hold her back from fatal recklessness. He backed away as soundlessly as he could on booted feet down the southward hall, while behind him the storm of debris raged. Just before he stepped around the corner, his wits caught up with him and he said in a low voice, "Di Studier—" Bullet impacts burst from the far plaster before a voice barked a cease-fire. He whispered, hoarsely, "Aye, it was a good, bloodcurdling shriek, wasn't it?"

"Come," said the voice—that of Stranhorne's one-armed lieutenant. He sidled around the corner, making himself the leanest possible target, and into the sonn of the group of a handful of men, advance guard on the corridor from a barrier built ten yards up. One of them, a jumpy marksman by the tremor in his hands, said, "But we heard—"

"They brought the roof down, and with it, one of th'ammunition boys. He's dead now."

"Stupid little sod," muttered the lieutenant. "Should have been at the muster already. Must have gone back to pilfer."

He must say that, Ishmael thought. *He must say that and believe it, that the boy deserved that death.* Reaction caught up with him, and he had to brace himself against the wall. "Fall back," he heard the lieutenant say, and two men caught his arms. The men behind the barricade pulled it down enough to let them scramble over, which Ishmael did well enough, and slid to his haunches in its rear, back against the wall. "Sorry," he said to the one-armed man. "Bit much, that."

"Aye, well, it's not over. Baron wants them well committed before—"

Ish lifted a cautioning hand. "Not sure how much they hear . . . There're three. Man, woman, boy. Shot the man; we'll find out if it sticks. He seemed t'be the leader, also th'one willing to talk," which might make the shooting regrettable, but he did not want to find out that the Shadowborn were stalling him to their advantage, even as he tried to stall them to his. "Strong mages," he said, grimly. "Very strong. Boy's a shape-shifter—probably came with us in the guise of one of Mycene's men, th'one supposedly laid up with street-cart belly. Darkborn or Lightborn mage that strong could pluck th'thoughts and plans out of our minds, though these don't seem to be behaving that way. May not be able; may be toying with us."

"Can't do anything about that; no sense worrying," the one-armed man said. "Baron wants you leading th'vanguard. He figures that anything needs to be fought through, you're best t'do it. Mycene will have the rear; nothing for them t'be a danger to there but Shadowborn, and he's a cursed good fighter. Be a good thing for th'Isles if he did get killed."

Ishmael noted the compliment, backhanded as it was; he'd had similar ones paid to himself, not the least by his own father. And Stranhorne's election of him as leader of the van was a high compliment indeed. But where did that put Stranhorne himself?

"People of Stranhorne!" Neill shouted.

Ishmael, to his shame, jumped.

"We are not interested in wholesale slaughter—"

"Could'a fooled us," someone muttered.

"If you lay down your weapons and surrender, you will be treated well."

Nervous snickers and scornful oaths, silenced by the one-armed man's throat-slitting gesture. Ishmael added the signal to mute sonn, which the one-armed man conveyed forcibly.

Ishmael started again as Lavender's clear voice called, "What do you want?"

"Who are you, *woman*?"

Don't tell, don't tell, Ishmael willed, and did not hear her reply as the pain in his chest wrung breath and thought from him—*idiot!* She wasn't even a mage.

The Shadowborn was saying, "We want the manor, and enough staff to keep it livable, and we want the family."

Was that brassy, confident voice the voice of a man whom Ishmael had mortally wounded not minutes ago, or of the stripling impersonator? And then his question was answered by the sound of his own voice. "Y'can tell them everything's all right. Y'can hear I'm fine."

Erich's hand slammed into his shoulder, pinning him against the wall, before he was even aware he had moved. He got the point: if he so much as hiccoughed, the hand would be over his mouth. He tapped the other man's wrist in acknowledgment, and waited, breath held, heart pounding.

"Do you really expect us to believe that?" Lavender said, without a tremor of uncertainty. *"Shadowborn."*

He could hear the quick breathing of the men around him—not the one-armed man, who knew how to make no sound, but one with a distinct wheeze, and two who were snoring, at least to his ears. From farther away, around the corner, he heard stones grumble and slide. Magic swelled sickeningly, and he heard stones grind on wood. "Down! Everyone *down!*" he roared, full voice, and threw himself flat, catching Erich by the belt and hauling him down, and twisting and kicking the feet of the nearest man out from under him just as the first stones ricocheted off the wall at the corner. A woman—*please not Lavender*—screamed from around the corner, and the improvised barricade before him shuddered violently under the barrage of brick, spars, and plaster. There was a thud of plaster on bone, and a man sprawled back from his place at the barrier. Ishmael rolled over and sonned, catching distorted shapes of fragments passing overhead. He heard yells from farther up the hall as the missiles reached the second barricade, but he'd noticed the barrage was thinning, seeming to travel high.

On the far side, he heard a crunch and a scrape, as of claws on wood, and felt the barricade tremble slightly—and his sonn caught the balewolf just as it scrambled onto the edge of a side-turned table. He rolled to his feet with a shout of "Wolves!" His left hand went out and caught the brute's shaggy throat, and with the power of his legs and back behind it, he heaved it backward off the barricade, a feat he would never have ventured, let alone accomplished, in cool blood and sobriety. It landed, leaped, and caught someone's bullet in its jaws. The entire corridor heaved with them. He heard yelling from the far corridor, and running feet approaching behind. Over his shoulder he shouted, "Fall *back, back!* We can't hold here." Maybe they could, but the enemy had to commit, had to come as deep as possible into the manor, and as long as they thought that the beasts were overrunning the defenders, maybe they would hold on the magic. Bordersmen could fight monsters, but magic . . . He caught the collar of one man who had not moved, who knelt still, fixedly firing and firing, and all but launched him down the corridor after the others. And then they were running back, two men carrying the one who had been felled by the stones. The one-armed man, covering the rear, went down beneath the claws of one of the brutes, but a second man ducked in with a knife the size of a short sword, impaled its open jaw, and slit its throat, while a third dragged Erich clear.

Above the abandoned barricade, the ceiling fell in, crushing the animals beneath it. He heard Neill's cry, "Midora!" with a choke of pain at the end of it, and the woman's laughter. Then from overhead he heard shooting—someone, two someones, firing through the cavity in the roof. Suicidally brave, with the ceiling coming down in pieces, but that let the defenders pile through the gap opened for them in the barricade, and fall to their haunches and knees for reloading. "Shit—," someone gasped. "Aren't I dead? Aren't we all dead?"

By some miracle, none of them were, though several were bleeding from stone or bite wounds, and the man who'd been felled at the barricade was unconscious with what looked like a grave head injury, and another was likely to bleed to death from his torn groin, despite the best efforts of his fellows to staunch it. It was a wound Ishmael himself could have dealt with once. The one-armed man recalled his attention from bitter regret. "If they've not held th'other side, we'll have some trouble on the retreat."

Truer words were never spoken. If the defenders in the north corridor had to fall back into the vestibule and entrance to the ballroom, then he and the others would be cut off. They would have to retreat into the cellars. He took a deep breath, aware of his own shakiness. How long since he'd eaten or, even more important, had anything to drink? He rasped, "Anyone got water with them?"

Someone passed him a flask; he drank, using the moment to think and to listen to the far side. He had not been able to listen to what was happening elsewhere while he was scrambling to save his own life, but from the sound of firing, he believed they were holding. Had to believe they were holding, and that Lavender was still alive. *So much,* he thought ruefully, *for Stranhorne wanting us in the vanguard.*

How long had it been? Long enough for the muster and breakout to be ready? He corked the flask and handed it back to its owner with a nod, then said to the one-armed man, "What's the signal, then? Ours, that we're breaking contact, or theirs that they're breaking out?"

With a crash, the ceiling collapsed, carrying the two snipers with it. Both were women. Ishmael surged to his feet. The defenders shot frantically, but there was just too little time—one had no chance at all to rise, while the other had no sooner gained her feet than a wolf leaped for her throat and dragged her into the mass. Her blank, terrified face and her wide, crying mouth seared into his memory. The man whom Ish had hauled from his post at the first barricade screamed obscenities and shot and shot and shot again, oblivious to the hammer falling on an empty chamber.

"Ishmael!" It was Lavender, her throat raw. "Break—break now." And then Ishmael heard a sound he would never again be able to mistake, any more than he would the magic that fuelled it—the *whumph* of erupting fire. He moved before he thought. Ten strides took him to the door into the central gallery, through which he plunged in utter disregard of what might be waiting on the other side. Nothing was; he sprinted the width, hit the door, threw it open; met smoke and the roil of heat and flame to his right. He yelled, "Lavender!" and heard her answer, from the far side. He shouted, "Y'have to run—run through. Run t'my voice. I'm clear." How long? He felt magic pour over him, heard a *whumph* behind him, and the gallery ignited. He roared, tasting blood, "Fall back, fall back to the muster!" The men on the other side had to come through the west gallery or hall, or go down to the cellar, and they had to do it now.

Two figures suddenly burst, solid, from the flame: Laven-

der, leading the young troop who had given up his horse to
Ishmael. She almost fell into his arms, as her sister had. He
did not greet her with an embrace, but with frantic slaps at
the smoldering edges of her clothing. She twisted and shouted,
"I'm through. Come! Come! Come! *Come!*" To her urging,
raw with need and nothing like command, they came in
twos and threes, bursting out of the fire on courses toward
her.

Jeremiah Coulter wore his buccaneer's grin. "Reminds
me of a ceremony on one of th'far south islands. . . ."

Ishmael heard running and stumbling feet on wood behind them, and turned to sonn the men and women from
the barricade. He could weep with relief that they'd found
their way. They helped him catch and slap down the men
and women emerging from the fire. The one-armed man
was not with them. The one on whom the leadership had
devolved said, "Erich went down to the baron. He said
they'd break out through th'south."

Through the bricked-up entrance they'd need to blow to
get free. *Sweet Imogene.* He caught Lavender as she moved,
with a harder grip than he'd ever taken of her. "No! Your
place is here." He couldn't tell her her father would be fine.
"We need t'get clear, and we need t'get clear now."

The last through the fire, a young woman, caught Lavender's arm. "Ronina and the Prescotts—they won't come—"

Ishmael stepped forward, almost up to the fire. "Y'come
and y'live, or y'die right here!" he challenged.

In answer, he heard three shots. Lavender, beside him,
made a sound like a puppy crushed beneath a wheel. He
said, hoarsely, "This is it—sound the breakout."

"The fire . . . ," she whispered. "If it reaches—"

"Erich's gone to warn." He caught her hand. *"Come."* He
led them, a ragged, wounded, indomitable band, into the
ballroom, but she had to force him to release her so she
could sound the bell—Mother bless that Stranhorne had at
least been willing to allow mechanical bells. She threw the
switch and the final retreat began to peal, thin against the
building roar of fire. She turned back to him, crying, but
unaware of it. He said, "We'll be back, lass. We'll be back."

She plunged ahead, toward the heaving mass of people pushing out the far doors, and Ishmael followed.

Balthasar

Cold roused Balthasar where he lay, rain, close to sleet, needling his exposed skin. Breathing hurt, every inhalation pulling at his side. Beneath his hand, he could feel icy rainwater pooling on the outstretched wing of a dead Shadowborn. He could hear the spatter of wind-driven rain, and a bell ringing in staccato bursts. And he could smell fire, the rank smoke of wood and fabric.

His hand jerked, twitching his soaked sleeve out of the puddle. He closed his fist, opened it. Not ensorcellment; the stiffness of exertion and cold. Making himself move, making himself lift his head, rise on his elbow, sonn around himself, was one of the most urgent efforts he had ever made in his life. Sonn caught shapes moving, and something growled. He froze. The movements came no closer, though the restless shapes continued to prowl. His sonn, probing the rain, delineated the gaping wall, the neat channel of cleared rubble.

Moving very slowly, he pushed up his shirt, explored the wound with his fingers. It was closed, though puckered and drawn. He remembered the Shadowborn touching him, the pain. Yet it had been a curative pain.

From deep within the manor came a low, rumbling belch. Through the flagstones he felt a vibration, and, with the next, louder—an explosion, he realized—he felt a distinct twitch, as though the earth itself were shrugging. The very walls of the manor wavered with the force of the third explosion, and the ceiling slumped into the gap. Warm air rolled over Balthasar, reeking of a munitions factory. From beyond the wall a bugle blared and a winch whined. Then a yelled command, a volley, another shout, another volley, and he heard wheels and hooves—a great many of both—on pavestones. A woman's voice screamed, hoarse with shouting, "*Drive! Run!* All speed to the Crosstracks. We hold the rear!" The manor shuddered again, though those massive walls remained intact. The woman—Lavender or Laurel—shouted, *"Father! We hold the rear!"*

This made sense of the whispers and exchanges he had overheard while he worked. The Stranhornes had planned for defeat, planned for retreat, planned even for betrayal. He listened with shuddering exaltation. The coaches would be carrying the wounded and those unable to keep the pace on foot. Anyone who could walk and run would do so, carrying those they could, and those who could fight would be on foot and horse in the van- and rear guard. Laurel and Lavender Stranhorne would be riding with them. But he feared now that he understood some of the silences that had fallen around Xavier Stranhorne, and the exaltation went out of him. Someone must have fired the charges placed inside the manor, someone who had chosen to risk being entombed with Shadowborn invaders in the gutted interior of his manor.

With a few more tired coughs, a few more tremors, the manor settled into its warrior's death. The wheels receded into the night. Wind and rain drowned the running footsteps. The bugle cried again in thin defiance, and then all that remained was the dwindling noise of hard-shod hooves. His skin was so numb he could not know either the temperature or the force of the rain. Sunrise would not be long coming.

At that thought, and regardless of what else prowled around those ruins, he staggered to his feet. The first step almost pitched him back into the puddles, but he shuffled toward the manor, though whether to shelter or succor, he did not know. What was not already destroyed in the explosion would be burning. Anyone living in that shell would not long remain so. Balthasar was dizzied by the war between free and ensorcelled emotions, an impotent, murderous rage that he knew was close to insanity, and a helpless pity for them all, including that child monster who held him enthralled. He hoped—how he hoped—that the Stranhornes had not left any of their own alive, but knew that some must have barred the entrance to the ballroom to the last, and some of the wounded would not survive the journey—he remembered Linneas's revolver—if they even began it.

Within the gap, he heard someone cough thickly. He barely caught himself from revealing sonn, and pressed his back against the wall, listening to the crunch and slither of stumbling feet on the untidy rubble.

"Don't—," a man's voice grunted.

"Let me —" Balthasar heard a bubbling groan, and the sound of rain-wet leather slapping and slithering against the wall. A familiar young voice gasped, "Neill—Neill, what do I do? *Help me*."

The ensorcellment jerked tight on his viscera at that "Help me" and dragged him forward. The boy crouched, his hands bracing Neill's shoulders against the rough wall. Neill's patchwork jacket was gone. Of the once-fine shirt, only its side panels and shoulders remained; the sleeves were in rags, and the front torn open. To the right of his sternum was a cavity in the flesh that frothed at every exhalation. With that wound, he ought to be dead. But he was obviously capable of healing magic, of a sort.

"I need—," Neill gasped, and Balthasar jumped violently as something bristled and muscular thrust against his legs, pushing first him and then the boy aside. The balewolf padded up to Neill and pressed its muzzle under Neill's hand and whined, like a solicitous hound. A second joined it. Silently, first one, then the other, sank to the wet rubble, their bristled flanks moving feebly as though they were exhausted. The cavity in Neill's chest no longer bubbled.

"Why didn't you—?" the boy protested, his tone hurt.

Neill said, roughly, "Don't be a fool. You'll need your vitality." He summoned two more of his surviving wolves to him, and their limp bodies joined the rest. The man stroked the nearest bristled heap gently.

Something moved within the smear of smoke and nascent heat, and from the ruined interior staggered a huge wolf moving on lacerated paws, its fur soaked—the smell was that of blood—and hide burned. Neill pushed himself painfully around to gather it in. "Ah, Mayfly," he said hoarsely, resting his face on the gory fur. The wolf let him lean on it, mild as a sheepdog.

"What—?" the boy began, plaintively.

With a swift strike that belied his injury, Neill caught his chin in one hand. "How, by the . . . Mother could you . . . *not* find out . . . that the cellar . . . was full of explosives?"

"It was not my fault!" the boy cried, struggling free. "How was I supposed to know? No one taught me enough."

The wounded Shadowborn gurgled a laugh. "D'you think . . . you're *alone*?" He fell back against the wall, throwing his hand up to bark knuckles against the stone. "I wanted this manor intact. Its *library* alone—" He swallowed down the confession and let his head drop back. "Midora's dead," he said, flatly. "Beam fell on her; couldn't help. Could barely keep myself alive." He snorted wetly and swept a wrist across his nose. "Speaking of overconfidence."

"I'd rather it was her than you," the boy said.

The man's expression was one common to the elders of antisocial juveniles everywhere. He turned his face toward Balthasar. "You're Hearne's brother. The physician."

"He's mine!" the boy said, sharply.

"I can sense that. You poor sod . . . not the least idea what's going on, by the look of you. Don't know whether to pity or envy you . . ." Behind Balthasar, something grumbled deep in its massive throat. He could now smell blood, ordure, and warm, wet, living fur. An atavistic sense told him he was ringed by Shadowborn. Neill raised his hand as he went to turn. "Don't—," he said, softly, and the ensorcellment reinforced that injunction. "They won't harm you, as long as you just stay as you are. I try not to repeat my mistakes." He rolled his head on its stone pillow toward Sebastien. "What happened in Minhorne?"

"We killed the Lightborn prince!" the boy blurted. "Set up the magic on the munitions—everything was going fine. Jonquil ensorcelled Vladimer, was going to let him slowly die, keep his people disorganized, but then Strumheller became involved. And even though he was accused of the ensorcellment and . . . and murder, he was directing other people toward us, and Jonquil thought he could hurry Vladimer's death as well as trap Strumheller's allies. But Strumheller was working with a mage, a *strong* mage—it wasn't the Broome woman; it wasn't any one of those we knew about—and she managed to resist him, and Strumheller . . . He *shot* Jonquil dead while *she* held him."

Telmaine, Balthasar thought, and desperately tried to stifle the thought.

"I got some of Jonquil's agents and waited at the station for Vladimer, but the mage was there again—I didn't think he was supposed to work with mages, and she turned my fires back at me. I was . . . I was alone. I was," he said in a small voice, "scared."

"I can understand that, Seb, but Emeya won't be in a mood to listen. You need to go back to Minhorne and finish up what you and Jonquil were ordered to do, and you need to do it before Emeya gets here. *Come!*" The boy jerked forward as though a rope had been hooked to his breastbone. "Trust me," Neill said, as he laid the back of his hand against the boy's cheek. "This is going to hurt me more than it hurts you." The boy stiffened and whined through his teeth, and Balthasar's body tensed in ensorcelled protectiveness, remembering the man's searing touch. But, fortunately, before he could otherwise react, the man's hand fell away and he slumped sideways onto his elbow, arm across the oozing hole in his chest. He had tapped his own vitality to work whatever magic he had on the boy, and paid for it.

Sebastien scrambled away, but only until he bumped against one of Neill's wolves, which growled at him. Then he crouched, staring at Neill, mouth opening and closing. Slowly, Neill raised his head. "I've shown you how; now would you *get going*, before *she* calls us back?"

The boy lunged out of his crouch to catch Balthasar's hand, though Bal's sensation of it was no more than of a jar at the end of a stick of wood. And then the boy threw his arms around him, and Balthasar felt an instant's disorientation before they fell.

Ishmael

Someone caught Ishmael—by his left arm, curse it—and hauled him close to shout in his ear, "Baronette wants you! Up front in the grand coach." He pointed, though how, in the shambles that was their retreat, he knew *where* to point, Ishmael did not know. He was supposed to be in the vanguard, but the van was already well up the road and Mycene had it. Stranhorne's plans notwithstanding, if ever a man was temperamentally unsuited to be rear, Mycene was. By the croaking shouts from his right, Lavender was mustering Stranhorne to guard the rear. Sharp woman, but with that throat, she'd be living on hot lemon and honey for the next week. So Lavender was with them, and Laurel. "The baron?" he shouted. "Boris?"

"Don't know about the baron. The baronet took a mauling. He's in the coach."

Holding his throbbing arm against his chest to spare it further insult, Ish struggled forward through the mob. He had not been privy to the planning of the retreat, but he had the essence: troops to the van, rear, and flank, running or riding; wheeled vehicles—everything from the Stranhorne state coach to a coal man's wagon—just behind the van, drawn by horses, mules, oxen, and teams of men harnessed together; and a long train of foot travelers following behind. With the fugitives from the west, the manor staff, and reservists, they had thirteen hundred people to get to the Crosstracks, five miles away. *And only two hours to do it in,* he thought, hand going out to steady a young woman who was lugging a screeching, thrashing child of three or four. In this press, a child that size could unknowingly be trampled.

Feeling the strength in his grip, she appealed over her shoulder, "Take him, please, sir. I can't carry him and keep this pace." He realized she was not a woman, but a girl, twelve or thirteen, tall for her age, but slender. Not a mother, then—a sister or cousin or nursemaid, or simply someone with a pair of empty arms. He accepted the burden. "I've to go forward past th'wagons. I'll find him a place." He hoisted the child over his shoulder, which spared his ears the howls and his wounded arm the little fists, and continued forward as rapidly as he could. The noise did seem to help clear his way.

He handed the winded but still gamely protesting child up onto a covered cart, where he joined a crop of small ones and their harried caretakers. The jouncing had already made several of them sick, and no doubt the rest would follow. He quickly assessed the solidity of the cover over their heads. It would do. It would have to do.

He found Laurel riding shotgun to one of her own coachmen, a rifle across her knee. Four members of the Stranhorne troop were keeping a high watch atop the coach. He swung up on the running board beside her, head level with her waist. She reached down, and they exchanged a lingering arm clasp. She wore a heavy leather jacket, too large for her frame, over her loose dress and stout riding boots, and someone—probably not she—had tucked a plump cushion behind her back. Her hair was caught back in a braid beneath her helmet. Her face was composed, even stern. He could sense her influence in the calm assurance of the people around her. He'd always known she had courage and a cool head, but this was more than he would ever have expected of her or her sister.

From beside and behind her, she produced a holster and a brace of revolvers, a pouch of ammunition, and a staff— all his own, he realized, as he took the holster in hand.

"Lavender's at the rear. Your father?" he said, knowing he could not spare her.

She shook her head once. "The way the manor was burning, the way it went up . . . he and the others may not have had time to get out." Her voice was small and tight. "We can't spare anyone to go back."

"Y'can spare me, I think, though your father'll take my hide, since his orders were t'get you clear. But it's still only a few minutes run t'get down to the southwest corner."

"Assuming," she said, "you meet no trouble."

"Assuming that," he said. "But I doubt I'd make any great difference t'you here."

"Then there's Dr. Hearne," she said.

"Who'd be th'first after me t'tell you you'd done the right thing by leaving him, if his mind was his own. But, yes, I'd try for the baronelle's garden as well."

"You shouldn't go alone."

"I'll move fastest, going alone." He hooked his right arm around the leg of the coachman's bench, and quickly checked both revolvers. Not that he didn't trust her, but he'd worked too hard to instill good habits in her and her sister.

"Ishmael . . . ," she said. "Please take care."

He briefly covered the hand on the rifle stock with his own gloved one. Being in the open air had restored him, and he felt as though he could run for hours. Illusion, but it should carry him where he wanted to go. "Who's the best we've got on th'south side?"

"Dyan." She pointed.

He wove through the crowd until he found the squad leader holding a firm seat on a young thoroughbred that had more spirit than sense; it was Boris's favorite horse. He should have asked after the baronet, but too late now. Trotting at Dyan's stirrup, Ishmael pointed out his course. He would fall out across the field, keeping level with Dyan and his squad until he was out of range of sonn. Anyone he found, he would bring up the rear.

I should do something about my cursed legend, he mused as he scrambled over a stile and angled his path across the new-mown field. *Anyone thinking to attempt this ought to be told he's daft, and tied up and thrown into one of the sick carts for his own good.* Stranhorne would have plenty to say, though a man who'd torch munitions in his own cellar was hardly one to condemn. But Stranhorne's trap had shifted a balance; Ishmael could feel it in the air. The rain had lightened to a drizzle and was almost warm, and he could sense very little of the Shadowborn's former strength.

On the far side of the field, he followed the wall until the corner and the gate, opened the gate, and slid through, onto the manor grounds. He moved as quietly as he was able at that speed. He could still hear the retreat: not even abject terror could keep quiet that many horses, carts and carriages, injured men and women, children and infants. But he could also hear the hiss of the wind through drying stubble, the chirp and flutter of an early rousing bird, the flap of a tarpaulin weighted down under stones—all the ordinary sounds of the area. The wind was in his face, blowing from the manor, so it would not betray his presence. Though with the heavy reek of smoke and munitions, he would be hard-pressed himself to smell anything before he came on it.

He knew the manor grounds, having spent a number of enjoyable nights training with the twins and cadet members of the troop, trying to teach them how to move silently and with the minimum of sonn, and how to place and number others in the dark. In addition, he had a perfect, and unwelcome, lodestone in the form of the Call. All he needed to do was keep driving himself away from it and keep from thinking that its strength made his leaving the retreat doubly foolish. With a momentary lapse in concentration, he might well find himself walking southwest.

He had the choice of following the wall of the manor or coming directly across the warning field. He chose the latter; the wall would be shelter, but would also restrict his direction of retreat. He wondered if he should regret that decision; the dry sticks were soaked, but he still had to navigate over sliding stones, crunching gravel, and deadfalls deep enough to break his leg, if he missed being impaled. The wind was blustering and shifting, pushing and lifting the smoke and stinging ash, and when the smoke shifted away, he could smell violent death and the beginning of rot. He stepped carefully around the crumbling edges of a pit occupied by several wolves. One struggled weakly on the stakes that pinned it, and a second was gnawing on the carcass of one of its dead companions. A few yards in, he came across the first of the Shadowborn brought down by the fire from the manor, more wolves, the first scavvern—a young one, by its growth—and one of the flying Shadowborn, crumpled and broken-backed in death. *Who might that have been before? . . .* Some thoughts were simply best not had. The wind shifted, and he shielded his face against the ash, trying not to cough, until it was done playing with him. Not far now. He moved forward, listening ahead of him, listening through the muffled crackle of the fire, the creak of heated stone, for the sound of voices, even for the sound of moaning. To his right, a wolf howled out its pain, and several more answered. He could no longer hear the retreat, and he was stricken by the sense that should he also throw back his head and howl into the emptiness, none of his own kind would answer.

He did not know when exactly he gave up hope, but it was gone by the time he reached the southwest corner. He could not even have said where the bricked-up entrance had been without going right up to the wall and examining where the stones lined up one atop the other. There was no breach in the wall, no place for Xavier Stranhorne, Erich, and the men and women with them, to have escaped.

He forced himself to move. He had less than two hours before sunrise, and he dared not linger around the manor. Even if there were nothing more dangerous than the dead, the snow and the battle might have scattered or silenced the wildlife he was used to using as a sunrise alarm. And he would not be safe to sleep out now, with the Call gnawing on him. It would be ironic if he were to be caught by the sun, after all these years.

The years of vagabondage and Shadowhunting saved him. Thought might be dulled by exhaustion and loss, but instinct was not. He heard *something*—a breath, a muted growl, the breaking of a wet stick—or smelled *something*, the sweat or breath that, rank though it was, meant something was living. At its very limits, sonn caught the shapes flowing along the south face of the manor, toward him, along the narrow, quiet band between the wall and the first layer of gravel.

Exhaustion was swept away by adrenaline. He shot, four times, to howls, and turned and sprinted along the base of the wall. He had no cover or vantage there, and if they were to come at him in numbers, he needed the gates and the gate towers, for cover, a vantage, a chance to reload. He could not hear movement behind him, for his own pounding effort and tearing breath, and, having committed him-

self to run, he dared not twist to sonn. And there, the
northwest corner, the wall around the courtyard, the turn —

The foul chill of Shadowborn magic rolled over him. Ishmael switched direction on a stride, zigzagging away from
the wall, across open grass toward the road. He heard and
felt the rasp of a wing close overhead, pivoted, and swung
with the staff, fouling its swoop. It grounded gracelessly, and
he shot it even as it spread its wings, then plunged back into
the dubious shelter of the wall. Back against the wall, he
sonned wolves closing in on him from the direction of the
road itself.

No chance to reload. He caught the first on the road,
switched guns, and shot the second on the embankment and
the third on the road. *Four more shots left.* Two wolves in
the lead from the side were dealt with, but there was more
movement beyond them. *Two rounds in the chamber, and
eighty yards to the gate.* He coiled to run, but even as he did
so, from the direction of the road came a whimper, the very
sound he'd heard a dog make, decades ago, just before a
Shadowhunt — only the third he'd ever been on — turned
into the bloodiest disaster he'd ever been in, barring this.

"The size of three stallions crossed with your worst
nightmare," he had said to Ferdenzil Mycene. This scavvern
was only somewhat larger than a cart horse, but that made
it all the faster. It rolled forward on the knuckles of its long
forearms, and as it reared to strike, his sonn caught the hard
echo of its talons and the envenomed spur on its wrist.

He shot it in the center of its mass. It reeled but did not
fall; scavvern were cursed difficult to drop with a single
shot, whatever his legend said. He dropped the staff and
steadied his revolver two-handed, readying his last shot,
knowing he'd have to try for a pith. Then it would be staff
and knife work for as long as he lasted.

A woman's voice said, "Ishmael di Studier!" He sensed
a surge of Shadowborn magic, as potent and vile as any he'd
known, and the Call itself, like a steel cable, wound round
his spine. The staggering scavvern, the milling wolves, and
he were suddenly moving as slowly as if caught in winter

honey. Only a small adjustment was necessary in his aim. A man shouted from behind the wolves, "Ariadne, look *out*!"

The woman screamed, "Lysander, no!"

Ishmael fired, and a second shot echoed his. He grunted at the punch in his belly, then agony briefly voided his mind of all capacity to reason and locked his jaws on a howl. His legs buckled, spine split, or as nearly as made no difference. He slithered down the wall and flopped facedown in the mud. The scavvern, toppling, barely missed him, sluicing him with mud from its fall. Half-smothered, mud filling his mouth, he remembered how, drunk, maudlin, and smelling nothing but the reek of the city, he had prayed to be able to mingle his ashes with Borders earth. Mud would do—his father would no doubt deem it fitting. He was bleeding hard, bleeding out, but he could still hear the approaching splashes of the mage and the man who had shot him. He could sense her foul power gathering around him. Well, they were welcome to his sorry carcass, but he'd make doubly sure. He reached into his magic.

<Not. Alive.>

Five

Balthasar

*T*he sense of falling was brief, and ended with a hard landing on tiled floor. Balthasar's knees bore the impact, and the pain left him braced on knees and elbows, dizzied. *Magic,* he thought, *this has to be magic. But to what end?*

"Yes," he heard the boy gasp out, "I *did it.* It's so easy. It's so *easy!"* he half wheezed, half screamed. "You lousy bitch, it's so easy." Then he slumped down on the floor, head on his arms, shuddering with reaction.

Beneath his hands, Balthasar felt dry tiles, not wet flagstone. The air was chill, but no rain fell. He could smell the dust and dried-flower scent of a house long closed up, though that was overlaid by a faint odor of rot, like neglected kitchen refuse. He turned his head away from Sebastien and softly cast, resolving an ornate arch over a doorway. To the left, another arch and stairs . . . the interior of a house.

He knew this house: it was in Minhorne. His brother had brought him here once, bragging of the scam that had ruined a man and laid his property in Lysander's hands. Perhaps it was justice that the house had been Lysander's own ruin. When he grandly gifted it to his inamorata, Tercelle Amberley—though her family owned half a dozen houses much finer—it provoked that last, fatal quarrel with his mistress, a possessive, volatile young actress. Which ended with her dead and Lysander sobbing in Balthasar's room, pleading for the help of his fourteen-year-old brother in smuggling the body out of the city, to leave for sunrise.

Help that Balthasar had, to his everlasting regret, given him.

This would be the house that Tercelle had fled to after she left her twin sons with him—the house Telmaine and Ishmael had traced her to. It was also the house she had died in, murdered, surely, by the Shadowborn.

"Get me something to eat," Sebastien said, faintly, into his arm.

In the kitchen, Balthasar exchanged his soaked jacket and waistcoat for an overlarge but thick servant's vest he found hanging on a peg. He retrieved bread, hard cheese, chutney, and honey from the pantry, not trusting the prepared meats, and made sandwiches sweet and savory. Also in the pantry were bottles of light beer, familiar to him from his student days, though that label was well beyond his budget then. Opening a couple of bottles hardly constituted a debauch, and the beer was probably safer than the water.

The boy had crawled over to the carpeted stairs and was sitting on the lowest step, head in his hands. He cast a wavering sonn over the tray as Balthasar laid it on the step beside him, but promptly seized a sandwich with each hand, eating alternate bites and swallowing almost without chewing. Balthasar had seen street urchins gorge so when set before food.

He had no appetite himself, but he knew he needed food to counteract the shock and hypothermia. He doggedly worked his way through a honey sandwich, each ashy bite washed down with beer. Turning the bottle in his hands, he supposed he should be glad to have no illusions that drink could rid him of his memories, because he understood as never before the desire to crawl into bottled oblivion.

"Why?" he said at last. "Why all this? Why Tercelle? Why Stranhorne?"

Sebastien shook his head. "You're better not to know."

Ignorance had not spared him before this. "Where is my brother?"

"Dead."

There was venom in that tone, enough to mark it as wish more than truth. Balthasar therefore did not answer it with conventional regrets. "And your mother?"

"Dead."

"She must have been a strong mage."

"I don't want to talk about them," the boy said. He lurched back against the stairs, pulling at the waistband of his breeches. "I feel sick. I've never *lifted* before."

The magical mode of transport, an instantaneous transfer between places. His sister, Olivede, had described it to him, though it required at least sixth-rank magic to achieve, and Olivede had not the strength. She had said more than once how glad she was to be spared both the burdens and the temptations of high-rank magic and not be other than she was—a skilled physician and reliable third-rank healer.

He turned over in his mind the scene he had witnessed just before they had come there. "Who is the woman you mentioned, who would have called you?"

"You shouldn't ask so many questions," the boy said.

It did not quite mute Balthasar, just thickened his tongue and made speaking laborious. He ate half of a cheese sandwich and finished his beer, feeling the slight detachment that came with beer quickly drunk. The boy sipped distrustfully at his bottle.

Balthasar tried again, "Why are we back in the city?"

Sebastien shrugged. "Orders."

Balthasar set down the bottle. "I'm going to try to light the stove," he said. "I'm soaked through. And—"

Sebastien's stiffening, his astonished gasp, interrupted him. The ground beneath them shook. An immense concussion cleaved the night. Balthasar came to his feet, swinging his head to try to fix the sound. He recognized it as an explosion, a huge one, larger even than the disaster of several years ago at one of the distilleries. But there were no factories in that direction, only more rows of streets, parkland along the river, the river itself, and the estates on the far side. He heard a bizarre screaming whistle from overhead, and then, from his left, another, lesser explosion.

Sebastien jackknifed, leaping to land on his feet beside

Bal. "Yes!" He punched air. "Yes, yes, yes. They've finally *done* it! *That* for your caution, Neill, and *that* for your power, Jonquil."

Oh, sweet Imogene, Balthasar thought. Sebastien had said something about ensorcelling munitions. Was that a ship or ships blowing up on the river? But who should have been bringing munitions into the city? Had the dukes insisted on arming themselves as well, now that the order of six twenty-nine was suspended? He heard another crash, another shriek of passing . . . artillery? Were they at war—Darkborn against Darkborn? Darkborn against Lightborn? He turned his head again, checking his orientation. In *that* direction was the river, the artery of trade and communication, and on its far banks, the great city estates of several of the dukes, including Duke Kalamay, hater of Lightborn and mages. And in *this* direction was the city center, the Lightborn prince's palace, the Mages' Tower.

From outside, he could hear screams. If Lightborn walls had been breached, anyone caught outside would die, swiftly if the light were more than a glimmering, and slowly and in agony otherwise. He could not leave anyone to that, whatever the risk to himself. He lunged past the capering boy, turned the door handle, and found it locked. He groped one-handed for a key that was not there, still twisting futilely. Even in its light-tight frame, the door shuddered from another barrage, and then he felt a wave of unease and dizziness, followed almost immediately by an explosion in the air, and another, even greater one, to his right. Then the reverberations faded away, leaving only a deep bell knelling and no living sounds outside at all.

Magic, he thought. *Magic enough even for me to sense.* He heard a whimper behind him and turned to sonn Sebastien on the floor, arched and shuddering with a convulsion. He dropped by his side, examining him for signs of injury, signs of anything that might have triggered the seizure, then rolled him over on his side, bracing him there with knees behind his back, protecting his head from the tiles. He did not know the boy's medical history; he might be epileptic, but from the coincidence, Bal had to suspect that this was magical. And if he were part of whatever had happened—as his triumph seemed to indicate—then he might be under attack by the Lightborn. Olivede, Balthasar's principal informant in the ways of magic, was merely a third-rank mage, and a determinedly peaceable one at that. He had no idea what might happen should mages turn magic upon one another.

Except that it was certain to be dangerous for the bystanders.

Even if he could run, he had nowhere to go in the light-polluted night.

Sebastien went limp, his head lying heavy in Balthasar's cradling hand. "They can't be . . . can't be . . . ," he whispered, drew in a whining breath, and began to convulse anew. Balthasar braced him, counting out the seconds. When the fit passed and did not immediately resume, he stripped off the servant's vest and wedged it behind Sebastien's shoulders, and bundled his wet shirt beneath the boy's head. Then he ran in search of the household's medicine cabinet.

To his surprise, he also found a full obstetrical kit, complete with forceps, anesthetic equipment, bottles of chloroform, and antiseptic. Initial, but not considered, surprise: Tercelle Amberley would have made alternate preparations for her confinement, had Balthasar turned her away from his door. His hands shook with chill and the intensity of his wish that he had done so, as he gathered bottles into a small pouch. But if the seizures continued, he would be able to anesthetize the boy.

When he reached the hallway again, Sebastien was lying curled up on his side, and for a moment of hideously conflicted relief, Balthasar thought he had died. Then he coughed, and the ensorcellment tightened like barbed wire. Balthasar knelt beside him, hand on his shoulder, sonning his face. "Sebastien?"

"They couldn't—," he whispered. "Couldn't have been able to—"

Balthasar probed his head, eliciting no wince; felt his

chest and belly, finding no tenderness; felt his pulse, finding it fast but strong. "Who couldn't have been able to do what?" he said.

"Shouldn't have been able to annul—"

Annul . . . magic in which the boy had invested his vitality? That might explain the seizure.

"Are you . . . safe?" Balthasar asked, stumbling over the words, the question, the conflict between ensorcellment, compassion, dread, and smoldering anger that made such a question a deeply resented obligation.

"They shouldn't . . . have been able to . . ." He managed to lift his head, and, with Balthasar's help, sit up. "They shouldn't have been able to *do that*," he said plaintively.

"Do what? What were those explosions?" Balthasar asked. He did not think he had ever less wanted to know the answer to a question.

"The Mages' Tower. We blew it up."

A simple statement, bereft of boast. The Mages' Tower was, by Floria's account, the dominant feature of the skyline, a tower occupied by high-rank Lightborn mages, men and women whose healing power granted them life spans four or five times the length of those of ordinary men and women, who could raise storms to their will, transport themselves and others between places . . . as the boy just had then. The dynamite needed—

Sebastien scowled at his skepticism. "We *did it*."

"You'd never have been able to place enough dynamite—" *Not with the vigilance,* he wanted to say, *not with the city watch.* But who knew how many in the city they already held under ensorcellment, to act for the Shadowborn or simply turn their attention away? How many other men and women had been forced into the position he was in?

"Not dynamite. *Guns.* Great big guns."

Great big guns. Despite his exhaustion, despite his resistance, he made the connections. "That was why you were interested in Tercelle." The Amberleys' industrial concerns were munitions and artillery. It was that, not the old love affair between Lysander and Tercelle, that had drawn the Shadowborn to Tercelle Amberley. As Lysander had said—

and Floria, more kindly—he was a sentimental fool. "They were the ones who—"

"No." A grin peeled back the boy's lips. "Duke Mycene and Duke Kalamay—*they* did it. We didn't even need to ensorcell them. They did it all on their very own. *We* just had to ensorcell the munitions." He drew his knees up to his chest and hugged them. "But they shouldn't have been able to . . . ," he whispered.

"Ensorcell the munitions to—"

"Make them extra lethal," the boy said. "This way . . ."

He put his clammy palm on Balthasar's wrist, and Balthasar's breath left him, crushed out of him by the pain in his chest, the overwhelming sense of dread and mortality. He could not even cry out.

Sebastien lifted his hand and released him, leaving him propped on his hands and gasping in shock. "*That* way."

Balthasar could not speak, so profound was his sense of near death and his realization of how much hope he had placed in the Lightborn mages having the will and power to end these atrocities. If even the Lightborn were vulnerable . . . Yet they *had* retaliated—he had sensed that himself. . . . "They *did* annul your magic, didn't they?"

"*No,*" the boy said, his voice breaking high. He forced it down to a growl. "Say that again, and I'll annul *you*. They *can't* annul our magic. They can't *sense* it. I just overreached. It was me and Jonquil ensorcelled the munitions, and Jonquil's dead, so it was just my vitality in there, and *I overreached*."

"What . . . do you mean that the Lightborn cannot sense your magic?"

"Just what I say—they *can't*. They can't sense us, and they can't sense our magic. Haven't been able to do it for centuries, but you can bet they've kept that a deep, *deep* secret. We didn't even know ourselves until . . . well, until. Lightborn can't sense Shadowborn magic; only Darkborn can. And Darkborn aren't that strong."

If the Lightborn mages could not sense Shadowborn magic, or if they could sense it but could not counter it, it made terrible sense of their indifference to the Darkborn's travails. The Lightborn mages had united to call down a rainstorm on the Rivermarch as it burned, but the target had been the fire, not the magic that set the fire.

"So they were no threat to you, but you still attacked the tower."

"We had to. They couldn't sense our magic, but they could still attack *us*."

"But *why*?" Balthasar said, angry now. "What is it all for?"

"I shouldn't tell you."

"Why shouldn't you tell me? You've ensorcelled me. I can't betray you."

"That's not—" He stopped himself.

Balthasar waited, shaking slightly with anger and exhaustion. *Not* what? *Not the way it works?*

Sebastien buried his face in his knees. "It's been happening a long time," he mumbled. "I don't know what it's all about—it's best not to ask—but there are two of them. Lady Emeya and another one. They fight each other, but they want the lands, the whole lands."

"And they hold you—and others—ensorcelled."

Sebastien lifted a face that held in it the same hopeless exhaustion Balthasar had sonned in child factory workers. "Some want to stay. *I* wanted to stay."

There was a time to ask, *And now?* But it was not now, and not because of the boy's readiness or uneasiness. Balthasar himself was not ready to hear. "But your will is your own," he said.

A silence. "My head really hurts."

"You've had a seizure," Balthasar said. "Had you had them before?"

The boy did not answer, his lower lip set sullenly.

"Let's get you upstairs," Balthasar said. "You'll feel better when you're warm and lying down." He helped Sebastien to his feet and steered him toward and up the stairs. In the first-floor master bedroom, he helped the boy out of his soaked clothes—the trousers soaked with urine as well as rainwater, he realized—and toweled him down, got him into a clean nightshirt, and coaxed a dose of chloral hydrate down him. The seizure, or the uncertainty about his magic, had left the boy dazed. Balthasar spread quilts over him, smelling the fragrant must of old herbal sachets, and started to turn away.

The quilts rustled. "Don't go." A child's voice, a child's plea.

"I need to change out of those wct clothes. I'll become ill otherwise." It was obvious that healing was not amongst the boy's skills.

"Come back quickly."

Balthasar obeyed, rummaging in the spare-room wardrobe for a heavy, smoky-smelling sweater and coarse trousers that were too large for him but would be warm. One of Tercelle's male relations, he presumed; they could not belong to either Lysander or Mycene, both of whom were slight. He stripped, washed the blood off his side, wincing at the tenderness of the closed wound, dried himself, and quickly rinsed and wrung out his clothing as bcst hc could. Then he dressed, drawing the waistband tight to hold it up on his hips.

Sebastien was still awake when he returned, fighting sleep like a child. Balthasar found himself straightening the covers, as he would for one of his daughters. Sebastien's eyes shifted—watching him?

"It's strange," he said. "Having you here. It's like having . . . him."

"My brother?" Wiser to say that than try "your father."

"He was . . . He looked after me. But then . . ." A long silence. "He wanted to take her away. He said he *had* to take her away. And if I wouldn't go, then he'd leave me behind. He said if it was her or me, he would take her."

The words were childish, the anguish was that of a young child's abandonment, and Balthasar could well imagine Lysander saying that to a child. He reminded himself that he could not imagine what Lysander had experienced among the Shadowborn. "Was she in that much danger?"

"Yes. No!" A long pause. "Emeya would have killed her."

"But you didn't know that at the time," Bal said. *Because people seldom do, even when it is there before them.*

"No," he said. He turned on his side, away from Balthasar. "I don't want to talk anymore. Be quiet. Stay."

Balthasar sat listening to the tolling of the warning bell, a sound he had heard only once before in his time in the city, when the collapse of an ill-built tenement had spilled light into the night. But those were poor artisans, with only enough light to last out the night, and though scores of Darkborn had been burned, few had died outright. The breached walls of the Mages' Tower would have blazed out like a beacon, and the Lightborn would have surely laid claim to the last hours of the night in a bid to rescue survivors. He could not escape and live, even if he had not been bound by the ensorcellment.

He heard a snuffling snore; the boy had rolled over to sprawl on his back. In sleep, he might have been one of the waifs Balthasar had treated in Olivede's Rivermarch clinic: half starved, half wild, street bred and street reared, neglected and abused. He could not hate the boy—and was that ensorcellment or pity? *Pity,* he thought, and rejected the thought—and then brought it back to reexamine it. His thoughts limped with exhaustion, but even in his weariness, he had a sense that he was close to something important. *Love me,* the boy demanded. An adult might thwart the wishes of a child out of love; as the father of two lively little girls, he found himself doing that more often than he ever wanted. For him to juxtapose his feelings for his daughters with his feelings toward this boy seemed an obscenity, but . . . if he had an escape, he sensed it lay there.

He would need his wits intact to know his way when it opened before him. Rather than strain against the ensorcellment by trying to leave the room, he found a spare quilt and a pillow, laid down the pillow, wrapped himself in the quilt, and stretched out on the rug in front of the cold grate.

Balthasar

Balthasar woke to the muted crackle of an untidily laid fire in the grate, and his brother kicking at his bare feet. "Up," Lysander said. "I'm having visitors. You get to play butler."

"Sebastien?" Balthasar said tentatively.

"Yes—oh, the shape." He smirked. "You like it?"

He did not like it. His memories of his brother were of taunting and torment shading to outright cruelty, ending in coercion to conceal Lysander's capital crime, but nevertheless he rebelled at the thought of his brother's living likeness being passed back and forth amongst these Shadowborn like an old sock. "No," he said. "I don't like it."

Sebastien scowled down at him. He was wearing a slightly outdated, formal suit that would have suited a lord's heir. It might have been Lysander's, since Lysander liked to dress expensively and above his station. The young mage seemed recovered after last night's collapse, but there was a hectic energy about him that Balthasar had seen in young addicts and young gamecocks intoxicated by their own recklessness. The first, he had treated; the second, he had, generally, outplayed. "I need to be older," Sebastien said. "Or they won't listen." He kicked Balthasar's feet again. "Get up. And dress decently. There's clothes in the wardrobe."

He left. Balthasar crawled out of his bedding. He could not tell what time it was; his watch, soaked once too often, had stopped. There were no familiar sounds to cue him. In his and Telmaine's home, the staff's routines demarcated night and day as crisply as the bells outside. In the old, narrow house he had inherited from his parents, he could tell the hour from the mutterings of the walls and roof as they warmed with the sun, and from the sound of Floria White Hand's movements next door.

His own clothing had barely begun to dry; he could still wring water out of the cuffs. Groping in the wardrobe, he found a shirt, pressed trousers—loose at the waist and slightly long in the leg—and a formal jacket and coat, both decently plain and smelling of tired lavender and long storage. He washed and dressed, wincing as he stretched the scar in his side, found a comb and pulled it through his unwashed hair, and decided not to bother to search for a razor. Despite his sleep, he was draggingly tired, but he knew his tiredness was as much of the spirit as the body, that it was despair that sapped him.

Sebastien was standing in the vestibule as he came down the stairs, toying with a large, ornate door key. "You look awful," he said, as though Balthasar's haggard aspect gave him personal offense.

"I can do what's needed," Balthasar said quietly. Sebastien would not hear the other meaning and the prayer in that.

Sebastien's response was interrupted by the doorbell. Key in hand, he crossed to the door. His smirk back over his shoulder, his expectant pause before he turned the key, jolted Balthasar to full understanding. Protest jammed in his throat at the realization that Sebastien knew precisely what he was doing—as Lysander knew what he was doing—and panic rendered him mute.

He had only enough time for a single step back, as Sebastien turned the handle and threw open the door on daylight.

Six

Floria

*P*olitics made for strange bedmates, Prince Isidore used to say, though Floria White Hand had never foreseen it applying to *her*. She was a vigilant; her prince's allies were her allies, and her prince's enemies her enemies. This she had learned when head-high to her father's belt, as he had learned from his father, and he from his, and so on, back ten generations.

How, then, did she come to be standing—albeit with her back to a solid wall—in a gathering of the very people she had spent eighteen years protecting her prince *from*?

In the center of the room, the dowager consort Helenja glowered at her sister. Helenja was a heavy woman, deceptively so, given how quickly she could move when inclined. She had a southerner's coloring, and the ornate construction of her dull auburn hair was in the southern mode. Her usual dress, southern in its earth-hued simplicity, was decorated with ribbons and a sash in bright red, in scant acknowledgment of her mourning.

In Sharel, Floria could see the young Helenja, despite the slight physical resemblance between them: Sharel was lean, dark, and straight nosed, where Helenja was bulky, auburn, and had a nose that had been broken by a fractious horse. Nevertheless, Sharel's arrogance and swift certainty of judgment evoked the arrogant young consort who had thought to conquer Isidore's court.

"Of course he's a hostage!" Sharel was saying. "You said Fejelis grabbed him just before they all disappeared. Orlanjis would never have gone willingly."

The dowager consort looked past Sharel, toward Floria. She was squinting slightly, as though looking at a bright horizon or suffering from a headache. "Orlanjis," Helenja said, grittily, "couldn't have made his support for Fejelis more plain. Mistress White Hand, come here."

Floria did not want to expose her back in this company, but she and Helenja had established a sketch of an alliance around their desire to find Prince Fejelis and his brother. Moreover, she'd never fight her way out. She obeyed.

"Tell my sister what *you* saw," Helenja said.

Why Sharel should believe Floria's account of the disappearance of Fejelis and Orlanjis, she had no idea. For eighteen years, Floria had been vigilant and food taster to Fejelis's father, Isidore, on account of the magical asset that protected her against poisons—most of which had been plied by the southerners.

Perhaps, she thought bitterly, *I have become credible because of the part I played in Isidore's death.*

Stonily, she reported, "The prince's sister"—to refer to her by either her birth name or the name given her by the mages was equally fraught—"came running up to Prince Fejelis and Captain Rupertis in the vestibule of the palace, to tell them that the high masters had Magister Tammorn, who had been working for the prince, and were planning to burn out his magic—"

"Why?" Sharel interrupted. "He's a mage."

"Magister Tammorn is a sport," Floria said. No need to explain what else the Mages' Temple had to hold against Tam, aside from his birth outside the Temple's carefully cultivated lineages. "Prince Fejelis went to the high masters and attempted to persuade them to release Magister Tam and to join with him in dealing with the Shadowborn."

In defiance of centuries of protocol shielding the archmage from earthborn contact, the young prince had appealed directly to the archmage for an alliance. His appeal had been bold and moving and might have worked, except that Fejelis had made a tactical error. "He let it be known that he believed that lineage mages could not detect Shadowborn magic."

"Was he mad?" said Sharel.

"Look out the window," Helenja said. "And tell me."

Out of the window was the Mages' Tower, that thrusting assertion of the mages' ambition, wealth, and power, which had shadowed the palace and streets beneath it for two hundred years. Its upper dome was gone, its upper stories collapsed in on themselves and fallen in slabs over the streets and buildings below, its middle and lower stories punctuated with jagged holes. The bright dust of its ruin was still settling out of the late-afternoon sunlight. That the destruction had been wreaked by material means—explosive shells from Darkborn emplacements on the far side of the river—everyone knew, but it was already widely rumored that the lethality had been magically augmented. And surely no enemy the mages sensed could have struck against them so preemptively.

"Mad, no," Helenja said, judiciously. "But unwise to have said so outright." She inclined her head toward Floria. "Continue."

Floria believed the silent archmage might have been weighing Fejelis's appeal, but her interpretation was unasked for. "Prasav"—that was Fejelis's oldest cousin on his father's side—"stepped forward to accuse Magister Tam of having been responsible for the prince's—Prince Isidore's—death, under Prince Fejelis's instigation. He suggested that the prince and Magister Tam were lovers."

Sharel snorted at this expression of northern bigotry.

"Fejelis asked the high masters to confirm that he and Tam were innocent of the prince's death. They made no move to do so. Vigilants under Prasav's command"—some of them suborned members of Fejelis's own guard, Rupertis among them, and she owed *him* an accounting at her first opportunity—"took aim at Fejelis. The mages raised no objection, though there was no formal rescinding of contracts."

That made Sharel's eyes widen: the system of contracts by which earthborn secured the services of mages were sacrosanct. "Orlanjis tried to push Fejelis out of the line of fire. Magister Tam deflected the bolts, and then he, the prince, and Orlanjis disappeared."

"The Temple staged a coup," Helenja said, bluntly. "They have set Perrin up as princess—a mage princess, against seven hundred years of compact. Fejelis and Orlanjis were removed by Magister Tammorn. *His* motivations are obscure and his destination even more so. None of *my* mages"—a cold glance in their direction—"claim to be able to locate them."

"And what are you doing here?" Sharel demanded of Floria. "You're Isidore's."

"And, ironically," Helenja said, with a smile that told Floria all their old antagonism was merely suspended, "the instrument of Isidore's destruction." She paused, letting Floria fully appreciate that statement.

"So that rumor about the talisman is true?" Tam believed that, under ensorcellment, Floria had carried to the prince's rooms a talisman enspelled to annul the magic of the lights on which he depended to survive the night.

Floria did not answer. The downward flicker of Sharel's gaze alerted her to her right hand, working on the pommel of her rapier. "Do *you* believe in the Shadowborn?"

For eighteen years she had guarded Isidore, as her father had Isidore's father and uncle before him, and her grandmother, Isidore's grandfather, unmoved by attempts at assassination, threats, seduction, and bribes. Nothing but magic could have made her part of the murder of her prince—yes, she believed in the Shadowborn.

Law might exonerate her of anything done under ensorcellment, yet she had murdered her prince and forfeited her honor, and she would do anything—make any alliance—to make and take recompense for that.

"Yes," she said. "I believe in the Shadowborn."

"And what do they say?" Sharel said, head turning toward the mage.

"The boys are not within the city; of that my mages are certain. Beyond that, they need a direction and distance, or time, to find them."

"If they are caught outside at sunset—"

Helenja glanced toward the window, at the slant of light and depth of shadows. "They won't be," she said.

"How can you possibly know?" Sharel said.

"Fejelis is levelheaded. If he has survived the *lift*, he will ensure they survive the landing."

She could not know. Tam's feat—*lifting* himself, Fejelis, and Orlanjis—should have been beyond a mage of his official rank, even before he had endured the high master's questioning. Misjudgment in such extremity was likely.

"Whatever," said Sharel, "got into Orlanjis?"

"The boy is fourteen, a bundle of emotions," Helenja said. "That mage won't have dropped them at random; it'll be a place he knows. Floria," Helenja said without turning, "you know this mage, I believe. Where would he go?"

Floria drew close the calm she had learned as a courtier in a mage-ridden court. "Magister Tam was born in the foothills of the Gyrheights—the Cloudherds," she explained, giving them their southern name. Tam would never return there, even in mortal danger, but Sharel need not know that. The southerners romanticized their origins. "I know he likes the west coast." It was not precisely a lie; he had visited the west coast once, but talked of it often.

Tam had not gone back, though, after he had met his artisan lady, Beatrice. They had a three-year-old son and a six-month-old daughter, and if Helenja did not already know about Tam's family, then Sharel's inquiries need not progress far before she came across them.

She would deal with Helenja to safeguard Fejelis's rightful position as Isidore's heir. Isidore had made her promise the night Fejelis came of age—the night Isidore died. But she also owed Tam her life; his magic had deflected those quarrels from her own heart, as well as her prince's. She had a blood debt to repay.

"No matter," said Helenja, when Floria said no more. "Start looking; I am expected in an audience with the 'princess.' Floria, with me."

If Helenja and Floria made for strange bedmates, Floria found herself thinking some minutes later, then whatever would Isidore have made of *this* orgy of the peculiar?

She stood at ease, back to a wall, gaze shifting around the room, clashing and glancing off the gazes of the other guards and witnesses ranked around the wall. Across the room, her former friends and colleagues in the prince's vigilance eyed her suspiciously, questioningly, or speculatively, according to their natures.

In the center of the room, beneath a rose skylight, was a round table, its edge and legs carved with ornate geometric scrollwork, decorated with silver, and inlaid with mother-of-pearl and ivory. On the far side sat Perrin, two hours' princess of the Lightborn, and aged a month for every minute of it. Whose idea was it that she sat in that chair, the high, flaring back of which diminished her to a child's proportions? She wore a prince's red-and-blue morning jacket, and her light hair had been hastily caught up in a style suggesting a prince's caul, with deep blue beads threaded through. No one dared re-create the true prince's caul, lost with Fejelis. By her height, her sandy hair, and her light gray eyes, she was Isidore's daughter, but Floria had never seen that hunted expression in Isidore's eyes, or even in Fejelis's.

On either side of Perrin sat the two whose alliance had pitched her into power. On her right was a solid, unremarkable-looking woman in crimson jacket and trousers. The crimson was higher necked and more opaque than any ordinary Lightborn should have been comfortable wearing, which meant its opacity was magical. Her glittering chains of rank showed her to be one of the surviving high masters, the leaders of the Lightborn Mages' Temple, and spokesperson for the archmage—definitely not unremarkable, was Magistra Valetta.

On Perrin's left sat Prasav, dressed as politic in crimson mourning and the green caul that marked his rulership of several northwest provinces. Beside him, sleek and predatory, was his daughter, Ember, in the guise of her father's secretary. She watched Perrin as a well-fed cat might a caged bird, idly considering possibilities for later.

Closest to Floria, Helenja laid her hand down on the table with a soft click of gold filigree rings. "So, Magistra," she said to Valetta. "Are you able to tell me yet where are my sons?"

"Regardless of whether we complete his deposition," Prasav added smoothly, "Fejelis is a disruptive influence."

"Nobody," Perrin said, "is completing Fejelis's deposition. I told you both," she emphasized, with a look at each of her power brokers, "I am not taking the caul stained with Fejelis's blood."

Floria had to appreciate her courage, if not her sense. A princess who refused the caul was no safer than a prince who had lost it.

"We are not interested in contracting to locate the princes, but we *will* find Tammorn, and we expect the princes will be with him."

Her use of "princes" could not be anything but designing. While Fejelis lived, only he was entitled to the address, but it was to the mages' advantage to have their brightnesses at each other's throats, not least because of the lucrative contracts protecting them against each other.

"When you do," Perrin said, firmly, "since my brothers are earthborn, not mageborn, they should be placed in the custody of the vigilance."

Where they will last only as long as it takes the first suborned vigilant to reach them, Floria thought. By chance—for it surely could not be the thought—Perrin's gaze intersected hers. The princess's face tightened, as though she had just tasted something unpleasant. The fading—Floria hoped—ensorcellment that lingered around Floria? Perrin, like Tam, was a sport mage. And sports, Fejelis had asserted, *could* sense Shadowborn magic.

"Well," she heard Prasav say, "shall we talk about the Darkborn? We've two hours before we meet with Sejanus Plantageter."

He and others cast an eye toward the sunlight shining in the west-facing window, low, slanting, and yellowing. Since the Darkborn archduke and his retinue could not travel by day, they would arrive at the meeting place after dark and cede the second hour of the night onward to the Lightborn.

"That assumes," Helenja said, "that he lives to reach the Council Chambers."

The meeting was to take place in the Intercalatory Council Chambers, the only space designed for such encounters, though it was hardly the environment their brightnesses—or the Darkborn aristocracy—were accustomed to. The council was of relatively low status, and its representatives not aristocratic. Floria's neighbor and close friend Balthasar Hearne had been serving intermittent terms on the council since he was of age to do so. He had described the chambers to her, the several rooms of various dimensions, to suit different-sized groups, each one bisected by an opaque paper wall supported and reinforced by heavy mesh. Darkborn and Lightborn could hear one another perfectly through the wall—as she could attest, having spoken to Balthasar through such a wall for most of the days of their lives.

Prasav stared across the table at Helenja, open distaste in his expression. "If you mean anything in particular by that, Helenja, may I suggest you think again, *now*. We want reparations from the Darkborn, not war with them."

Helenja snorted. "Ever the mercenary, Prasav. Do you really think that what they did last night—last *night*—can be paid for in money alone? If you have any doubt, look out there." She stabbed two fingers toward the window.

Magistra Valetta's was the only head that did not turn. Rumors ran through the palace of high masters crushed in their beds or quenched as their lights were buried.

Helenja leaned forward slightly. "Magistra, how are we supposed to decide on our demand for reparations from the Darkborn if we do not know what lives were lost?"

"The value of even one life is incalculable," the mage said without expression.

"Yet we are going into negotiations with the archduke of the Darkborn and the men who were directly responsible for this atrocity," Prasav said. "We will demand justice for your murdered people, but we will also demand reparations. And it will not come cheap."

"The city," Helenja said.

The others looked at her, Prasav frowning, Ember with eyes narrowed in speculation, Perrin with pale, parted lips.

Valetta blinked.

"Tell them we want Minhorne," Helenja repeated.

"I very much doubt they'd agree to that," Prasav said. "No matter what we held over them."

Helenja's fist closed. "The Darkborn live here on our sufferance. They depend on our goodwill. Our light is more deadly to them than their darkness is to us: any light kills them, but only complete darkness does us. Minhorne's the only city of any size where we have to live like this. It's unnatural."

"I refuse to put my name to—," Perrin said.

"Minhorne's the largest, most prosperous city in the Sundered Lands." Ember's voice glided smoothly over the princess's objection. "Arguably, it is this way because Lightborn and Darkborn economic interests have become intertwined to their mutual advantage, at least among the earthborn. Losing their industry and innovation at this time would cost us more than we could afford."

Prasav's daughter, indeed. Where the entire Lightborn realm was impoverished by hundreds of years of contracts with the mages, Prasav's scrupulous—plenty said "ruthless"—economies had let him husband his wealth.

"Then let them live underground," Helenja growled, "the way they used to. There's a whole network of underground streets."

The buried streets linking the older parts of the city were hundreds of years old, and Floria had heard Balthasar's description of their condition—most damp, some collapsed, others more sewer than thoroughfare.

"What about you, Magistra Valetta?" Ember said. "What do the mages want from the Darkborn?" She leaned back into the sunlight to regard the mage, her face grave and concerned. The only death Magistra Valetta would acknowledge was that of Lukfer, a reclusive mage of strong but uncontrolled magic whom the mages accused, with his student Tammorn, of spreading false rumors about the Shadowborn.

"We have yet to measure our injury," the mage said at last. "But we wish to hear what the Darkborn have to say. .The streets *will* be safe for them."

Magic kept those lights burning. Magic—particularly high-rank magic—could quench them.

Perrin spoke softly. "We, too, must live to reach the council chambers."

Prasav said, with distinct impatience, "We have it taken care of, Princess."

Perrin turned her silvery eyes on him, and for a moment Floria saw her father in her.

"My daughter," Helenja said, before she could speak, "has a point. Please describe how exactly we are to avoid Isidore's fate."

"When the bell sounds, runners will leave the palace, carrying lights. They will string the route so that it is as brightly lit as the corridors of the palace. We will not travel together, and we will carry lights of our own. If there *were*"— a cut of the eyes sideways toward Magistra Valetta—"such a thing as Shadowborn, I doubt they would be able to swallow the magic in that many lights." He folded his hands and said to Helenja, "*I* am satisfied with the arrangements; whether you are is up to you."

Helenja acquiesced with a tilt of her head.

"Shall I suggest," Ember said, evenly, "that we hear what the archduke has to say—how, for instance, he plans to deal with those responsible—and assess our injuries further before specifying the reparations we seek?"

Prasav said, "I think not. I am in a mood to demand." He smiled coldly across the table. "So let us demand the city, and let them take the proper measure of our outrage."

Ember dipped her head slightly in acknowledgment.

Magistra Valetta said, "Agreed."

Perrin, the princess, licked her pallid lips and said nothing.

Balthasar

I should, Balthasar told himself, *have realized what Sebastien was capable of.* Given what Tercelle Amberley had said, given what Sebastien had said about his parentage. But first there was that moment of sheer, abject terror to pass through, before he realized that he should already have been dead, if he were going to die. Sebastien was half Darkborn, half Shadowborn, and perhaps immune to the Curse—he had at least wondered about that possibility. But *he,* Balthasar, was not immune. . . . Yet here he stood, before a door open on daylight. Sebastien had been mage enough to bring them here; now the boy had proven himself mage enough to shield them both from daylight. Not even the Lightborn high masters had achieved that.

How can we fight these people, Balthasar thought, *Telmaine, Ishmael, Vladimer, and me?* He swayed where he stood.

Sebastien thought it a fine jape and greeted the newcomers with suppressed glee more suited to the boy he was than the man he was pretending to be. "Welcome, Captain, Johannes. Come in; bring your lights. Don't mind my brother; he's a little nervous about the sun."

A gust of heated air swept around the two men standing on the doorstep. Balthasar reached out with a shaky burst of sonn. The younger had the build of a man who labored for a living and the clothing of one who did no more than subsist by it: his vest was sleeveless and his trousers ended in a ragged hem. He wore thick-soled sandals with heavy, close lacing. His only adornment was a knot-work bracelet on one wrist. The older man was lean and supple, and Bal's sonn picked out the indistinct texture of fine, soft lace in his sleeves and leggings. He carried a rapier and a pistol on his belt, and the fluid balance of his movements reminded Bal of one of the Rivermarch enforcers who was also a fencing master; it was how he imagined Floria would move.

"Balthasar," Sebastien said airily, "fetch us some of that excellent beer."

"None for me," said the older man, gravel in his voice.

Lightborn would not accept food and drink from those they distrusted.

"Nor me," said the younger.

"Then come through to the sitting room."

"I'd as soon speak here," the older man said.

With the door open? Balthasar wondered. His mind was beginning to clear of the panic inspired by the threat of sunlight. He took in more details of their stance, their position—close to, within lunging reach of, the door. Their distrust could not have been plainer if they had shouted it.

"Balthasar, these gentlemen represent two of our allies, Captain Rupertis of the Palace Vigilance, and stonemason Johannes of the artisan's progressive movement. Gentlemen, my brother, Balthasar Hearne, Darkborn."

Heads turned toward him for a long moment. Was he so obviously Darkborn to sight? It must be so; Sebastien appeared pleased by their reactions. Then the older man turned his attention back to Sebastien, while the other continued to face Balthasar. The self-styled progressive movement demanded revolution and the formation of a republic, and simultaneously rejected all forms of technological innovation, especially Darkborn. They were marginal, but not as marginal as Balthasar would have preferred. But Rupertis . . . He knew Rupertis by name, as one of the several watch captains of the Palace Vigilance. A captain of the Prince's Vigilance, suborned or ensorcelled . . . What did that mean for Floria?

"Now," said Sebastien, with Lysander's smile, "what have you to tell me?"

"Why didn't you tell us that you planned an attack on the tower itself?" Rupertis said.

"Why should we?" Sebastien said, folding his arms. "You didn't need to know."

The man's jaw tightened. "Well, here's something *you* need to know. Isidore's dead. Fejelis has disappeared. And the Lightborn now have a *princess*—Princess Perrin, ruling with the backing of the mages. Your shells *didn't* kill the archmage *or* the head of the Temple Vigilance. And they've taken over. Is that what you wanted?"

Sebastien's smile had faded. "Who's Perrin?"

"Isidore's and Helenja's eldest daughter. She showed at ten as a mage and was taken into the Temple."

Sebastien shrugged. "Not a problem, as we've told you before."

"Are you sure? Perrin's a sport—born outside the Temple lineages. Fejelis claimed that lineage mages can't sense your type of magic, but sports can."

"That's impossible," Sebastien said, voice rising. "Lightborn can't sense our type of magic."

"You'd better hope they can't," Ruportis said, flatly. "Fejelis contracted with a sport mage, name of Tammorn, perpetually on the outs with the Temple, but strong. Fejelis claimed the shells that hit the tower were ensorcelled, and the sports dealt with them."

Sebastien's breathing was quick and shallow. "It didn't happen that way."

There was a grim satisfaction in the set of the man's lips, hearing, as Balthasar heard, the wavering. "Fejelis put this to the archmage and high masters, in front of their brightnesses. They didn't like that, I could tell you. Prasav made a play for Fejelis's deposition, right there and then—had to, I figure, since if Fejelis had made the contract with the mages he was asking for, we'd never have shifted him—and the high masters stood aside when we drew on Fejelis. Cursed shame, I thought, but I had my orders." From his tone, one would never know that he spoke of the murder of a nineteen-year-old man. "That sport mage of Fejelis's swatted the quarrels aside and *lifted* himself, Fejelis, *and* Orlanjis out of there. If the mages know where he took 'em, they're not saying."

He waited for a reaction, and then said, dangerously, to Balthasar's ear, "But it doesn't actually matter to you who is prince, does it?"

Sebastien, too, heard that undertone. "Of course it matters," he said quickly. "That was the agreement: we help deal with Isidore and with Fejelis, and leave the way clear for Prasav. We'll help deal with Perrin and the mages. They're lying; they're hurt."

"Was it Beaudry's own plan to quench himself after he put a crossbow bolt through Fejelis?" Rupertis said. "We found his residue bundled up in a black tarpaulin. He didn't even try to get away."

"I don't . . . ," Sebastien began, and checked himself. "I didn't order him to do that."

"Floria White Hand is still alive," Rupertis said. "Fejelis put a warrant out on her himself, sooner than we expected. We sent a team after her, but the woman's as sharp as her rapier. She cut through the screen into her Darkborn neighbor's house. Got out that way—" His face swung toward Balthasar. "*That's* where I've heard the name. So you're part of this, too."

"*No*," Balthasar said, fiercely; that much the ensorcellment did not forbid. "Never of my own free will."

The captain's face clenched, as if he heard an accusation. "You'd understand better if your rulers had beggared you with taxes to pay mages to protect them against other mages. My family used to have lands and a name—his did, too." He gave another jerk of the head toward Johannes. "We were bled white by taxes from our lord and by our own Temple contracts. We turned vigilant, hired swords, but decades of service, decades of practice . . ." He flexed his sword hand. "We're no more than glorified footmen, hired for a show of wealth, because earthborn are *cheap*, and when the money finally runs out, we'll slip another step down toward begging in the streets."

From his council service, Balthasar knew the price that the Lightborn had ultimately paid, both for the original compact with the mages and for their own murderous customs. By the compact, mages could not use magic against earthborn in their own interests, but could be contracted to do so by earthborn—and thereby indemnified of the consequences. Over time, as the tradition of deposition of heads of houses established itself, anyone at risk must contract with the temple for their protection, against threats both magical and secular. Now, after hundreds of years, much of the wealth of the princedom resided not in the hands of the prince and their brightnesses, but in the hands of the mages, who had much less interest in employing earthborn. And every year the number of starving in the provinces and vagrants in the city increased.

"Isidore tried to fix it, but he's been bled white, too." A grim smile. "They're all fussing about the prince's caul having gone with Fejelis, but the thing's no more than wire and glass. Some of our lineage turned jewelers, and I have their word on it. Prasav is the only one who's been able to hold on to his wealth; he seemed the best bet, the best gamble, for those of us who'd rather not be eating the garbage from the streets."

"I have served several terms on the Intercalatory Council; we know, as much as anyone can know on the far side of sunset, how it is with you. What"—another question for which he did not want to know the answer—"was the warrant for Floria—Mistress White Hand—for?"

"The deposition of Isidore. Fejelis said she'd been ensorcelled to take a talisman to the prince's rooms, a talisman that would annul the lights around it."

"*No*," whispered Balthasar. "She served him all her adult life—"

"Tasted every dish he ate," the captain confirmed. "Closer than a wife, to Helenja's ire."

For a long moment, ensorcellment or no, Balthasar simply hated the Shadowborn. How many people's loyalty, how many people's despair, had they used to craft their way to power? For their design was power, he had no doubt of that. They did not care which Lightborn became prince, because their aim was their own ascendancy. Did Rupertis know what he worked for?

Johannes spoke for the first time, his voice suffused with anger. "We've got the Prince's Vigilance out on the streets. We'll have mages' vigilant investigating, and assets questioning. Tempe Silver Branch is questioning the people arrested in front of the railway station. No one can lie to her."

"That's their problem," Sebastien said. "If they were stupid enough to get caught. You *said* you wanted a revolution. What's that song you sing?" He affected a nasal, though true-pitched tone. "*Streets running with blood and fire.*"

"There was a servant with Isidore when the lights went out," Johannes ground out. "Nobody cares about *him*—it's all Isidore, Isidore—but he was my cousin, one of *us*! You're no better than the rest, you callous bastard." His hand went to his knife—and was enveloped in flame as the scabbard and pommel caught fire. Rupertis slashed with his dagger at the ties on the sash, yanked them, let the scabbard fall with a clatter of metal and a scattering of ash. Even in those few seconds, the blaze had almost completely consumed the leather.

Johannes slowly folded to his knees, holding out his burned hand before him.

Balthasar started to go to him, but Rupertis spoke, and the tone of his voice made him pause. "Fejelis said something else. He gave a name to the magic and to the people who practiced it: Shadowborn."

Sebastien was breathing quickly, suppressed glee and horror in his expression. "Shadowborn are a Darkborn myth."

"Moving from dark to light," Rupertis said, half to himself. "Ensorcelling men, burning—" Balthasar took a step forward. Ever after, he would be uncertain whether it was his professional instinct to defuse conflict or an impulse born of the ensorcellment to draw Rupertis's attack on himself. He was too late for anything more. Rupertis's rapier came from its scabbard like a breath driven out by a blow. Sebastien fell backward with a screamed, *"Stop!"* but Rupertis had already started to uncoil in a lunge, as oblivious to command as a falling boulder. Sebastien shrieked a word or a curse, and the captain's body exploded into flame of such intensity that Balthasar threw his arms up to shield his face. He heard the man's last breath roar out in agony. The blazing corpse dropped to the tiles with a meaty crunch that—like the sizzle of meat and fat, like the stench, like the postmortem spasms as muscles cooked—Balthasar knew he would be revisiting in his nightmares. The blade clattered to the tiles and broke.

Too late, far too late, Sebastien cried, "Stop!" and the flames went out.

Johannes staggered to his feet, eyes bulging with horror. He backed away, one step, two, three, stumbled backward and through the door, colliding with the lintel without a cry. Sebastien did not appear to notice his leaving. "He made me do it!" he cried.

Balthasar, repelled though he was by the sentiment, could not entirely disagree. Perhaps death had been Rupertis's intent; perhaps it was simply a risk he had accepted in trying to kill the young mage.

"I've never burned a *man* before," Sebastien blurted, still facing the body of the man he had killed. "I'm not a monster. I'm not. They said I'd be if I stayed. Just like they said."

Balthasar swallowed. "It was a reflex," he said, and before the boy could seize too hard on that as exoneration, he said, softly but sternly, "But if you are going to use your magic to defend yourself, you *must* learn different ways to do it."

Sebastien turned on him. "How am I supposed to learn?"

"Neill seemed willing to teach you."

"*She'd* stop him. *She* doesn't want me taught."

He was tired of pronouns and circumlocutions. "Was your mother the one who warned you about becoming a monster? A powerful mage needs training, or even with the best will, he can do great harm."

"None of *them* want to teach me. Save Neill, and *she's* got him so ensorcelled—"

"Sebastien," Balthasar said, "what do you want? *You*, not Emeya."

"It doesn't matter what I want."

"Your mother and father got away from her."

"They left me behind."

"You *chose* to stay behind, you said. I doubt, with your strength, they could have taken you against your will. But I don't think you know what you chose then. You know better now."

The boy did not answer, his face sullen. "*Smell, Sebastien,*" Balthasar said, almost in a whisper. "Is this what you want to be?"

Sebastien's throat worked on a suppressed gag. "I *hate* you."

Balthasar flinched, but said steadily, "You ensorcelled me to care, and therefore I must care if you court destruction. From what Captain Rupertis said, someone did counteract the ensorcellment on the shells. You felt that last night."

"I *know* it worked. I *felt it*."

Balthasar was courting destruction himself now. The boy need not call fire to burn him, not with the door open to daylight. "If you make the Temple come for you, they will destroy you. If you go to them now, they may spare you. You have a form of magic new to them, and if you can prove that you were acting under the influence of another, then their laws may protect you." He could not convince himself that it was a certainty, even under Lightborn law. Yet he was certain that if the boy continued on this course, it would be to his own end. Under Darkborn law, Sebastien would be condemned to death for sorcery. If nothing else, if he had fathered Tercelle's twins, he was guilty of sorcerous seduction.

"You don't believe that," Sebastien said dully. "You think they're going to kill me."

"You haven't been taught what you need to know," Balthasar said, "about magic and about morality. I would make them understand that."

Sebastien stood a moment longer, head turning from the charred and reeking corpse to Balthasar and back.

"You do not have to do this," Balthasar said.

Sebastien suddenly straight-armed him, hand to the chest, making him stagger. "Be quiet. Go back to your room. You're not turning me against her. You *can't*."

Floria

Floria raced sunset across the bridge. Conspicuous to hurry, and risky to go straight, but what else to do with the time she had? As it was, she would have to return after dark, under the archduke's proclamation granting the Lightborn part of the night, and hope to make it back before anyone thought to look for her—whether with benign or malevolent intent.

Breathlessness forced her to slow from a sprint and then to a jog. Her ribs ached; her throat was raw. She was still feeling the effects of being nearly drowned in the fountain outside Bolingbroke Station. Up on the crowded hill of New Town, sun warmed red walls and white roofs. To her left was Darkborn land, the estate of Duke Kalamay, and the raw, brown wound of the mages' retribution and the explosion of the guns and stored munitions that had carried away half the hill. Nestled in deep shadow, the house itself still stood untouched, but the sky above it was smudged with smoke from outbuildings near the crest of the hill. The last time she had crossed this bridge, there had been smoke in the air, too, the smoke of the burning Rivermarch.

She glanced down at the dock below the estate; it was intact. If the occupants of the estate were wise, they would leave later tonight. Fejelis had today put almost every vigilant at his command on the streets to protect Darkborn, but she would be surprised if Perrin extended the order tomorrow, so she doubted Kalamay's grand house would be standing by tomorrow night. Mycene's estates were in the country, in Darkborn lands, but pity help the city household that had had him as a guest, if the rioters knew.

As she reached the far side of the bridge, on the road approaching, she met a party of two dozen guardsmen and -women. They looked like they'd had a long, hard afternoon, and were dusty, weary, cut, bruised, and carrying three of their number on stretchers. "Mistress?" one called, though it was a hail, not a challenge.

Barely checking stride, she rasped, "Nothing for you, unless one of you's a midwife."

They shifted to let her pass, with weary well-wishes. There was more than one gray or balding head with experienced eyes in it, who might well think to ask a few questions about a fair, running woman with her particular collection of bruises, dressed for court and armed for trouble. It would be too much to hope that her rash stand in front of the railway station would not be one of the stories told in the barracks tonight.

Worry about that later. Up the hill she ran, feeling every stride in the center of her chest. The bundled lights in her backpack bounced on her shoulders. She had her hand on Tam's gate when she thought to wonder what kind of talismans and protections he kept around his house. Would they recognize her as a friend in his absence? What if he had thought to ensorcell them against Shadowborn magic, including the ensorcellment that still lingered about her?

From the house there came an infant's screech: Tam's daughter had a voice proportioned to her will. *Nothing else but to take the risk.* She eased cautiously through the gate. No unseen barrier stopped her, no sudden weakness collapsed her, no roar of thunder met her. She padded across the garden, trying to steady her breathing enough that her voice would sound normal. Beatrice was wary of her at the best of times.

Her pull on the doorbell elicited a sweet carillon and a clamor of, "Mama, mama, mama, atta*door*, *attadoor*." There was a thud, as of a small body striking the door, and Floria winced. For some, "head-on" was not merely a metaphor.

The viewing hatch opened; Beatrice's pale face floated in its frame. "Floria?"

"Issadaddy?" the unseen child demanded.

"Let me in," she said. "Please."

"Tam's not here."

"I know. And I know when and how he left the city. Will you just let me in?"

Beatrice closed the hatch. Floria drew her stiletto—if the woman would not let her in, then she would force an entry—and pushed it quickly back into its sheath as she heard the bolt slide back. The door opened slowly. Beatrice stooped to keep a hand on her son's collar, her posture wary. Disappointment filled his upturned face and eyes at the sight of her. "Isnadaddy."

A crash behind her made Beatrice whirl, releasing the boy. The red-haired baby, propped up in a chair, had hurled a wooden toy onto the tiles, and was glaring at Floria. She could feel the little boy trying to squirm past her legs.

"Is there someone who can take the children while we talk?"

"Have you come to tell me he's dead?" Beatrice said tensely.

Tam would surely not have left her uncertain of his survival after the tower was destroyed. "He's not dead. But he's in trouble. Do you have anyone you can go to for the night—someone you know who would shelter you?"

The baby screeched. Beatrice moved to collect her while her son mounted an assault on the door. "Did he send you?"

"Tam *lifted* out of here with Fejelis and Orlanjis, saving Fejelis from deposition. Helenja has Sharel trying to find where he might have taken them, which means learning more about Tam. It won't take her long to learn about you."

Beatrice's lips pinched. The southerners' reputation in New Town was dismal; they were loud, reckless, destructive in their entertainment, and careless in making reparations. They had disrupted more than one market with their rumpus, and while more lay behind the failure of Beatrice's family business than a single stall full of broken crockery, Beatrice's thoughts about southerners were far from charitable. "It's too late to go anywhere now," she said.

"There's to be a meeting between their brightnesses and the Darkborn court, and an hour after sunset the bells are to be rung to allow their brightnesses to travel to the meeting place. The Darkborn will keep to their houses. You can move then."

"I never—"

"It's not common knowledge. We don't want any mischief done under its cover. We'll not meet anyone in New Town."

And if we do, she resolved, *I will deal with them.*

"I don't think— No." Her fine lips set. "*If* I decide to go, I'll go first thing tomorrow."

"And if the southerners come for you tonight? They're used to the desert, used to traveling by night."

"I'm not taking the children out on your word alone, Mistress Floria," she said, narrowly. "For one thing, I hardly think it will help us to make our way to safety if my son and daughter scream in terror the whole time. I thank you for your concern, and I will act on it if I choose."

This was the woman who had refused Tam for nearly five years, though he was as decent a man and besotted a lover as anyone could ask. And she had a point about the children and the noise they would make. Floria might have been able to concoct a potion, even from household herbs, to sedate the children; if she hadn't had water on the brain as well as in the ears, she would have *brought* a potion.

"All right," she said. "When you go, don't take any talismans with you that Tam made. Nothing, not even protection or toys for the children." Some of Tam's uses of magic were playful and inventive. "Mages would be able to trace you through them." She wondered whether to mention that the Temple might be taking a renewed interest in Tam's lineage, given the strength he had shown. If they were, there was probably very little any earthborn could do, and they, at least, would treat the children well.

She had her hand on the door when she heard the sunset bell begin to ring. The first hour of the night was for the Darkborn. She turned back, ignoring the resentful expression chased off Beatrice's face. "Make yourself at home, Mistress White Hand. I must go and put the children to bed."

That was a ritual that would occupy her for the better part of the next hour, Floria suspected. She made her way through into the social room and sat down on one of the long couches. Her first glance had already measured the room and eliminated all threat in it; now she studied the brightly painted tiles mounted on the walls and in brackets in alcoves, Beatrice's former livelihood. In the corner was a clay sculpture, a tree with coiled and twisted roots and huge, enameled copper leaves. The tree drew her eye and made her uneasy. It suggested turmoil, unhappiness. Though when she had said as much to Tam, he had laughed and said she did not understand artists. Being a mage, he could not avoid knowing what his lover felt, that she liked him well enough, but she did not love him—though he could be consoled that she loved no one else better.

She was hardly one to judge the bargains others made, she who frequented the vigilants' house of companions, when she felt the need. Perhaps it was time to engage a matchmaker, as more than one of her relatives had suggested, and cease to be so choosy. Or accept that the priceless magical asset against poisons she had inherited from her father would pass to one of her cousins or their children.

Old thoughts, useless thoughts. Better to spend her time thinking what else to tell Beatrice that would make the woman move the moment the sun came up.

Balthasar

Sitting in the room, resting as best he could, Balthasar listened to the sunset bell and then to the voices in the vestibule beneath. This time, Sebastien's informants were Darkborn; he was sure of it, though he could not hear the words. The ensorcellment would not permit him to leave the room. Presently, he heard the door beneath close, and feet come quickly up the stairs. The door gusted open, slamming back against the wardrobe behind it. "You!" The carpet around him burst into flame. Balthasar scrambled into a crouch on the cushion of the chair.

"You didn't tell me about your *wife*!" Sebastien shouted, in Lysander's voice.

Balthasar started to stand, and then realized that standing would place him above the full heat of the blaze. "No," he said, more faintly than he would have liked. "I didn't."

"You ought to have. She was a danger to me! She helped murder Jonquil." That last seemed to turn his anger more calculating. "Well, it doesn't matter." It wasn't just the shimmy of the flames that distorted his face, Balthasar realized. His voice completed its shift toward the boy's. "Your wife's *dead*."

The edge of the cushion was catching. "Put out the flames, please," he said, arm shielding his face.

Sebastien quenched the flames with a sweep of the hand, his expression ugly. *"Did you hear what I said?"*

"I did," said Balthasar. He took a precious moment to compose himself, and stepped down and over the scorched carpet. "I have no reason to believe you."

Sebastien's hands closed into fists. "She tried to use *our* magic and lost control. She nearly killed the archduke, and then she came back to heal him, and they captured her and he had her executed. They put her in a room with a skylight and opened the skylight."

That made two of three implausible statements. The only one believable was that if Sejanus Plantageter were hurt, Telmaine would try to help. "As I said, I have no reason to—" And he remembered what Ishmael had sensed from Telmaine while they were in Stranhorne, and what Stranhorne's son had telegraphed to his father. And that the archduke, judicious ruler though he might be, had a profound distrust of magic. That was enough for the ensorcellment. An abyss of belief and despair gaped beneath him.

The boy's hands loosened their clench, and his lips eased into a smirk. That was worse; that was Lysander's smile of considered cruelty. "You *ought* to have told me," he said. "I'd have been able to save her."

"She would never give in to you. And I refuse . . . to believe she is dead."

"Believe it," the boy said.

At the words, the ensorcellment twisted inside him, trying to tear out his hope, tear out his heart, tear out his love. It wrung a sound from him that was midway between a gasp and a groan, the sound of a man who had taken a mortal injury. There was no argument reason could make against the imposed conviction that Telmaine was dead. "I *will not*," he said, strangled. "I will not."

"Tidy yourself up," he heard the boy say, dismissively. "We've a visit to make."

His body moved, somehow. He wondered that a man could endure so much pain and still live. He could barely draw breath for it; he found himself leaning, dizzied, against the side of the wardrobe.

Promise me, Telmaine had said, as they began to reckon the danger they were in, *that if anything does happen to me . . . promise me you will still live for, love, and care for the children.*

Their daughters, who were sheltering with Telmaine's formidable elder sister. Florilinde, who had a fascination with all things mechanical, and little, strong-willed Amerdale, whose sixth birthday was a mere two weeks away, and whose one immovable desire was for a kitten of her own.

Amerdale will not have her birthday in a city ruled by Shadowborn. Whatever had happened to Telmaine; whatever happened to *him.* Balthasar pushed himself away from the wardrobe. His hands sought the pouch of bottles he had taken from the medicine chest and obstetrical kit the night before. He remembered the pleading *Don't leave me* from the night before and set the thought, *Chloroform, for painless surgery* first and foremost in his thoughts as he wrapped the small bottle of chloroform and pushed it into his pocket. *Morphine, for the relief of pain,* and a syringe, in the other pocket. He did not count himself as religious—it had always seemed to him that religion was a product of psychological frailty as well as a triumph of imagination—but now that he stood face-to-face with his own psychological frailty, he whispered a prayer as he rose: that he be given the moment he needed, the opportunity he needed, for he surely could not choose.

He followed the boy, once more in his Lysander form, down the steps, to the tolling of a warning bell. Sebastien had said the night had been ceded to the Lightborn to allow their brightnesses to travel to negotiations. The air that brushed his skin felt like night air, just after sunset, though with Sebastien's ensorcellment on him, he did not suppose it mattered whether it was night or day. Nothing much mattered. Not the tolling bell, not the eerie, huddled quiet of the city beneath it. He heard no voices from the streets, no carriage wheels, no horses, not even any machinery. Only the wind stirred. Sebastien said, disgruntled, "There aren't any coaches. I don't want to waste myself *lifting.*"

He is afraid, Balthasar thought, insight penetrating his dullness. He roused himself. "Where . . . arc we going?"

"Your council chambers. The Lightborn princess—whoever she is—and her nobility. They're *all* going there to meet the archduke and his council."

Balthasar forced himself to pay attention to the undertones of that gloating. He said, quietly, "You do not have to do this."

The boy in his brother's shape halted and swung on him. "Do *what*?"

"Whatever you are planning to do—" No, that was weak. "Kill the archduke, kill the princess—is that it?"

"You don't think I *can* do it? I'm a strong mage."

"Yes," Balthasar said. "I think you are entirely capable of it."

"Good."

"I also think you do not understand what you are doing. But for me to make you understand—for me to even start to make you understand—between here and the council chambers is quite beyond my capacity."

The admission stirred a vague impulse of alarm. He needed to care—he needed something to use against the ensorcellment. "Tercelle's children—they *are* yours, aren't they? Truthfully?"

"You don't think I'm old enough?" Sebastien challenged.

No, thought Balthasar; he had been nearly ten years Sebastien's elder, and still not old enough, when the midwife set Florilinde in his hands. She had thoroughly disapproved of him, he recalled. Telmaine had told him later that she had been outraged to have a husband underfoot who fancied he knew *something* about childbirth. He stopped with a gasp, remembering her laughter. It felt as though he had just scraped a scalpel across the raw wound of her loss. "Did you feel anything—anything at all—for Tercelle Amberley?"

Sebastien caught him by the arm and swung him around, wrenching aching muscles. "I *loved* her, stupid! She was so beautiful. The way she spoke, the way she held her head, her grace—she wasn't like the women where . . . where I come from. It was just once, for me and her, the first time I ever . . .

I didn't expect . . . I didn't think about . . . I didn't even know she was pregnant. I couldn't even look for her because Jonquil would have known. And it was all for *nothing*. Jonquil had her killed. When I felt him die, *I danced*. And if anything's happened to my sons because of you, you'll die—*horribly*." He spun and started running, slowing to a walk halfway down the block. He might have been sobbing. But if he had been, he was composed again when Balthasar caught up with him.

Balthasar considered and rejected several questions, among them whether the men who had nearly beaten him to death had been sent by Jonquil or Sebastien himself. "What . . . would you like to do after this is over?"

"What do you mean?"

"I mean, once you have done what has been laid upon you to do," Balthasar said, choosing his words carefully. "What will you do then, if you had a choice?"

"Get away," Sebastien said, head down. "Take my sons and . . . live far away from people. I'd set magical talismans all around, so that no one would approach, and if anyone dared, I'd raise storms and lightning. I'd build a house for them, out of stone and earth. We'd eat fruit and berries, and we'd raise oats and barley and potatoes, but not lettuce—I hate lettuce. And meat. We'd collect stones—beautiful stones—and make mosaics. You're laughing at me."

"No," Balthasar said. "No, I'm not."

Perhaps he did not entirely keep the sadness from his voice, for Sebastien halted. "You didn't believe all that, did you? *That's* where I'm really going to live."

Balthasar oriented himself to Sebastien's grand gesture and the direction, and realized he must be pointing at the Lightborn palace. "I've heard it's very beautiful inside," he said, "though much of the beauty is in the colors, and would be wasted on such as myself."

Sebastien stared at him. "Would you *like* to *see*?" he said, unexpectedly. Balthasar tried to conceal his sudden dread that the boy was about to turn his magic on him. "Doesn't the dark . . ." His voice suddenly trailed off, but Balthasar heard, quite clearly, *frighten you?*

"I was born in darkness," Balthasar said, mildly.

"You nearly wet yourself when I opened the door."

"So would you have," Balthasar said, "if you'd known your whole life that sunlight would burn you to ash.... I wish I understood magic better, to know how you were keeping me from burning. It's an ... exceptional thing. Your people must understand the Curse very well."

"Yeah," Sebastien said, "we do."

The Intercalatory Council Chambers were just within the boundaries of one of the newer Darkborn districts, small row houses occupied by the homes and offices of minor civil servants and not-yet-established professionals. Had he married according to his station, he might well have had his first home there. A couple of streets away was the start of an equally modest Lightborn district that for two or three hundred years had been home to Lightborn artisans, artists, and craftsmen. He liked to believe both districts had prospered in unexpected ways from their proximity. The outer walls of the council chamber had been plastered smooth, so that the Lightborn could paste posters, which offered the people's commentary on politics and society. He could rely on Floria to describe those that his colleagues on the council were too politic to translate.

He set a hand on the wall as they approached the steps, and felt damp, lumpy paper. The lumps compressed as he pushed at them: fresh paste, hastily applied. And then his hand brushed something tacky, and he caught the smell of blood. He halted, midstride, the memory of those hours in surgery coming back to him. Sebastien, on the stairs, turned. "What is— Ugh! Leave it! Leave it. Nasty thing."

"What—"

"Leave it! It's vile!"

Balthasar pulled a handkerchief from his pocket and wiped his hands, keeping his mind closed to the stickiness. Sebastien rattled the handle. "They're locked!" He threw his weight against the doors, unavailing. "I'll burn through!"

"No!" cried Balthasar, remembering the stench of smoke rolling out from the gaping wall of Stranhorne. "I know where there's a key."

Distrustfully, Sebastien watched as Balthasar hoisted himself up to the lowest rank of gargoyle. Floria had been appalled when she learned about it—why, she demanded, didn't they just leave the door unlocked? His groping hand found the key, spilling it onto the paving stones with a clatter.

Sebastien simply stared at it, while Balthasar slithered down, collecting moss on his borrowed formals. "Tradition," he explained, as he bent stiffly to collect the key.

Sebastien stood at his shoulder as Balthasar plied the key and pushed the door open. Deep in the building, a bell rang, and Sebastien started. "What's that?"

"The council works day and night—it's best someone's warned when the door is opened."

"You didn't tell me." He caught Balthasar's arm. "Do they keep explosives here, too?"

"I don't know any reason for them to."

"You'll die, too," the boy threatened.

"I might count that a mercy," Balthasar said, and cursed himself for the indulgence. He said, more quietly, "We don't have to go in."

"Yes, we do."

He opened the inner door, and found himself caught by the sonn of half a dozen armed men of the archduke's guard. Instead of the pistols that formed part of their usual ceremonial regalia, they held revolvers as modern and, he had no doubt, deadly, as Ishmael's.

Sebastien jarred up against him, catching his arm. "What is it? It's dark." Belatedly, he used sonn, and caught his breath.

Balthasar croaked, "Wait!" What inspiration might have come to him, he would never know. A door flew open at the end of the hall, and a compact, handsome man built like an athlete threw himself out to confront them, followed a step behind by his own sister.

"Lysander!" Olivede cried out.

"No!" the man said. *"Shadowborn."*

Bal recognized Phineas Broome, the fourth-rank mage who was one of the coleaders of the commune that Olivede belonged to. "Kill them!" shouted Phineas.

And Balthasar heard the thunder of revolver fire from behind him as Sebastien *lifted* both of them the length of the hall. Shouts, an explosion. His wild backward cast of sonn caught the guards as they spilled aside, thrown or throwing themselves away from a figure who was simply falling amidst a feathery echo that Balthasar knew as spurting blood. He started back down the hall in trained response, and behind him he heard Phineas Broome groan deep in his throat. The mage stood with arms outspread as though to bar the door, face contorted with extreme effort, the muscles in his neck like ropes. The smell of smoke thickened the air, though Balthasar did not know where from. He gasped, "No, Sebastien. *Remember how it smelled!*"

A backlash of heat seared his face as Sebastien fleetingly wavered and the weaker mage prevailed. And then Phineas cried out and fire flashed up his clothing, from trouser cuff to collar. The door to the main chamber slammed open and a revolver boomed. Sebastien lurched; the flame unwrapped from Phineas like a cloak, and then Balthasar heard a man's mortal scream, felt the heat, and heard and smelled, for the second time, a man being incinerated alive by Shadowborn fires.

In the move he had rehearsed in his mind a dozen times, he pulled cloth and bottle from his pocket; twisted out the plug; dropped it, freeing his hands to sluice the chloroform onto the cloth; and discarded the bottle in turn. He caught Sebastien around the chest, clamped the rag across his mouth and nose, and held him with all his strength in a travesty of an embrace. He could feel, against his wrist, the warmth of the boy's blood. In Sebastien's ear he rasped his half-deranged babble of justification: "*I can't let you do this. I can't let you destroy yourself. You would destroy yourself. It is because I care for you that I am doing this, because you demanded I care. . . .*"

The boy wailed something unintelligible, muffled by the rag. Bone and muscle rippled and swelled beneath his arm; claws dug into his wrist. Heat mounted around him; he could smell the acrid stench of singed wool and hair, and pressed his face to Sebastien's neck, praying that the mage could not turn the fires on them both. With one last uncoordinated rake at his hand, Sebastien slumped against him. Balthasar half collapsed, half guided him down to the floor, and then squirmed urgently out of his smoldering jacket. In unconsciousness, Sebastien had shed his borrowed form, and Balthasar, panicked by the memory of the Shadowborn who had transformed as he died, tore open his collar until he had exposed the bleeding wound at the join of neck and shoulder, and sonned the pulse in his throat. *"Olivede,"* he said, *"help me."*

"Busy," she gasped, from inside the council chamber. *"Sweet Imogene—"*

He heard, then, a pistol hammer being drawn back. He dropped forward onto his hands, shielding the unconscious body. Two men dragged him to his feet, their expressions murderous. Both wore the livery of the Duke of Mycene. "No," he shouted, trying to struggle free, as a third man went down on one knee and laid his revolver behind Sebastien's ear.

And then, blessedly, the archduke's voice cut through it all. "Hold."

The moment teetered; Balthasar sonned the tension in the finger that rested on the trigger. Then one of the men who held him rasped, "Aaron, wait. This is too cursed quick."

Balthasar felt, more than heard, a growl of approval from the gathered men.

Olivede said, breathlessly, "Please, someone give me a hand here—"

Of Phineas Broome, he could sonn only his booted feet. The archduke gave some quiet orders; someone in the rear ranks dragged him clear.

"Balthasar Hearne," the archduke said.

"My lord archduke." The expression on the archduke's face killed his last hope that Sebastien had lied. He could not imagine any other reason why he should sonn shame as well as raw-nerved suspicion on that face.

At his feet, Sebastien moaned. Revolvers leveled. Balthasar crouched and held the chloroform-soaked rag over Sebastien's nose until the boy stopped twitching. He could not even say "I'm sorry," in case regret weakened him fatally. "I'm going to stop the bleeding," he said, asking no one's permission.

"Explain, please," said the archduke, "how you come to be here? Who is this . . . boy?"

"I have heard," Balthasar ground out, "what happened to my wife." He went on before anyone could speak. "Whether I shall ever"—*forgive* would have been the honest word, if not the most politic—"reconcile to it is . . . a question for another day. I am still a servant of the state, still *your* servant. But this boy is my brother's son, and I claim his life."

No one questioned his assertion, but, then, the proof was there in the resemblance. Nor did they respond to his claim. It was enough for the moment that they not interfere. He opened the boy's jacket and shirt to expose the narrow, childish chest, pulled off his own shirt, and tore strips from it to make a compress and bind it down. It was awkward, clumsy work, but he got it done.

"Lysander was living among the Shadowborn," he said as he worked. "He fathered a child by a Shadowborn mage. There are at least two factions of Shadowborn. Lysander and his wife fled from one to the other, but they did not succeed in taking their son. I first met him, though I did not know it, at Strumheller Crosstracks; he arrived in the guise of a member of Mycene's troop. In Stranhorne . . . do you know that Stranhorne was overrun by Shadowborn?" Stark, and not the way to break such news, but he was past delicacy.

"We do. The details are scant and we don't have time; the Lightborn should be here very soon, unless it pleases them to make us wait. Go on."

"With the help of another mage who survived the destruction of the manor, he brought me here."

"As what? His collaborator or his captive?"

"His captive." He paused to wind a strip of bandage around his wrist, and from his pocket fumbled the morphine and syringe. He cleaned his hands as best he could, and with still-tacky fingers he filled the syringe and used his knife to slit Sebastien's sleeve and expose the thin arm.

Sebastien moaned and rolled his head weakly. Balthasar placed the tourniquet, braced his arm, slipped the needle into the vein, and injected the drug. He released the tourniquet and hung over the boy until sure his breathing was steady. He could hear men moving past him, three men carrying another, and Olivede giving steady instructions despite the strain in her voice, to the accompanying drone of a prayer from Duke Kalamay.

"You seem most concerned for someone who has held you captive," the archduke observed.

"The boy is sixteen at most, and has been cruelly used," Balthasar said. "Ill taught—fire and shape-changing seem to be the magic he knows best. The other mage, the one Ishmael di Studier killed at Vladimer's bedside, was the elder and the dominant partner."

"You will have to keep him drugged," the archduke said, "and if that does not kill him, and he does not die of thirst or hunger, we shall—"

For almost the first time ever, he heard Sejanus Plantageter fail to complete a sentence. He was glad of it; his desperate accommodation with the ensorcellment would not survive a threat of execution for sorcery. He shuddered, the ensorcellment racking him. "I know," he gasped, "that this situation cannot pertain indefinitely."

"Indeed," said the archduke, grimly. "The situation will assuredly change, and possibly not for the better. Let me be plain: is your will your own?"

"As long as I believe that I am acting in *his* interest"—a desperate belief, held fast, despite accumulating evidence of harm—"then I believe my acts will be my own. I am quite certain that permitting him to continue on his planned course would only lead to his destruction."

"So ensorcellment is amenable to solipsism."

"He is a *boy*, Your Grace, uneducated, unsophisticated, abandoned, and abused. He has the emotional maturity of a young child. He demanded first of all that I love him as I love my own children—impossible, but it gave me latitude to act for him as a father would. As his father," he said harshly, "*should* have."

Sejanus Plantageter pinched the bridge of his nose. "I am under the impression that the Lightborn could not sense this ensorcellment," he said, slowly. "Thus your acquaintance, Floria White Hand, was able to deliver the ensorcelled talisman to the prince's room."

Balthasar realized a beat too late that the statement had been a test of what he himself knew, and his reaction had betrayed him. "I was not thinking . . . about that, Your Grace. About other things, but not that."

"Mistress Floria was, I understand, quite unaware of her own ensorcellment. That was why I permitted your wife to be condemned to death. I had no other way of being certain that my mind was my own."

Balthasar said, in a voice that shook with repressed feeling, *"You were wrong."*

There was a silence. "I am truly sorry," the archduke said, and his face twisted as he heard his own words. "I said that to your wife—"

"Wait," said Balthasar, forcing himself to reason through numbing grief. "Sebastien said . . . Sebastien said that none of the Lightborn could sense Shadowborn magic—he believed that no one could. But Ishmael di Studier could. Phineas Broome could—sense it and fight it. And when the attack was launched on the tower, Sebastien reacted as though the Lightborn had somehow counteracted or annulled it—"

"They demolished the gun emplacements."

"But there was also an ensorcellment on the munitions, Sebastien said, to make them . . . to increase their harmfulness. The boy's vitality had been used to support the magic—"

"Only that?" said the archduke, very still.

"I don't know," said Balthasar, "but I do know he suffered a seizure immediately after the emplacements were destroyed."

"Sejanus." Claudius Rohan, the archduke's closest counselor and friend, shouldered through the group of guards. "Sejanus, the Lightborn have arrived."

The archduke turned away, paused. "I'll spare the boy's life for the moment," he said, his back to Balthasar. "I will not promise more."

Telmaine

So this is life after the worst has happened, Telmaine Hearne thought, as the Borders-bound train rattled south across an uncertain landscape toward an uncertain end. Across the train compartment from her, an old man sat kindling a taper made of newspaper with the touch of his fingers, a delighted smile on his imp's face. Even with her inexperience, she could sense his magic delicately eliciting a fine rill of flame along the edge of the paper, like a feather stroking sand.

A feather plucked from a very dead bird, she amended. Farquhar Broome was himself Darkborn, but the magic he was toying with had originated with the Shadowborn themselves. And though Shadowborn magic did not actually smell, it left her with the unsettled conviction that she *had* smelled something thoroughly foul.

"Father," protested Phoebe Broome, but resignedly.

Her father quenched the flame with a belch of that nauseating magic, and held out the taper to Phoebe. "Try it, dear girl," he invited. "Just do as I did."

Dutifully, Phoebe took it. She was a tall, switch-thin woman several years older than Telmaine, her dress so plain as to be masculine, and her manner awkward and self-conscious—except when she forgot where she was and who her traveling companions were. Her father, too, was tall, of an indeterminate age, with a wizened-apple face that wrinkled into merriment at the least invitation. His suit and coat had to be at least four decades out of date. Had Telmaine encountered them under other circumstances, she would readily have typed them: difficult father with long-suffering daughter; he charming in his disregard of social convention, and she carrying a double burden of it. But had someone been so indelicate as to mention the name Broome to Lady Telmaine, the duke's daughter, she would have cut the speaker dead. Mages, even the leaders of the largest and best organized commune of mages in Minhorne, were not discussed in polite society.

And yet here she was, sharing a train compartment with Farquhar Broome, said to be the strongest living Darkborn mage, and his daughter. Here she was, a condemned sorceress, spared execution by the archduke's last-minute, secret orders, carried out by Vladimer with imaginative scrupulousness. Would anyone, even the archduke, know that that heap of ash in the execution room was not hers, with her own wedding rings and Balthasar's silver love knot cushioned on it?

She imagined some footman or courtier laying the jewelry in Balthasar's hand. She imagined her husband's face—imagined what she would sense if she touched him—and bit her gloved index finger until it hurt. She had not even dared leave Balthasar a message—save an oblique word to Floria White Hand, of all people, safe on the other side of sunrise and accomplished in keeping secrets—for fear she might compromise the ruse. But when would Floria be able to pass the word on, if she even would? How long would Balthasar think her dead, and what would he do in the meantime?

Phoebe Broome slipped her gloves from her long hands and laid the gloves aside, and then unwound a thin, controlled ribbon of magic, quenching the flame almost as soon as it came into being. Farquhar Broome beamed approval. "Not nearly as unpleasant when you do it yourself, is it, now?"

Phoebe smiled back, reluctantly. "No, Father."

Telmaine sank a little deeper into her seat, determined not to attract their attention. Earlier, she had demonstrated Shadowborn fire setting to them—having learned it, entirely against her will, from the Shadowborn themselves—but even her most tentative and careful coaxing had created a burst of flame that had instantly burned the taper to a strip of ash. She had just managed to quench it, leaving their compartment reeking with smoke.

That was not the worst. Across from her, Lord Vladimer

had jolted upright in his seat, snatching at his revolver. She had gone utterly still, terrified, knowing what he remembered: that catastrophic breakfast, Telmaine's uncontrolled fires blazing up around Vladimer's brother, the archduke. She herself remembered her dear friend Sylvide crying, "Lord Vladimer, no!" and throwing her arms around Telmaine just as Vladimer fired. He had been aiming at Telmaine—aiming to kill her magic with her—but with his right arm wounded and his aim unsteady, he had mortally wounded Sylvide instead.

After a moment, Vladimer deliberately removed his hand from his holster, his bony face a sick mask, pulse beating hard in his temple. He apologized to the Broomes for alarming them, and excused himself—to rest, he said, completely ignoring Phoebe Broome's efforts to ease the atmosphere or mind his comfort. The mage was as gauche as a provincial sixteen-year-old. *But, then,* Telmaine thought, *how should Miss Broome, mage and social outcast, know how to behave around a duke's daughter and the archduke's half brother?*

She heard Farquhar Broome tear another strip from the broadsheet and fold it, and sensed another pulse of Shadowborn magic. "Now, my dear"—Telmaine sonned him holding out the unlit taper to Phoebe—"try to set it off. No, don't take it; I'm not quite sure how vigorous—" The taper burst forth with a jet of flame several inches high; Farquhar Broome promptly dropped it. Magic leaped out from father and daughter and the taper was snuffed, leaving a scorched ring in the broadsheet. Farquhar Broome shook his fingers, then lifted the sheet and explored the hole.

"I wonder that they have not refined it," he said. "It should be possible. It's an intriguing approach to latency. I'm sure it could be applied in other areas."

It already has been, Telmaine thought. The murder of the Lightborn prince had been carried out with a talisman, spelled to annul the magical lights Lightborn needed to survive the night.

She sensed, passing between father and daughter, a ripple of magic, such as she had sensed passing between Phoebe and her brother, Phineas, when she had listened to—spied on—their conversation with Lord Vladimer. Then Phoebe got to her feet, politely excusing herself so she might check on the well-being of the fifteen or so mages who comprised the rest of their party. As though the group was not well able to communicate even through walls. Telmaine repressed a sour little smile. She could recognize an engineered opportunity.

Farquhar Broome turned his face toward her, his smile now only a memory in the lines of his face, though his expression was gentle. He was as circumspect in his use of sonn as Ish, she had noticed; perhaps magic substituted, or perhaps he was simply accustomed to other people taking care of him. "Dear lady," he said, "what a shock this must be to you."

Statements of the obvious were not confined merely to vapid society matrons, apparently. She said tightly, "I have lost my reputation, my place in society, and but for the archduke's clemency"—belated, secret, and ambivalent clemency—"I would have lost my life. I am well aware that with another man"— Duke Mycene, perhaps, or, Mother of All avert it, Duke Kalamay—"I *would* have lost my life. I don't deny what I did. I don't deny my responsibility."

He nodded, as though none of that took him by surprise. "It was a serious thing you did, and a brave thing in coming back. Your sureness in healing is remarkable, for a young woman who has kept down her magic for most of her life. With your strength, my dear, *someone* should have recognized what you are."

"I was always careful to stay away from mages," she said. Until Ishmael, who had guessed within minutes of meeting her. But, then, Ishmael did not allow prejudice to interfere with his perceptions, and *he* could hardly reject outright the notion of a nobly born mage. "My husband is a physician, and I had Ishmael's—Baron Strumheller's—guidance, too," she said, challengingly. Phoebe Broome had come close to expressing the sentiment that Ishmael was not a suitable preceptor for her.

"You do understand, dear girl, that you cannot go on in

this fashion. Your magic—well, it is like a ball gown. Once it is out of its box, then it will not be pushed back in again, not without violence to its fine fabric."

And what could a seventh-rank mage and a man know about ball gowns? But she understood. The magic she had kept tucked well within her skin was restive now. "I know I need to learn how to control it," she said.

He smiled his imp's grin. "And I believe you will do well."

Assuming, she thought, *we survive what we find in the Borders.*

As though one of his threads of ambient magic had snagged the thought, he said, "There is another painful matter I must bring up, dear lady. That nasty thing in your mind will give you no trouble in and of itself now, although had Ishmael been less timely and sure with those firearms of his, you would likely not be sitting here."

"That nasty thing" was a legacy of her battle with the first Shadowborn that had tried to kill Lord Vladimer. She had come away from that encounter with a cyst of Shadowborn presence in her, an infection or parasite of magic forced on her by the Shadowborn. With the Shadowborn's death at Ishmael di Studier's hands, the magic in it was extinguished and it could no longer ensorcell her, except that the Shadowborn had also given her its knowledge. Her experiments with that knowledge had awakened her magic in dangerous ways.

"I will not use it again," she said, a heartfelt wish.

"Dear lady, you must. Or, rather, you may have no choice. Why do you think we have been amusing ourselves with tapers and fire? It is because we must understand this magic before we meet it. We are already under strength—I am quite sure of that. You have not sensed ahead, have you? I thought not."

"Why?"

He shook his head. In the last few sentences, the fey manner had slipped away. "We may have right on our side, but we simply do not have the numbers or might to match the Shadowborn. We are fortunate in Lord Vladimer, who is certain to favor an oblique approach—he is renowned for it. But he will be the first to insist that we need all the information we can get if we are not to blunder into a confrontation we cannot win."

"I will tell you everything I can," she said.

"Though it pains me to say, that may not be nearly enough, because your understanding of magic is a novice's, strong as you are. It would be of immeasurable help to us if you would permit me or my daughter, Phoebe, to examine the Shadowborn's *gift* directly."

For a moment, she resisted understanding that he wished to touch the thing in her mind, magic to mind. Through stiffened lips, she said, "I cannot believe you are making such a suggestion to me, sir."

She hoped—she fervently hoped—that she was convincing in her outrage.

His smile was very sweet. "I am," he said, without apology.

Should she leave the compartment in umbrage? Order *him* out? She had a distinct feeling that he would not oblige. He could sweep the knowledge from her mind with the barest effort, as she had the knowledge of his plans against the tower from Duke Kalamay, and then he would know. . . . Frantically, she pushed down the thought.

"I know this is far too soon," he said, as though, she thought dizzily, he were an impulsive suitor offering a premature proposal, "but please give it some thought. Neither Phoebe nor I would ever force you, *especially* now that we face a living demonstration of violation of our principles. Compose yourself, dear lady; we do not want to alarm the good people on this train, or disturb young Lord Vladimer's rest."

Then she was alone in the backwash of his magic, for he had not even opened the door to the compartment. She gulped at such a casual display. How could she possibly resist? She thought she smelled smoke and frantically made her mind blank, holding her breath. When she had to breathe, it was only the stale air of the compartment, like old cigar smoke, that she inhaled. Perhaps she had only imagined the smoke.

Sweet Imogene, the thought of Farquhar or Phoebe in her mind appalled her, though not nearly as much as it would have before she had met Ishmael. Ishmael she would, and had, let into her mind without hesitation. Society had not the least notion of all the improprieties possible through magic—*she* had not had the least notion.

If she could only speak to Ishmael, she would have laid her confession before him, even though . . . even though . . . Would he understand how she had come to know about Duke Mycene and Duke Kalamay's plans to launch an attack on the Lightborn Mages' Tower, undeclared and unprovoked— except that to such men, the very existence of the tower, and the mages it housed, was an offense. Would he understand why she had misused her magic so? He would understand why she had taken the knowledge to Vladimer, trusting him to act on it? Ishmael was deferential to Vladimer's greater cunning. And she thought he would understand why Vladimer had chosen to do nothing.

But that was because, after years of service and friendship, he knew Vladimer, and Ishmael's was not a nature given to outrage or bitterness. He would not hesitate to condemn Vladimer's silence, but he would understand it. She could not trust that the Broomes, who barely knew Vladimer, would be forgiving.

Vladimer—and she—could not do this alone. They needed the Broomes and their commune. She could not—

A woman screamed in full-voiced horror. Telmaine lurched to her feet, sweeping aside her skirts, and threw open the door as Phoebe Broome cried out, *"Phineas!"*

The mage was standing in the corridor, bracing herself against the walls, her father at her side. "Phineas! Oh, Mother of All, *Phineas*." She stretched out an arm, back along their track, and Telmaine could feel the magic streaming out of her.

"What is it?" Vladimer said, harshly, from behind Telmaine. He was framed in the door of one of the two state-

rooms, supporting himself against the lintel, coatless, hair disordered, and shirt loosened.

Phoebe gave another cry of "Phineas" and fell to her knees, curled palms held up before her, as though cupping water or life. Behind them, mages crowded the corridor; behind Vladimer, the door to the engine opened and one of the engineers stepped through, revolver drawn.

Phoebe lifted her face to her father. "Why didn't he call on us!"

"It was too quick, dear girl." He put his hands beneath her elbows and lifted her with an implausible ease. Telmaine sensed magic. Phoebe hung, limp as a pennant, on its prop.

She heard Vladimer dismiss the engineer, assuring him that he would take care of it.

"I just felt my brother die," Phoebe told them all, between sobs. "I don't know what happened. Olivede is there, but I can't get her to respond. I could feel her pouring out magic . . . healing. . . ."

"It is not death you felt, dear girl," Farquhar said.

"Then why— Oh, *no*. He feels like Ishmael. He feels just like Ishmael. Phineas—"

"Telmaine," said Vladimer, so close behind her that she could feel his breath.

"I *don't know*," she answered the implied demand for information. Phineas Broome had been lately in the service of the Duke of Mycene, though exactly why he had taken such service, perhaps only he knew. He claimed loyalty to the state, protecting Vladimer and the archduke from a dangerous mage—Telmaine herself. Vladimer inferred he wanted access to the Mycene armory for his revolutionary associates, and using that inference, Vladimer had struck a deal with the mage: silence for silence on Telmaine's escape. Telmaine had been immensely relieved that Phineas had not joined them, that his actions appeared to have estranged him from his family, because Phineas *knew* about Vladimer's silence over the tower.

If Phineas had remained with the Duke of Mycene, and Olivede Hearne had been there, then it was not too far to assume that the archduke was there also. And if by "he feels like Ishmael," Phoebe meant that he felt dangerously over-spent, burned out, that meant the *Shadowborn*—

Vladimer said, "In here," in a voice meant to be obeyed.

"My dears," said Farquhar to the rest of his party, "we will tell you as soon as we are able."

He steered the stumbling Phoebe into the compartment, moving as steadily as if he were walking through the halls of the immense, immovable archducal seat. Phoebe sub-sided limply into her seat, with a murmured, "I'm sorry."

Vladimer sat down. "Magister Broome," he said, in a voice that caused Telmaine's stomach to clench. "Inform me."

Farquhar Broome sighed. "I wish I could, dear boy. . . ." Vladimer's lips thinned dangerously at that, though whether it was the evasion or the solecism, Telmaine didn't know. "I cannot sense either Phineas or Olivede now; there's too much Lightborn magic blocking me. They are quite a bit stronger than I."

"Lightborn?"

"It is customary, particularly when sensitive negotiations are proceeding, to block magical surveillance."

"Magister Broome, I could order this train to turn around, this minute."

"Dear boy, what would that possibly achieve? What is happening in Minhorne would be long over by the time we reached there, and what is happening in the Borders very much needs attention."

Vladimer accepted that with obvious reluctance. "Were the *Lightborn* responsible for the attack on your son?"

"No," Phoebe said, faintly. "It *was* Shadowborn. It felt stronger than Phineas. He was trying to stand against it. . . . There was fire . . . and he . . ." She put gloved hands to her face. "I'm sorry, Lord Vladimer, but he's my *brother*—"

"And was *my* brother there?"

She swallowed. "Yes," she said, more steadily. "Yes, I think he was. I don't know where they were, but I don't be-lieve it was in the archducal palace. There were other peo-ple there—you'd know who should have been there better than I. But the first thing I sensed for certain was Phineas's alarm, and panic and pain—agony— as he tried to quench the flames. And then I felt him wring himself out with the effort, and—from Olivede, Dr. Hearne's sister, and not as strong as Phineas—I sensed only healing effort, on a man. Two men. And . . . emotional turmoil, something to do with family. She wouldn't, or couldn't, respond to me. And then I lost all sense of them."

"The Shadowborn have used the guise of Lysander Hearne in the past; perhaps they did so again. That would certainly disturb his sister—it did his brother."

"Yes," said Phoebe. She put out a hand, groping, and after a moment, her father took it.

Vladimer braced himself as the train shook and rattled over uneven tracks. "When we arrive in Strumheller Cross-tracks, I will immediately wire north for information. But if you learn more by other means," he said through his teeth, "I need to know."

Balthasar

Duke Mycene was dead, despite Olivede's efforts. Phineas Broome was still alive, but barely so, his heartbeat irregular and his blood pressure very low. They had no stimulants for him. One of the archduke's guards had been gravely injured when his revolver exploded; only his fellows' quick work with tourniquets and pressure bandages had kept him from bleeding to death. The others were all burned, lacerated, and half deafened, but still standing. The archduke had left two with the physicians and casualties in a side hall, and taken the remaining three with him into the main conference room. Balthasar could just hear the voices from there, the words themselves indistinguishable.

"Balthasar," his sister said, lifting a face that seemed to have aged twenty years in minutes, "I am so sorry about Telmaine. I had no idea that she was mageborn. If she had only trusted . . ." Her voice faded.

For Olivede, there had never been any question of not following magic, or any expressed regret at the life and place in society that she gave up to do so. But the open, sensitive girl had become a guarded woman, bruised by the many hurts the world dealt her kind, and Balthasar was not certain that she knew how much she had changed. He did not think she could understand—could have understood—his wife.

Olivede pushed herself to her feet and came along to where Balthasar sat beside Sebastien, whom he had made as comfortable as possible on a long, padded bench. The bleeding had almost stopped; the boy snored slightly in his drugged sleep. There was a suppressed revulsion in Olivede's face as she sonned the boy, though whether it was at his magic, his actions, his resemblance to their elder brother, or all three, he could not know.

She took Bal's bandaged arm—he had strapped it properly with the help of one of the guards—in hers, checked it, and let it go. Wasting magic on so minor an injury was out of the question. "I can't annul the ensorcellment on you," she said in a low voice. "I haven't the strength, even if I had much left after"—a twitch of the head toward where the body of Duke Sachevar Mycene lay in an improvised shroud. Even so, the smell of his death tainted the air. "He so *willed* to live. He gave everything to the struggle. How could I give less?" Her smile twisted in a peculiar mingling of compassion and repugnance. "To him, the only profanity in magic was that he had none himself. He liked power."

"Be careful," Balthasar breathed. "If Kalamay—"

"Between Mycene and Kalamay and the Shadowborn, they murdered dozens of Lightborn mages," Olivede said, as though she had not heard, her head still turned toward the dead duke. "But that death was obscene." She sonned him. "Balthasar, you're in as much danger as I am from Kalamay. You *cannot* protect this boy."

"I *must*," he said, throwing all the weight of meaning he could into the two words and imploring her to understand.

She masked her face with her hand, denying him the chance to sonn her expression. "The Lightborn are preventing me from reaching anyone, but I don't suppose Master Kieldar could come, until the curfew is raised." Even in here, they could hear the warning bell. "Phineas needs more than I can do for him, and Phoebe must be frantic. I didn't respond because I . . . didn't want to explain." She sighed and sat down beside him, her worn skirts folding almost silently—unlike Telmaine's starched, scented rustlings—and slipped her arm around him. "My poor little brother," she said quietly, "you've sustained a dreadful loss. I cannot imagine what you have been through. But you have your daughters to think of. Just remember—"

She brought up her hand as though to draw his head against her shoulder. He sonned the bare skin, thought of the ensorcellment, and ducked out of her embrace. And then realized what she had meant to do: spend the last of her magic in rendering him unconscious. "I am not distraught with grief," Balthasar said angrily. "At least not distraught beyond reasoning."

"Balthasar," she said. "Please let me—"

From the main chambers, they heard a shout: "Will you listen to me!" Balthasar's experience of the archduke was slight, generally gained as part of a large audience to Sejanus's masterful public performances. He had never heard the veteran statesman even raise his voice in anger, much less shout. He took a step toward the door.

"Not with that ensorcellment about you! If any of them can sense it—"

There was real fear in her voice, but, still angry with her, he disregarded it. "I know more about the Shadowborn than anyone here. I'm used to conducting business with Lightborn—six terms on the council, Olivede! And if there *is* someone who can sense it, my ensorcellment would be proof—"

"Of further Darkborn involvement. *Don't*, Balthasar. There's at least one high master in the building—I can sense the strength. It's important—it's vital—that this is dealt with as a matter between earthborn. If the Lightborn mages decide *we* had anything to do with it, they'll crush us like cockroaches. Phineas—"

"If it were to be dealt with earthborn to earthborn, would they have a high master with them?"

"Archduke's orders were that none of you were to leave," one of the guards said civilly from his station beside the door. In deference to his injuries—his face was bound with cloth torn from a pennant—it was a seated station. But if his hand on his revolver was not quite steady, it was purposeful. *Brave men,* Balthasar thought, *knowing what they guard here.*

Olivede wrapped her arms around her ribs. "Phineas went to warn Dukes Kalamay and Mycene about Vladimer's mage, who was your own Telmaine. But because he was involved with them, he might be accused of ensorcelling the munitions that destroyed the tower."

He could not keep his temper; she sounded so frightened and forlorn. He lifted his scorched jacket and put it around her shoulders. She leaned against him with a sigh, and he rested his cheek cautiously on her hair. "I'm sorry," he whispered. "I'm sorry you have to fear your own people as well as the Shadowborn."

She pulled away, wrinkling her nose. "Ugh, Bal, that ensorcellment is revolting."

She had worn exactly that expression at twelve when he had run to her in outrage after Lysander had pushed him into a pigsty. Though the muscles of his face moved like clay, he smiled at the memory.

They heard the door to the main council chambers slam open, and a moment later, Sejanus Plantageter swept into the room, a brace of Mycene's guard scrambling ahead of him. Balthasar found himself up and standing between them and Sebastien before he was aware of having moved.

Dukes Imbré and Rohan followed the archduke together, Rohan lending an arm to the oldest duke. Then came a young man who, by his resemblance to Xavier Stranhorne, was surely Maxim di Gautier. At his shoulder was a stout older man who steered his young baron with the gentlest of touches and cast a challenging sonn over Balthasar and Olivede. In his other hand, he held a staff in a grip that dared anyone to menace his baron. Duke Kalamay followed, fingers kneading an amulet that Balthasar recognized as one distributed to followers of the Sole God as a shield against magic. Behind Kalamay came his heir, whom Balthasar knew as a clever man of malicious wit and considerable theological knowledge, and one who took as much pleasure in demolishing the fallacies of faith as those of skepticism. He stumbled on the threshold, caught himself against one of the benches, and lifted a face sagging with shock. "You said there was nothing to it. Nothing," he said, to his father's back.

Imbré laid a hand like a gnarled root on the archduke's shoulder. "Well, Sejanus, now we know."

"W'can't yield, of course," said a stocky man in a Borders accent, setting his stance before the archduke.

"You shall not treat with mages," Kalamay said.

The archduke ignored him. "Lord di Gruner, while yielding is as repugnant to me as it is to you, I cannot ignore the fact that, should they choose, they could trap us in our homes, day and night both, with their lights. I doubt most households have more than two weeks' sustenance to hand, and the poorest will have less. Not to mention the havoc it would cause for business and trade."

"Are they," Maxim di Gautier spoke up, hesitantly, "a legitimate government? Is this princess a legitimate ruler, or does authority still properly vest with Fejelis?"

"Of whose whereabouts we have no idea," said Rohan.

"I got the impression," the archduke said, "that neither did they." He started to pace. "I should not have let myself be thrown by the fact that they brought forward a woman. I think even Vladimer stopped keeping a dossier on Perrin when she dropped out of the succession. I thought if Fejelis went down, it would be Orlanjis. And his mother, likely—Odon's granddaughter, indeed. I wonder if this order of expulsion was her idea."

"Our people won't stand for it."

"Indeed they won't—and I wonder if theirs will, too. Oh, there's feeling against the Darkborn—the riots and the vandalism tells us that—but there are sectors of the economy and parts of the city that owe their prosperity to trade with us." He paused, his expression one of concentrated thought. "We are vulnerable to the light, but we have other, subtler means to hand. But I think I do not want to discuss *any* of our options until we are well out of this building."

Balthasar got stiffly to his feet. "Your Grace," he said, "am I to understand that the Lightborn still insist this is a matter between Lightborn and Darkborn—that they do not accept the part played by Shadowborn?"

Sejanus hesitated briefly—whether because of Balthasar's insignificant status or his involvement—and then said, "You understand correctly, Dr. Hearne. As far as the Lightborn are concerned, the attack on the tower was entirely Darkborn. As to what happened just before their arrival—they didn't even acknowledge that."

But even lineage mages should have been able to sense Phineas and Olivede's efforts, and the injury and deaths of Darkborn on this side. So how much of the denial was authentic and how much politic? First and foremost, the Mages' Temple served its own interests, and those interests would not include admission of so profound a vulnerability. Mages contracted to the various members of the Lightborn nobility would obey the letter of their contract—no more. But what of the princess herself? She was born outside the lineages, to a family with no known magical members. Was her magic of the sport form?

He said, slowly, "My ensorcellment makes me immune to daylight. As long as that ensorcellment lasts"—as long as Sebastien was allowed to live stood implied, he hoped—"I would be able to go into the courts of the Lightborn and act both as envoy and as living proof of the existence of the Shadowborn. To my best knowledge, even the high masters would not be able to reproduce the feat of allowing a Darkborn to survive in light, or a Lightborn in darkness. If they cannot sense my ensorcellment, yet there I am, alive, they must ask themselves why."

"Bal—," Olivede began, and fell silent at a gesture from the archduke.

"If they do not simply kill you to restore congruence to their worldview," Plantageter pointed out.

"I believe that I will be sufficiently intriguing and offer sufficient possibilities that they will keep me for study."

"Why should you take the risk?"

Because I hope the Lightborn will spare the boy, he told the ensorcellment. "Your Grace," Balthasar said, "I have served several terms on the Intercalatory Council, as my father did before me. I know about and care about the relationship between Lightborn and Darkborn. I have a family connection to the Shadowborn. I have been their victim—it was only by my wife's and Ishmael di Studier's doing that I did not die twice over. I have lost my wife to a series of events that *they* initiated. Regardless of what happens to me, I do not want my daughters—or even my brother's twisted child—to live under Shadowborn rule. By their acts, I know them. I can do this. I am *uniquely* qualified to do this."

"How much of this is your own will, and how much . . . his?"

"He has never intimated that I should cross the sunrise, but as long as I believe that I am acting in *his* interest, then I believe my acts will be my own. As I have demonstrated, I believe."

"And how is your crossing over in his interest?"

Balthasar swallowed; he had not wanted to be asked that question, much less answer it truthfully. "Because I believe that Lightborn law will be more lenient to his crimes than Darkborn, and that the Temple mages have the strength to train and discipline him properly, which we do not."

There was a pause. He could not tell, from the archduke's face, what he was thinking. "We have received what amounts to a demand for complete submission to Lightborn rule and a surrender of the city itself. The Lightborn deny that Shadowborn exist, and blame Prince Isidore's death on us, though they cannot say how we might have achieved it. Mycene's and Kalamay's guilt in the destruction of the tower and the deaths of mages is inarguable. One more offense, and I do not think they will refrain from tearing down our walls. How am I to know you will not be the agent of that offense?"

"It is my belief," Balthasar said, "that Floria's ensorcellment was the work of the other Shadowborn mage, who was also the one responsible for ensorcelling Vladimer." A muscle ticked in the corner of the archduke's mouth at the mention of his brother's name—Bal wished he knew more about Vladimer's condition. But what was said was said. "That Shadowborn could keep Floria unaware of what had been done to her. The boy does not have that ability. I have been aware of my actions all along."

"While unable to control them," the archduke said. Balthasar turned in appeal to Olivede, but the archduke said, "Miss Olivede is your sister, and I am barely acquainted with her. Her efforts to try to save Mycene's life and case his passing speak well of her—but I cannot take her word regarding you."

"Your Grace," Balthasar said intensely, "*am* I the man you would send on an assassination? My marksmanship is risible. I am no mage. I may know drugs, poisons, and anatomy—but I would be entering a Lightborn court where assassination is a mechanism of succession and their brightnesses surround themselves with layers of secular and magical protection. The fact that Floria had to carry a talisman to the prince suggests that such magic cannot be centered in a living body, and therefore I argue that I cannot be carrying such an ensorcellment. If you are concerned about anything else I might be carrying with me, then have me stripped and searched before I go.

"You *need* the Lightborn to accept the existence of Shadowborn, Your Grace. I am the best proof you have."

Seven

Fejelis

A hand on his shoulder woke Fejelis, a hand that snatched itself back as he snapped upright. His head connected with a chin; she thudded back on her rump on the floor. "Ouch!" Watering, honey-gold eyes squinted at him.

Wit finally overtook reflex, and Fejelis recognized his hostess and surroundings: Jovance, mage turned railway woman, in the hut in the Darkborn Borders that she shared with three others—her brother, Jade, and a young couple, Midha and Sorrel. Rather too few hours ago, by the way he felt, he had stretched out and gone to sleep on a pallet on her floorboards. He had simply trusted to Tam's judgment, and his own assessment of her—which was admittedly not unbiased, another unexpected aspect of the situation. He tried to untie his tongue for an apology.

"Sorry to startle you, your brightness," Jovance said. "But we've been asked to mount a guard outside for some Darkborn trains coming through. How are you with a rifle?"

". . . Isn't it still . . . ?" He just avoided asking the obvious question; of course it was still night, and of course she knew that. ". . . Depends on the size and speed of the target. Overall, fair to middling." Against a target, anyway; he had never had a taste for hunting live game. "Jis—Orlanjis—is better than I am."

"Sooner have a crossbow," his younger brother said. He was nervously finger-combing his long red-gold hair, trying to worry loose a snarled residue of his ornate coiffure. His face was pale beneath his desert tan. But Orlanjis had spent seasons in the desert with their southern kin; he had hunted and bled his kill, dressed, cooked, and eaten it.

"If we need one of you, we'll need both," Jovance said, rising smoothly on strong legs and reaching down a hand in a worn leather glove to draw Fejelis up. He tried to convince himself that the shirt he had slept in was long enough to preserve decency, groping drafts notwithstanding. Her eyes glinted with mischief, noting his knees-together, slightly hunched posture.

The need to distract her, as much as the need for information, prompted him. "Trains, you said?"

"Yes. It's an hour after sunset—again, I'm sorry I had to wake you so soon, after you walked all that distance, carrying Tam." *Which my body doesn't need to be reminded about—thank you, Jovance.* He felt nineteen going on ninety. "The Darkborn manor of Stranhorne reports being overrun by what they describe as an army of Shadowborn, which seems to have swept through some of the outlying territories. They managed a retreat to Stranhorne Crosstracks just before sunrise last night—they're ferocious fighters and well organized, which means anything that could overrun them is thoroughly bad news. Now they're trying to evacuate wounded and noncombatants by train. They'll have armed guards, but they want us to mount a watch in between trains. It's good we're six." She did not count Tam, who had been incapacitated by his exertions getting the three of them there, and was lying unconscious in the small bedroom. Her lips compressed. "Not quite what Tam was hoping for, bringing you down here to supposed safety."

Another, less stupid, question occurred to him, about how they could shoot, looking out into darkness from light, but he decided he would let that, too, answer itself. As well as the one after that: if she were able and willing to use magic offensively, they need only wait to find that out, too. He suspected she was strong, but did not know how strong.

Jade lobbed Fejelis underwear and a pair of trousers that were short in the shank but otherwise a passable fit. His own clothes were impregnated with the dust of the fallen tower. Fejelis pulled the clothes on, tucked in his shirt, ran his hands over his unkempt hair, and accepted a rifle offered him. He confirmed it was unloaded, noting that it was of Darkborn manufacture. *The blind Darkborn are certainly accomplished at killing at a distance,* he thought grimly. The rifle had an interesting attachment, a long tube set parallel to the barrel with a lens mounted inside. Peering down it, he could see the glint of curved glass, the wink of focused light at its center. "One of Tam's artisans thought that one up," said Jovance, "attaching a telescope to a rifle."

He knew Tam's artisans, or some of them. He considered them *his* artisans, too, since, in a guise other than heir, he had been an irregular visitor to their cafés and workshops. Jovance said, "Tam described the design to my"—a small flinch—"grandfather." The grandfather who had died in the destruction of the tower. "Lukfer arranged for some samples to be made up and sent them down for us to try out. He worried about us. If you can tolerate having your eye right up to the end of the cylinder, it gives remarkably good magnification, and cuts out ambient light."

Fejelis sighted the grain of the scarred wooden floor, the knobby edge of the carpet. The prickling around his shaded eye grew into an ache like severe eyestrain. ". . . I think I can do this," he said. ". . . But the fog . . ." When Tam had set them down, the fog had been too dense for them to do more than find and follow the railway track itself.

"Still there. The telegraph says Stranhorne's had snow, wind, violent rainstorms; a mage in their party said it was mage weather. The first train left Stranhorne an hour and a half ago, so it has roughly another hour before it reaches here, and another half to reach the Crosstracks. It's carrying a couple of the Stranhorne family themselves. There's another about half an hour behind it. So we've time to go out and drill getting the lights and ourselves into and out of place fast. We'll get a signal as it passes each station, so we'll know when to close up."

She glanced at Midha, who did not speak, and went on. "Everyone get four lights and sling them to either side, and then take up ready positions." Midha opened the door on darkness. Fejelis's mouth went dry, remembering the hallucinatory chiaroscuro of the night before as they hunted for survivors in the rubble of the fallen Mages' Tower, but Orlanjis all but threw himself down the black maw, and Fejelis had to follow. The hut stood on a platform, fifteen feet in the air, with a covered deck all around, so that—in light, without fog—they should have had a fair vantage. Now they could barely discern the line of the railroad tracks.

"Too slow," said Midha to Jovance. Fejelis guessed that he would ordinarily have been in charge, but he, like the other two, would rather Jovance deal with their unnerving guests. She had once been a Temple mage. Thus prompted, she had them try their deployment in pairs, with two riflemen covering the diagonals while the others slung lights; that went better. While Sorrel went back into the hut to monitor the telegraph and put on the kettle for what promised to be a long night, Jovance had both Fejelis and Orlanjis shoot several rounds at a marker, the nearest of those they used for target practice, and the only one they could make out in the fog. They established that though Orlanjis was the better shot, he could not use the closed sight. Jovance exchanged Orlanjis's closed sight for an open one, warning Orlanjis of the difficulty he might have seeing.

"I've night hunted," Orlanjis began ... and in the middle of the sentence brought up his gun, squinted through the sight, and fired, lurching a little at the recoil. In the mist across the tracks, something howled its outrage. Orlanjis fired again, steadier now, and the howl ended.

Jovance said to Midha, "Let's ask Sorrel to telegraph the Crosstracks, get details of what we're up against." To Orlanjis: "What was it?"

"Don't know. Large ... animal." On the last word, his teeth chattered and he clenched his jaw.

She clapped his shoulder. "Bigger target, then. There's too much light for Darkborn out there, and too much darkness for Lightborn, so feel free to drop anything that's not us."

She has a vigilant's gallows humor, Fejelis thought, exchanging glances with Orlanjis along the length of the platform. Bright though they were, the lights were chill and dim compared to sunlight, and Orlanjis's face was wan and damp with the lack of sunlight, settling mist, and fear. With his vivid imagination, the night must be full of horrors. For Fejelis, the greatest horror was the possibility that he might have brought Orlanjis here to die. After years of having had his brother held up to him as the southern faction's favorite and his nearest rival, the last thing he had expected was that a single, impulsive act on his part would have won Orlanjis's loyalty.

Then he saw Orlanjis swing his rifle toward him and thought for a brief and terrible moment that he had won nothing. Orlanjis fired, and just behind Fejelis something scraped against the railings. Fejelis threw himself flat, rolling, and stared up at the man-sized but not man-formed creature clinging by one hooked talon to the rail. Its chest was deep, with a prominent breastbone and hollow belly, and its pectoral muscles worked as its wings fluttered. The jaw and lower face were a man's, but the eyes were barely visible. A fine pelt covered the head and torso. Orlanjis and Jovance fired together, each from their corners. Skin split, blood gushed, and the Shadowborn thudded down to straddle the railing and slither like a half-filled bag of sand off the railing to the ground below. "For the Mother's sake, *watch*," Jovance yelled at him. "The fog conceals them!"

In the doorway, Midha said, "Stranhorne Crosstracks says that some of them can fly—"

Panting, Jovance said, "We *noticed*. You want to take this corner? I'll cover the front, get us ammunition. Your brightness—"

". . . Yes, fine," Fejelis said, before she or Orlanjis turned to look. He climbed to his feet, picked up his rifle—thanking the Mother of All Things Born it had not discharged—drew a deep breath, and stepped up to the rail. The mist roiled, its motions disorientating; he fired twice at phantoms before he saw his first creature and spooked it into Jovance's line with his misses. He heard several shots from Orlanjis's direction, followed by an unnerving pause. From between them, Jovance rasped, "When you're reloading, say, 'Cover me,' so we can."

Fejelis shot at ripples of mist, at dark, solid, moving shapes on the ground. Twice he left a wounded Shadowborn that Orlanjis or Midha dispatched. "Reloading," he croaked, and had just realized he had nothing to reload with when she pushed a pouch into his hands. "Your little brother remembered *his* ammo," she chided him, before Jade's *"Cover me,"* summoned her around to the far side.

The mist seethed, though his adrenaline-sharpened vision and even the uncomfortable sight found nothing solid. Orlanjis yelled alarm and shot wildly. Fejelis broke discipline to throw one swift glance over his shoulder—

—To see one flying Shadowborn tear two of Orlanjis's lights from their hangings, even as another dropped on him from the roof. Orlanjis pitched forward, without a sound, beneath its weight. From the far side of the hut, Jovance shouted, "Hold your posts!" Fejelis remained mesmerized as the falling Shadowborn seemed to rebound, thrust skyward against gravity, and then both Shadowborn simply burst as though an immense fist had crushed them. Meat, bone, and gore spattered the platform, the roof, the ground, Orlanjis. The unstrung lights whirled above Orlanjis's head.

"Fejelis—*outward*!" Jovance shouted, dropping to her knees beside Orlanjis. "I have him." He whirled, eyes raking the mist, his finger twitching on the trigger. He had no idea how many hours later it was that Jade said, quietly, from his side, "They're gone." He pried the rifle from Fejelis's grip and turned him to face Jovance, who was supporting a trembling, blood-spattered Orlanjis. Jovance released Orlanjis to his embrace; under his hands, he could feel rent fabric part over whole skin. "Thank you," he breathed over his brother's shoulder. "Thank you."

"I, for one," Jade said, "might have wished she'd done that sooner. That was a bit close."

"Easy for you to say," said Tam's tired voice from the door. "It wasn't your magic."

"I didn't want to find out they could sense me when I

couldn't sense them," Jovance said to Jade. "But, yes, I nearly held back too long." To Tam she said, "What're you doing up?"

"Well . . . ," said the mage, burying his hands in the pockets of a ragged dressing gown. "I might have slept through the shooting, but when one of those things landed on the roof above my head—you have no idea how vile that magic is—and you let rip . . ." Fejelis hoped his face wasn't as green as he felt at the reminder. Yet he grinned with relief at seeing Tam awake and upright, if as heavy-eyed and ashen as a man recovering from a three-day bender. The mage smiled back with a rueful shrug of the shoulders as he glanced around them, apologizing for the failings of their haven.

The bell, loud, insistent, made them all jump. Jade said, in horror, "Mother's milk, the train—" The Darkborn train, which they'd all forgotten, with Darkborn guards riding outside. "*Inside*, now." He and Jovance dove right and left, harvesting lights, while Fejelis half carried Orlanjis into the hut, lowering him carefully into the chair nearest the fire. He'd apologize for the stains later. Orlanjis's eyes were dilated, black pupils in dark irises. He looked as he had looked when he learned of their father's death in darkness.

Tam said, "Get warm water with honey or sugar down him; it will take the edge off the shock."

By the time Fejelis came back into the little living room, Jovance was spilling an armful of lights onto the floor inside the door as Midha dropped the bar on the door. They looked at each other with the stunned expressions of survivors, expressions Fejelis had grown far too used to seeing around him.

"Have they gone?" Midha said to Jovance. "Is the train in danger? Is there anything on the track?"

The mage's golden eyes became hooded. She stood quite still, except for the flexing of her left hand, in the center of the close little room. Tam's brow tightened as though in discomfort. "Now it's clear," she said, and took a step toward the chairs. Finding them occupied, she sat down on Fejelis's pallet, beside the stove, knees drawn up to her chest, face hidden.

"Hot water and honey for her as well," Tam said, mildly. "Maybe something stronger for the rest of us."

"Don't you dare," said Jovance, lifting her face. "Coming over all fatherly doesn't mean you're not overspent. So stay out of this."

Tam silently parsed that sentence, his lips moving. Jovance made a gesture that Fejelis knew from the streets and the vigilance, caught his eye, and looked sheepish. He managed to grin at her.

The "something stronger" was bedeeth tea, an infusion of a desert root with stimulant properties, with a jolt of what he supposed was brandy before it ate its way through the cask. He wondered how Floria White Hand's magical asset would have reacted to it. Tam docilely sipped hot water and honey. Fejelis crouched at Orlanjis's side, steadying his cup and ignoring the tackiness on his hands and the tears trickling down his brother's face. They fell silent, listening to the growing clatter of the approaching train, riding its tracks under control of a Darkborn driver, in the faith that the combined efforts of Darkborn and Lightborn kept the tracks clear. The noise was joined by a fine vibration Fejelis felt through the soles of his feet. Then the vibration coarsened to a shake, and to the accompaniment of chattering crockery in the kitchen, the train passed beneath them and receded into the night. Only the reek of engine smoke remained.

He was not the only one who let out the breath he had been holding.

"Eight carriages," Jade said, "maybe nine." He looked at Sorrel, who nodded. "The Crosstracks said nine."

"Engine'll need some maintenance after."

Jovance opened and closed her left fist, staring at the wall in the direction of the departed train. "I don't sense anything ahead of them," she said, sounding strained. Then she dropped her face onto her knees with a poorly muffled obscenity. "That's a trainload of pain and grief," she said, face hidden. Jade eased himself down on the pallet and put his arm around her shoulders.

Sorrel got up hastily. "I need to check if the other huts are all right."

"Mother's milk," said Jade, grimly. "If any of the others— No, save your strength," he said to Jovance. "We'll wait for the telegraph. There's nothing much we could do anyway."

They waited in silence, listening to the tap and clatter of the telegraph. Sorrel returned, mug in hand; by that and by the ease of her movements, Fejelis could tell that the news was good. "Several skirmishes just outside Stranhorne Crosstracks. No one seriously hurt."

"Nat and Les?"

"Checked in fine."

Jade said to Tam, "Les—Celeste—was the first Lightborn ever taken on by the Darkborn railways, forty years ago. She didn't tell them she was a woman and six months' pregnant at the time. She's worked most of the track from Stranhorne to the Southern Ocean, and what she hasn't, Nat—that's her eldest son—has. They've got family at every branch office who've been after her to give up the huts and move into town—and been agitating even more since she broke her hip a few weeks back. *She* says she plans to end her days as grease on the track."

A gruesome image, Fejelis thought, who had recently seen far too many residues of quenched Lightborn, but at least Orlanjis was no longer staring or crying. He seemed distracted by the character sketch, and hopefully missed the allusion.

Tam stirred. "Do you know whether the train had to fight off Shadowborn?"

"I can't say, Magister Tam," Sorrel said, diffidently. "The train has not stopped, so we haven't had any reports from it, but it is within five minutes of schedule . . . which means it hasn't had to slow down."

"And none of the other huts came under as strenuous an attack."

By Midha's expression, he, like Fejelis and Jovance, knew where Tam was going, and did not like it.

The question had to be asked. ". . . Is it us—me?" Fejelis said, correcting himself.

"Or me," Tam said. "Or me and Jo. It can't be Jo alone,"

he said to Jovance. "They attacked before you started using power." He hesitated. "Jo—"

Her head snapped around. "Don't be stupid." Tam put a hand to his head, his freckles even more prominent. He had, Fejelis realized, just attempted to speak silently to her. She glared at Tam, then Fejelis. "Your brightness, he'd like me to take you out of here. I could, but I won't abandon my brother and my friends."

He did not like the idea, did not like it in the least, but he owed it consideration. *You'll never have the luxury of doing something simply to impress a girl,* he remembered his father saying, dryly. If he were the danger, if their attackers were still working according to some plan that sought the decapitation of both governments, and they knew he had fetched up here, then they would all be safer with him gone. But where to?

Tam, watching him, sighed. "Forget I asked," he said. "Curse it, Fejelis, I'm—"

"We're *all* still alive," Fejelis said, firmly.

Jovance put her hands down on the pallet on either side of her and stretched out her legs. "At least we've ammunition and a defensible position here. I just have to hope that my chucking magic around hasn't *attracted* attention." Her eyes flicked sideways, and met Fejelis's briefly. She was not talking only about the Shadowborn.

Midha said, "We'll just have to deal with what happens when it happens. Jo, can you keep a sense of what's moving outside, say for half a mile around, until we get organized?" She nodded. "Then let's all have something to eat and work out watch schedules. Master Orlanjis"—Fejelis was relieved at how quickly Orlanjis lifted his head—"you're first up for a shower and change of clothes. Don't stint on the hot water; we've plenty. I'd like two of us outside, except when there's a train passing, and one on the telegraph, but the others have to get some rest—"

"Should we go down and check the line?" said Jade.

"We'll not be able to cover enough line to justify the risk. We can barely see two hundred yards with the fog."

"Is clearing the fog a higher priority than sensing for

Shadowborn?" Jovance said. Tam opened his mouth; closed it. Mages seldom tried weather manipulation solo, even on a very limited scale. Even Tam, with his aptitude for handling inert matter, found it exhausting.

Watching Midha's expression, Fejelis thought that although Jovance's magic was no secret among them, her companions had never seen it so decisively demonstrated. Perhaps they did not understand her limits. ". . . Since it's dark," Fejelis tendered, "and our vision and ability to move would be restricted anyway, I feel it would be a waste of strength."

She gave him a grateful glance. "So we hold out here for the night. There aren't many Shadowborn come out by day, usually, even though the Curse doesn't seem to affect them— or so the Darkborn say."

"There is one other possibility to consider," Tam said, slowly. He looked down at his hands. "You, or even I, contact the high masters—"

"No," said Jovance, and then looked sideways at Fejelis, conflict in her face.

This wasn't the time to think his argument through before he spoke, he sensed, though he would have appreciated the chance to consider. His impulse, which, as ever, he distrusted, was to refuse. "If another attack comes, we should surely have some sense that our situation is becoming desperate. *Then* we could call for help."

"And if the high masters cannot make up their minds as quickly as you can?"

"Don't . . . refuse just to protect me," Tam said.

Fejelis cleared his throat. ". . . And who were those three crossbow bolts aimed at? Besides . . . my mother's family has an ugly history with the Darkborn. I would like a chance to rehabilitate it. The Borders seem to have become a front for this war, and though we Lightborn are not many, we have three assets that the Darkborn do not: the ability to see, to move by day, and strong magic."

"Two mages, one of whom is gravely overspent," Jovance pointed out. "And we're just here to do a job."

". . . I know this is not fair. I know it. Yet all four of you were prepared to stand guard in the night, at risk of your lives."

"That's our job: safety on the railroads. Not the whole Mother-blessed Borders."

"Jo," Tam said, "stop arguing for the sake of argument."

She rounded on him. "Someone has to. Oh yes, you read me right: I've never had any sense of self-preservation. But what about them?" Her snapping hand indicated her friends. "He's his brightness Prince Fejelis Grey Rapids. Are any of you going to argue with him?"

"I'd like to think I would," Midha said, though he did not look at Fejelis as he said it. "If it were to keep us all safe. But we've got too many friends on the other side of sunset—" Now he looked at Fejelis. "The routine can get cursed dull at times, so we write a lot of letters, and the owners don't mind if we use the wires when there's no official traffic. We've come to know and like a number of Darkborn rather well, in Stranhorne Crosstracks and along the lines. We're in."

Floria

Beatrice spun out the exercise of putting her children to sleep, but returned before the hour was over. Floria laid before her the other information she had: that Tam had successfully escaped the Temple's binding, that the Temple might therefore be interested in the lineage they had before this disdained. As the bells changed their rhythm from warning of darkness to warning of light, she left the woman sitting on the couch, staring into space. She had done what she could. In the foyer, she unpacked and strung lights around her waist and across her back, leaving both hands free. Below ground level in the palace was an unlit room that vigilants used for practice in moving and fighting, with only the lights they carried. Nothing and no one should hold the power of terror over a vigilant.

Or so her father had said, the first time he pushed her through the door into the darkness.

At first, she saw nothing but the near walls, the dim forms

in the garden at the edge of the spray, and beyond that, nothingness. She closed her eyes and listened for any movement out there, besides the wind that came up around dusk. She and Balthasar had used to play listening games, ear to ear on either side of the paper wall. She could not match his hearing, but listening with him, she had learned how to use her own better. Hearing no threat, she opened her eyes and moved away from the door. Now, across the river, she could see a faint linear glow that marked the route to the council chambers. There appeared to be no other lights in the dark streets: *good*. She moved quietly to the gate and leaned against it. She could afford to wait a while, to ensure that no one would use the curfew to come for Beatrice.

She waited until she saw that the lit route traced out by the princess's party had begun to shorten; their brightnesses must be on their way back. Once they had reached the palace, once the lit way had been dismantled, the night would be returned to the Darkborn. If the mages remained adamant about that, they had the means to enforce it. She did not intend to outstay her welcome. She retraced the route as quickly as she could and more easily, since it was now downhill. The moon was just coming into view over the slopes to the east, giving an eerie glitter to the water on the river. A false promise, since should her lights fail now, the moon would merely illuminate her death. The thought raised a cold sweat, chilling the shadowed skin of her scalp, and despite her training, fear forced her on until she was almost running.

She had almost reached the palace, almost reached the wide street—now dark—that had been used as their brightnesses' corridor, when she heard scuffling, and then an angry, familiar voice. ". . . What you are doing is criminal."

The reflections on the walls lurched as she halted. It could not be—no Darkborn could be alive, not with this much ambient light.

She drew her revolver. If it were not Balthasar, then there was only one other person it could be.

She heard the voice gasp in pain. She remembered that gasp: she had heard it from the other side of the wall as two men manhandled Balthasar on a search through his house. He spoke again. "The curfew was laid for one purpose and one only: to permit your princess to travel to a meeting with the archduke—"

She stepped around the corner. Three men and a woman—southerners, by their dress—encircled a fifth person. Seven servants, personal light bearers, ringed them. She recognized two of the four as members of Sharel's retinue. One of them held an ax at half ready. Another, a pry bar. The third was restraining *him*. She had an impression of a lean frame; dark hair; pale skin; mottled, stiff clothing; a back arched in an attempt to ease his pinned arms. The southerners were too close for her to take a clear shot without the risk of one of them fouling it, and if they held what she thought they held, they were dead or enslaved already. They just did not know it.

"—not," he finished, "to terrorize Darkborn with gratuitous *breakings*."

He sounded so like Balthasar in his quiet fury at the greed, stupidity, and indifference that crippled factory workers or kept the old underground streets a disease-breeding sewer. How *dare* the Shadowborn mock her by so perfect an impersonation?

"What are you, cripple?" the woman mocked. "Some kind of Darkborn-lover? Some kind of darkness freak?"

Cripple? Floria remained still. Should she call out, hoping they would give her a clear line as they turned?

The man who held the pry bar lowered it, saying uneasily, "Marle, there's something off here. Where are his lights?"

"I don't need lights," the creature who was not Balthasar said. "It's complicated to explain, but I must speak to your princess or to your archmage as soon as possible."

"I don't think so," said the man holding him. His movement took Floria by surprise—took them all by surprise. He pulled his captive backward, pivoting. Floria glimpsed a white profile, whiter than any Lightborn she knew. She tracked with the revolver, her wonder intensifying. Why was the mage letting himself be manhandled? She heard the woman say, "But we can't—"

"Got to," the man said with a grunt. "Don't want him telling anyone." He heaved; Floria glimpsed a shape hurtling into the shadows. She heard a body land and another of those sounds of pain terribly familiar from the far side of the wall.

The revolver cracked before she knew she meant to fire. One of the hanging lights shattered, raining glowing fragments down on the head of the servant who carried the stand.

One of the southerners went for the rifle slung over his shoulder. She shot him in the leg. He fell, shrieking. Then she shot out another of the lights. She didn't have nearly enough bullets to threaten them all, but the psychological effect should be enough. She said, making sure her voice carried, "Leave one set of lights and go."

"Mistress White Hand—"

"*Go!*"

The woman was crouched by the wounded man, trying to get him to release the hands gripping his thigh. "He needs a mage," she said, urgently.

The man glared out of the circle of lights, his longing to fight palpable even across the distance. But the most belligerent of his companions was wounded, the woman had abandoned all fight, and the other man was standing paralyzed. He seized one of the stands of lights from a servant and threw it down, and then gestured the other man to help the woman. Floria watched them go, unmoving, guard up, revolver trained. Yes, he turned once, his eyes promising vengeance. She had made an enemy there.

And she'd have him up before the judiciar for this night's work. Even if the judiciary were indifferent to the Darkborn, they'd care that he had intended murder by darkness—never mind that what he intended to murder well deserved it.

On light, deadly feet, she ran forward, revolver raised.

He was still sitting on the ground with the fallen lights beside him. He was holding his left wrist, which must have taken the impact of his fall, in his bandaged right hand. She realized immediately why the southerner had called him "cripple." She had seldom seen a blind person, and never one whose eyes were not visibly marred by the process that had destroyed his sight. Yet his dark eyes were flawless, with a brown, healthy iris and glossy cornea, except that his pupils were constricted and his wandering gaze did not fix on her.

As quietly as she approached, he was still aware of her. "*Floria?* Was that you speaking?"

She sighted the revolver on the center of his forehead.

"Please," he whispered. "Of all people, not you."

Her lights spilled over his face, lighting the pallor of an invalid who seldom saw the sun. A narrow, intense face, a scholar's—or a fanatic's. Blinded Lightborn, knowing themselves destined to look on darkness for the rest of their days, frequently committed suicide or lost their minds. On one side of his face she could see the red, shiny marks of newly healed wounds—like knife marks—from his ear to his jaw. His clothing was too thick, too opaque, to be wearable, particularly in this light, and with that uneven, natural dye reminiscent of the little box that Balthasar had given her—and that the Shadowborn had used to craft the talisman that had killed her prince. On his index fingers were matching silver rings. She had seen a pair of rings identical to those when Balthasar had slipped them into the *passe-muraille* to show her. Sitting against the paper wall, he had talked until he was hoarse about his wedding and the marvel that was his wife.

He said, almost in a whisper, "I wrote you a letter when I was thirteen. It was the first love letter I ever wrote. I imagined a meeting between us. This isn't . . . what I imagined."

She still had the letter, read once and unopened all those years since. She had been eighteen, Prince Benedict had just been deposed, and childish imaginings had seemed very distant. "No," she said. "Because you are not Balthasar."

He took a shallow breath. "I told you what Tercelle Amberley said: that her lover had come to her through the day. I now know who the man—men—were who used her so, how they moved through the day and what they wanted from the Amberleys. I know why the children were born sighted."

"A Darkborn can no more live in light than a Lightborn can live in darkness."

"I am living proof to the contrary. Which is why I *must* speak to your princess and the mages of the Temple."

"I can't allow that."

"Floria," he said, so familiar. "It *is* your voice. Were you with the party that spoke to the archduke?"

"No, I had a separate errand."

"How much do you know?"

"I know," she said, "that their brightnesses do not believe in such things as Shadowborn. I know that I do."

A beat; pain crossed his face. "Prince Isidore," he said, compassionately.

She did not answer. She would not let him feed on her pain, whatever he was.

She heard the bells change their rhythm, signaling warning to the Lightborn that their part of the night was at an end. If she let him up, if she risked leaving him alive, dared she bring him to the palace for questioning and punishment?

Whom did she serve? Isidore, who was dead, but who had commissioned her to watch out for his son, and Fejelis, whose steadiness in the midst of chaos and disaster had won her respect.

Would it help either of her princes if she took a Shadowborn into the palace?

It would be proof of her innocence, and of Fejelis's. And a . . . curse on their enemies.

Her voice rasped. "Stand up."

He did, clumsily, holding his wrist close to his body. She ignored that; injuries could be faked to put an opponent off guard. But his clothing jarred her. Mages could ensorcell clothing to appear opaque, but the cloth usually retained the texture of the sheer cloth most wore.

And he carried no lights, nor did he ask to pick up the fallen stand.

"Turn around," she said, testing him. "Walk. Back to me—look round, and I'll shoot."

He turned without hesitation to face the darkness, and began to walk in the direction of the palace. "Floria," he said, "I am so very sorry about Isidore, about the tower. If we'd realized faster what it was we faced—"

"Don't talk," she said. For all she knew, he had woven an ensorcellment into the words.

He continued a half block in silence, then spoke again. "Telmaine . . . is dead. Part of me simply does not care if you do shoot me. Except that I would rather it not be you. And I have undertaken to do what I can to persuade their brightnesses that another force has been working to destroy the peace between us."

"Your dukes had more than a little part in it themselves."

"Yes," he said. "Duke Mycene is dead—he faced down a Shadowborn. Duke Kalamay—I think the archduke will deal with him as soon as he can, but his power is compromised. Telmaine—I don't know how much you heard, how much they told you, but my wife was a mage."

"A *mage*?" Prejudiced, proper, jealous Telmaine . . . She reminded herself, forcibly, that this *could not be* Balthasar, but why should any impersonator think she would care about Telmaine, with whom she had no more than a speaking acquaintance?

And who could not be dead, whatever he said, because she had freed Floria from her prison before her lights ran out.

He was speaking again to the night before him in as bleak a voice as she had ever heard. "She had had no training, and she went up against—fought—a Shadowborn. I don't know what he did to her, but something went wrong with her magic. I can't believe she would willingly have harmed the archduke, much less nearly kill him." He halted without warning, and she nearly jammed the revolver into his back. "Keep moving," she said.

"She healed him, but they took her prisoner. Took her prisoner and put her in a room and opened it to the light— they executed my beloved wife for sorcery, and I was not there to protect her," he finished in a gasp, suffocated by pain.

She remembered Telmaine—or the voice that sounded like Telmaine—saying, "Tell Balthasar we spoke. It is very important."

If this were a Shadowborn, it might think to disarm her with Balthasar's grief, not knowing that she would know it lied. Or be soliciting information, if Telmaine were, implausibly, a mage. "Keep moving," she ordered.

After that, he did not speak again until they reached the walls of the palace and passed through into the gardens. And then she saw him falter before her, heard him faintly breathe, "Sweet Imogene. I never imagined . . ." She did not have time to walk him around to the rear, bring him close to the terrible ruin of the tower, which was just as well—if he were Shadowborn, she would not give him the chance to gloat, and if he were not, if he were, impossibly, Balthasar, then she could not inflict such pain on him.

When, she wondered, *did I begin to doubt?*

Since she was not in attendance on their brightnesses, she had not come to the door of greater privilege, but one of the doors of lesser privilege favored by the vigilance, because it gave them quick access to most of the places vigilants needed to be, including their own internal barracks. At the top of the steps four vigilants stood within a shelter of light, watching them. She recognized Captain Lapaxo, the most senior surviving of the captains. Parhelion had died at his post with Prince Isidore. Beaudry had apparently committed suicide or been murdered after making an attempt on Fejelis's life. Although, given that Rupertis had apparently transferred his allegiance to Prasav, perhaps *he* was in charge of the vigilance and Lapaxo exiled to guard duty. The captain's eyes, tired and suspicious, moved from Balthasar to Floria and back again, seeing exactly the same anomalies she had. "Mistress White Hand," he said, neutrally.

"I need a mage to question this man, urgently."

Her prisoner said, "A lineage mage won't be able to—"

"Would you kindly *be quiet,*" she said, tense with doubt and the potential for disaster.

Lapaxo said, "Go through; wait inside." She heard him

ordering one of the other three, the last two to take down the lights and close up, to follow. He joined them, flanking Floria and watching her prisoner. It was easier to think of the prisoner as such now, to believe that whatever he was, it was not what he appeared to be. Out in the night . . .

Inside was a short, wide vestibule with another vigilant post at the end. To those guarding it, Lapaxo signaled, *Bring a mage.* A woman disappeared through the door beyond the post.

"I would quite like to sit down," her prisoner said diffidently.

"It won't be long," she said.

It wasn't. The vigilant returned not only with a mage wearing the badge of the palace judiciary, but with Tempe Silver Branch of the judiciary—not mageborn, but magically endowed to detect lies, as Floria was magically endowed to detect poisons. The mage was less than Floria had hoped for, merely third rank, born of the lineages, and quite likely as young as her oval face. She was dressed entirely in mourning red—tunic, trousers, headband, and gloves. Her wheat-colored hair was meticulously braided into multiple neat loops, attesting to vanity, poise, and an understanding of the need to maintain appearances. Despite that understanding, she had something of the harrowed, heavy-eyed look common to many of the younger mages in the aftermath of the tower's destruction. Though where most of them looked merely stunned, her eyes smoldered with rage.

Floria said, "Magistra, could you please tell me what this man is? I warn you, he may be dangerous."

"How so?" said Lapaxo, and she realized that her prisoner was not the only one under suspicion.

"He claims to be Darkborn. Indeed, he claims to be a close friend of mine. That is, as we all well know, impossible."

"Even so, you don't quite believe that," Tempe said, quietly.

Floria laughed bitterly. "My notion of what is and is not impossible has been somewhat tried of late."

"Where did you go tonight?" Tempe said.

"To warn someone that the southerners might be about to take an unwelcome interest in them. I would prefer not to say who." Especially not in the company of a mage. "I will say—listen to me, Tempe—that the party I went to warn constitutes no danger whatsoever to any of their brightnesses, the vigilance, or the Temple."

"Truth," said Tempe, somewhat reluctantly. She turned her attention to Balthasar. "Who are you?"

Floria had been vainly hoping that she would not start with that question.

"My name," said her prisoner, "is Balthasar Hearne."

Both Lapaxo and Tempe looked at her; they recognized the name. The mage did not. She had not moved, had not shown any indication of initiative. Absorbed by her own anger, she would do nothing without a direct order.

". . . And, yes, I am Darkborn."

The mage's lip curled. "Do you want me to examine . . . him?"

There was a silence. Tempe said, as uncertain as Floria had ever heard her, "He is speaking the truth—as he believes it. Lapaxo—"

Lapaxo returned the mage's glare with his own, one of a captain of vigilants. She was the one who dropped her eyes. "Please, Magistra."

She jerked off her red glove and tucked it into her belt. "Fine," she said. "Hold him."

"There's no need," their prisoner said.

"I'll determine the need," the mage said, shortly. "Hold him."

Floria took one arm, Lapaxo the other. The mage said to Balthasar, "I'm going to touch your face."

"I know," he said. "My sister is a third-rank mage."

The touch was almost a slap, though it quickly softened as she took hold of herself, her hand molding to his cheek. Floria watched her face as her magic penetrated his thoughts, watched her expression shift from anger to confusion and then, abruptly, to deep pity. Floria could not see his, though he shivered a little in their grip.

The mage dropped her hand and stepped back. "He

needs a healer, not me," she said, staring at their prisoner in undisguised pity and dismay. "He's—he's quite mad. He is convinced he *is* Darkborn. He believes he was held prisoner by these Shadowborn, ensorcelled by them, made able to walk in daylight. He believes he is on a mission to prove that the Shadowborn exist and are responsible for everything that has happened. He believes he is blind, believes it so strongly that I cannot see through his eyes, yet he behaves as though he is able to see. Something terrible must have happened to him. . . . If you were to make inquiries among the people who lived around the tower, you might well find someone who knows him."

Their prisoner made a sound that might have been the ghost of a laugh or the ghost of a sob.

Tempe said, "Does he intend anyone harm?"

"No," she said, with certainty. "He wants to save us—Darkborn and Lightborn both. Even the Shadowborn. He cares. He cares passionately. And he grieves." To their prisoner, she said, awkwardly, "I'm so sorry."

Floria said, "Do you sense any ensorcellment about him?"

"No!" The mage bristled at that question, taking it as accusation.

As a pure-lineage mage, she would not.

"Thank you, Magistra," Lapaxo said. "That answers some of my questions."

She dipped her head, turned away, and left at a walk just shy of a run, fleeing the presence of a man driven mad by tragedy.

Their prisoner sounded shaken. "She's wrong. I'm not mad."

Lapaxo said, tiredly, "We'll hold him here, under guard. Find his family in the morning." If they had survived. And even if they had survived, what was the likelihood of their being able to pay for a healer to restore a mind so broken?

Yet that voice. That manner. Every word he had spoken, every action he had taken, *was* Balthasar. Perhaps she was as mad as the mage said he was. She said, choosing her words carefully, "May I look after him? I brought him here."

"And why was that?" Tempe said, promptly.

"I couldn't leave him out there," she said, truthfully. "We were due to hand over the night, and he'd already run into some of Sharel's retinue, who'd been amusing themselves by battering in Darkborn doors."

"They came through half an hour ago," Lapaxo said. "Spitting fire and swearing vengeance against you."

Their prisoner said to Tempe, "Then I wish to lay charges against these four individuals, by the compact of eight sixty-four, dealing with matters of legal transgressions across sunset. The charges will certainly involve property damage and assault." He held up his wrist, the swelling and new bruising prominent on the pale skin. "I was in imminent danger when Mistress Floria stepped in: by their words and behavior, they did not intend me to survive as a witness. There may be further charges, depending on what else they did."

For once, Tempe seemed at a loss, caught between the insistence of her asset that he believed every word he said, and her own certainty that he was severely delusional. She said, weakly, "I'll . . . send a clerk to take a statement."

"Thank you," said their prisoner.

"Permission granted," Lapaxo said. "I'll want a guard on you both."

That was precisely what Floria did not want, but she took what she could get—them past the guard post and into a small holding suite. It was starkly lit and equally starkly furnished, with a modest living and eating area, three beds in separate rooms, and toilet facilities. The prisoner investigated the stretched mesh of the seating with interest before sitting down and leaning back. "Floria," he said, in a strange, wondering tone. Then, purposefully, "Do you think I could get ice and a strapping for this wrist? I don't think it's broken—there's no tenderness at the expected spots—but it's swelling. And then I *have* to speak to a mage who can actually detect this ensorcellment."

She was not going to tell him that the only sport mage in the palace, as far as she knew, was the princess herself. She decided to deal with the practicalities, and spoke to their guard, requesting bandages, ice, food, and drink, and a dose of painkiller from the vigilant's store.

The vigilant returned with the medical supplies and the food and drink. She mixed a dose of the painkiller into juice, sweetened it with honey, and tasted it. She had half expected recent events to have undone her efforts in educating court in the futility of poisoning her. But it was unadulterated.

She offered it to him, not certain whether he would take it. He put their shared thought into words. "I'm trusting you haven't put something in here that will knock me out until morning." He did not mention a simple, lethal dose, though if he did not think about the possibility, he *was* insane.

"I'll call in Tempe, if you want. Let you ask me in front of her. She wouldn't let me poison you."

He considered her thoughtfully for a few heartbeats longer and then drained the glass. "I must get you to teach me how to make medicines palatable," he remarked. "Most of the ones I was taught to prepare taste thoroughly vile."

Despite his seeming calm, she saw his relief as moments passed and he felt no ill effects. "My wrist?" he prompted.

Wary of touching him or letting him touch her, she pulled up a stool. It was her turn to feel relief when she took his arm and nothing happened. His skin was pale and cool, with a slight rash or chapping across the back of his hand, and no calluses of manual work or sword training. She examined the wrist, feeling the tendons and probing the fine bones, ignoring his flinches—provoking them, even. He let her hurt him, enduring. "I don't think it's broken, either," she said at last.

He relaxed as she wound the coarse mesh of the bandage deftly across his palm and around his thumb. "Do you remember," he said, "mixing up a hangover cure for me, after my friends and I celebrated passing our final exams?"

She did; she had been worried about him—about Balthasar—as he had been so miserably ill. She finished strapping the wrist. "Let's have something to eat."

Somewhat to her surprise, Tempe did respond to their request, sending a clerk to record both the prisoner's statement and hers in his impeccable shorthand. The prisoner's account was precise and well observed, including details of appearance and posture. The mage must be right; he *could* see.

Or he was Darkborn, and Balthasar Hearne.

She needed to know for her *own* sanity.

The clerk gathered together his materials and started to rise. The prisoner said, "Wait." And when the clerk looked at him—and away from those disturbing eyes—he said, "I have a request that you take down another statement, under the seal of the judiciary."

"Under the seal of the judiciary" meant that the statement would enter permanent record. The judiciars considered the integrity of their records as sacrosanct as the Temple did their contracts.

The clerk looked at her for confirmation; she nodded slowly. Whoever and whatever their prisoner was—mad or sane—he understood Lightborn law, and under that, he was fully entitled to make such a statement.

"It may take a little time. Would you like something to eat or drink?"

The man shook his head vehemently, and Floria felt the corner of her mouth twitch. Of course not; not in the presence of a notorious vigilant assassin whose asset made her immune to poisons.

In a measured voice, the prisoner began, "My name is Balthasar Hearne, and I am a physician, born Darkborn in the city of Minhorne. I am an adult of sound mind and a citizen in good standing, and I make this statement of my own free will to place on record my knowledge of the troubles that beset Minhorne, specifically the burning of the Rivermarch, the assassination of Prince Isidore, and the destruction of the tower of the Mages' Temple."

She knew part of the story, but not all, and certainly not what had happened in Stranhorne and after. His account of Captain Rupertis's treason and death brought her to her feet, fists clenched. She rang for a guard and demanded that Rupertis come down and see her. The guard told her that Rupertis had not reported in, having left on an errand during the day. After that, she could not sit down again, but paced while, in a still place in the center of the room, the man told his story. The clerk's moving hand faltered several times during the narrative, as did their prisoner's voice, but he told it to the end, listened as it was read back to him, and signed in an uncertain but recognizable script when the last sheet was offered to him. "Put that before your Mistress Tempe, if you would."

He managed to hold his composure until the clerk left, and then he laid his face in his hands.

Her last disbelief had crumbled, listening to a voice she had known for close to thirty years speaking without a mis-chosen word or misplaced inflection. She sat down beside him, resting an arm along his spine and gently kneading his neck as though he were another vigilant. "You need to pull yourself together," she said, quietly. "As soon as Tempe reads that, she'll be along, wanting to hear you confirm it to her asset. You're liable to find yourself up before the Temple or the princess very shortly after that." She closed her hand on the tendons of his neck, pulling gently back. "Balthasar, sit up and listen to me."

He let her draw him up, his head in profile to her. She said softly, "It's a dangerous thing to show weakness in the Lightborn court. Whatever you feel, whatever anger or hurt or grief you're carrying, you *must* conceal it. Otherwise, you won't be believed. Otherwise, you'll be a target." Those were, she recalled, the very words her father had used to her, nearly thirty years ago. They were words she had used to any number of vigilant cadets in the years since.

He turned his head. "You said my name. You believe me."

"I believe you. But if others do . . . you have to know that they may decide this ensorcellment makes you too danger-ous to live." First, they would want to extract all the infor-mation from it that they could.

He leaned back, his face drained of emotion. "Why do you think I dictated it under a judiciary seal? Even if I die, my testimony has entered the record."

Clever. And no less than she would have expected of Balthasar. She reached for the dish of hot towels that had come with their meal, finding them still somewhat warm. "Let's get you tidied before they come for us."

Telmaine

"We'll be into th'Crosstracks in a matter of minutes, m'lord," the engineer addressed Vladimer, ignoring his companions. "All seems t'be clear."

Vladimer was sitting with his sound shoulder propped against the wall. He roused himself. "You've made better time than I expected. My compliments to you and the rest of the crew."

The engineer paused. "Aye, well," he said, in his Borders accent, "I'd as soon we none of us had t'do this again."

"I would add my wish to yours," Vladimer said, dryly, "if I thought it would be heeded." The engineer touched his cap lightly and started to close the door, but Vladimer spoke again. "Even if it does appear to be clear, I want you and your crew to be on the alert as we come into station. Given what happened the last time I got off a train." When he and Telmaine had been ambushed by a Shadowborn and his agents, leaving Vladimer wounded and an engine and carriages blazing.

"Aye, my lord," said the engineer. "That y'can count on."

"Though I trust," Vladimer said with grim satisfaction, "that should the Shadowborn try an ambush here, they will meet with an unpleasant comeuppance."

The bordersman's expression flickered at the reference to Vladimer's traveling companions, though not with the prejudice Telmaine might have expected; he appeared almost gratified by the prospect. Telmaine wondered if he were from Strumheller. If he were from Ishmael's barony, that might explain it.

"Do you expect there to be trouble at the Crosstracks?" Phoebe said as the door closed.

Vladimer leaned his head back. "Better to expect trouble and have none, than not expect trouble and walk into it. I have no idea of their numbers or how they communicate, although I would deduce that at least in Minhorne, they are relatively few, since they have caused as much mayhem through their agents as directly. It may be we have been able to keep ahead of them—assuming that none of the nonmageborn in your community were serving them without your knowledge." Phoebe did not rise to that lure. "And assuming that Sejanus and his staff have been able to maintain the fiction of my incapacitation."

The drawn cast to his bony features gave the lie to that "fiction," in Telmaine's opinion.

There was a silence; then Phoebe Broome drew in an audible breath. "Lord Vladimer, I would like you to let me hold your revolver until after we arrive."

The extraordinary demand startled Telmaine into sonning her. She found her leaning forward with a determined expression, all trace of the gauche, socially intimidated woman gone.

"If you will not let me or one of my people heal you, then you should let me have the revolver. If Ishmael were here, he would insist."

"Would he, indeed?" said Vladimer, in that brittle tone that intimidated Telmaine every time she heard it.

"He might weigh the risks differently. But, tell me, Lord Vladimer, would *you* leave a man in your condition in charge of a loaded weapon?"

There was a silence—in which Vladimer must remember, as Telmaine did, Sylvide's death—followed by a rasp of clothing, a snap of a holster. Telmaine's sonn caught the passing of the revolver, hilt first, from his hand to hers. "Thank you, Lord Vladimer. I would feel better if you would let one of us deal with your wound. You would think more clearly if you were not in so much pain."

"That is not acceptable."

"No," she said with a sigh, checking the revolver's safety before slipping it into her own pocket. "I suppose not."

Should Telmaine mention that Lord Vladimer's cane was as lethal as a revolver in his hands? She had been there when he had killed a man with it. She found she didn't dare.

"What do you want us to do when we pull into the station?" the mage said.

"I would suggest you leave nonmageborn to the railway crew. You deal with mages. I would much prefer that you immobilize rather than kill them, since we need information. However, the magical aspect of this is your command; I cannot advise."

Arrival in Strumheller was a welcome anticlimax, in one sense. There was no Shadowborn ambush waiting for them. But in another, it was immediately apparent that this was no normal night. They disembarked into a cordon of railway workers and were promptly set upon by a brace of reporters from the local broadsheet and several officials from the railway. On the opposite platform, Telmaine could sonn a shifting crowd and the panting profile of a waiting train. Vladimer raised his voice over the racket to order Phoebe to secure carriages for their party to take them to the manor, and insisted on being taken to the telegraph office before he would answer any questions. The reporters descended upon Farquhar, demanding to know who they were and why they should be traveling with Lord Vladimer, and were they aware of what had happened to Stranhorne, and what were these reports of the archduke having been mortally injured. The strongest living Darkborn mage beamed at them, whipped four beanbags from his pockets, and began to juggle. Telmaine's momentary relief that he was not going to tell them anything swiftly passed when the reporters switched their attention to her; in a traveling dress made for an archduchess, she was the obvious anomaly amongst the plainly dressed mages. She backed up under their barrage; reporters were a species the sheltered Lady Telmaine had little experience of.

She was saved by an incursion of armed men. Farquhar Broome's beanbags swooped down into his hands—something hopefully not too conspicuous to the nonmages around—and she felt a surge of magic between the others, a massing of defensive powers. A man in railway uniform thrust himself between her and the reporters, setting his back to them and addressing her. "M'lady, we need t'clear the platform for an unscheduled train from Stranhorne. They've got wounded."

"Wounded?" she managed.

"Aye. There's bad trouble in Stranhorne."

Trouble . . . "What," she said, aristocratic accent to the fore, "is happening in Stranhorne?"

"Don't rightly know," said the station guard tersely. "If you'll go into th'concourse, you can talk to th'agent there — he'll tell you what's possible for getting y'back up the line. Excuse me." He shouldered past her.

"This is the second evacuation train," the younger of the two reporters said at her shoulder. "First one came through with the worst injured, children, physicians, the young baronet and baronette—"

"Physicians," Telmaine caught. "Where—where are they? Did you speak to anyone? Did you hear anything of a Dr. Balthasar Hearne?"

"Hearne? Wasn't he the man that—" She could not miss their suddenly keener interest. "Is he a relative of yours, m'lady?"

"Dr. Hearne is my husband," she said. "So if you would kindly tell anything you know, I would be much obliged."

"My colleague was going to say that a man by that name had been arrested by Lord Mycene and—taken off toward Stranhorne. Why was your husband—"

The train, reeking of smoke and burned *something*, drew into the station. The younger reporter said, "That engine's a Stetler nine-oh-four. What are they doing running a nine-oh-four on this line?"

"Best they had, likely."

In a long, expiring squeal of brakes, the train halted. The doors crashed open, swinging back to rebound off the train's flanks. Men jumped down, began lifting down children, women, injured men and women. Someone shouted, "Help here!" Telmaine, straining, sought any line of profile or plane of cheek that would identify Balthasar before extending her mage sense in desperation. The sense of pain, of panic, of grief, of terror, nearly made her cry out. Her knees buckled. Phoebe's voice in her mind said, *<Don't open yourself!>* and the shock of that intrusion jerked her rigid. She recoiled, both from the crowd and it.

Phoebe shouldered her way through the crowd, using deference to her femaleness, and where that failed, her height and elbows. She put her mouth close to Telmaine's ear. "Some of us are going to stay here, if they'll accept our help for the worst hurt."

"Mistress— Miss—," said the younger reporter.

"Magistra," growled Phoebe. "And if you don't want your beer to taste like horse piss for the next month, you'll keep your next words behind your teeth."

Vladimer, accompanied by a four-man guard, arrived before the reporter found a rejoinder. "We're leaving."

The guard swallowed up Telmaine and Phoebe; Phoebe attached herself to Lord Vladimer's side, hastily explaining the mages' deployment, while Telmaine wavered along behind. She did not know what had shaken her most: her sense of the refugees or having Phoebe address her so.

They arrived to be greeted by an argument in Borders accents so broad as to be unintelligible. The mages' end was being upheld by a fiery man in his late twenties; Telmaine remembered, from the flurry of introduction in Minhorne, that his name was Bryse, and that he came from Strumheller. Vladimer interrupted crisply, "I'll pay what they're asking. Let's get going."

The collective surprise over his ability to make sense of the argument was good enough to get them aboard; Vladimer, Telmaine, Phoebe, and Farquhar shared one carriage. Vladimer said, "They'll need something to make up their losses on the Stranhorne passengers. Horses have to eat, never mind men." With one of his thin smiles: "At one point in my misspent youth, I drove a cab for hire. Excellent way of gathering information." He paused; he did not need to be a mage to be aware of his companions' nervous anticipation of his next words. "Stranhorne Manor and the lands east of it have been overrun. Baron Stranhorne himself is believed dead. He and others used explosives to set fire to and collapse the manor to trap the Shadowborn who forced entry. My informants say that the explosions were probably premature, not entirely unexpected given the Shadowborn's casual way with fire. Ishmael, Ferdenzil Mycene, and the young Stranhornes led a fighting retreat to Stranhorne Crosstracks. Unfortunately, although Ishmael escaped with the others from Stranhorne, he made a bid to reach survivors from the baron's party, and has not been heard of since."

On an exhale, Phoebe Broome said, "No."

"And Balthasar?" Telmaine heard herself say in a thin voice.

"No one who knew your husband, or knew of him, had reported to the railway authorities. Perhaps we will learn more when we arrive at the manor."

Tam

Tam rolled on his side in the hard bed, trying to find a less painful position. He'd been born a peasant and spent his young-adult years one meal away from hunger and one mischance away from prison, so he wasn't soft, but the overreach had left him aching in bone, muscle, and joint. If he regained his former station, he was buying new mattresses for this household.

It wasn't his aching body that kept him awake. Nor had he retreated to bed purely because he felt awful. If he had stayed in the main room, either Jovance or Fejelis would have asked him what had happened between him and the high masters. Jovance, whatever her bitter differences with the Temple, was a high-ranked mage, and Fejelis had a keen eye for deception. They would realize very soon that what he had supposedly done was impossible.

He had already been exhausted when the high masters summoned him, exhausted by grief at Lukfer's death and from annulling the Shadowborn death magic that riddled the ruins of the tower. He had welcomed the masters' examination, desperate that they should know what he knew—until he realized that, horrific as the shattering of the tower had been for him, it had been far more so for them. Lukfer had warned him that the archmage and the oldest high masters—centuries old themselves—had received the memories of mages who remembered the first years after the

Curse. Only the earthborn's utter dependence on the lights they created had saved mages from extinction then.

I should have warned Fejelis, he thought, made him understand how their friends among the artisans threatened not only the Temple's current wealth and status by their experiments with generating light from electricity, but raised atavistic terrors in ancient minds.

He had struggled at the end, which had decided his fate. He still did not know who had sent Perrin running to warn Fejelis that the high masters planned to strip his magic and probably his mind from him. Perhaps she truly did not intend Fejelis harm, since she had tried to warn him when she realized the treachery planned in her name. By then it was too late. Tam had been bound, body and magic, able to hear everything and do nothing. He had heard Fejelis argue for Tam's life, heard him tell the high masters outright he knew about the Shadowborn and their powerlessness against their magic, and heard him appeal for the formation of an alliance. He had heard Prasav accuse Fejelis of conspiring to undermine the Temple, and offer Fejelis and Tam himself as scapegoats for the Shadowborn's crimes. He had realized, from the silence of the mage's spokeswoman—who with one touch could have confirmed Fejelis's innocence, and who *knew* Tam's—that Fejelis was about to die.

And then he felt the archmage's magic slip through the binding like a sharp knife, felt the archmage's strength extended for him to grasp. He had swatted aside the crossbow bolts, reared up, and seized and *lifted* Fejelis—and Orlanjis, too, apparently—and dropped them all here. Here in the Borders, where Lukfer had brought his granddaughter six years ago.

Once more he should be grateful for Fejelis's steadiness. If he'd been alone, he would have died at sunset, sprawled unconscious on the bracken beside the railway tracks.

Instead, he lay on a hard bed and waited for the high masters to find him. Or for Fejelis or Jovance to ask that question.

Overspent, aching, preoccupied, he missed the first

questing touch of magic. A newly familiar magic, tainted with the sense of their enemies, but fundamentally Dark-born.

He felt her sense him. <Telmaine.>

Telmaine

Without an introduction, Telmaine would never have known the woman who greeted them as Ishmael's sister. She was so unlike him: dainty, pretty, and fashionably dressed. But Noellene di Studier did have her brother's phlegmatic temperament; she received them—the arch-duke's illegitimate brother, Telmaine, and a posse of mages—without fuss or fluster, directed her housekeeper to find everyone suitable rooms, and escorted Vladimer, Phoebe, and Telmaine into a large, well-appointed apartment to meet the Stranhornes.

The apartment was kept at sickroom heat by a fire in the grate. A lanky young man, no more than a teenager, lay on a couch, his shoulder and chest heavily bandaged. A woman in her early twenties sat beside him, coaxing him to drink from a medicine glass. She wore a maternity dress—she was past the stage where it was proper for her to be out in society—and riding boots, her hair woven back in a simple braid. *Wife?* No, too close a resemblance; the two shared the same wide, slightly prominent brow, the same strong features.

"Lord Vladimer Plantageter," Noellene said. "May I introduce Baronette Laurel and Baronet Boris Stranhorne. My friends Lord Vladimer Plantageter, Mrs. Telmaine Hearne, and"—the barest hesitation—"Magistra Phoebe Broome."

Telmaine heard the baronette draw in her breath sharply, not at Phoebe Broome's name, but her own.

"As you are," said Vladimer firmly, as the baronet moved to push back his covers. "You will accomplish nothing by fainting at my feet." *You should know,* thought Telmaine, reproachfully. Had Vladimer not been faint with pain and blood loss when he first tried to convince the archduke of the emergency and Ishmael's innocence, Ishmael and Balthasar might be with them now.

Vladimer allowed Noellene di Studier to move a chair in place for him and sat down, leaving the baronette to seat the rest of them. Telmaine could not prevent herself wondering, albeit fleetingly, whether Noellene knew that Phoebe Broome had been her brother's mistress.

"Lord Vladimer," Laurel Stranhorne said, extending a hand to him. He took it, dipped his head, and released it, a sketch of courtesy. "It is an honor finally to meet you. Ishmael has spoken of you often. I can offer you a summary, and then explain more fully as you need. Ishmael preferred his reports that way—the essentials first, then action, if need be, and then the details." Her smile was almost too fleeting for them to catch the quiver at its corners.

"Ishmael always has a sound grasp of priorities," said Vladimer, with a suggestion of warmth. "Go on."

"Stranhorne Manor and, as far as we know, the villages to the south and west beyond, were overrun by the Shadowborn almost a full night ago," the baronette said. Her studied detachment was effortful. "We had scant warning, and still don't know the extent of the force against us—it consisted of Shadowborn, animals, and . . . ensorcelled Darkborn. The leaders were mages. We took in those of our people who had managed to reach us before we had to close the gates, and set to defend the manor. We had been stockpiling munitions in case the Isles asked for our help." Vladimer's expression did not change at that admission. "We tucked them away in the cellars of the manor when Lord Mycene arrived. When the manor came under heavy attack, our men moved the explosives to structural points within the manor. The plan was that if the Shadowborn forced entry, our father"—she stopped, pressed her lips together, and composed herself to go on—"our father and others were to fire the munitions while the rest of us broke out through the front gate and made a dash for the Crosstracks. Father and the others meant to get clear, but the Shadowborn were using fire. We think the explosions were premature." The baronet threw his undamaged arm over his face. His sister slipped her hand into his and squeezed. "We were attacked twice on the way to the Crosstracks and lost another twenty or thirty people. But they didn't move on us during the day, and we're evacuating as many as we can tonight. We've had to fight off raids on our trains, but we have succeeded so far."

"I now appreciate," said Vladimer, slowly, "why the Stranhornes have earned the respect of such very different connoisseurs of warfare as Ishmael di Studier and Lord Sachevar Mycene. What of Ishmael? Is he . . . ?"

She shook her head quickly, sparing Vladimer the word at which he had balked. "He left the manor with us, but he went back to try to find Father, and he has not returned."

Vladimer's expression turned bleak; if he called anyone friend, it was Ishmael.

"I wouldn't give up hope," Noellene di Studier said. "I've learned not to."

"Lord Mycene and his men are still at the Crosstracks. With Lavender—my sister. People are still filtering into the Crosstracks from the surrounding areas. You know how extensive the underground complex is, so now that we have reinforcements from Strumheller, we hope we can hold. But, not knowing the extent of the Shadowborn forces, we cannot promise."

"These reinforcements—I trust they do not represent a substantial portion of Strumheller's own defense." He sonned Noellene di Studier's scowl. "I have no wish to insult your brother, but by Ishmael's account, he does not have the experience—"

"His troop commanders do," the baronette said. "My brother—*both* my brothers—are the quintessence of Borders stubbornness when it comes to each other, but they know their duty to their people and they are neither of them fools."

"Please," Telmaine interrupted. "Where is my *husband*, Dr. Balthasar Hearne? Is he back in the Crosstracks?" She could not imagine, if he were already in Strumheller itself, he would not have come to find her. "Or did he . . . ?" She could not voice the thought that he might have stayed behind in Stranhorne. Or *died* in the manor. Hopeless as he was with a firearm, he would put himself between any patient, woman, or child, and the Shadowborn. He might even have volunteered—

"I am sorry, Lady Telmaine," Baronette Stranhorne said. "I am truly sorry. We don't know what happened to your husband."

She lies, Telmaine thought. "That is *not*—"

With an edge of desperation, the baronette said, to Vladimer, "Ishmael said that you knew about the Shadowborn, Lord Vladimer, that they can, apparently, change their form—"

"Yes, we know about them," Telmaine said, beyond courtesy. "Tell me about my husband!"

Vladimer, too, must have sensed something in Laurel's manner. He said, "Baronette, if you would."

"We had one of those Shadowborn in Stranhorne Manor," she said, slowly and unhappily. "We think it arrived with Lord Mycene, as one of his men. Dr. Hearne had been helping our surgeon, quite capably, so I didn't suspect him, but I caught him, or something in his shape, opening a side entrance to let in the Shadowborn."

"No!" Telmaine cried out. "Balthasar would *never* do that."

"Not willingly," said Vladimer in a tone that made Phoebe's head turn toward him.

"Whether it was or wasn't, your husband did not escape with us. I'm terribly sorry, Lady Telmaine."

Her ears were roaring. She heard Noellene di Studier say, "Put her head down." She would have welcomed fainting, welcomed escape from the terrible choice between Balthasar as betrayer, ensorcelled by the Shadowborn, and Balthasar left behind, living or dead, in the ruins of Stranhorne Manor. But someone—*Vladimer?*—pushed her head down to her knees and held it there.

Slowly her head cleared, and her wits and resolve returned. She would not believe it until she had sensed for herself that Balthasar was gone, that his essence was no longer in the world. She need not rely on others' reports or wait, perhaps in vain, for some relics of him to be returned to her. She could thank magic for that.

And she could thank it for something else, too: if Balthasar were dead, she would be able to do more about his death than weep for him. Unlike other wives, she would not have to beg others to punish or avenge his death . . . or beg them to do nothing, for their own lives' sake. She had power; *she* could deal with his murderers.

"Lady Telmaine!" hissed Magistra Broome. Farquhar Broome's softly scolding, <Tsk,> brushed her mind. Smelling burning, she reared up—Vladimer had removed his hand—but all that remained was a faint scent of smoke and a tingle of magic.

"Yes," Vladimer said. "There is that." He let a beat pass, but neither of the Stranhornes challenged that cryptic statement. "Thank you, Baronette Stranhorne; that was most succinct. Your father is a great loss, to Stranhorne and to the archdukedom as a whole. I will ask for further details in a moment, but first I owe you, I think, a summary of events in the city."

Telmaine realized he was going to begin with Balthasar's opening the door to Tercelle Amberley. He certainly would not begin with his own encounter with the Shadowborn. She did not want to hear her part of it again; she would surely scream or weep. She stood up. "Please excuse me. Hearing it again would only distress me."

The threat of magical vapors was even more potent than the threat of the ordinary kind. The door was well closed behind her before Vladimer said another word.

Out in the hall, she had nowhere to go; if she had been given a room, she did not know where it was. She did not want to join the mages; they might be her kind, but the train journey had amply demonstrated that they were not her class. She simply let her feet take her where they would, and when they led her through an unobtrusive door into a small library that smelled disquietingly familiar, she realized then that she had been guided by Ishmael's memory.

Centerpiece to the library was a molded relief of the region as large as a dinner table and surely as heavy. When she was much younger, her brothers had had such a relief in their part of the nursery, across which model huntsmen, soldiers, and rogues skirmished on those nights when winter weather barred them from outdoor make-believe. This had a far more serious purpose.

She paused before it. She could not imagine Ishmael being careless in the placement and orientation of something so essential to his planning. So if she stood thus, then Stranhorne should be ... Cautiously, she extended her mage sense outward, seeking her husband's familiar vitality. It had never been a vibrant vitality—Balthasar lacked the brawny energy of her brothers and Ishmael—but it had a distinctive constancy and sweetness.

And then, out there, she brushed up against something potent and vile—Shadowborn magic, but so concentrated that she crumpled her magic back into her skin with such violence that, between the action and the Shadowborn magic, she found herself leaning over the table, fighting dry heaves.

<Telmaine?>

She nearly screamed, but the mental contact was not Shadowborn; it had a ground-glass abrasiveness that she had learned to associate with one Lightborn mage. <Magister Tammorn?>

<Thank the Mother,> Tammorn said. <Can you hold this contact? I'm—> But she already knew what he was; she had felt burnout before. He felt her recoil, read the memory that surged to the forefront of her thoughts. <No! Curse it, don't drop it. I'm not going to die on you!>

His exhaustion was even greater than his irritation, but she did not sense the excruciating pain she had sensed from Ishmael, or that terrifying sense of his life draining away. Cautiously, she assumed the burden of the contact. Immediately, he demanded, <What's happening? What are you doing in the Borders? How did you break my binding?>

The binding that he had imposed on her as the price of his help when she went to save the archduke. <I won't let you do that to me again.>

<Lady Telmaine, in my present condition, I couldn't bind dandelion fluff. What were you just doing?>

<I was trying to find my husband. I sensed>—she gagged, and managed—<Shadowborn.>

"Mother of All," he muttered aloud. <Could you *please* try to organize your thoughts? My head's about to split as it is.>

Control, she urged herself. Feeling her way, she moved hesitantly to the hearth and sat down on it, drawing her legs up beneath her. The slate was cold under her hips, even through the layers of fabric, but it was not combustible. <My husband, Balthasar, was in Stranhorne when the Shadowborn invaded. I thought I might be able to find him. Instead, I sensed Shadowborn—nothing but Shadowborn.>

"Shadowborn," Tam said, to whoever was with him. "Yes, I know we knew that, but she says strong mages. No, I promise, I won't try—" <Lady Telmaine, I'm in a railway man's hut on the Strumheller–Stranhorne line, half an hour's ride out of Strumheller Crosstracks. There's me and six others. We've already fought off one Shadowborn attack. We've no means of travel, not even one of the rolling platforms the railway uses for maintenance, and I'm flat-out spent getting down here. We need help.> The urgency wasn't for himself; she sensed that. Someone with him . . .

And the door to the library burst open, reminding her, terrifyingly, of the moment when the Duke of Mycene and his men invaded the archduke's bedroom with revolvers drawn and took her prisoner. Magistra Broome led with skirts flaring, Vladimer several limping strides behind her. Farquhar Broome followed, that familiar expression of impish fascination on his face.

"Lady Telmaine," demanded Phoebe, "what are you doing?"

"Speaking to Magister Tammorn," Telmaine said. Etiquette as taught a duke's daughter had no protocol for providing introductions by magic and across distance and sunrise. "He's . . . not an enemy." Which was as accurately as she could characterize him.

"Magister Tammorn?" said Vladimer sharply, thrusting past Phoebe Broome with little care either for propriety or his wounded arm. "Can you interpret for me?"

"You want to talk to him?"

Vladimer propped the cane against the hearth and gripped the mantel, standing over her. "I most certainly do."

<Vladimer?> Tammorn said, when she asked. A surge of emotion, foremost of which was rage, and memory of a beloved master and friend becoming a corpse under his touch, of the great, lifeless body in his arms, of the cold stour of Shadowborn magic from the ruins of the Mages' Tower. <The one that let them . . .> No word. No word, but impressions and emotion as dense as lead.

"He *didn't do it himself!*" she blurted in defense, not only of Vladimer, but of herself.

At Tammorn's end, someone had a hard grip on his shoulders. Someone was speaking to him in a tone of urgent concern, but no words penetrated through the mage's anger.

<I can't possibly think what he has to say to me,> Tam said, savagely. <I can't possibly think how he dares.>

"Telmaine," said Vladimer, looming over her.

"He's angry," she said up to him. "He's— He says he can't possibly think what you have to say to him."

Vladimer drew a sharp breath. "Please tell him . . . tell him that my failure to take action was the worst misjudgment— the worst mistake—of my life. It cost me my place at my brother's side, and his trust and high regard."

She relayed the message. And was promptly clubbed by the mage's rage, grief, and more memories, as by a wave that knocked her off balance, bowled her over, sucked her down. She was gasping, drowning in the undertow of his grief and her own. Vladimer suddenly released the mantel, seized her arm in a bruising grip, and shook her, an exertion more punitive to him than to her. "Tell the man he can have my life if he wants," he said into her face. "Tell him he can do with me whatever he cursed well wants—*after* he has listened to me."

She did. There was a long silence. Tammorn's anger receded, sinking in exhaustion. The someone with him—by the mage's emotional response, it was the young Lightborn prince himself. But what was the prince of the Lightborn doing in the Borders?—was supporting and steadying him. <What does he want?> Tammorn said, at last.

"He wants to know what you want," she said to Vladimer.

Vladimer released her, set his hand on the hearth, and buckled down onto the stone beside her. "An alliance," he rasped. "Between our mages and theirs."

"But the Lightborn cannot *sense* Shadowborn magic," Telmaine protested.

"Lightborn can speak to Darkborn using magic," Vladimer said, tersely. "As you are demonstrating right now. Darkborn can sense Shadowborn with magic. And Lightborn can destroy with magic. Darkborn perceptions can direct Lightborn force. Together, we can fight them." He paused. "*Tell him*, Telmaine."

She did. The connection popped like a soap bubble under harsh sonn.

"He's gone," she said.

"What do you mean *gone*? By the Sole God, woman, can't you use words properly, without all this genteel circumlocution?"

If the carpet ignited underfoot, it would be all *his* fault. "I mean *gone*. Broke the connection. Is not talking to me anymore."

"Contact him," Vladimer ordered.

"No," she said, more forcefully than she had ever spoken to him. "He heard. He understood." Vladimer drew breath, and she twisted to brace a hand on his chest, shocking herself more than she did him. "Lord Vladimer, *listen*. He's not in Minhorne; he's down in the Borders. He is badly overspent in his magic—bad enough to be ill with it. He says he's with friends in a railway hut. He needs transport out. When he speaks to me again, if I can say that a train will stop and collect them, I think it would help."

"This is more important than—"

"I think one of the people with him is the Lightborn prince himself." Deliberately, she said, "He did not tell me, but it's the way he feels. He thinks of Prince Fejelis as a beloved younger brother. When he tried to bind me, back in the city"—a circumlocution, if ever there was one—"it was because he thought I was Shadowborn and had hurt Fejelis."

His drawn face set in his old, calculating expression. "I'll order a train to pick them up. They can bring lights with them and ride in a closed carriage. I need those Lightborn here. I need that mage to listen to me. Unless"—he sonned Phoebe Broome, who had been standing very still—"unless you have a mental telegraph line to any other high-ranked Lightborn mage that I do not know about." His head turned slightly to expand his challenge to Farquhar, who shook his head soberly. "They're refusing to have anything to do with us, dear boy."

"Lord Vladimer," Phoebe Broome said, "before we take this any further . . . *Did* you know of the attack on the Lightborn Mages' Tower before it happened? Because that is what that sounded like."

The silence was long, and Vladimer's breathing quick and shallow.

"You referred to a misjudgment. A mistake that cost you your position and your brother's regard. May I know—as the person responsible for my people being here, as your ally in this, or so I believed—whether you knew, and, if so, why you chose not to warn the Temple or us?"

"Magistra Broome," Vladimer said, "you heard my offer to the Lightborn. It was meant. If he leaves any part of me, it's yours."

"What use is your life to me?" Her voice shook with distress. "Do you have any *idea* what this plan of yours will mean for us? We are mages, Lord Vladimer, and the one characteristic that is common to the lowest and highest of mages is that we sense vitality, which means we sense life, we sense death, and we sense suffering. And there are times when that pain is *unbearable*."

"Magistra," Vladimer said, coming to his feet. "The creatures that slaughtered us also appear to have magic, and no such fine sentiments as these."

"They are not fine sentiments to *us*, Lord Vladimer. They are the truths we live by. Before we accept your orders to do *anything*, did you stand by and permit the slaughter of the Lightborn mages? If so, *why*?" There was a long silence. "That's right, your *life* is easy for you to give up. But the *truth*, no."

Telmaine, rising, thought she had never seen Vladimer look so sick, not even when he learned of Casamir Blondell's death. She said, almost in a whisper, "There was more to his ensorcellment than coma."

"How so? The Shadowborn died; any ensorcellment was broken."

She wished Phoebe Broome were a woman of her own class, because there were ways of communicating the unsayable to those who understood the code.

"If it makes any difference to you," Vladimer said, starkly, "I realized my error when the relic of my loyal lieutenant, Casamir Blondell, was laid in my hands. He denounced my decision—in fact, he accused me of treason—and went on his own to investigate. He was caught and killed, or incapacitated and left for sunrise. But between my receiving his relic"—an amulet Blondell had worn to protect himself against magic—"and being rendered unable to act, was a span of minutes. I was on my way back to ask for my brother's ear when Magister Tammorn attempted to bind Lady Telmaine. In attempting to stop Telmaine's magical outburst, I shot the blameless Lady Sylvide, and was promptly overpowered and drugged into a stupor on the excuse of insanity."

"I thought . . ." Phoebe's hand moved slightly, the gesture as stillborn as her initial thought. "No matter the shunning, the denunciations from pulpits, the expulsion from work, from families, from society—no matter all of that—I thought there must come a time when we would by our virtue prove ourselves, *prove* that magic was not what the Sole God's Church said it was, what history said it was, what the slander in the broadsheets said it was. I thought there would come a time when you—all of you—would understand that all we wanted was to live and do our work as well as we were able. . . ." Her voice trailed away.

"Magistra Broome, I am truly sorry."

A half shake of the head, perhaps of negation, perhaps simply to clear her mind. "And you," she said to Telmaine. "Did you also know? Did you also keep silent?"

"I . . . ," she said, weakly, remembering listening to Mycene and Kalamay toying with Bal's life and her sister's happiness. Phoebe would never understand what had made her probe Mycene's thoughts. In a low voice she said, "I thought Vladimer would—"

"Vladimer," Phoebe Broome said, flatly, "but not you."

She shrank under that tone, and for a heartbeat hated her. What did *she* know of the stifling restrictions of society that punished the least initiative in a woman—she with her father and her brother and her commune? But in the shabby little boardinghouse where her flight had brought her, Telmaine had gathered both responsibility and power into her hands, despite the fact that by doing so, she had lost society, virtue, the self that was. She said, simply, "I did not know how then."

"Curse you. Curse you both," Phoebe said, and turned away.

"*Wait*," said Vladimer, in raw appeal. Phoebe halted, but did not turn. He spoke not to her, but to her father. "Magister Broome—" He choked to a halt.

Farquhar Broome tilted his head to one side, considering him. "Dear boy," he said gently, "we have built a tradition and earned trust by only practicing magic upon the willing. You are as far from willing as a man could be. And that is something I need no magic to know. "

"I do not *want*," Vladimer said harshly. "Indeed, this is the very last thing I want. But I *will* that it should be done. If this is what it will take for you to work with me, then *do it*."

Phoebe drew breath, her expression a mingling of outrage and protectiveness. But magic flowed, and she did not speak. The elderly mage smiled at Vladimer, the creases in his face falling into well-worn pleats. "I am quite old, dear boy, as I suspect you already know, given the dossier you will have compiled on me. Life was not always as kind to me as it has been in these last years, when it has given me a home, a community, and a son and daughter to cherish me. There is not much in the way of men's natures and conduct toward one another that I do not know. If you entertain some notion that I will be more forgiving, perhaps you are right. But I will remind you that it is the young ones, the ones like my daughter, you must also convince."

"You are their master, Magister Broome. If you accept, *they* will," Vladimer said, intensely.

"Oh, dear," Farquhar Broome said. "It is not quite like that, but, yes, I do have some influence. You *should* ask my daughter, but you find betrayal by a man the less painful to contemplate, for all you pretend such dislike of women." He clicked his tongue at Vladimer's recoil. "I have met it all before, as I said. . . . Shall I ask the others to leave?"

"No," rasped Vladimer. "Let them witness it done."

"Then sit down. I will be quick."

Vladimer did, lowering himself painfully onto the hearth again. Telmaine resisted the urge to move away. The mage took Vladimer's head between his hands, turning his face up with gentle pressure. The magic was no more than a breath, but Telmaine felt the healing in it. Then Farquhar Broome stooped and kissed Vladimer on the forehead. Unexpected as the gesture was, it was not theatrical or absurd. Telmaine's throat filled: she remembered her own father—not a demonstrative man—kissing her so, when he gave his last gift to her: permission to marry Balthasar.

"Dear boy," the mage said, "I dare not urge you to be easier on yourself. You are able—and you are willing—to do great evil. But you are equally able—and equally willing—to do immense good. Which you do is a choice you will make every day." He straightened, released Vladimer, and stepped back.

Vladimer's cane toppled slowly to the carpet as his hand went to his arm. His face and entire posture relaxed at the sudden release from pain. "What an extraordinary sensation," he murmured; Telmaine was not sure that he was aware he was speaking aloud. She felt a discreet nudge of magic, and the cane hopped upright again, coming to perch by Vladimer's knee.

Phoebe was standing with her hand pressed to her lips. With her attention on Vladimer, Telmaine had not sensed any exchange between Phoebe and her father, but obviously it had happened. "Lord Vladimer," Phoebe said, in quite a different tone, and her father tapped her arm. "We shall just let that settle a while, shall we?"

"No!" Vladimer said urgently, surging to his feet. His cane spilled again, but when Telmaine tried to pass it to him, he ignored it. Speaking quickly, overriding any question or offered sympathy, he said, "Notwithstanding their apparent magical strength, the thing—one of the things—that perplexed me throughout this is how capricious their actions have appeared, a mixture of the subtle use of ensorcellment and coercion and the gross manifestations of magic. It may be they are capricious by nature, but I have found the assumption of caprice rather than logic to be a dangerous one to make about one's enemies. We must think this through, and quickly. Was Stranhorne merely the first, geographically, or was there a reason why it should suffer the first mass attack?"

He started at a forcible knock on the door: Noellene di Studier, with Laurel di Gautier at her shoulder. "Lord Vladimer, excuse me. There's a telegram from Minhorne—"

He almost lunged at her, snatching it from her extended hand without a word of thanks. Telmaine sonned the momentary surprise on Noellene's face, and the more speculative attention on Laurel's, as he used both hands to tear it open. He dropped into an armchair, spreading the telegram on his lap to sweep his fingers over the text. They held their collective breath.

He lifted his head. "The Lightborn have delivered an ultimatum to my brother. They wish the city surrendered to them in reparation for the attack on the Mages' Tower. They rejected all arguments as to the existence of the Shadowborn. They gave this ultimatum at a meeting, and immediately prior to the meeting, the archduke's party came under attack from a boy of some fifteen or sixteen years, manifesting Shadowborn magic and purporting to be the son of Lysander Hearne—Balthasar Hearne's brother." To

Telmaine, he said, "I suspect this is the individual you and I encountered at the train station. . . . The Lightborn gave no indication they were aware of the incident. The Shadowborn was accompanied by Dr. Balthasar Hearne."

Telmaine heard Laurel di Gautier breathe, "Oh," but was too dizzy with relief to wonder why.

"Dr. Hearne managed to physically subdue the Shadowborn mage"—Vladimer's brows rose as he read—"using chloroform, but not before the Shadowborn had incapacitated Phineas Broome and killed the Duke of Mycene."

If the rumor that Suuhovar Mycene had fathered Vladimer had any truth to it, no one would know from his manner. "Chloroform," Vladimer noted with approval, "is less flammable than ether. . . . Hearne claimed to have been ensorcelled by the Shadowborn, but the ensorcellment obviously had its limits. He also claimed the ensorcellment allows him to survive in daylight. He volunteered to offer himself to the Lightborn court in a living demonstration of the existence of Shadowborn magic."

"No," Telmaine breathed. *"Why?"*

"Despite considerable reservations that he is acting according to his own will, my brother decided he had no choice but to take the risk, in hopes that Hearne could provide the evidence needed to convince the Lightborn." To Farquhar Broome: "Can someone be ensorcelled to move during daylight?"

"Not by us," Farquhar said. "Nor, to my knowledge, by the Lightborn. How intriguing."

By his expression, "intriguing" would not have been Vladimer's word for it. To Telmaine, he said, "Your husband appears to have survived the transition. They were able to exchange words with him through the wall."

"Are they sure it is him?" Laurel said.

Vladimer nodded approval. "His sister—who is a mage— vouched for him, as did two members of the commune working at the palace who had no known contact with the Shadowborn. They all confirmed he was Darkborn, ensorcelled, and the man they had known in the past as Dr. Hearne. Which passes for certainty, I suppose, in these times.

"According to Hearne, there are two factions of Shadowborn, led by two very strong, rival mages. One goes by the name of Emeya; the other name Hearne could not learn. Their ambitions appear to be territorial, though Hearne could not say why they chose to act on them now." He refolded the telegram. "Admirably succinct. I owe Casamir Blondell another debt of thanks; he trained his successor well. What is unfortunately apparent is that we are unlikely to get immediate reinforcement from the north—"

"Did my husband know that I am still alive?" Telmaine interrupted. She would be *cursed* if she let this question go unasked. "Did anyone tell him?" If *only* she had made herself known to Olivede at the train station and not shirked that personal awkwardness. If only the—she could say this in the privacy of her own mind—*cursed* Lightborn were not obstructing the mages from speaking to their fellows in Minhorne. If only Balthasar had never opened his door to the pregnant Tercelle Amberley . . .

"If anyone did know to tell him," Vladimer said, "then my ruse with Blondell's ash and your jewelry was not nearly as convincing as I intended it to be."

Farquhar Broome was shaking his head at her with the expression of a benign tutor. His magic drizzled around her, dampening her fires.

"I will inform my brother of your survival when I telegraph in return." A wintry smile. "We did arrange that he lay the blame for your escape on me." To Noellene di Studier he said, "I need to speak with your brother and his advisers. This makes it exigent that we use every asset and advantage we have to keep up the pressure on the Shadowborn. . . ."

Telmaine hardly heard. Balthasar, gone into the light and ensorcelled by the Shadowborn. Ishmael, lost around Stranhorne. With tight fists and a tight throat she said, barely audibly, "Magister Broome . . . I retract all suggestion of impropriety around the request you made of me on the train. You had every right to ask, and I . . . have an obligation to answer."

He gave her a broad smile. "My *dear* girl."

Balthasar

The summons to the archmage's presence came a half hour later. By then, Floria had badgered him not only into self-possession, but into putting his appearance in order. She sent for a pair of eyeshades, two oval pieces of smoked glass held in a fine frame of wire, to cover his sightless eyes. His eyes disturbed Floria; it was plain. Lightborn were averse to physical infirmity, but he had never thought of himself that way.

He was glad she was at his side, though he had not expected to find her so disconcerting. In the sentimental manner of boy and youth, he had presumed she was beautiful, but it was a shock to find that she truly was, even with her hair scraped and netted back and that wary, hard expression. Hers was an elegant, bone-cast beauty that would last into old age. He knew women who had labored all their lives as domestics and at the factories, but he had never met one whose strength had been groomed like a fine racehorse. She asserted herself in space like a man—indeed, like a nobleman—expecting others to yield to her. Only her voice, familiar to him since early childhood, was the same.

Six vigilants, including Captain Lapaxo, escorted them. From Floria's descriptions of the palace, he knew that the walls had been painted by some of the finest artists in the land. He could even have said what the panels depicted, had he known exactly where he was, from her descriptions. But to sonn alone, they were featureless.

"Who?" Floria murmured to Lapaxo.

He replied, "Helenja."

The dowager consort, mother of the princess, and descendant of Odon the Breaker, a southern lord reviled in Darkborn history.

"Why?"

"Y'think she'd tell me?" Lapaxo said. And even lower, though not low enough to escape Balthasar's hearing, "You believe him, about Rupertis?"

So the captain of vigilants knows about the report, Balthasar thought. *Good.* The more who knew, the better.

"He hasn't been seen since, has he?"

They finished the walk in silence, passed by a wide double door, and were shown through—threaded through—a narrower side door into a suite of rooms even hotter than outside.

Helenja, dowager consort, was a heavyset woman with a broad, handsome face oddly enhanced by a once-broken nose. Perhaps among the southern clans, such an injury did not merit a healing. Perhaps it was even a mark of beauty or vigor. At her side was a lean man with a fine, crafty face and a caul marking him as one of the highest in the land. His clothing, though of Lightborn style, had panels of lace that Balthasar recognized as Darkborn work and that Telmaine would have priced to the penny. Balthasar suspected he could put a name to him: Prasav, Isidore's cousin and nearest rival. The young woman with him, whose resemblance suggested she might be kin, wore an expression of covert fascination, her face not quite turned toward him.

He swept sonn over the others, making himself pay attention to their positions, groupings, and alignments to try to distinguish advisers, attendants, and hangers-on. A few he recognized: Mistress Silver Branch, with her clerk, who was trying to make himself as small as possible. Balthasar hoped he had not endangered the man by making him record his testimony. The young mage who had tested him at the door, and—he realized this with a pang of visceral alarm—two of the group whom he had challenged on the streets.

Helenja waved them forward. "This is the one?" she said to them.

An unnerved silence. Then they tried to answer together. "Yes, Mistress Helenja." "But we—"

"'Yes' is sufficient." To Floria: "Why did you not bring him directly to me?"

"I was stopped at the door."

"Mmph," said the dowager, swinging across to stand in front of Balthasar, studying him up and down. "I admit, I expected something a little more impressive." Her head turned toward the door, then back to him, and she pointed to one side. "Over there."

He did as indicated. At a hand signal from Lapaxo, two of the vigilants joined him. Helenja did not object to them, but she stopped Floria as she made to accompany him. "I want you there."

On the opposite side of the room. Floria went, a threat in her expression.

Helenja returned to her place midway between them and waited. There were few chairs, which was in keeping with the Lightborn's aversion to showing infirmity. He should maybe have accepted Floria's offer of a stimulant, except he remembered too well the effect of her stimulants on the unaccustomed constitution. He hardened himself to endure.

Some minutes later, the double doors abruptly folded back. "The princess, Mistress Helenja, Master Prasav." Vigilants and mages filed in, followed by a tall young woman with an elaborately woven cap of hair who stopped three strides in and spun to face him with an expression of appalled revulsion.

"So," Helenja said, with a long sigh of satisfaction.

The newcomer controlled her face, though her throat worked involuntarily with nausea, and turned to face Helenja. "Your message said you needed to speak to me urgently."

"Princess," Helenja said, "I presume you have not yet had a copy of that extraordinary report prepared by Mistress Tempe's clerk. Meet Dr. Balthasar Hearne, Darkborn."

So this was the usurper princess. Floria had cast aspersions on her courage and honor, but Floria was a woman of slow-shifting loyalties, and one who preferred her world ordered, and all those in it predictable. The mage princess offended both loyalty and order, and no one could have predicted her ascent. To his sonn, the princess seemed far too young for her role, tired, nervous, and overburdened— another person rolled over and harried by events and others' wishes. He felt a great empathy for her.

She tried to recover her balance. "That's . . . not amusing, Helenja."

"No, it's not amusing at all that the Temple has lied to us."

"I don't know what you mean," she said on an exhale.

"Of course you do." Helenja's waving hand scattered hard echoes of metal and gems. "Fejelis claimed that lineage mages could not sense Shadowborn magic, but that sports could. For that, the Temple allowed his unrighteous deposition, because they could not afford to have us believe that they were unable to defend themselves or us against Shadowborn magic. You, however, are not a lineage mage. What do you sense about that man?"

"He cannot be Darkborn," the princess said, a little desperately.

"I have witnesses who found him walking the streets without lights," Helenja said. "Shall we try that?" she said to Balthasar. "Put him in a darkened room."

"If that is what you have to do," Balthasar said, "do it."

Helenja rewarded him with a smile. Floria's stance gave the impression of a cat about to pounce. "She"—Helenja gestured toward the young judiciary mage—"tested him at the door. She thought his mind had been broken by the horror of the tower's destruction. But you have another explanation, don't you?"

"Mistress Helenja, Mother, I can't—"

"You can't *what*?" The dowager's voice was a growl. "Two-thirds of the contracts held within this palace are contracts to protect us against hostile magic. If the Temple cannot protect us—as the attack on its own tower showed—then those contracts are invalid."

Balthasar drew a breath. "Princess," he said, "Mistress Helenja. Forgive me, but the integrity of your contracts is an internal matter between the Temple and you. I am here to prove the existence of the Shadowborn, and to assert Darkborn innocence in crimes you have held them responsible for."

Helenja's expression was one she would have turned on a potted plant that had rustled its leaves and spoken aloud.

"Princess," Balthasar pressed. "You may be the only person in this palace able to sense this ensorcellment, but you *can* sense it. Your reaction showed it."

"It was Floria—"

"You turned toward me, not Floria," he said gently. "My

ensorcellment is the more recent, and probably the stronger."

A shiver passed through her; her face changed. "Come with me," she said, in a voice deeper and more authoritative than before. He had taken a step forward before he recognized that there was magic behind it, magic working on him. In sudden panic, he struggled against it. From the far side of the room, Floria shouted, "Under whose contract do you use magic against us?"

The compulsion stopped. The princess said in her own voice, "The high masters will see you now. Please come with me."

"Take him," Prasav said swiftly. Helenja merely gave a sour smile at his preemptive gamesmanship. "We will speak again," she said to Balthasar, a statement that had the quality of a threat—though against whom, he could not tell. He forced himself to walk steadily forward and not even to turn his head toward Floria. Pride and honor precluded his taking her into danger with him. Then he found her at his side once more, her face showing something of his own panic and resentment at being overpowered so—when she shouted out, she had said "magic against *us*." He tried to take her hand, but she shook herself free with a frown and set her hand on the hilt of her rapier.

Three men and two women waited for them in an upstairs suite. The most remarkable of the men was a small, wiry man wearing nothing more than a loincloth and sandals. The less remarkable of the women was a plain, middle-aged woman in a featureless tunic that covered her to midshin.

He dipped a bow to the man in the loincloth, as though to the archduke himself, taking a bold guess at his identity. "Magister Archmage."

The high masters also regarded him as they might a speaking plant. There was no revulsion in their reaction, despite their far greater strength than that of the second-rank princess, further confirmation that they could not sense the Shadowborn ensorcellment. He felt a movement behind him, and Perrin passed by him, her face working, to stand between the archmage and Valetta. The archmage glanced aside at her, questioning; she gave a jerky nod. And then the nausea and the personality in her face simply drained out, and she stood silent, swaying slightly.

"Balthasar Hearne," Valetta said, "we wish to examine the magic that Magistra Viola—Princess Perrin—senses on you, through her. We will try to do you no harm, but we cannot promise that harm may not come to you."

"Magistra, this is what I came for, in expectation"—he stressed the word—"that my presence here, and the ensorcellment on me, would convince you that what the archduke said to you is true. I consent to your examination."

He had no sooner finished than a great, disorientating surge of magic rolled over him. He was aware of Floria first gripping his arm and then supporting him. <You did not tell us,> a voice said in his mind, <that you were mageborn.>

"I'm not," he gasped out. All he had ever had was the ability to sense concerted, powerful magic—like last night—and a diagnostic acumen that Olivede reckoned was due to a tenuous sense of the inner workings of the body that might, were it stronger, be magic. But otherwise, he could not even touch-read, could certainly not heal, and could anticipate no longer a life than any other earthborn. Conversely, he had been spared the stigma his sister lived under.

<For our law, what you are will be sufficient,> another voice intoned. <That will make this much easier.> Another wave of magic rolled over him and drowned his wits.

He came back to himself lying on a wide, comfortable bed of stretched netting. His sonn picked out a circular relief on the ceiling above him, a stylized sun whose rays extended to each distant corner. Many Lightborn rooms had such a device, and he remembered Floria telling him that it was a potent symbol even to those who did not associate it with any divinity. This one was as molded and detailed as any Darkborn ceiling decoration. He said, vaguely, "That would be painted gold, wouldn't it?"

Floria leaned over him, her expression anxious. "I'm all right," he said, and demonstrated so by sitting up. He didn't realize until he was upright that he had used his sprained wrist without pain, and that the bandage was gone from his other hand. He felt his face; the tenderness from the scoring was also gone; he could no longer feel the seams. And he did not ache. He felt astonishingly well.

They were not in a holding cell—his swift cast around the room showed a large, strangely furnished suite—but he would study his surroundings later. "What happened?" he said, urgently. "What did they say? What did they decide?"

"To me, nothing," she said, unhappily.

"I'm all right," he said again. "No more ill effects than a day of very disturbing dreams, and physically, very well. Did I pass out?"

"No," she said. "You stood, you walked, but you simply—like Perrin—seemed to disappear from inside yourself."

"Disturbing," he acknowledged for her; he would examine his own feelings later. "So you noticed a change in me, and then, even if they did not say anything, could you describe what happened? Were you also"—he could not, he found, say the word "ensorcelled," could not apply it the actions of those he hoped would be, needed to be, allies—"held as I was?"

"No," she said, frowning. "I was aware throughout. They were much more interested in you."

"They'd have had plenty of time to study your ensorcellment, if they'd wanted." He frowned in turn, a new thought occurring to him. "If the ensorcellment is still active, then it was not due to the Shadowborn Ishmael killed—Jonquil, they called him—or the one called Midora, who died in Stranhorne Manor." *Was that Sebastien, too? Or one of the others?* Was Floria's connection to his family the reason the Shadowborn had chosen her to carry the talisman to Isidore? A shudder of sheer rage went through him, unattenuated by the ensorcellment.

No, unattenuated by *any* ensorcellment.

"Balthasar?" she said, her tone wary, almost warning. She had advised him about keeping his composure. But how else should he react to these . . . atrocities now that he no longer needed to warp his own thoughts and emotions simply to survive?

He heard his voice, distorted by the intensity of his emotion. "They've annulled the ensorcellment on my will. They've left the ensorcellment protecting me against light, or they've assumed it—or I'd be dead by now."

He had to think. Why should they have lifted the ensorcellment? Why might they have assumed his protection? Was he their chance to practice with Shadowborn magic? Could they do so through the princess? Did that trace of magic in him mean that they cared about the ensorcellment on him? That they had healed him suggested it might. He wished he knew whether they had removed the ensorcellment on Floria. "Did you get any sense of what they might do now?" he asked her, desperate for *some* answer to any question.

She shook her head. "As I said, they exchanged not a word after you spoke."

But by the set of her shoulders, there was more. He was already learning to read her. "What is it, Floria? You said they mostly concentrated on me. What did they do to you?"

"Raised the memory of my ensorcellment," she said, rising to stand with her back to him.

He waited. "A lover?" he said, finding the question unexpectedly difficult to ask.

She turned, eyes narrowing.

"You are not the first," he said, turning his face a little to the side, so that he would not seem to be probing or challenging her. "It seems to have been the way they liked to turn people."

"*Curse him,*" he heard her whisper.

Hands upturned on his lap, he sighed. "We can but hope."

She sat down beside him on the bed, the slump on her shoulders betraying her weariness. He remembered this was night for her and that she would not have shown her vulnerability to anyone. "He was one of the men in the companion house. I've always been so careful, as my father insisted. . . ."

It seems a bleak approach to intimacy, he thought, as he

had thought before. The promiscuity did not trouble him as much as the lovelessness. "I'm sorry," he said.

She gave a twisted little smile. "Nothing to do with you, Bal. You always urged me to find a true partner—a husband, in your terms. You could be quite insufferable on the subject."

He supposed he had been, happy as he himself was then. "You deserve to be loved, Floria," he said, quietly. "No doubt you will tell me that my Darkborn prejudices are showing, but what was right for a man is not right for a woman. What was right for your father was not right for you."

She turned her head, a smile gentling that hard, beautiful face. "You've said that to me before."

This close, he could sonn the slight thickening and change in texture of her skin, and realized that her face was bruised badly. Her voice had sounded husky, which he had put down to strain. "You're hurt," he said, shocked that he had not realized.

She shrugged. "Met with a mob outside Bolingbroke Station on the way back from the palace. Did something stupid and needed to be fished out of the fountain."

He touched her face gently, but the pretense that it was a clinician's touch failed as soon as he felt the silken warmth of her skin. There was no wall between them now. Their weight on the mesh of the bed created a subtle, in-falling force. It took no effort for him to tilt sideways, to close the distance between his lips and hers; the effort would have been in resisting. Her lips were cool and firm at first, then softened as they parted. Her breath stroked against his lip, quickening with her breathing. Her hand caught the back of his neck hard, and her fingers spread in his hair.

Then that moment of abandonment passed, and he pulled back. She held him briefly, and then yielded, her hand sliding away. His sensitized skin remembered the track; his sensitized mouth, her lips.

"I'm sorry, Floria," he muttered, deeply ashamed of his behavior. "This is not right."

"You'll notice," she said after a moment, "that you are

not sitting on the floor, wondering what hit you. Which you would be if I objected."

He opened his mouth to say "I'm sorry" again, and closed it. Nine years of marriage had taught him that a wise man did not apologize for doing something a woman wanted, no matter how foolish or wrong that thing might be.

"It would have been strange," she said, "if we had met and this had not happened."

"I'm not myself," he said, inadequately. "Everything that has happened . . . Telmaine . . ." Remorse mingled with his grief now, that he had come so near to betraying both the women he cared most for. "It's too soon. Maybe . . ."

"Yes," she said, in a tone he could not interpret. "Telmaine. I had a conversation with her just before I left the palace. She told me it was very important that I tell you we had spoken."

"Thank you," he whispered. "But I'm not . . . sure I'm up to hearing her message at the moment."

"That *was* the message. When Telmaine returned to the palace and was taken prisoner, it was night. When she spoke to me, it was daylight. Why would her jailors let her speak to me? Why would they let her release me when they'd shown no sign of caring that I'd have been dead when my light failed? Balthasar, she's a mage—a strong mage. Unless she *wanted* to stay in that cell and die, it would not hold her." She paused. "All she said was that it was very important that I tell you she and I had spoken, not *what* I should tell you. I did not make the connection immediately myself, and then I waited to tell you because I needed you to hold together before the court." She waited, stoically, for his response, her face like a carved mask.

So stupidly simple a chain of reasoning. He had held most of the links himself—he *knew* what Ishmael had told him about Telmaine's strength as a mage, and he *knew* she would not submit tamely to death. He should have connected them, would have connected him, but for the abomination of the ensorcellment. In a raw whisper, he said, "Floria, even if you'd told me before, I *couldn't* have believed you."

A moment for understanding to come, and then she swore, softly.

He put a hand over his face, dislodging the spectacles. If his loss of composure disturbed her, he was going to shock her now. "Could you please . . . give me a few minutes to myself?"

He felt her rise, the netting release. She touched his cheek, her fingertips calloused, scratchy, and warm—except for the warmth, unlike Telmaine's. To his lowered head, she said, "I would lie with you, Balthasar, for the asking. All these years demand more than a kiss. I would never have made you my enemy by deceiving you on something that important. . . . But I'll leave you now."

Eight

Tammorn

<*Tammorn.*>
　　He had known this contact would come ever since he spoke to Lady Telmaine. Indeed, he had known it would come since he recovered enough to think clearly. Though he had not expected the archmage himself, there was no mistaking that immense strength. The archmage's replenishing touch across distance had the healing warmth of sunlight. Tam all but groaned in relief as his pain and leaden exhaustion dissipated. He sat up: one did not address the master of the Temple while supine in bed.

<*Why?*> He cut to the essence. <*Why release me?*>

<Why not? You told us no more than the truth. You are not our enemy ... and we need you to do something for us.>

<I won't leave Fejelis unguarded.> He put force of feeling, if not force of magic, into the statement. He showed the archmage a swift succession of impressions: waking to the reports of bullets, hearing talons scrape the metal roof overhead, sensing that vile aura, hearing Orlanjis cry out and Jovance shout, and then the painfully intense burst of matter manipulation. He was aware of the archduke's gratification at the last, but he could not have concealed Jovance's presence, even if he had tried. <The Darkborn are letting us ride one of their trains into Strumheller; we heard over the telegraph. Archmage, they are desperate for our help.>

He felt a moment's base relief that he could not conceal the information that Vladimer had known about Mycene's and Kalamay's plans, and done nothing to prevent it. He was glad not to be tempted.

<It is of no account,> Magistra Valetta said. Unlike the archmage, her magic stung like static sparks. <The earth-born have always hated us.> This close to her, he could tell that she returned their hatred in equal measure. <This is not the first atrocity they have committed, but we have determined it may be the last.>

<You can sense Shadowborn magic, and you are the strongest surviving mage who can,> the archmage said. <We want you to be our envoy to the Shadowborn.>

<To the *Shadowborn*?> he said in disbelief.

<They are mages, Tammorn,> Valetta said.

<They are *murderers*,> Tam said—and sensed Magistra Valetta's startlement at being so fiercely contradicted. <They—not the Darkborn, *they*—murdered *dozens* of us. They'd have murdered more, but for Lukfer sacrificing his life. How dare you darken his memory by pretending he lied about the Shadowborn?>

<The Darkborn were the ones who fired the cannon,> Magistra Valetta said. <We cannot know, until we speak to the Shadowborn, who was responsible by law.>

Were they really going to pretend that this had been done according to compact, to pretend that the Shadow-born had been working under the orders of the Darkborn and so were indemnified, even for *this*? <If you could have sensed what Lukfer and I sensed in the tower—>

<We did,> the archmage said. <Through you.>

<But Lukfer mastered that magic. Perhaps . . .> Valetta paused. <Perhaps it was his native form.>

He sensed the calculation in that thought, but even so, Lukfer had been born a sport, and his strength had been immense but dangerously uncontrolled. Ever since he had been received into the Temple's care as a young child, he had been the high masters' ward. He had used pain—mostly the pain of living in poor light—to bleed his energies in healing effort. Tam had assumed that he had achieved his final act of mastery because of his mortal injuries, but he remembered how even before, Lukfer had cast fire and effortlessly annulled an ensorcelled crossbow bolt that was killing Fejelis. If the high masters were right, there could be no crueler irony—

<If this magic is peculiar to sports, you have the potential for the same mastery. We know he *gifted* you at the last.>

He had had neither the time nor the heart to examine that gift yet. It was the gift of the master to his or her favored student—a distillation of the master's essential knowledge of magic, imparted magically as a nucleus of insight and memory. It was a precious, perilous gift. Given too soon, it could overwhelm the student and distort his maturation. Given maliciously, as the Shadowborn had done to Lady Telmaine, it could induce possession. She should be grateful for Ishmael di Studier's steady hand.

But given at the right time, the *gift* could accelerate a mage's realization of his full capacities. And that, he knew, was what Lukfer would have wished for him.

<You *know* how strong you are, Tammorn. We have felt how strong you are.>

<No!>

<Would you waste his *gift*, Tammorn?>

That was rich of her. The high masters would have burned out his magic, Lukfer's precious gift or no, for the impertinence of exposing their weaknesses.

<That was merely theater.>

What he had sensed, facedown on the floor within the circle of high masters, was not theater. He told them so.

<Tammorn, you broke the compact. And, yes, we remember all the justifications you offered, but you broke the compact. You intervened when Fejelis was poisoned, although you were not contracted to the palace—>

<Fejelis was *dying*. The contracted mages might not have reached him in time.> He had never said he was sorry and he never would, though they had bound his magic for five years after and seemed set on holding it against him indefinitely.

<You sheltered and encouraged artisans working to import Darkborn technologies—>

<Their work has nothing to do with magic! The compact—>

<*Enough,*> said the archmage. <Tammorn, you will do this thing, whether of your own free will or not. It is our best chance of a peaceful resolution.>

<*Peaceful*—with that?> He threw his impressions at them, of that swirl of violence outside the hut, of the corrupted vitality and magic of the Shadowborn.

<The compact reached seven hundred years ago has run its course,> the archmage said. Centuries whispered behind his voice. <We have damaged the earthborn; we freely acknowledge it, and they in turn have damaged us. It is time for us to seek the society of our own kind. We can offer them wealth and knowledge, and they can offer us land.>

<You'd have us move to the Shadowlands?>

<There are older, better names for it; it is time those were brought back into use. It seems a reasonable solution, does it not?>

Not for me, Tam thought. His heart and causes were here, with Beatrice and the children, with Fejelis, with the artisans, with the immigrants from the provinces who trod the road he had trodden a quarter century ago. <What of the people who depend on light?>

<We will make sure they have enough,> the archmage said. <It would be immoral to do otherwise. Perhaps the Darkborn might run one of their Borders trains into the Shadowlands. Or we could build one ourselves. Powering it would be simple enough.>

He was going to laugh or scream curses at them, both equally futile. <I *will not do it.*>

He could feel the weight of Valetta's magic, Valetta's will, readying to bear down on him. Others stood behind her. <You have no choice,> the archmage said, no gentleness in that ancient voice. <We must do what we must to survive.>

<*They*—>

<*Shhh.*>

<We will make sure your prince is safe,> the archmage

said into his stilled mind. <I promise. He makes me think ...>
of a striding man sweeping across a wide, tiled floor and
turning to gesture, every long line of him radiating vitality.
A chieftain or prince of an age remembered only by the
high masters.

But remembered, Tam thought, *as I would have remembered Fejelis a hundred years after his death.*

<He would have caused us great trouble in the ordinary
way of things, but he is what they will need; we will leave
him as our gift to them.>

<It is *night* out there,> he said, a last, desperate objec-
tion. <If I take light with me into their camp, and they are
Darkborn by lineage, they'll die. If I don't take light with
me, *I* will die.>

<Not necessarily so.> He sensed deep satisfaction. <The
Darkborn have given us the means.>

Ishmael

"You might as well wake up," a man's voice said. "I know
you're faking; I'd do the same in your place."

He might have taken the voice for Balthasar Hearne's,
except that it was crisper and more forceful in delivery, and
slightly deeper in timbre. Without moving, Ishmael said,
"Lysander Hearne, is it?"

He rolled over on the sheets, propped himself up on his
elbow, and sonned the speaker. He perched on a stool well out
of lunging reach, one foot hooked on the crossbar, revolver
resting on his knees. The man's resemblance to Balthasar
Hearne was notable, though he was sinewy rather than slight,
and casually dressed in clothes that would let him move freely.
There was about him no taint of Shadowborn, only the air of
a man who lived hard and wary and on the edge of the law.

"So you've met my weakling brother," the man noted.

"'Twas your weakling brother set your plans in disarray."

Lysander Hearne snorted. "And which particular plans
are those?"

Ishmael, reclining, spread his free hand. "Th'ones upset
by the birth of Shadowborn-got sons to Tercelle Amberley."

Muscles tensed in Lysander Hearne's face, enough to be noticeable, not quite enough to constitute an expression. "It so happens," he said, levelly, "those weren't *our* plans." He paused. "You're very calm. Case you don't recall, you were dead as mutton back there."

As an effort to disconcert him, that missed its mark entirely, because he had just realized something far more disconcerting. Carefully, he turned his magic on himself, eased vitality from his bones to his tissues . . . and felt nothing. There was no breathtaking pain, no faltering heart, no sense of his life draining uncontrollably into his magic. He caught a breath, shaken with equal measures joy and fear. Not even Magister Broome had been able to undo the damage done to him. Now he had the measure of the mage who held him prisoner.

And something else was gone, as though it had never existed: the Call.

So he was where the Call wanted him. Nowhere he recognized, in a bedroom easily as large as the baronial suite in Strumheller, furnished with pieces whose style and materials he had met only in museums. There was not a join or a seam in them, not in the curving headboard, the rounded edges of the dressing table, or the bowed front of the wardrobe. *More to the point,* he thought, *none of them can be easily moved.* This was no traveling camp.

But the bite of the arid air on his throat had already told him he was no longer in the Borders.

He tossed the covers back, swung his legs over the edge of the bed onto solid floor, and stood. "Now what?"

Hearne jerked a thumb over his shoulder. "There's the wardrobe. Our lady wants you."

"Your lady?"

"Lysander's and mine," said a woman's voice from beyond the end of the bed. A long step carried him sideways, away from her, and his pivot placed both of them in front of him.

She came forward with no apparent embarrassment at his nakedness, a lovely, foul-tainted creature in a dress faithfully Darkborn. The gown covered her from high collar to cuffs to ankles in layers of silk and lace, and if he recalled his sister's digressions on fashion, she was at least a decade outdated. In the Darkborn manner of a mage, she wore gloves. Her face had a sculpted refinement, with full lips, a narrow, straight nose, wide brows, and distinct cheekbones. A face such as he had sonned on celebrated actresses and lords' mistresses, who were often one and the same.

"M'lady," Ishmael said, dipping his head.

"Charming," she said, "but insincere, Ishmael di Studier." Arms folded, head tilted, she added, "Given that you greeted me by firing point-blank at me."

He set his jaw, trying to hold his composure at the aura of magic around her. Its mere strength would have set his head spinning, even without the Shadowborn aura of it.

"I'd thank you for saving my life," he said at last, "if I thought I'd like what you mean me for."

"Ah, well, Ishmael. That's not for me to explain."

"And your name is, m'lady, since you make so free with mine?"

"Call me Ariadne." She turned her head toward Lysander Hearne. "Sander, if you would?"

Lysander frowned, but pushed himself off his stool and went to the wardrobe, producing from its depths an evening suit in the Darkborn style, more formal than Ishmael would have chosen for himself. "Put it on. Or we'll do it for you."

"Need t'relieve myself," he said, accepting it from Lysander's hand, and turned his back on them to walk, with studied steadiness, into the bathroom. As he expected, there was no way out, and no weapon more threatening than hard soap and a back brush. He'd go before their lady as stubbled as a vagrant.

He managed the suit, though not nearly as well as his manservant would have. It was tight across the shoulders, but otherwise a passable fit. He gave the cravat his best shot and then let it lie, returning to present himself for their inspection. Lysander Hearne passed him socks and shoes, and he sat down on the bed to pull them on.

"Are you hungry?" she said, the social hostess.

Not with that magic around him. "I'd sooner get m'fate settled, if you'd be so kind."

Lysander gave an odd smile. "Oh, she is that."

With Lysander at Ishmael's elbow and Ariadne at Lysander's, Ishmael left the room, finding himself in a corridor as wide and fine as any in the archducal palace. Except for one feature: windows with shutters turned back. He tried not to be disconcerted by the gusts of warm wind, and wrestled briefly with the urge to ask what time of night—or day—it might be, but pride precluded that. Lysander Hearne wasn't alone in his posturing. Otherwise, Shadowborn stronghold or no, it had the feel of any large household. Of all the perils he had associated with capture by the Shadowborn, being run over by a dashing housemaid with a stack of fresh-laundered towels was not among them.

Ariadne's magic thrust open a door, and they herded him into a wide receiving room. Lysander said, "Ishmael di Studier, my lady."

His sonn caught movement at the far end of the room. A harsher stroke outlined the woman standing on a raised dais. Her simple dress, a knee-length tunic and trousers suitable for this warmth, was far more revealing to sonn than a Darkborn woman's. His first absurd reaction was chagrin at the impropriety. He halted.

Lysander Hearne tapped his elbow. "Go on."

"No need." The woman forestalled his response. "Thank you, Lysander, Ariadne. Please go now."

Lysander bowed and withdrew, as quietly as Ishmael himself might have. Ishmael heard a sandal brush tile and sonned the woman as she stepped down from the dais. She was small, her figure described by the straight lines of childhood or age. Her hair was short and untidy, a jumble of crisp curls; her mouth was generous and her nose, almost snubbed, no balance for it; her cheekbones were flat and indeterminate. An ordinary face with a winning smile. If it were her true face, any more than her apparent age were her true age.

"Ishmael di Studier," she said, pleasantly. "I've wanted to meet you for a very long time."

He had no sense of great strength about her, but that very absence was suggestive. He set his stance, hands relaxed and open at his side. "You'll pardon me if I say I've had no like wish."

"Apparently not," she said. "I've seldom known anyone to hold out against Ariadne's Call so long."

"Then that'll give you the measure of my will t'cooperate, if it's cooperation y'want, or submit, if it's submission y'want." For all the good it might do him.

"Come here and sit down," she said, "and we'll talk."

A quarter century of rough work had taught him to conserve his strength. He followed her out onto an open balcony, dense with plants in pots and planters, and took the chair she indicated.

"Have my people seen to you?" she said.

"Aye, as much as I'd allow," he acknowledged.

A feathery eyebrow lifted, but she did not inquire. They sat in silence, each waiting out the other.

"What is it y'want with me?" he said at last. "You've gone to some trouble, it seems, to get me."

"What do you think I want you for?" she said, temporizing.

Ishmael shrugged. "We've always thought th'ones who followed th'Call wound up in something's larder or someone's belly." She frowned, but did not contradict him. "It comes t'me now, meeting Hearne there, that you've another use for Darkborn. But I'll not serve you willingly, whatever it is you want of me."

"And who do you think I am?" she said.

He tapped his abdomen with a lightly closed hand, conveying part of his answer: a mage, and one powerful enough to pull him back from a death he thought assured. "I fought you for twenty-five years. I thought t'die fighting you."

"You would have. Does that not tell you something?"

"It's hardly worth you making a point of raising me only t'break me. My people will regret my fate, but nothing you do t'me will weaken them. And if you send me back to them ensorcelled, they'll know."

"Ishmael," she said, gently, "you fear all the wrong things

of me." There was something in her voice that chilled him — not merely that she deflected, but did not deny he had reason to fear. "My name, which you are too stubborn to ask for, is Isolde." She paused, waiting for recognition. Then with slight resignation, said, "My mother was Imogene."

As the name of the mage attached to the Curse, the supposed leader of those who had worked the great Sundering of peoples, it had not been used on either side of sunrise for eight hundred years.

"Think it through, Ishmael," she invited.

All he could think of was that Xavier Stranhorne had been right.

Yet he could hear Vladimer asking why, if the Shadowborn had such might, would they hide in the Shadowlands all these years. Why only now move against the north, and in such an oblique, chaotic way?

"I'm the younger sister. The one who did not make it into the history books."

"Aye, well, it's not usual that the living do," Ish said, still suspended between belief and disbelief. "And the Shadowborn. What are they t'you? Are they your making?"

"*No.*"

"But th'Call. That was your handmaiden's. As I said, if th'Call's how you bring people t'serve you, I'm not minded to." Futile bravado; ensorcellment could make him serve, willing or no. He drew a deep breath and steadied his tone. "Explain t'me what you want, if y'would."

There was a silence. His sonn caught the small smile curling the corners of her mouth. His mother had smiled so when he pleased her. She had been a sensitive, sophisticated woman who had no patience with childishness.

That, too, she could no doubt pluck out of his mind, if so inclined.

"What do you already know about the Sundering, Ishmael?"

"I'm no scholar," he said. "A scholar I know" — no need to tell them that Xavier Stranhorne was dead, if they did not already know — "says th'final break had something t'do with geography or perhaps weather. But I've th'experience t'know it was probably nothing of th'sort at root. Factions, ambitions, rivalries; whether it's dukes or dockside gangs or market stallholders or mages, it's the same."

"Not *quite*, Ishmael."

"I'll have t'take your word for it. How long have I been here?"

"Less than a day, Ishmael. Be still." He was not aware of having moved, but inside, yes, he had reared up at the realization that time had passed without him. "They took Stranhorne Manor, but moved no farther yet."

"Not allies of yours?"

"Definitely not allies of ours."

"Do y'mean t'oppose them, or do y'mean just to stand by?"

"That," she said, "may depend on you."

"And how's that?" he fired back before he could think better of it.

She straightened up. "I'm afraid you will have to put up with some history. At the time of the Sundering," she said, in a voice that was clear and somehow younger, "I was a child of eight. Imogene and her followers knew that laying the Curse would burn them out, if not kill them. Yet for the Curse to survive them, it had to be anchored in vitality and magic. For the anchoring in magic, they chose nine of their children—younger brothers and sisters, children and grandchildren."

He could imagine what Phoebe Broome would have said to that. The Broomes were fiercely principled in their use of magic. "Y'make the distinction between vitality and magic," he said. It had been deliberate enough to catch his ear, whether she meant it to or not. "And th'vitality?"

"In everyone born into it. Could you imagine it being done any other way?"

If he considered only the execution, he could not. A mage, even a low-ranked mage such as he himself had been—was—could draw on another's vitality as well as his own, whether mage or nonmage. There was a cost; he was always laid up for days if he pushed himself into overreach. The Broomes' commune's code of contact prohibited them from doing so except when it made the difference between life and death, and all involved had given full, knowledgeable consent. The Lightborn Temple did not even allow that between mageborn and earthborn, although he had heard rumors of the practice behind mages. But a work of magic that drew on the vitality of all those living and yet to be born, with magic that was anchored in children . . . "And th'purpose of it." Ishmael growled. "Th'Curse."

"Revenge," the woman said, sounding slightly surprised. "Imogene's revenge upon everyone who failed her, betrayed her, let her daughter die."

"And was th'Curse meant to turn out this way?"

"Why do you ask that?"

"Because it makes cursed"—he caught himself too late to avoid the idiom—"little sense. Why, if they'd t'doom themselves in the setting of the Curse, not simply kill and be done with it?"

"You don't understand revenge, do you, Ishmael?"

His thoughts glanced off memories: his father's bitter words, sending him on his road; his words to his father, demanding his inheritance; his thoughts after Athelane had rescued him from the glazen and died in doing so; his realization that half a dozen men of his own barony had set out to murder him on his return for his father's laying out . . . a dozen other experiences to sear a man's heart and rouse his anger.

But he realized she was right. Anger he understood, not revenge. He'd always made sure of a merciful final shot, no matter how monstrous the enemy, and no matter the terms of his hire or mood of the mob. It was safer, but that had not been the entire reason. Killing didn't turn his stomach; torment did.

And surely the object of the Curse had been torment, to leave those who survived the first sunrise, the first sunset, living in dread of the next and the next and the next. He smiled grimly. He had no idea how many Darkborn had survived that first sunrise, or how many Lightborn that first sunset, but they and their descendants had lived to build twin civilizations on either side of sunrise.

He was a son of that civilization, and he was done with being toyed with like a mouse trapped by an overfed lap cat.' What did it matter what Imogene's intent had been, or how she justified herself? She was eight hundred years gone. "I don't care about the history. What matters is now."

She rocked back ever so slightly at the change in his voice.

"If y'won't come to the point as to what y'want of me, then I'll tell you what I want of you: I want the Shadowborn—th'ones who have overrun Stranhorne, and all their ilk—turned back. I don't care if they live or die, as long as I never hear of them—claw, bristle, fang, wing, or Call itself—whether in the Borders, th'offshore waters, th'Isles, or the land itself, from this day onward. Do you have the strength and the will t'do that?"

"With your help," she said, and he thought he might hear a little caution entering for the first time.

He barked a laugh. "I'm a burnt-out, first-rank mage."

"But I'm not," she said, softly. The softness chilled him. "I'm not the mage Imogene was, and I'm not the mage my sister was. But with one exception, I may be the strongest living mage."

"Th'exception being your enemy, the Mother of Shadowborn."

"Mother of Shadowborn . . . no, you cannot blame her for them. But never mind. Emeya was a couple of years older than me. . . . Well, I don't suppose you would care what else she was. Her mind did not survive the Sundering. We were able, while more of us lived, to contain her. Now there is only me."

"And what killed the rest of you?"

"Time. Despair." Her narrow shoulders shifted. "If I were not Imogene's daughter, I would have succumbed centuries ago."

"What is it y'want from me?"

"I have borne nine children and outlived them all. They in turn fathered or bore children, none of whom survived."

"Survived Emeya and th'others?"

"Until Ariadne came to me, I had no other mage even

approaching my strength. I could not risk myself, because without me, there would be no one to stop her."

"Ariadne . . . came over?"

"She's Emeya's granddaughter. It was Emeya's great-grandson, Jonquil, you killed—though how you achieved that, I do not know. But it gave me even more hope of you."

"T'do what?"

"With Jonquil and Midora dead, she has only two mages as strong as Ariadne."

He waited.

"I need you as an ally," she said, simply. "You are a mage, experienced in fighting Emeya's monsters, and with abundant vitality. There is no one else quite like you."

"I'm first rank."

"Ariadne and I can augment your strength, Ishmael."

"That's not possible."

"Am *I* possible?" she said, distinctly amused. "Is the fact that you are able once more to use your magic possible? They told you it was not, didn't they? I can augment your strength."

He found himself standing, driven there by the urge to run from the greatest lure she could possibly cast before him.

She spoke as though she had not noticed his reaction, as though he were still sitting in the chair. "You're not much use to me as a first-ranker, that's very true. But I can augment your strength." She moved her hand; he sensed the first flicker of magic—Shadowborn magic—he had received from her. Out in the corridor, a bell chimed. "I'll have Lysander take you to get something to eat while you think about what I've said."

Floria

Voices woke Floria, voices from the sitting room outside. She rolled to her feet with revolver drawn and sighted through the open door of the bedroom, even as she recognized them.

Lapaxo sat at ease on a high-backed chair to one side,

wall at his back. Balthasar, on the couch, faced the outer door: that much of her instructions he had heeded. The corner of the low glass table was between him and the captain. Bal twisted to face her, and the shift in his expression made her aware that she was untucked and mussed, with her hair unraveling down her shoulders.

"Floria," he said. "It's all right. The captain had some questions for me."

"I told you to wake me if anyone came to the door." She had left him alone, as he asked, though she resolved she would find a way to tell him she did not despise him for the intensity of his emotion. So when he came back out into the sitting room, pale but in control of himself, she had honored his offer to take watch while she slept.

But she had *told* him to wake her.

"I would have, shortly."

"*Shortly* could have been too late," she said. The captain seemed entertained, which did nothing to reassure her; Lapaxo was the most serious man she knew. But she put up the revolver. Had Lapaxo meant harm, he would have acted as soon as he heard her stir. She could afford the two or three minutes it would take for her to tidy herself.

She listened through the door as Balthasar continued to describe how the Shadowborn had killed Rupertis, in detail that was brutally clinical even by a vigilant's measure. Not something she would have expected of Bal—though she would not have expected him to open the door, either, with her safety depending on it. She had to remember that Balthasar had his own purpose here.

As she returned, Lapaxo was saying, "We know Johannes. He was cousin to the servant we lost with Isidore, and to two or three others who work in the palace. He drinks their lager and talks revolution to anyone who'll listen, and Parhelion took him for a blowhard. But if he knew Rupertis, then that's my first choice for how Prasav knew that Fejelis had ties to the artisans. We'd had Isidore's orders to keep it close, just to those of us assigned to Fejelis." He pounded his thigh with a fist, his mouth grim. "If I'd had the least suspicion Rupertis was suborned, I'd never have left him in charge." He shook his head. "That mage, he's the one your father found, isn't he?"

"Yes." Tam had arrived in the city destitute, unaware that what had blighted his fortunes for a dozen years or more was poorly emerged magic. He might have struggled on for a dozen more years—if someone had not cut his throat first . . . had he not crossed paths with Darien White Hand.

"Darien thought it was hilarious that he'd see what a city full of mages could not. . . . You know where he'd go, that mage, when he took Fejelis? I heard you told Helonja west, over the border and into the mountains."

"Last place he'd go."

"You haven't switched sides?" the vigilant captain asked, bluntly.

He was entitled to the question, though it angered her to have him, too, question her loyalty. "I was Isidore's vigilant. His last orders to me were to look out for Fejelis."

He gazed at her; she returned the gaze levelly. A one-sided smile curled his lip. "I'll tell you now that my heart nearly stopped when Fejelis insisted on interviewing you alone. I'd have placed even odds you'd have put a knife in his heart."

"And five minutes later, I'd have been dead, and Fejelis already healed." If Fejelis had been responsible for Isidore's assassination, she would have set out to depose him, yes, but she would not have been stupid about it. "Fejelis did not succeed by unrighteous deposition; therefore he is the rightful and righteous prince, and I will do what I must to see him restored."

"And the Darkborn?"

She glanced at the listening Balthasar. "An old friend."

"Vigilants don't have old friends," Lapaxo said, citing a well-worn maxim.

"Vigilants don't have lovers, either," she returned, pointedly. Lapaxo had lived with the same woman for more than twenty years.

He signaled a touch over his heart.

She wondered why he had come. At forty-five, he was old for an active vigilant, and unlike her, had no long family tradition of service behind him. Twelve years ago, he had

been a captain in the city watch, and even now he thought
like a watchman, paying far more attention than most vigilants to the city outside the palace walls.

"Lapaxo, why are you here?"

Lapaxo turned to look at Balthasar, and Floria's hand
shifted to her revolver as he slipped a hand into his waist
pouch and drew out a printed sheet of paper. "Two dozen
copies of this came in with the mail bag with the reports
from the Darkborn public agents. Every other mail slot ac-
cessible to the night has them pushed through it, and I don't
doubt that there have been hundreds more distributed
overnight out in the city."

The sheet was printed in solid black type on thin white
paper, Lightborn make—Darkborn paper tended to take
ink poorly—but unmistakably Darkborn in content. Type-
setting could be done by touch as easily as by eye. In plain
language, it laid the responsibility for the burning of the
Rivermarch, the murder of the prince, and the destruction
of the tower on the Shadowborn, who had influenced people on both sides of sunrise to work for them. It accused the
Temple of failing in its contracted duty to protect the earthborn, and their brightnesses of exploiting the disaster to
demand that the Darkborn cede their rights to the city. It
asked for the readers' support in resisting this injustice.

She read it aloud for Balthasar, slowly, so that Lapaxo
could appreciate how he flushed with anger and then paled
as he listened. Bal took it from her hand and ran his fingers
over the featureless surface. "So that was what he meant."

"Who?" Floria and Lapaxo said together.

"The archduke spoke of other measures. What he meant,
he would not say in front of me. But we know how restive
some of your people are against their brightnesses and
against the Temple. This aims to redirect their anger away
from the Darkborn, toward older grudges—"

She remembered the mob she had confronted outside
Bolingbroke Station and imagined them battering at the
gates of the palace itself, howling for the blood of their
brightnesses.

"They've forced his back to the wall," Lapaxo said, appreciatively, though whether his appreciation was directed at the Lightborn strategy or the Darkborn response, she could not tell. "This could be very effective. The spark's already been set to the tinder—we saw that yesterday. This will throw oil on it. Who will burn? We'll know after sunrise. Tell me, Hearne—and know that I can have it confirmed— were *you* sent as an agitator?"

"No," Balthasar said, forcefully. "I knew nothing of this, and if I had, I'd have wanted nothing to do with it. And I will so declare before Mistress Tempe, or anyone else you want."

She waited, ready to counter Lapaxo's first threatening move, and aware that he was aware of her readiness. But all Lapaxo did was sigh. "You'd better get him out of here," he told her. "He's a dead man otherwise."

"I am not going anywhere," Balthasar said.

Perceptive as he was, he had missed the meaning of Lapaxo's sigh. Balthasar himself was spark to the oil, living proof of the existence of Shadowborn. The more widely he spread belief in himself, the more widely he spread belief in the assertions in these papers. That he had persuaded Lapaxo of his innocence had done no more than make Lapaxo regret the inevitability of his death. Their brightnesses would not leave him alive to lend support to this.

Her eyes shifted to the back of his dark head. One blow would be enough, but, stunned, he would not be able to travel by himself, and she could not carry him out until sunrise. Though Lapaxo might help.

Then Bal's head came round, and she thought for an instant that he had somehow deduced her thought, but his attention moved beyond her to the door, his head angled, listening. She heard nothing—but he was Darkborn. She raised her hand to stop him from speaking and signaled to Lapaxo. The captain slid from his chair, moving to the door. She pulled Balthasar up, meaning to get him into the bedroom. Behind a wall, he'd be shielded—

She heard the lock turn. As the door burst open, she kicked Balthasar's feet from underneath him and dropped him into the shelter of the table, snagging the collar of his thick jacket to soften his descent. That consideration earned her a knife in the side and the sting of a second across her neck. Two more knives clattered off the table. She jerked the knife out of her side—a small throwing knife, not dangerous outside eye or throat—even as the mandala on the skin of her abdomen started to burn. Lapaxo flowed around the door with a sweetly economical slash that opened the nearest woman's body from rib to hip. A third pair of knives fell from her hands.

"Poison!" Floria grunted, half doubled over. If the poison was giving the asset this much trouble, Lapaxo or Bal could die of a scratch. Lapaxo shied from a blade, and two more assassins forced their way through the door. They wore light armor and were armed with rapiers. *"Bal, stay down!"* she barked, and leaped to straddle the arms of the chair, brazenly exposed—a flamboyant idiocy her father would have whipped her for, but one that kept their attention on *her*. A knife lodged in the muscle of her shoulder; a second, aiming to split her throat, hissed past her ear. She shot the man who had thrown them above the right eye. With a ceding parry and bind, Lapaxo slipped his blade neatly through the seam of the nearest man's armor. The downed woman twisted violently with a flash of bluish intestine, and lashed out. Floria's shout of warning came too late. As Lapaxo sprang clear, Floria shot the last assassin, and jumped down from the chair to land beside the table, revolver swinging from the fallen to the door and back. Her hands were slippery with cold sweat.

Behind her she heard a scrape and a scuttle, and movement caught the corner of her eye—Balthasar dropping to his knees before Lapaxo, who had backed to brace himself against the wall with one hand, rapier still raised, eyes still on the door. The fabric covering his right shin was bloody. Balthasar slashed a strip from his own jacket—Sweet Imogene, with one of those cursed poisoned knives!—and flipped the strip around the captain's leg below the knee, cinching it tight. "I need water," he said over his shoulder, to Floria. "Something to wash the wound. And a clean knife."

"Identify them," rasped Lapaxo.

There was only one identification she cared about: who was still a threat. Her eyes flicked over the assassins, taking in their attire: that of ordinary palace staff, complete to the red morning jackets, stained a much darker red with blood. Two of the four were dead, or indistinguishable from it. The woman was lying curled up around her spilled intestine. The fourth was sprawled on his back, gargling and trying spasmodically to roll over. The corridor outside was empty for now. She wondered what had become of the guards outside; nothing good, she expected. She flicked away all the knives she could see, and then risked leaning over the assassins to frisk them and strip them of other weapons. There were no apparent firearms, but the rearmost was carrying a rolled-up black tarpaulin. A quiet assassination, then—Balthasar with poison, Floria with poison assisted by steel, and her body, at least, quickly disposed of.

She whirled as Balthasar lunged for the table. Oblivious to her reaction, he caught up the carafe and a glass and smashed the glass and used the broken stem to open the poisoned cut, raising new blood. Lapaxo's face was gray and he was breathing heavily, but he was still standing, back flat against the wall. Balthasar, his fingers on the pulse at his groin, said, urgently, "Floria, I need some digitalis, some stimulant—"

"I've nothing with me." She would have, she *should* have, if she hadn't been knocked from crisis to crisis.

"Then *get me some*," Balthasar said, lurching out of his crouch to catch the captain as he began to slide down the wall. The rapier fell with a clatter. "*That* or a mage."

Arguing the matter was pointless if Bal couldn't see that moving them from a defensible position could kill all three of them more surely than lack of help would kill Lapaxo.

The sound of running footsteps from outside sent her back behind the table. She'd have grabbed Balthasar if she'd thought he would come, but—"Quiet!" she barked at him, and in a burst of adrenaline-fired strength, heaved the glass table on its side. It made an inadequate shield, but its crash was enough to command the attention of the new arrivals.

Who were half a dozen vigilants wearing judiciary

badges, with Tempe Silver Branch at their back. The lieutenant in charge swiftly assessed her and the casualties, and then directed two of his men to clear the way for Tempe and the young mage who had questioned Balthasar. Tempe walked, seemingly unaware, across the tacky floor, while the mage followed her with mincing step, her face working in horror and revulsion. Adamantly, Floria pointed to Lapaxo. Tempe said to the mage, "Him first," and the mage went. Balthasar ceded his place with profound relief, whispering urgently to her.

A ferocious cramp bent Floria over. Hands braced on knees, she grunted out an assurance that she'd be fine. Tempe scowled; she hated it when appearances contradicted the truth told her. "You're bleeding."

"Scratches," Floria rasped. Tempe took her arm, examining the wound, and unstuck the side of her tunic to check the other, carefully avoiding the blood. "*Bitch* of a poison." If it had come to her against the assassins, she'd have been fatally off form, even if no poison could kill her outright. She freed a hand to knead her abdomen, willing everyone to go away and leave her to her misery. Maybe she could deflect their attention. "You'd better get the mage on to them soon if you want answers."

"Helenja or Prasav? Take your pick. The two who were posted to guard you are dead." She put a hand on Floria's shoulder, knee behind her knee, and pushed her down onto the mesh couch. "We've been having an interesting night, while you two were snug in here." Her suggestive tone earned her a sour look, which she met with a quizzical expression. "Been two letters for him, heavily ciphered—and, yes, I know they've not been delivered. We want to know what's in them. Also leaflets"—she nudged the paper on the ground with a toe—"pushed through every available mail slot and newspaper drop in the civil-service sector and servants' quarters. Variety of texts, all the same theme—the Shadowborn are your enemy, we're not, their brightnesses and the Temple are obstructing our alliance. You can say this for the Darkborn: they're thorough. I'd venture to say this wasn't all thought up in a night; someone had it planned ahead of time."

"Lord Vladimer," Balthasar said, from beside Lapaxo. Lapaxo's eyes were closed, but his skin had already warmed several tones from death gray. Then Balthasar noticed Floria's hunched posture and came quickly to his feet. "Floria!"

"I'm *all right*!" she said, sharply. "The asset protects me." If he couldn't read her eyes, she willed him to read her expression: *Watch what you say.* Both for her sake and his.

He started around to the rear of the couch, but was intercepted by Tempe's outstretched arm. "You don't want to get behind a vigilant just coming off a fight." She looked him up and down. "Vladimer? Word came to us that he had lost it mentally."

Floria, craning her neck, saw him realize that he had spoken too freely, particularly to a woman with an asset of veracity. He said, "Lord Vladimer would have thought about the implications of tension between Darkborn and Lightborn before. He received the council's reports, and it is his job to assess and deal with threats to his brother's rule."

"I've read some of your council's writings. This isn't without precedent."

"We—the council—write leaflets when we feel we need to inform, not to agitate," Balthasar said, adamantly. "Floria, won't you let me—"

"There'll be poison mixed in with the blood," Floria said, straightening up. "No point having you poison yourself now."

The mage drifted over to them, leaving Lapaxo with two of the vigilants. Tempe glanced toward the door. "If you would see to the survivors, Magistra."

"I cannot, Mistress Tempe," she said, stiffly. "They attempted to harm a mage."

"A mage—," said Floria, baffled. Tempe said to Balthasar, "*Are* you?"

"Not by any useful measure," he said, quick mind visibly working. "I can sense anything on the scale of weather-working, but nothing smaller. I never thought it amounted to anything."

"It doesn't, ordinarily. Well, well, well. So now you're under *Temple* law." Tempe looked at the mage, a glitter in her eye. "Magistra, does this man look harmed to you?"

"No," the mage said, warily. Floria had heard that same tone in a junior vigilant greeting a veteran's invitation to play a friendly dice game or practice a no-fail fighting move.

"Exactly. The vigilants are the ones who are poisoned and bloody, while he hasn't a hair out of place." Not strictly true, but any further bruises and sprains were strictly Floria's doing. "How do you know their intent was to harm him?"

The mage opened her mouth. Closed her mouth. Said finally, "You want to know," and turned and picked her way across the tacky floor to the fallen.

"She'll go far," Tempe predicted. She glanced toward Lapaxo, who was being lifted to his feet by two of the vigilants. "Good not to lose another captain tonight. Nice work with the tourniquet."

"Yes," Floria said, obscurely resentful that she had not been allowed to say it first. "It was."

Tempe drummed her fingers on her knee. "So, did whoever ordered this do it before or after the Temple had laid claim?"

"I don't understand," said Balthasar, perching on the edge of the upturned table, his worried attention more on Floria than Tempe. She was irritated; she had survived much worse, and she needed him not to assume Tempe was an ally.

"Several possibilities. The Temple wants you completely under their control. Ordinarily, they don't bother themselves with less than first-rank mages, but you are unique."

Floria had a sudden, uneasy feeling that she did not want to hear the rest, not with a mage likely to lay a healing hand on her in the next few minutes.

"The compact prohibits mages from using magic to either benefit or harm earthborn, except under a negotiated public contract and at the request of an earthborn. You understand?"

"Yes." By the tight tendons in Balthasar's neck, he did not like the way this was going, either.

"The compact does not apply to *mages,* although there is governance on the use of magic by stronger against weaker mages."

Governance, Floria thought. *That depends upon strength.* She suddenly discovered an unwelcome sympathy for the princess, a mere second-rank mage in possession of knowledge that her superiors were determined to deny. Little wonder she seemed hardly more than a puppet.

The mage approached somewhat warily. "Two of my colleagues have arrived," she said, primly. "They're seeing to the prisoners."

"Was it Prasav gave them their orders?" Tempe asked the mage. "Or Helenja?"

"Sharel," said the mage, pointedly. "And they were to kill him, too."

"Of course," Tempe said, relaxing slightly. This was retaliation against Floria and Balthasar for that incident in the night, not some wider political scheme. Floria wondered if she could possibly cozen the Mother of All Things into letting her be there when Helenja found out that Sharel had ordered the assassination of a man claimed by the Temple. At the very least, there would be a substantial fine.

"Mistress Floria," said the young woman.

Floria, resenting the need, gave the mage her best intimidating stare. Tempe scolded, "Don't bully the girl."

She was good for a third-ranker. She dealt with the trivial wounds and left the poison and the asset to fight it out without interference. Her eyes widened, though, at the strength of the asset. Neither of the mages maintaining it had been in the tower last night, or this skirmish would have had quite a different outcome.

"You can go and report now," Tempe said, watched the mage leave the room, then turned back to Floria.

"What are the other possible reasons for the Temple ... adopting me?" Balthasar said.

Tempe smiled thinly. "Control, of you as a source of information and a source of disruption. Possession, of an example of some very interesting magic. I understand magic only as much as the next nonmage."

Disingenuous of her, in Floria's opinion, given her asset and her relentlessly inquiring nature.

"But I do know that until now, nobody has known how to keep a Darkborn alive in light, or a Lightborn in darkness. I don't think your archduke quite grasped the implications of this, for the Temple; if I had been him, I would not have let you come over. It may even have bearing on our understanding the nature of the Curse itself, a puzzle for eight hundred years. . . . Yes, I think they'd want you alive."

Assuming, Floria thought, *that the high masters have not already learned everything they needed from Balthasar.*

"That makes it less likely they'd use you as bait," Tempe added. "Though not inconceivable."

"Bait for whom?" Balthasar said with strain in his voice. "And for what?"

Tempe gestured suggestively toward the door. "Enemies of the Darkborn. Enemies of the Temple. Enemies of the status quo. This court is riven with factions, but in the main, enemies know each other; we exist in a balance of tensions and oppositions. We do not like them to be disturbed. Now Isidore is dead, Fejelis has vanished, and you have come in from outside, bringing with you rumors of unseen forces of unknown potential—This isn't a simple place you have come to, Balthasar Hearne."

"I've known Floria for decades," he said, by way of answer.

"Yes," she said, with that annoying glint of speculative amusement.

Floria bit her tongue; she did not want to invite Tempe's curiosity.

"It's different, being on the same side of the wall." He turned his face to her, then to Tempe—sonning, Floria realized. "Please advise me."

"Next time I say, 'Stay down,' *stay down*," Floria said. "Save me grandstanding."

He looked abashed. "I . . . understand."

But wasn't sorry; she heard that distinction. And she'd be

a hypocrite if she pretended she'd respect him more for cowering under the table.

The corner of Tempe's mouth drew down. "*My* advice: get out of here. The Temple's protection goes only so far, particularly now that they've torn up the compact. Tell your archduke this is not a good idea, trying to stir up the populace. Their brightnesses won't forget it."

"And the Shadowborn?" Nothing in Balthasar's face betrayed his feelings—so he could do it if he needed to.

"Are magical, yes? Therefore the Temple's problem. Or their brightnesses, should they choose to contract with the Temple to deal with them."

"That's not enough," Balthasar said.

Tempe sighed. "That man Johannes—his cousin was summoned to his bedside, found him raving about Shadowborn who could turn a man into a flare, burn him to char in seconds. Half the servants had heard that story, or versions of it, by the time we knew."

"Did he mention Balthasar?" Floria said.

"Not in any version I heard—but who's to know who else from that household will be talking—or the group he's part of?" She stood up and said, deliberately, "So take your lover home and leave him there, if you want him alive by tomorrow's sunset."

"We are not lovers," Floria said, not looking at Balthasar.

Tempe snorted. "Woman, I've an asset of veracity. Whether you've lain with him or not, you've loved this man as long as I've known you. While he was on the far side of sunset, you were safe to be the perfect vigilant. That kind of accommodation has the habit of breaking down, though seldom as spectacularly as this."

"Thank you for your counsel, Mistress Tempe, and for your intervention tonight," Balthasar said, steadily, though Tempe's words had brought a flush to his pale skin. "But until the Shadowborn are dealt with, I shall stay. May I have the letters addressed to me now?"

From his pocket, he slipped a cipher. Tempe's irritated glance at Floria rebuked their collective negligence in not finding it and questioning him for the key. He worked the cipher one-handed with some dexterity, reading the messages with the fingers of his left hand, lips moving slightly as he committed the translation to memory, and apparently quite oblivious to the activity around him as Tempe's people gathered up the dead and wounded.

He lacked most of the basic instincts of survival in the Lightborn court, she had to admit. She had to assume that was nurture, not nature: with the exception of his brother Lysander, his lineage was sound, producing generations of civic-minded, intelligent men. Quiet men, with the kind of courage that was proven only on testing, as Balthasar had proven his. The women were less distinguished, but she suspected the diminishing effects of Darkborn expectations of their sex; Balthasar's small daughters were promising enough.

A daughter of hers would be spared that impediment. Her lineage offered the health and athleticism and survivorship of ten generations of vigilants, plus her asset. The Mother of All determined how those offerings would be endowed—except the last—but at least they would be on offer. Even if a child inherited Balthasar's blindness, the example of Ishmael di Studier and the Stranhornes had proven that was no handicap. . . . Though if a child required an ensorcellment to live under light . . .

And there was Telmaine, and Darkborn expectation of sexual fidelity in marriage, which Balthasar, unlike many of his peers, practiced. She did not need Tempe to explain to her that in a court of alliances that formed and dissolved overnight, governed by contracts that could be torn up even before the signatures had dried, that she had learned to prize, even idealize, such loyalty. If she asked him, would it lessen her in his eyes . . . thoughts . . . or herself in his? *Think highly of yourself, don't you, woman? Assuming he'll be yours for the asking . . .*

His movement drew her eye as he returned the cipher back to his pocket, and folded up the letters. With a shake of the head in response to Tempe's extended hand, he pocketed the letters as well. As he drew breath, she converted the silent request into a staying gesture, and motioned forward the secretary who had just arrived. "I think it best we enter this into the record under a judiciary seal."

Balthasar began to explain how Lord Vladimer had taken the Darkborn mages—and Telmaine—south to the Borders to contend with the Shadowborn, and were requesting Lightborn assistance. Floria, listening, thought, *And first we all three have to survive.*

Fejelis

"Tam's gone *where*?" Fejelis demanded.

Jovance was a step behind him as he threw open the door to the small bedroom, on the empty bed and empty room. He turned to face her, and she put a strong hand on the center of his chest and firmly pushed him backward over the threshold. "Give us a moment," she said, over her shoulder. "Get everything together, and tell us as soon as you hear the train."

As she kicked the door closed, he seized her shoulders, answering her disrespectful handling of her person with his own. *"Where has he gone?"*

"He has been *sent*"—she laid stress on the word—"to negotiate with the Shadowborn."

He should not have such difficulty understanding simple words. He looked around at the bed, its covers trailing off the edge, the sheets still creased with Tam's restless movements. If he touched it, might it still be warm? ". . . I didn't even know he'd gone."

"You're not a mage, Prince Fejelis."

The title—reminding him who and what he was, and why this might be a disaster much larger than betrayal by a friend. ". . . Gone to the Shadowborn?"

"Sent," she reminded him, forcefully. "It wasn't voluntary; that I can tell you."

"But Tam's—"

"Very strong. My grandfather said seventh-rank potential, sixth-rank fulfilled, fifth"—a sour expression—"acknowledged. But against the high masters, he had no chance."

". . . He got us away." He felt dazed and blundering, and knew it showed.

"Only with the archmage's help, he told me. They anticipated needing him to do this—and the archmage had taken a liking to you. You remind him of someone from his past."

". . . And the Shadowborn?" Fejelis said, disregarding anything else for the moment. "Has he a chance there?"

Her eyes asked him not to make her answer that question. "Not . . . if they're hostile. Tam . . . said to tell you goodbye, to give you his love, to give you his regrets. He made me promise I'd look after you. Said you'd look after me, Beatrice and his children, the artisans. . . ."

Fejelis felt his shoulders bow under the weight of all Tam's love and lost hopes.

She tipped her forehead forward, bouncing it lightly on his chest. With him pinning her arms, she could move neither forward nor back. "He didn't have a choice, Fejelis. If nothing else, you must understand that."

". . . Could we go after him?"

She lifted her head, honey-colored eyes narrowing. "*No*, Fejelis. He . . . gave me an impression of what he sensed just before he *lifted*. It's ugly and it's very, very strong."

"Where?"

"West of us. I'd say close to the Darkborn barony of Stranhorne. Directing or driving the force that overran Stranhorne. *No*, Fejelis."

Can I believe her? he thought, with a sudden and too-welcome suspicion. Suppose it was the Temple who had found Tam, seized him, and took him unwillingly—Fejelis believed that, at least—back to Minhorne? He'd rather have her a willing traitor and a liar than Tam a traitor, a tool of the high masters, and a prisoner of the very monstrousness that had produced the things they had fought.

She was still in his hands, and he realized that through his grip on her shoulders, through the coarse weave of her sleeves, she could know everything he was thinking. He let her go, like a coal that had fallen into his hand, and at the flicker of pained emotion in her eyes, promptly regretted that. ". . . I'm sorry."

"I know." She hesitated. "I should have cloaked my touch-sense, but . . . I had to peek."

His lips formed something that was not a smile. "Now you know."

She sighed. "I too wish it had been that way, Fejelis."

". . . Is there nothing—nothing we can do for him?"

"No. If the Shadowborn kill him, then we can try to avenge him. It didn't occur to him to veto that."

Her smile was wondrously cold, but in her eyes was the knowledge that death was not the worst that might await Tam. The silence was punctuated by a chime. "We need to go," she said quietly. "The train's coming."

He opened the door just as Jade was raising his fist to knock.

"We wait until they stop and blow the whistle twice," Midha said, as they gathered around the door. "That's the usual routine if we have to come down to a train in the night. Either the caboose will have been cleared for you, or someone in it will shout instructions."

They had Jovance's assurance that there was nothing living nearby except for those on the train and themselves, but Orlanjis was still shivering slightly at the thought of going into the night. Fejelis put a hand on his shoulder, drawing his gaze, full of unspoken questions and uncertainty. Fejelis managed, from somewhere, to summon a grin. "Have you ever actually ridden a Darkborn train?" His brother had shown a surprising—perhaps lifesaving—knowledge of the Darkborn railways, and admitted to a desire to escape court to the railways. "This'll be a first."

Orlanjis managed, from somewhere, to summon a pout. "Don't tease."

Then the whistle sounded, and Midha opened the door. They dropped a rope with lights down either side of the ladder and climbed down one at a time, with only Jade staying on guard above. Orlanjis suddenly blurted, "I have to get something."

Midha, frowning, nodded to Sorrel. "Make it quick."

Lights in hand, she flanked him on his dash underneath the platform to a tarpaulin that, from its profile, covered a

stack of drums. He reached underneath and withdrew a
bundle of red: Fejelis's ceremonial caul and jacket, which
Orlanjis had hidden in a futile attempt to disguise their
identities. He was sweating when he returned, his arm
blanched with exposure to shadow.

Fejelis accepted the bundle and tucked it under his arm
with a quiet "Thanks." He could feel the hard wire of the
caul against his ribs.

The door to the caboose opened with a crack that made
them all jump, and a great fan of light spilled across the
gravel and scrub alongside the tracks. A man's huge silhou-
ette waved at them and a voice barked from inside. "All
aboard that's coming aboard. This train's got a schedule to
keep." By its pitch it could be man or woman, aged but still
strong.

"Les?" said Sorrel. "Les!" Their boarding was briefly ob-
structed as Midha and Sorrel crowded into the doorway to
confirm and shout greetings; then the train whistle blew
warning and Midha boosted Jovance aboard. Fejelis and
Orlanjis scrambled after. Midha closed the door and bolted
it behind them.

"They ordered me out because of this cursed hip," explained the railway legend in frank disgust to Jovance. "Put
Lomand and his gang in place. Didn't know anything about
it until the train stopped and they all got out. I'll skelp the
lot of them if we don't find our hut entirely as we left it."
She was a small woman whose weight made scarcely a
bulge in the netting of the hammock slung for her. It seemed
implausible that the deep, forceful voice could be hers, or
that the hulking Nathan could be her son. He had an inch
on tall Fejelis and at least half his weight.

Then again, Fejelis knew within two minutes of climbing
into the caboose that if personality had mass, the engine
would have been in for a hard pull on the hills. Celeste in-
spected them with pale blue eyes, unimpressed. "Who're
these'uns? New blood? Look an unlikely pair. Pair of city
lads run away from trouble?"

"In ... a sense," Jovance said, with a quick, cautious
glance at Fejelis.

Gently, so as to show he had taken no offense, Fejelis said, ". . . I am Fejelis Grey Rapids. This is my brother, Orlanjis."

She scowled. "If you're going to pull my leg, my laddie, pull the one that's not broke."

His thoughts seemed to hit an unseen obstacle—*thump*. At his side, Orlanjis started to quiver and sank down to rest against the rocking wall of the caboose. Fejelis realized his brother was laughing. Jovance said, tremulously, "It's so, Les," and undermined her assertion by collapsing, giggling, beside Orlanjis.

After that, Celeste could not be convinced, particularly since, when she chose to fire some testing questions at them, Orlanjis had the answers. "Why would a prince's son learn about trains?" she demanded. To that, Orlanjis had no response. To Fejelis he might confide his dream to flee court for a simple life as a railway engineer, but not to others. Fejelis left them to talk trains, glad to have Orlanjis distracted from the horrors of the night. He had heard the undertone of hysteria in his brother's laughter.

He had no such diversion. "What am I going to tell Lord Vladimer?" he murmured, as he and Jovance sat side by side on the floor, backs against the rough wall of the carriage.

She made a small hand gesture, one he knew from Tam when he sealed a conversation against eavesdropping. He had always thought it was a quirk of Tam's, but perhaps it was one they had both learned from Lukfer.

"What can you tell him?" she said, close-cropped head bent close. "He should know he's reaping what he sowed."

He twisted to face her. "The only thing he is guilty of, by Tam's testimony, is inaction. The rest was other men's doing."

A flash of yellow eyes, unreadable.

He took his best guess at an answer to that flash. ". . . Jovance, I'll treat with whomever I have to, to achieve my ends."

"Which are?" she said, neutrally.

He let out a breath. ". . . My position back, of course." He bounced the red bundle on his hand and had to snatch at it before it unraveled, sending the caul skittering across the cabin. "Unlike Jis," he said, "I've never given any thought to an alternative occupation." Then, more soberly: ". . . I have to speak to the archmage again. I'd like to be able to convince him that this is folly, but if it's not—if it's quite simply that the Shadowborn are too-strong mages and we have the choice of death, enslavement, or collusion—then I must know that. It may be"—he rolled his head on the rough wall to look at her—"that I too must treat with the Shadowborn, to try to secure the best possible terms."

"For whom? For you? Their brightnesses?"

". . . For myself, their brightnesses, the palace staff, the artisans and craftsman and merchants and indigents . . . for us, the Lightborn. I would count it my failure if Minhorne suffered what Stranhorne Manor has and I had done nothing to avert the stroke."

Jovance's hand opened and closed. Something moved in her face, something grim, powerful. Despite himself, he remembered the viscous red rain of a body ruptured in midair.

"Fejelis," she said, slowly. "If it's death or enslavement, I'll take death. I'll not have done to me what's been done to Tam."

He felt the words physically as a pang in his stomach or beneath his heart. He drew up his feet, bracing himself with his angled legs, and wondered what to say to her. Her determination would not change his decision—could not, even if he knew that by some choice or conciliation of his own, he could save her. Yet to say so aloud seemed cold, and he did not feel cold toward her fate.

She said, quietly, "I didn't tell you that to influence your decisions, or make what you have to do more difficult. It's difficult enough. I told you so you'd not be taken by surprise."

". . . 'Difficult enough'?" he picked up from that bleak tone. "Do you mean 'hopeless enough'?" A hesitation, longer than his usual. ". . . What do you sense?"

She shook her head. "I also told you," she said, "so we'd

not waste the time we have." She slid work-hardened fingers under his jaw, turned his head, and kissed him.

"That's playing dirty," he said, huskily, when she drew back.

"So it is."

"You're not going to tell me."

"No, I'm not. It's a matter for mages, and it would do you no good to know."

He chose to accept that, for now. At least she had not pointed out that none of the mages were under contract to him on this matter.

A far too few minutes later, the train drew into Strumheller, giving them no opportunity for more than that kiss, an interlude of the desultory, uncertain conversation between two people exploring a mutual attraction, and another kiss. Celeste gleefully observed, "That's no prince, though the lad's got taste." Orlanjis looked worried, as well he should. Neither tradition nor compact allowed for a mage consort to the prince, and the Temple would still want Jovance's strength for their lineages. Fejelis doubted he would meet the obscure fate of her first earthborn lover, though, who had been lost on his travels, possibly through the Temple's doing. Whatever Fejelis's fate was to be, it would not be obscure.

And if they escaped death or enslavement, the relations between princedom and Temple would change. He would see to that.

They listened as doors slammed open, so forcefully the train rocked, and the people inside spilled out. He heard bellowed orders from men, and shouts from men and women—if Darkborn women were submissive and meek, he did not hear much evidence of it—and children crying. At one point, there was a shot, followed immediately by a thoroughly profane rebuke from one of the voices in charge. Someone knocked hard on their door to tell them that they'd hear the bell when it was safe for them to come out. They waited more or less in silence. Talking was difficult with the racket outside, and flirting inhibited by tension, and by Orlanjis sitting on the floor on his other side. Though his young brother made a negligent chaperone, since by the time they heard the bolt slide back, Orlanjis had dozed off, propped against Fejelis's shoulder.

"Wait until y'hear the bell," the voice said from outside. "Lightborn quarters are off the west end of the platform—you'll know from th'signage, if y'haven't been here before. When you get inside and th'door shut and all, throw th'switch t'turn off the bell t'let us know. The baron and some'll be down to join y', very shortly." He rapped on the door again, and they heard his booted feet move away.

Nat helped his mother to her feet, and she tucked crutches under her arms. He could have carried her effortlessly, but Fejelis had no doubt, even on this slight acquaintance, as to how she would receive that. He prodded Orlanjis awake and resisted the temptation to tease him with the request that he witness the formalizing of a contract, less on Orlanjis's account than Jovance's. They heard the bell, and Nat opened the door on chill night air; shivering, they climbed down.

Strumheller Crosstracks Station was an open station. He did not linger to look around, aware of the courtesy their hosts were extending them, surrendering even so small a portion of their precious hours of darkness on a night like this. The Lightborn quarters were easy to identify, even without the painted sign. It was the one building where the paintwork was truly decorative, not merely functional, the door, trim, and mounted panels on the sides brightly painted in a rustic, slightly garish style. Ordinarily the mounted panels would have held posters, but there was no one to read them here.

They closed the doors behind them, gladly putting the stone walls between them and the night. The building was surprisingly large, accommodating a dozen people in three bedrooms and a six-bed dormitory, and very well lit. The lack of posters outside was more than made up for by the many sheets of notice and instruction inside, which Nat and Les completely ignored. They staked their claim to their favorite rooms.

Jovance threw the lever to turn off the bell, saying, "The

meeting room is through here." She steered them into a modest-sized room dominated by a long glass table and an equally long glass sideboard. Six chairs of Lightborn design were pushed in on one side of the table, so that the occupants would face what looked like a large watercolor painting on paper, with a fine silver mesh over it: the paper wall. The painting would be backed by several layers of opaque black. Orlanjis, who had not had many dealings with Darkborn, eyed it dubiously. It looked flimsy, but any breach would be more dangerous to the Darkborn than to themselves. Jovance said, "Shall I get you something to drink, your brightnesses?"

She was prompting him back into a role; he supposed he should be grateful. "I'm not sure my stomach is up for more bedeeth tea," he said, "but I need something to keep me alert. It has been a long night."

"I'll see what I can do," she said, and left.

Orlanjis said in a low voice, "Fejelis, she's a *mage*."

". . . I'm fairly sure there's no ensorcellment involved," Fejelis said.

"That's not what I meant," Orlanjis said. "I mean, she's not eligible to be consort. And if you're not serious, I mean—" He flushed deeply, to Fejelis's well-hidden amusement. So his indulged younger brother had a sense of ethics in romance.

". . . I could be quite serious. And if it comes to that, we will deal with it then."

"But why should she—"

"Who's he insulting?" Jovance interrupted, coming into the room with a tray. "Me or you?"

She must have used magic to heat the water that quickly. She offered them their choice of cups and dispensed tea from the common pot. Orlanjis's scowl dissipated as he fell on the bannocks and cheese. Self-appointed food taster or ravenous adolescent? Finding himself in a losing race for the spoils, Fejelis concluded it was the latter. Jovance helped herself to a portion and then simply watched the scrum with a sisterly smirk. She never did get an answer to her question.

Fejelis was halfway through his second cup of bitter Darkborn tea and wondering if there was any more cheese in the stores when they heard the door open on the other side. He put down the bannock he had been holding, and, wanting a napkin, wiped his mouth on his sleeve.

Jovance leaned down to breathe in his ear. "Eight people. Three mageborn. Two pretty strong."

A voice from the other side of the wall said, "Your brightnesses?" A prompting murmur. "Magistra?"

"Yes," Fejelis said. He made himself speak steadily, without his habitual hesitation. "This is Fejelis Grey Rapids, prince of the Lightborn; my brother, Orlanjis; and Magistra Jovance." He realized he had no idea how she styled herself on such occasions. Earthborn Lightborn clung to a fashionable minimalism in using titles, although they were as prideful and hierarchical without them as the mages with their ranks, or the Darkborn with their layers of nobility. It did help, when dealing with either of those, to have a title to brandish, but he was not sure she would want to use her Temple rank, even if he knew it.

"I am Baron Reynard Strumheller," the Darkborn on the far side of the wall said, in an aggressive, light baritone, as though daring Fejelis to dispute his claim. "I have with me Lord Vladimer Plantageter, the brother of the archduke" — Jovance's face hardened at the name — "Baronet Boris Stranhorne, Baronette Laurel Stranhorne, Lady Telmaine — Mrs. Balthasar Hearne, formerly Lady Telmaine Stott." That a woman, but not a man, could gain or lose rank by marriage was one of those Darkborn nuances that had taken hours of study to understand. "Magister Farquhar Broome" — he saw Jovance nod in recognition — "and Magistra Phoebe Broome."

Jovance leaned over to whisper, and he pointed to his ear and the wall in warning, and indicated the paper and pens and ink laid out on the sideboard.

"My companions and I are deeply grateful to you for your timely retrieval and hospitality, Baron Strumheller," Fejelis said.

Jovance dealt out pens and paper. Orlanjis eyed his dubiously. Incongruously, the pen was of Darkborn manufacture, the wooden barrel carefully carved, with a metal nib and hidden bladder that stored ink. The first time one of these had been laid before Isidore, the prince had laughed himself breathless at the cheek of the Darkborn, out to best the Lightborn there as well.

Fejelis uncapped the pen, tapped it to start the ink flowing, and scribbled, *3rd mage lady T.* He had not named her when he told Jovance and her colleagues the background to Tam's, Orlanjis's, and his sudden arrival beside the railway tracks, and he did not think Jovance or Orlanjis would connect name and account now. Even so, Jovance gave him a searching glance.

Vladimer Plantageter said, "I expected that the mage—Magister Tammorn—would have been with you."

Straight to the heart of the sticky questions, Fejelis thought. "So did I," he said. At least he had had a chance to decide beforehand how to meet it. Which was directly. "Magistra Jovance tells me that he has been sent by the archmage and high masters to open negotiations with the Shadowborn."

There was a reverberating silence from the other room, no spurious or stalling questions as to his meaning.

"That is not news I wanted to convey," Fejelis said, "any more than it is news you wished to hear. Magister Tammorn did not go willingly—he is a sport, and able to sense Shadowborn magic in a way that lineage mages do not, and his sense of them was of something hostile and dangerous—but being under Temple law, and being fifth-rank, he had no choice. If he had defied the high masters' orders, he would have been coerced into it."

"Well," they heard the baron mutter, "that's that, then."

"That most decidedly is not that," Vladimer said, his voice gritty. "That is not welcome news, but not, perhaps, unexpected." And what exactly did he mean by that—that he expected treachery of the mages? Or the Lightborn? "However, Prince Fejelis, your being here in the Borders is unexpected. The report I had from Minhorne is that you had been deposed."

And in the usual course of such things, should have been dead, yes. "My survival was Magister Tam's doing. He *lifted* my brother and me out."

"Why bring you here?"

Despite himself, he hesitated a half beat. ". . . He brought me to someone he trusted—Magistra Jovance, granddaughter to his master, Lukfer. Magister Tammorn is more than a contracted mage to me. He is a good friend."

"That is not the usual relationship between earthborn and mageborn," Vladimer said, crisply. A slightly reproachful murmur from the other side. Jovance scribbled, *F Broome.*

"You're not the first to tell me that, Lord Vladimer."

A woman's voice spoke up, slightly hesitant but determined. "Lord Vladimer, neither my father nor I can detect any sense of Shadowborn about them."

P Broome, wrote Jovance. *Checking us.* Orlanjis shuffled his chair closer, craning his neck to see.

Fejelis decided that he would not acknowledge that they themselves lacked a similar advantage. He scratched, *Cn they tell yr lineage vs sport?* She squinted, deciphering, and shook her head.

He'd be better reassured if her expression were more certain, though if any of the Darkborn weren't Darkborn or were Shadowborn-held, he might be dead or ensorcelled before he knew he'd misjudged. The paper wall was a fragile thing. The vigilants would be disgusted with him for sitting still, so his voice could be placed, but instinct told him that he should stay where he was; the tension on the far side of the wall was palpable.

"And what do you plan to do now?"

Orlanjis was frowning at the other's tone. Fejelis wished he were able to signal that he was choosing to let the Darkborn have control for a while, to let them settle. "Get back to Minhorne," he said. "Hope to be able to influence the archmage—"

"To do what?"

That, too, he had thought through. ". . . To consider the interests of the earthborn as well as the mageborn in their actions. I don't know why the high masters have chosen the course they have taken. Perhaps it was anger for your people's attack on the tower." He'd get it said, rather than leave it leering through the silences. "For me, I don't think that in itself was enough, but if they felt themselves weakened by it, so that they did not feel they could fight . . ." *Assuming,* Fejelis said privately to himself, *that they wished to fight under any balance of powers.* His fear was that the Temple had decided that their loyalty lay with magic, whatever the nature of that magic. He could not say that to the Darkborn, and deepen their hostility against magic. Or was that what Vladimer had meant when he said that the Temple's move was not unexpected? ". . . I could continue to enumerate reasons, but won't know until I ask."

"Which may satisfy your curiosity, Prince Fejelis, a motive with which I find myself in sympathy. But what will you do when you know?"

Jovance's pen beat a soft staccato on her paper, leaving dots of ink. He quirked a smile at her; Lord Vladimer was obviously accustomed to provoking a reaction and letting others do the soothing. Sejanus Plantageter was superb at it. ". . . How is your brother the archduke, Lord Vladimer? I had had some bad news of him earlier."

"If you are asking as to whether I have power to negotiate," Vladimer said, "I do."

"I'm glad to hear it, but no. I was asking because, when I return to Minhorne, it will be reassuring to me to know that I have Sejanus Plantageter on the other side of sunset, rather than a regency council." *Composed,* he thought, *of bigots and old men.*

And are those in charge of the palace any better? queried an internal voice that sounded remarkably like his father's.

"You need not worry about Mycene anymore," the Darkborn said. "The telegram I had earlier said that he had been killed by a Shadowborn. The present Duke Mycene is fighting Shadowborn in Stranhorne Crosstracks. Kalamay continues alive, but I don't doubt Sejanus will deal with him. My brother is quite well."

Which was a relief, but left more than a little unsaid. Fejelis well knew that Plantageter was strongly opposed to having magic in his city, but despite his prejudices, the arch-duke insisted on scrupulous respect of Lightborn rights under the letter and the spirit of the law. Fejelis could only hope that had not changed. "The injury was magical, was it?"

"Yes . . . Shadowborn, indirectly."

Gracious—or politic—not mentioning Tam's part in it. Might Vladimer suspect that Fejelis already knew more than he was saying, from Tam?

Vladimer, suspect? With a name that was a byword for suspicion? Very well. He would put Vladimer's trust to the test. "What is your plan, Lord Vladimer?"

"To retake Stranhorne Manor and the territories on the far side," Vladimer said. "We have reinforced Stranhorne Crosstracks all night by train with troops and reserves from Strumheller and Telemarch, farther around the border, but, unfortunately, our ability to reinforce by day is limited by the design of this station. Stranhorne has also received further reinforcements from the estates and towns on the inner Borders, including Mycene lands, and they are close to the numbers that they can safely shelter."

Fejelis breathed out: Vladimer seemed prepared to treat him as an ally after all. "Both Magister Tam and Magistra Jovance warn me that these are very strong mages. If you come into contact with them, you will take high casualties, possibly to not much advantage."

"It has th'full support of the baronies," Baron Strumheller said—growled, rather.

"If it comes to that, we may," Vladimer said. "But that does not imply we will lose. Ishmael—the former Baron Strumheller—killed a Shadowborn mage at my bedside, admittedly with the help of Lady Telmaine here." *Rank?* he scratched, to Jovance, and she, *6?* "Baron Stranhorne's sacrifice stopped the advance across Stranhorne lands, and we have information that one of the mages present was killed. I ask you: if they are so potent, then why are they employing such familiar tactics of assassination and social disruption—earthborn tactics, not mageborn? Why use people, such as your Mistress White Hand, or the dukes of Mycene and Ka-lamay? Why take such care to turn us against each other before they emerged into the open?"

All good questions, Fejelis acknowledged. "You assume that you have seen their full strength."

"I assume nothing. But we have no choice but to fight or be overrun. By doing so, we may also ease the pressure on the city, which is no small concern of mine, and perhaps provoke your Temple to find its courage."

"You are not the one to judge the Temple's courage," Jovance said, sorely provoked.

"I may have no right, Magistra, but others do: my brother, the archduke, who knew nothing of this until after the tower was down; Baronet and Baronette Stranhorne, who both fought in the defense of their home, though the lady is with child and her brother not yet eighteen; Baron Strumheller and his brother and predecessor, who built much of the defense we are now mobilizing, and who is a mage himself."

A mage who knew Shadowborn . . . "Is the previous Baron Strumheller still alive?" Among Lightborn, he would almost certainly not be, but Darkborn convention allowed for the deposition of the living.

"Unknown," Vladimer said. "He was lost in the retreat, but I've learned not to discount his survival."

That sounded as though it was directed to someone else's address, likely the brother's. How much did he wish to risk alienating one or another of the Darkborn by inquiring further? And if the high masters would not listen to their own, why should they listen to a Darkborn sport mage? ". . . I will support you in any way I can," Fejelis said. He decided it was time for a little provocation of his own. ". . . Here we are, three Lightborn, essentially alone in the barony. Why not simply take us hostage?"

"I thought about that," the Darkborn spymaster said, unruffled. The muttering this time sounded as though it was coming from Baron Strumheller; Fejelis thought he heard the word "hospitality" in a resentful tone. "But who would ransom a prince they'd tried to depose, especially in the coin I needed? And the mage with you would be more trouble than you're worth."

Point to Vladimer. Jovance's smile showed teeth, and Orlanjis's eyes on the decorated paper wall were white ringed. Fejelis quickly sketched two stick swordsmen, the cauled one with arms outflung as he was impaled on the other's blade. As an artist, he would have starved on the street, but the sketch eased the tension along the glass table while leaving the Darkborn listening to silence for a little while. ". . . We will see which one of us is right about my importance," he muttered, knowing the Darkborn would hear. He raised his voice. ". . . I'll be leaving for Minhorne first thing in the morning, Lord Vladimer." And if he had any sense, he should have asked Jovance beforehand if she would take him. He had a mental image of himself riding in triumph into the city on a hay cart, but that was beyond his drawing skills. He corralled his wandering thoughts. ". . . The high masters are mine to deal with, but I'd appreciate any additional information you have on what has happened over the past day and night."

Ishmael

Lysander Hearne was waiting in the hall outside her room, lounging against the wall as though he had idled away hours there. He returned Ishmael's sonn and shrugged himself upright, then strolled over and fixed Ishmael's cravat with a few brisk tugs. There was something cheerfully brazen about him that Ishmael, in his shaken state, could not help appreciating.

"Ready to get something to eat?"

"As long as there's none of their magic close enough t'turn my stomach, or I'll get no good of it."

The corner of Hearne's mouth twitched slightly. "You're a rock-nerved bastard; I'll grant you that. I know what she just put to you."

He steered Ishmael into an interior room where the air was still and all walls sonned as solid. The hexagonal table in the center was large enough to seat twelve luxuriously, and eighteen at a pinch. Lysander directed the servant who arrived at the ring of a bell to set the table for two. He pulled out a chair for Ishmael. "Sit."

Ishmael sat. Hearne dropped into the nearest chair on the next edge of the hexagon. "So," he said, "any questions?"

"Aye," Ishmael said. "A few."

"And you're wondering whether you can trust me."

"No," Ishmael said; about that he was quite clear.

Unexpectedly, Hearne leaned back and laughed. Ishmael's sense was that the laughter was unfeigned, even pleased. "If you know my brat of a brother, I'm sure you're wondering how I came to be here."

Ishmael was entirely content to let him tell his story; he'd take what he would out of it. Servants set down fresh rolls, with pâté and preserves, fruit and cheese, and newly made tea.

"I was twenty-one years old," Hearne said, while Ishmael cut and spread a roll, "and a very bad little boy. I was clever, and I didn't care who I hurt, and I knew what I wanted. I was well on my way to wealth and I'd have found my way to power, for all there wasn't a title in the family. But I made a mistake. After that, if I didn't leave, I'd have to deal with the one person who knew what I'd done. I found I couldn't, I could make the brat's life a misery, but I couldn't kill him—not with the fresh feel of that girl's throat cracking under my hands. You ever felt that?" The question was rhetorical; he did not wait for an answer. "So I ran. Nowhere's far enough when a man's trying to run from himself, but I didn't know that then. Down at Odon's Barrow I crossed some of the local enforcers and was knocked senseless and dumped out in the middle of a field. They'd been feeding troublemakers to the Shadowborn."

"They were," Ish said. "We put a stop t'that."

"I woke up on the march to Emeya's midden, a prisoner. You'll hear more about Emeya presently. Over the centuries, she and our lady have pulled in tens of thousands, and those tens of thousands have begotten others. Emeya's— barony, I suppose you'd call it—is probably seventy, eighty thousand strong now. Earthborn here do what earthborn have always done: farm, hunt, spin, craft, flirt, gossip, intrigue, marry, breed, and die. I'd no desire to be a peasant groveling in the dirt, so I maneuvered my way into her stronghold itself."

His face was utterly devoid of expression. "I said I was a bad little boy, but that's all I was—a little boy. Though I expect I'd have grown up and made out all right—but for Ari.

"Besides Emeya, she had four strong mages—and I mean eighth-rank, if not more. That's the kind of power our lady's offering you, di Studier. There were Ariadne, Neill, Jonquil, Midora—all of Emeya's lineage, as mages reckon it. There'd been more, but a while back—a couple of hundred years—they tried to take over and lost. Ari was the youngest, and Neill was Emeya's favorite, then. Neill wanted to wait for Ari to come round to his wooing, but Emeya wouldn't have it. She set an ensorcellment on them, meaning to force them together. Ari had enough strength to bind another man in that ensorcellment—me. I could no more have refused her than I could have flown. It made me an enemy of Neill and a target of Emeya's anger, and I hated Ari for it."

If there was an ensorcellment of that sort on him now, Ishmael could not sense it. He certainly did not behave as though he hated her—not even counting the bullet he'd put through Ishmael. Head lowered, Hearne said, "That was the way we started, but along the way, something changed. I never thought I'd care about what someone else felt. And when the boy was born—well, I've a cur's way with the small and weak, but this one was different, too. This one was *mine*." He sonned Ishmael with a harsh stroke, his expression defensive, and a warning. "I wanted her safe, I wanted him safe, and the only place to look for safety was here. It was cursed slow doing, convincing Ariadne to take the risk, and by the time I did, the boy had will and strength of his own, and Emeya had made a pet of him—they all had. He wouldn't come. He said he'd bring Emeya down on us. He forced me to choose, and I chose Ariadne."

There was a long silence. "Ariadne's strength and knowledge were gifts to Isolde. If the uprising hadn't reduced the numbers of Emeya's strong ones, not to mention made her so suspicious she put a choke chain on the survivors, Emeya'd already be the only one left."

"Emeya's got one less of the th'strong ones," Ish said. "I shot th'one called Jonquil at Lord Vladimer's bedside; two bullets in the body, one in the brain. It's possible that Stranhorne got others, including your Neill."

Lysander sonned him with that close attention he recalled from dealing with his brother, though it was plain the two were very different men. "Did you, indeed?" he said. "Frankly, that surprises me."

"I'd th'help of a brave mage. And"—before Lysander could ask who—"it's likely I met your son at Stranhorne."

The father leaned forward, ready, Ishmael thought, with any of half a dozen ordinary questions. *How did he seem? Was he all right?* But he eased back without speaking, his lips tight, his expression one of hard-schooled composure.

"I took him for your brother th'first time I sonned him. Seemed t'me as though he could do with steady feeding t'flesh him out, steady labor t'build him up, and no small amount of education. I've known street children less neglected. He's got th'one trick of fire down fine—nearly broiled me—and he's learned something of ensorcellment." He would hold back, for the moment, how Sebastien had used that skill, or how the near broiling had been provoked. "I also got th'sense that your leaving had lost him favor," he added.

"It would," Hearne said, taking the information straight.

"If Emeya were t'lose this war, you'd have your son."

"If he lived."

Ishmael chewed bread and considered. Lysander had all the characteristics of a virtuoso liar—someone who lied merely to keep in practice—but Ishmael could not tell which part of this might be fabrication. The one part he believed was Hearne's feeling toward his son. Briefly, he entertained the thought of asking the man if he could touch-read him. But he knew the answer, because as sure as sunrise killed, there were things that *none* of them were telling him.

"If she's got th'ability t'augment mages, where are th'others?"

Unease passed across Lysander's expression. "What do you mean?"

"Th'question's simple enough. If she can do this t'me, why not t'others?"

"It's . . . not exactly like closing a cut, di Studier. It's going to be very taxing for both of them."

"And?" said Ishmael. Lysander sighed and toyed with a fork, flicking the tines with a nail to make them chime. "They were children when this was done to them. They lost most of the higher knowledge of magic that existed from before the Curse."

"Seems t'me some things are better lost," Ish rumbled.

"Isolde knew it was possible; it was done to her, after all. But she did not know how. When Ariadne came over, it filled in what she did not know. Between them, they could do it."

"You're telling me I'll be th'first to have it tried on me," Ishmael said.

Lysander laid down the fork. "You're not exactly the usual low-rank mage. You've pushed your magic to its limits and beyond, you fought Shadowborn for some twenty-five years, and you held out against Ari's Call for nearly ten years. If anyone's got the constitution for this, you have."

And I'm not fool enough to be flattered into noticing you've not answered my question, Ishmael thought.

"Frankly, now, whether you do or don't do it, whether it succeeds or doesn't, if Isolde cannot take down Emeya, if she tries and loses, you're as dead as we are. And if you live, you're looking at a cursed lot of power. I'll not believe any man who tells me that makes no difference to him." He snorted. "I've been trying to persuade her to do it on me, but I've as much magic in me as a mud pat."

"So it's t'the death, her and Emeya. And after, if she wins, what then?"

He committed his attention not to sonn, but to his other senses, allowing Lysander to think himself unobserved, but listening hard for the change in Lysander's breathing, for the timbre of his voice as he answered. "Trust me, you *don't* want to live in a land ruled by Emeya."

That, at least, sounded sincere. "So th'choice is rule by one or rule by th'other, is it?"

"If it comes to that—and I'm not saying it will—"

"But y'think it likely," Ishmael interposed. He was in no mood to indulge prevarication. "I'll thank you for the feeding and the counsel, Hearne. I'm the better for th'one at least. And now I think I'd best have another word with the lady."

They found her not in her grand receiving room but on a small balcony that, like the other, was crowded with planters and pots. She was weeding. Ishmael, stepping firmly onto the balcony, suddenly felt a one-sided heat, like the heat of a fire, or the heat he felt through his day shade when he overnighted outside. He checked himself midstride. He had heard neither bells nor dawn chorus to mark the dawn, nor had he sensed his own ensorcellment in the miasma of Shadowborn magic. He did now.

"You'll get used to it," Lysander Hearne said with false cheer.

She circled a planter and shook her head reproachfully at her servant. "Shall we go inside?" she asked, gently.

In the cool of the interior, he recovered his equilibrium; there was nothing to do about the ensorcellment but be glad of it. "You'll do with me what y'want, m'lady, I've no doubt of that. But if it matters t'you that I'm willing, then let me have a sense of you." He jerked off his gloves, demonstrating, if not conveying, his meaning. It was ridiculous of him to propose this, to pretend that she would be unable to deceive him or suborn his will—but she need not touch him to do that. He said, "If the sense convinces me, then you can have me willing. If not, I'll fight you with all that I am, puny though that may be."

"Not so puny, Ishmael," she said. She extended her hand, as a lady might for a formal greeting. The hand was smooth skinned and evenly fleshed, younger than her face. Even so strong a mage had her vanities. Her hand did not tremble. His, he noted, did.

To have actually taken her hand would have seemed too

much an intimacy. He lifted his fingers, offering his palm. She turned her hand likewise, and set palm to palm.

Telmaine

"I shall want you with me" was all Vladimer said as they left the conference with the Lightborn. He had moved on before Telmaine understood what he meant: that he was taking her with him to war. She pushed after him, forcing her way through pressing lines and tight huddles of men, skirts snagging on stacked crates and heaped, stuffed bags.

She caught up with him as he intercepted the stationmaster, who had been trying to dodge him. Little wonder, given the way their last encounter had ended, with the stationmaster telling Vladimer there was no way on this cursed earth that he could convert an open platform into a covered station in the few hours remaining before sunrise, and Lord Vladimer must apply elsewhere for magic or a miracle. Vladimer said only, "Will this train be ready by sunrise?"

"Aye, it'll be ready," said the stationmaster, deflating from posture of war. "It'll leave within the half hour, if I've anything to say about it, and be into Stranhorne less than two hours after sunrise. It'll be stopping for lookouts; I don't want it traveling without a Lightborn guard."

"Good," Vladimer said. "Have someone call me when it's ready to leave."

"Aye," the stationmaster said, and, with no "excuse me" turned away to bellow, "No, you'll *not* load that in there, unless y'want to be blown t'very small pieces."

He sounded so like Ishmael, her heart hurt. She tried for imperious and failed. "Lord Vladimer, did I hear you correctly?"

"I regret you do not have time to send to the manor for luggage, but I am certain that if you use your charm, some of these gentlemen would be delighted to oblige you."

Given what she wanted at this *particular* moment, which had nothing to do with luggage, probably not. "Lord Vladimer, a *word*, if you would."

He did not so much find as clear a corner; the quartet of

men occupying it flowed out like putty. "Now," he said. "What is unclear about—"

"What could I possibly do in Stranhorne Crosstracks? The Broomes don't want me using magic, don't want me to be part of their group." Which had been more humiliating than she would have thought possible, given that she had had to be backed, resisting, into magic, and forced into their company. Given that she had let them into her mind, let them explore the Shadowborn *gift* The worst of it was that she knew they knew how she felt, and she knew they were probably right. "I haven't the experience, and I'm too strong to be safe."

"So I am informed," he said. "I am willing to take that risk. I know you can communicate over distance without adverse effects on your contact, and it occurs to me that I might need that."

"You're not thinking to talk with the *Shadowborn*?" she breathed.

All expression left his face. "No."

There was a silence. She stood quivering slightly with the urge to apologize, even for a question that had to be asked in this night of betrayals. "If the Mages' Temple does not repent of its decision," Vladimer said, in a whisper like sand blowing through dry reeds, "then I shall unrepent of my silence."

She pressed her back against the wall, fighting the impulse to scramble away—like the nine-year-old Telmaine whom Vladimer had surprised in his private sanctum, years ago. He said in a slightly less deathly voice, "I trust that they will, for if not"—he raised his head, turned as though to cast, but in the end did not; his hearing would have told him everything he needed to know—"it is likely we are all going to death, ensorcellment, or enslavement."

"Does that not *bother* you?" she whispered. "All these people."

"I recall we had a previous conversation along these lines," he said. "And while things that have happened since have made me reconsider some of the things I said then, I do not believe that I have done anything to regret, here." His expression changed, disturbingly, at some thought. She would not have been surprised if he was remembering what Magister Broome had said to him; she certainly was. "If the Temple does repent its decision or find its courage, it will be immensely useful for me to be able to speak to Fejelis or his mage."

"I don't . . . think the Lightborn mages will be best pleased with me." Not if Tammorn was anything to go by. She tried not to sound as frightened as she felt.

"A risk we must both take." He turned his head, and this time cast over the platform. "They're nearly ready. You recall that I said—not very long ago, if one merely thinks in hours—that there might come a time to contact Ishmael. I may ask you to do that once we reach Stranhorne."

"I'd be glad to," she said. "I'd have done it already, but—"

"I will give you an order, if you wish," he said.

"I don't *need* an order," Telmaine bridled. "Ishmael may need help."

"Good." She expected him to move, aware that the crowd on the platform was thinning, that there was almost no one near them. Aware, too, of the presence of the Broomes and their commune: Farquhar Broome's vast, quiet power; Phoebe's tightly disciplined strain; the others she was learning to recognize. She could sense about them the foul taint of Shadowborn magic, from their hurried rehearsals. That sense of exclusion scraped her spirit, but shriveled into pettiness as she sensed something more about them: resolve, almost resignation. They had taken the measure of their enemy and their enemy's magic, and they did not believe they would be returning.

Then Vladimer said, "I have one more request of you, Lady Telmaine. I will not be made a slave to the Shadowborn again. If it comes to that—if I give you the order, or if I fall to their ensorcellment, I want you to kill me. Shoot me in the head, use your fires, do whatever you must to do it quickly and *thoroughly*. I will it, and I *wish* it."

Nine

Tammorn

*H*e did not die. He stood on scrub and heather, in night's very heart, and did not die.

He did not realize until then how much he had wished the high masters had been wrong, even if it meant his death. But he could sense the protective ensorcellment on him, sheathing him but not caging him—he still had all his strength to answer his will—and they had somehow managed to make it feel more like an itchy suit of clothing than a coating of sewage. He would sense the strength and vitality of the high masters in it, but the guiding magic had been Perrin's, second-rank sport though she was.

Fejelis would chide him for not having paid better attention to what they had been doing, and he would accept the chiding, knowing that Fejelis would not have sunk into passive misery. He hoped Fejelis would understand, and that Tam could return something for his betrayal. The high masters had sent him to negotiate for themselves, for the Temple, and he had no choice in that—but he would also negotiate for Fejelis and the earthborn, if he could.

The thought made him look out of himself and around. His eyes seemed to be adjusting to the darkness, rendering it less absolute with every minute that passed. There was even a thin glaze of light on the barren hills around him, like the luster on one of Beatrice's pots, from a three-quarter moon rising to the east.

Beatrice ... Years ago he had promised to protect her, promised her—standing amidst the shards of glazed crockery and tiles, the sticks left of shelving and workbenches—that she need never again fear the bullies of her own guild. She had come to him on that promise. In that, too, he had failed; the Temple would surely look again at his children, and if it chose, would take over their rearing.

He shivered. The night wind, sweeping in with the moonlight, was cold, and his clothing was styled for the heated interior of the palace and the Temple. He was standing on a dirt path on a barren heather and bracken slope. He knew such dirt paths—he had spent his boyhood driving herds along them, herds that dwindled year by year, sold off for the taxes. The soil here was even poorer than the soil in the foothills of the Cloudherds. But this scraped land was Darkborn; here the barons cared whether their people starved. He smiled bitterly into the darkness. If it were only their brightnesses suffering here, then he would do nothing for the earthborn, a peasant mage's revenge for the centuries of oppression.

The night seemed darker, now that he could see the moonlight, than it had before. Shadows cast by moonlight seemed far denser than those cast by sunlight. The shaded lee of the hills, the roots of the bracken, the sides of the path, all might have been folded out of the world. He shuddered and raised his eyes to a sky so filled with stars as to replete even a Lightborn eye. He had not looked willingly on the stars for more than thirty years, since his younger brother had been murdered, but even then, he had never seen their full plenitude. If Artarian had been here, he would have flung himself down on the night-damp bracken, green eyes huge with wonder, and not stirred until the sun came up.

Magic surged, sudden, close, and Shadowborn enough to make him swallow hard. Thirty yards down the path was the figure of a man, briefly dark and then radiantly illuminated. Tam stared, the light painful to his dark-adapted eyes, at his right hand, which seemed to be holding the light. Behind the light was great strength not entirely controlled. In the

Temple, with his training complete, the man might have been one of the high masters—a contender for archmage, even. He felt the magic rake his ensorcellment, and the man whistled. "Tammorn, I take it? I'm Neill. Emeya sent me to meet you."

Still staring at his hand, Tam said, "How do you do that?"

Neill turned up his palm, showed the coldly blazing stick within. "This. It's quite straightforward."

"Not for Lightborn, it's not," Tam said. "Our lights need recharging by sunlight."

"I'll show you when we get a chance." Neill looked like a man in his early twenties, but then so did Tam, who was nearly fifty. He was quite tall, with an underdeveloped build, as though unaccustomed to using his muscles when magic would serve. His face was angular; hollow-cheeked; and all brow, jaw, and nose, with a lupine cast to it. His dark hair was coarse, wavy, and windblown. His eyes were deep-set, and Tam could not tell their color. He wore a long, patchwork coat of hides and furs, open over a ruffled shirt and heavy trousers. There was an ensorcellment on him, a binding of the will. The invested vitality had the feel of the mage he had spoken to when he had reached into that roil of Shadowborn power south of Stranhorne.

He swallowed again and breathed slowly to calm his stomach and his nerves. "I am ordered by the archmage and the high masters to open negotiations with the Shadowborn."

"Then, first of all, don't refer to us as Shadowborn. Our home's Atholaya."

He had heard, or read, the name somewhere, but could not recall where—Lukfer had more than once had sharp words for him for his studied indifference to Temple history. If the dead could speak, it would be to say, "I told you so."

"Are you taking me there?"

"She sent me here to make sure you weren't a danger to her. We've been dealt a few unpleasant shocks of late." He did not sound as though he entirely regretted those shocks—but, then, would the Shadowborn archmage ensorcell a loyal follower so?

He felt Neill's magic playing around him, prying at his own ensorcellment. "How fascinating," he said. "How long have you known how to do that?"

The instincts of a tower-trained mage prevailed: above all, impress. "A few hours, since the Darkborn came with the ensorcellment on him."

"Darkborn . . . Ah, Sebastien, what have you done? Was this Darkborn named Hearne, by chance?"

"They didn't say." And to his regret, he had not asked.

"I am sure it was." He sighed. "Foolish boy. So the Temple sent you here with a just-learned, completely untried ensorcellment on you. To impress us, I presume, with their aptitude and the obedience they can command from a strong mage." A glint of tooth. "Are you expendable, Magister Tammorn?"

Tam matched that cynical smile with one of his own, but did not answer.

"So . . . the Lightborn Temple wants to treat with us. For what?"

"Should I not wait and take that up with your archmage?"

"You could. The problem is that Emeya is insane. Come at her direct, with reasoned argument, and you will meet only unreason. I know how to deal with her."

"Is that why she has you ensorcelled?" Tam said, coming at him direct.

The lantern sank in his hand, throwing angled shadows across his face. Of the deep-set eyes, only a hint of bluish sclera remained. "I failed to take Stranhorne, and a valued one of our number was killed. She does not think there is any such thing as failure, only willful defiance."

Tam lowered his voice. "You don't have to put up with that."

Neill lifted the lantern and held it out, almost between their faces. "Are you trying to suborn me? Better and more beloved than you have tried. But it's less a case of where the bread's buttered as who's holding the knife." Teeth showed in his smile, sharper than before. "But I suppose you've earned something for that. So I'll give you some advice: go back to your Temple; go back and tell them that Emeya recognizes no peers. If she did, she would have to recognize the one who surely is. If they don't agree, they can test themselves against her power. I expect they will lose, though I'd much prefer that they win. Oh yes, the ensorcellment only prevents me working against her will. It does not prevent me saying what I think."

There was another Shadowborn as strong, and an enemy of Emeya? "Emeya's presence was the strongest I sensed."

Neill's feral smile flashed. "You'll not get me to spill that way, Tammorn. If you're not going to go back to your Temple, then I suppose I'll just have to take you to Emeya. What are the Temple's terms?"

"I think I should best take that up with your lady."

"As opposed to a mere minion? On your own head be it." Magic surged, caught him up, and, despite his reflex resistance, *lifted* him.

His first sense was of magic all around him—hideous, tainted magic that reminded him of nothing so much as a slaughterhouse in high summer. If he could endure the assault of rotting blood and hot urine and manure on his senses then, he could endure the assault of this on his magic now.

"I don't know why it takes your kind that way at first," Neill said. "We've had the occasional mage follow our Call, though all have been low-ranked. The distress will pass, or you'll be past feeling it. This way. Stay close."

Tam followed at Neill's shoulder, stumbling despite the light the man carried. He had trodden rough ground before, but never by a single light, and he was repeatedly deceived by shadows and pits impersonating shadows. Some great violence had been done the land here, leaving it gouged, deeply scored, and stripped of scrub, bracken, grass, and tree. Only tussocks and fragments of root remained, barbs for the ankles and snares for the feet. He was aware they were on a downslope, but between trying to control his revulsion to Shadowborn magic and trying to keep his footing, he was not aware how the torn earth had been reshaped until Neill stopped moving and he looked ahead—up at a towering earthworks molded from the dirt and the embed-

ded fragments of the plants swept up with it. His mouth fell
a little open: he had a gift for inert-matter manipulation
himself, but he could never have imagined having moved so
much of it. . . . He could just see the top of the wall, and
though the curve of it was perceptible, it must easily exceed
the circumference of the tower. The slope they had just
climbed down was the pit scoured to raise it. They reached
an arch of earth that was not only packed but fused into
clinker, and, passing through, entered a midden of sleeping
animals.

Sleeping monsters—no farm animals these, brought into
the village stockade for shelter. He could smell fur and
urine and feces, and instead of grain or hay, the odor was of
rotting meat and old blood, for real, this time. From a
mound of gray pelt that was waist-high at its apex, a spear-
shaped head rose on a long neck and four slitted eyes glared
at the light. Neill murmured a word that seemed to carry as
much affection as command, and the creature sighed and
laid its head down once more.

A huge wolf shouldered past Tam to butt Neill's knees.
Tam had had a herd dog who liked to do that, thinking it a
merry joke if he could dump people on their rumps, but it
had done it to Tam's father, and he had sold it at the low-
lands fair. Neill crouched to fondle the wolf's ears, allowing
it to nuzzle his face and chin as though those jaws could not
have torn his throat out with a snap. "Hey, Mayfly, good
hunting out there?"

Tam took one look at the dried blood on the beast's ruff
and averted his gaze. Behind the beast—Mayfly—came several others, sizing up Tam for the eating and making up to
Neill, whose magic spun out and around and through them.
Their maker, perhaps, because Mayfly and several of the
others were nearly twice the size of the foothills wolves
Tam had hunted in his youth. Their master, certainly. Neill
clucked at Mayfly like an old village wife feeding her chick-
ens, gave it a parting pat, and led Tam to stairs that followed
the inner shell of the earthworks upward. Tam could not
help but look back, remembering Fejelis and the others
talking after their defense of the railway hut and railroad,

and measuring the numbers that might yet be turned against the Darkborn and against his own earthborn. And then up, apprehensively, toward the lair of the flying Shadowborn.

The stairs, like the arch, were built of clinkered earth, rough and uneven. Neill held the light at his side, showing him the edge, for which Tam was grateful. He wondered why, with such power as he clearly had, Neill did not simply let it carry him to the top. Unless that, too, was bound.

And then all speculation ended with an obliterating sense of Shadowborn magic, and only Neill's quick clasp saved him from a stumble and possibly a fall. "She's back," he said, quite unnecessarily. "And she wants you. Now."

He let Neill haul him up the last several yards, aware of the urgency in his manner. Yet at the top of the stairs, at the first sight of the person who stood there, he halted in commonplace shock.

She was a *child*, a fair-haired girl of no more than thirteen. No taller than his chest, her figure barely budding, her dress a simple blue frock with a pattern of rushes and dragonflies and grass stains over the knees, and a circlet of wilting purple daisies around her curling crown. Her skin was translucent in Neill's light, like his son's, who had inherited Beatrice's lovely complexion. Almost he might have believed that she was an innocent trapped at the center of this vortex of magic, rather than its focus, because no child commanded that kind of power. She peered up at him from beneath transparent lashes and smiled shyly.

Before her magic tore his mind apart.

He was not aware of falling to his knees and then to his hands and knees, but that was where he found himself when the magic let him go. Helpless, shaking, he vomited himself dry. In the one, two, three—however many infinite—minutes she had pillaged his mind, she had taken from him his past, his knowledge of the Temple, his knowledge of magic, and even—something the high masters had refrained from doing—Lukfer's last *gift*. His life had been pulled from him in a tumble of faces, places, experiences, emotions: his hardscrabble boyhood, his muddled youth, Artarian's death, his years of wandering, his rescue by Darien White Hand, meeting Lukfer, saving Fejelis and being punished for it, falling in love with Beatrice, finding a friend in Fejelis, his children's births, Isidore's death, Lukfer's death and the carnage in the Temple, rescuing Fejelis, the high masters' orders, the high masters' wishes, his own hopes . . . Knowledge and memory, she had taken it all.

He felt Neill's hands light on his forehead and the back of his head, but he barely felt the touch of the man's magic, except that his stomach finally stopped wringing itself out. The Shadowborn mage hooked his hands beneath his armpits and hauled him upright on his knees and then to his feet. "I warned you," he said, through set teeth. Angry, Tam realized, and on his behalf. The Shadowborn mage pulled Tam's arm across his shoulders and walked him around the curve of the earthworks. They were on an inner ramparts, with another level above them; there he sensed the presence of the flying Shadowborn.

Another earth wall loomed before them, with a smaller archway closed by a hanging. With a snap of the hand, Neill tossed aside the hanging to allow them through. Inside, another gesture lit several illuminated wands jammed into the walls. He dropped Tam into an armchair. The chair, the bed, the table—all were carved with a detail that any Darkborn would have coveted, though the wood was deep, even, rose brown, and highly polished. Except for its disturbing opacity, for its ability to cast dense shadows, it might have graced a bedroom in a guild master's house. "I refuse to sleep on dirt," Neill said, observing his interest.

In the corner, in a carved basket, tawny fur stirred. A small wildcat hissed at Tam from where she lay curled around her kits. "Where's your sister?" Neill said to her, and a thread of magic looped the room, drawing a second wildcat out from under the bed. Decades-old habit made Tam tally the bounty on the skins. Neill folded himself down on the floor, which he had covered with a camp mat in the southern style, allowing the cat to sprawl across his lap. Her flank bulged with her own unborn litter. "I'd best send you back, hadn't I?" the mage said to her. "Too many things with big teeth around. I'll do it as soon as she lets me." He looked up at Tam; in this light, his eyes were a deep blue. "Not much of a welcome for the emissary from the Temple."

"Why?" Tam said hoarsely.

"Her? Me? You? The world? Life?"

"She could have *asked*."

"Simplest answer: because she can, and now you and your Temple know she can." He shook his head. "You should have let me handle it."

"You're stronger than I am," Tam said bluntly, "but not that strong."

The corner of Neill's mouth tucked in. "And how, may I ask, did you survive in the Temple so long?" He met Tam's startled look with raised brows. "Did you think we didn't study our enemy?"

"We didn't sense your magic."

"We didn't send up fireworks. We knew the Darkborn could sense Shadowborn, even if we weren't aware that extended to Lightborn sports. We kept to the minor magic: shape-shifting when we had to"— *minor?* thought Tam— "ensorcellment of mind"— *Floria*— "some talismanic magic."

"The"—he cleared his throat—"the munitions that destroyed the tower?"

"Dealt with at the factory outside the city. All right," he said to the wildcat, who had taken his stroking hand in her jaws, teeth not breaking the skin. "I'll leave well enough alone." She heaved herself off his lap and squeezed back into her refuge under the bed.

"Who is Emeya? How did she get . . . the way she is? The strength she has."

Neill did not at first appear to hear the question, his eyes following the wildcat. But he let her go, rising to settle in the second chair. "How much do you know about the origin of the Curse?"

"Laid by the mage Imogene and her followers in revenge for the death of her daughter in a war between mages," Tam said, promptly.

"And why didn't it die with them?"

That was the subject of endless speculation amongst student mages, and like most such exercises in speculation, one Tam avoided. He was a peasant; what was, was. Magic was supported by the mage's vitality and will, and when those ceased, so, too, did the magic. The Curse was the exception. Those were the facts; speculation was specious.

Then he had a sudden, appalling thought. "Did *all* the mages who laid the Curse die?"

"The obvious question, but the answer is yes. All died, and more. If you think Emeya's a monster, you should have met Imogene . . . Be patient," he said in response to Tam's stirring. "I'll come to your answer. But first, Imogene, a monster beyond compare. She'd specialized for years—centuries, even—on ensorcellments of the will, and anyone who came within her reach was made subject or driven away, with the exception of her daughter Ismene, whom she doted on. Ismene took an earthborn lover—not by his choice, you understand. It meant nothing to her that he was plighted by custom and honor to another woman, or that he killed himself in shame when she cast him off. Earthborn law could not touch Ismene; and mage's law barely, but that man's betrothed—her name has not come down to us—did not forget. Thirty years it took her to have her revenge. How'd an earthborn kill a mage?" A smile, with sharp teeth. "The Darkborn seem to be learning the way of it. In this case, she found allies—many allies, who'd been injured by magic, who were jealous of magic, who feared magic—and what she couldn't find, she bought. She found ways of setting the mageborn against each other, made sure that Ismene had enemies enough among the mageborn that her magic was worn down—not that that was difficult—and finally lured her underground and dropped a mountain on her head. And *that* is why the Curse, why Imogene took such revenge upon the earthborn, for all those who were part of her daughter's murder. . . . I sometimes wonder what became of that lady after, though she probably did not survive too long."

"Did nobody try to stop her . . . Imogene?"

"Oh yes, and either joined her or died refusing. *That* was

the war between mages, there, between those who'd joined Imogene and those who opposed her. To ensure the Curse would survive them, Imogene anchored it in the vitality of everyone born into it, and made her and her followers' children the keystones of the magic. Of those, seven survived the first century. Six were alive at the end of the third. Four after the fifth. Two at the eighth."

Magic anchored in the vitality of another, one of the lost skills that the high masters had tried to retrieve for generations. He knew how the high masters would react to this, greedy as they were. "And those two are Emeya and . . ."

"Imogene's younger daughter, Isolde."

"And you are?"

"Emeya's great-great-grandson. *She* was so clearly deranged that even the other children knew it, so they kept her under ensorcellment. In the end, they were too few. Five hundred years had passed while she slept. You can imagine what that did for her. She let herself mature enough to bear a son, and then let others do the bearing for her."

Five hundred years and then five generations . . . This man might be older than the archmage's three hundred years. He had the strength for such longevity. "And Isolde?"

Neill released a long breath through his nose. "Imogene's other daughter, the one who was not the favorite, the one of whom nothing was expected. I'm sure her mother would have been surprised to find Isolde had outlived them all. I don't think she's sane, either."

And how much of that should he believe, given that between Emeya and Isolde there was at least rivalry and possibly outright war? He wished he had Fejelis here—the prince made a study of the ways people revealed themselves. Mages could grow lazy.

"Why, after all these centuries, should the two of you be looking north? Why attack the manor?"

"Emeya decided that Atholaya was too small for the two of them." The tone was easy, but the shift of his eyes in their deep sockets betrayed a lie. Then he sighed and leaned back on his hands. "Emeya is afraid of Isolde."

That might be truth, but the Temple mage distrusted

such a ready admission of vulnerability. What else did it disguise? "Has she reason to be? Is Isolde the stronger?"

"As to the manor, the Stranhornes and Strumhellers have been nothing but trouble for centuries. We wanted the manor. We'd have had *both* manors by now, but that we—*I*—got overconfident. Baron Strumheller, the man said, and I knew that name, but I've never sensed anything so weak and ripped up with overuse besides. So I was talking to him, waiting for Sebastien to join us, and he simply *shoots* me—calm as you please, with a bullet that would drop a scavvern. I suppose I should be glad he stopped at the one. And while I'm putting my viscera back together, Midora and the idiot boy start burning up the interior of Stranhorne, until—*boom*." He gave Tam a dark look, then let out a sigh and snapped his fingers in the direction of the basket, following it with a prod of magic.

The wildcat hissed, but obediently caught up a kitten in its jaws and carried it, dangling, to Neill's knee. She crouched, glaring at him, while he examined it, inserting a finger into the small mouth, running a hand down the spine, testing the thrust of its hind legs. The diversion seemed to calm him, and he smiled engagingly at the angry cat as he handed her kit back. "She's a beauty, isn't she?" he said to Tam.

Her pelt certainly was thick and healthy, though small for full bounty. "The creatures—are they all yours?"

"They are now. I inherited them from Durran—my father—along with my bent toward fleshworking. He'd the original idea to use what the Darkborn call the Shadowborn to drive the Sundered out of Atholaya and keep them out. They were all terrified of what they'd do if they found us, he most of all."

"And . . . the transformed Darkborn?" Tam said. He'd been too overspent and sickened to characterize the magic around the flyers, but this man could rework flesh, so if any mage could . . .

A white glimmer in the shadowed eyes. "Ah, you realized that."

"Your doing?" he said, quietly.

"Emeya would not have let them live otherwise. Transformed, they're useful to her."

"Do *they* agree with you that life is worth accepting on any terms?"

"You don't have the slightest idea what you are talking about," Neill said, without temper.

"Do you not realize," Tam said, in a low voice, "that what you are doing is an atrocity?"

Neill tipped his head back, the light catching on the long, vulpine planes of his face. Its cast was not quite man, now Tam saw it fully in strong light, as though Neill had chosen to emulate one of his beloved animals. "I realize it. And I repeat: you don't have the slightest idea what you are talking about. Believe me, there are worse atrocities."

Tam was tired and sickened and ready to despair, but he struggled on. "And Sebastien?"

"My cousin Ariadne's son. Emeya wanted her mated—didn't matter to whom—but without waiting for them to find their way"—his eyes glittered with anger—"she set an ensorcellment on them. Ari was just strong enough to twist the ensorcellment toward another man, and just to add insult, she chose a new Darkborn slave, bound him to her and herself to him. The child born to them was mageborn, and strong, so Emeya let them live. But they were marked from that day. Hearne's a survivor, if nothing else. He persuaded Ariadne to make a run for Isolde. They'd have taken the boy, but he was Emeya's pet then, and he didn't want to go. Knowing what Emeya would do to her, I helped them get away." He grimly contemplated the pattern of the carpet. "If I'd known then what I know now, I wouldn't." He glanced up. "Emeya needs this Temple alliance; she just won't face the fact."

"Why?" Tam said.

The deep-set eyes looked directly at him, blue in their depths and calculating. Tam wished again to be Fejelis or one of the high masters, old and crafty, instead of a blunt, muddled peasant.

Neill said nothing; plainly, he was not going to answer that particular question, at least now.

"Why do you stay with her?" Tam said.

Neill said, "I'm a mage. I want knowledge. I *crave* the exercise of my power. That's what binds me. I couldn't live with all your Temple rules."

Tam knew that craving. At its best, that desire expressed itself as it had in Lukfer, in the long years of study and unceasing efforts to master his unruly strength, and in the generosity that had made him willing to offer his knowledge to anyone who would receive it from him. It was not his failing that so few had. At its worst . . . he thought he had taken his measure of it at its worst, when the high masters had him lying bound before them and ransacked his mind for his knowledge. But now . . .

Now he had met Emeya, he knew her strength exceeded that of the archmage, exceeded that of the archmage and high masters who had bound him—for all he might try to tell himself that she had taken him unawares and they had not. And if she knew magical protocols lost since the Sundering . . . the high masters would want those.

"You look quite horrified," Neill observed. "What are you thinking?"

"About magic. And your archmage. And the high masters."

"It's not an unendurable life, ordinarily. Just lately . . ." And then the color drained suddenly from his long face. "She wants me," he said. "Don't leave this room, whatever hap—" In a knot of Shadowborn magic, he was gone.

Tam gagged. "'Not an unendurable life,'" he quoted hoarsely, to the empty room. Hissing answered him, from the basket and from under the bed.

Could he escape, while Emeya was occupied with Neill? He might yet have the strength for a *lift*, drained though he was. He was desperate enough to try—to Stranhorne, even Minhorne. As Lukfer had repeatedly reminded him, distance was more a psychological barrier than a physical one; his body's memory of all those miles walked barefoot or in holed boots refused to yield to magic alone. But should he succeed in leaving, dared he take this information back to the high masters? Would it repel or entice them—all this power, all this knowledge? Would they believe him or think

him mistaken about her strength? Would they send him
back to accept her terms? And what hope for Fejelis and
the earthborn then?

He had a dreadful vision of himself set up as master and
protector of earthborn, as Neill was master and protector of
beasts. Had his stomach not already been empty, he would
have vomited. A voice insinuated itself into his thoughts.
<No, then.>

The vision had not been his own temptation, but hers.

He extended his magic toward the archmage, the high
masters; reached in blind desperation and met only her
presence, her strength, pressing down. She said, <Be still,
or—> and his sense of her magic reaching to twist the core
out of his protective ensorcellment against darkness, of
himself melting away, was so strong that for heartbeats he
believed it had happened.

He fell back into the chair, feeling half dissolved. He did
not sense the wolf enter the room, though he heard the
wildcats hiss. He blinked tears from his eyes in time to see
it regard the basket with intelligent yellow eyes, and lurched
forward in his chair in an absurd protective reaction toward
one predator against a greater. Then froze as the wolf turned
its malign gaze toward him. It whined, padded forward, and,
even as he mustered the magic he would need to defend
himself, propped its jaw on his knee, its brows quirking,
doglike, as it contemplated his face.

He was still sitting there, pinned in place by his guardian,
when Neill reappeared. The mage landed on his feet and
promptly dropped to hands and knees. Tam could see the
stripes across his face and neck and arms, wheals like those
he had seen on a man who had fallen into a swarm of skull
jellyfish. Mayfly abandoned Tam to snuffle at Neill's ear.
The mage slung an arm around his pet's neck and leaned
against the shaggy shoulder. The wheals along his jawline
seemed to bubble as magics battled within them, hers to
hurt, his to heal.

Her magic intensified. The wheals suddenly split and the
bubbling spread across his entire face, and he rolled away

from the wolf, curling into a fetal ball. Far later than Tam would have expected, he screamed.

Her magic swirled away, and Neill slumped over onto his back, the blisters sealing themselves over, the raw flesh drying and dulling and going pink. He stared at the ceiling for several minutes, chest rising and falling, then worked a hand into the wolf's ruff and pulled himself up. "How d'you like that demonstration?"

"Not," said Tam.

"As you can perhaps gather," Neill said, sounding slightly breathless, "she is not receptive to the idea of an alliance. I think she mismeasures your high masters' strength, myself." His skin was as unmarked as it had been before, but Tam noticed that his face had lost the angularity and length of jaw and was now entirely a man's.

"Come outside," Neill said abruptly. "I know you'll never have seen this. I know I need to, just at the moment. It gives me strength."

In trepidation, Tam followed him outside, and with even more trepidation followed him up a final series of steps to the ramparts of the earthworks. He could see around him the crumpled mounds of sleeping Shadowborn, each one with a mat for a mattress and its folded wings for blankets. He could feel Neill's magic flickering around them, soothing. On the edge of the earthworks, not too close, Neill pointed east. The sky, so dark when they had met, had lightened along the horizon to the cobalt blue of a fine glass, draped with cloud. "Dawn," Neill said.

"I've seen dawn," Tam said. He would take no gifts from this cruel paradox of a man.

Neill glanced at him. "Not like this, I'll warrant. Enjoy it. It may be our last."

A wave of magic rose from beneath them. A boy's voice screamed rawly. Neill closed his eyes in sympathetic pain. "I have to go. You stay. No one will bother you. Mayfly." The wolf, summoned, pushed between them like a jealous child. "See no one does."

Neill was right; seen from this side of sunrise, daybreak was astonishing—the transparent yellow, the intense orange, the blinding break of sunlight. Artarian should have been here. Beatrice should have had these colors to glaze on her pots. Fejelis would have watched with his usual interest in the new. His son ... would no doubt have tried to throw himself from the ramparts or down the gullet of a wolf. He wiped his face. How could a sight so beautiful elicit such despair?

Neill returned, climbing the stairs, looking weary beyond words, but with no physical hurt on him, to Tam's peculiar relief. The beast mage put a hand on Mayfly's back and leaned briefly. "She brought the boy back," he said. "She needs his strength. And he wanted healing."

He straightened and turned to face Tam, half his face brilliantly lit by the new, orange sun, half in shadow. "You asked why Atholaya was too small for Emeya and Isolde, why Emeya needed new territory. I told you that Imogene and the others anchored the Curse in children. So think about the fact that magic often doesn't mature until late adolescence or after. Even mageborn children wouldn't have had the strength to support magic like the Curse. Imogene changed those children. We think that Isolde is close to rediscovering how—with Ariadne's help. She may already have. Should she succeed, she will destroy Emeya."

"And why," Tam said, harshly, "would that be worse than allowing Emeya"—*and you*—"to continue unchecked?"

Neill gave him a very long look. "This: how do you think many of Isolde's own children and grandchildren died?"

Telmaine

Every train journey with Vladimer seems to take longer, Telmaine thought. They did not even have the compartment to themselves, she and Vladimer; the five officers of the Strumheller troop had been shoehorned into it. She ought to be grateful that, unlike Vladimer, she was sitting hip to hip with only two men, not three. The floor was muddy and sticky and littered with scraps of oiled cloth, odd bullets, and pieces of newspaper. As the train labored up a hill, a hip flask skidded out from under her seat and bounced off her foot before sliding under the opposite bench. At intervals it, or some other detritus, reappeared. The compartment was too crowded for anyone to grope after it. The air reeked of sweaty men, soap, old smoke, damp wool, oil, and ammunition. The carriage was not designed to travel by day, so all the vents had to be closed.

Vladimer and the men seemed unperturbed. They were planning, fighting verbal campaigns, just as her brothers and their friends had on those interminable summer journeys to and from the estate. All it wanted was her sister, Merivan, at her side, fingers poised to pinch should Telmaine try to join in the boys' talk.

Ishmael, Telmaine thought irritably, *would not spend all this time talking about it.* Ishmael was practical. Ishmael would prepare his weapons, settle his people, and then go to sleep. Let Vladimer work himself up to a pitch—she had the sense that this was the way he was—Telmaine would emulate Ishmael. She shifted until her head was more or less propped against the inner wall, shoulder hunched uncomfortably, and breathed slowly, remembering Balthasar's efforts at hypnotizing her before the girls were born. When this was over—and she must believe it would be over, somehow—she would delight in doing something as commonplace and removed from magic as having another child.

She became aware of the smell of lemon tea, drifting pleasantly through the reek of men going to war, though that was there, too, both in her dream and out of it. Ishmael was sitting on the floor of a train carriage, cleaning his weapons. She could sense great heat coming from him, furnace heat, as though he had been newly cast in clay and set out to cool. He was slow to lift his head when she spoke to him. And the weapons were strange. Was there such a thing as a two-barreled gun? It could not be safe, pointing both ways. He lifted his head, sonned her with a terrible regret, quite unlike any expression she'd known on his face, and pulled the trigger. She watched him fall away, as the man on the platform had fallen, the dart from Vladimer's cane in his belly. She touched her own abdomen and felt her hands sink into the wound he had made in her.

A man's voice said, "M'lady, are you all right?"

She was back in the carriage, her face wet with tears. One of the men handed her a handkerchief that was clean and well made, but had the smell of too much laundering. She nodded her gratitude nevertheless and dabbed her face. "Bad dream," she whispered. They murmured understanding, though she was sure they did not.

"We're nearly there," said the donor of the handkerchief. "It's gone sunrise."

After Ishmael had *gifted* her—tried, through mind-touch, to convey to her his accomplishment in magic, she had found herself dreaming his dreams, running through the Shadowlands, fighting remembered battles. But even when he was held in prison, in peril of his life, his dreams had not threatened her or himself, or despaired.

Or burnt so, with magic.

If she understood one thing, it was that he needed help. She could not endanger these men by using magic in such close confines and with only a train's siding between themselves and daylight, even if she was certain that this time, Vladimer would not miss his shot. Nor did she particularly want to die. She knotted her gloved hands, one in the other, and endured the last, interminable minutes as the train paused before Stranhorne Crosstracks to let their Lightborn guard disembark, listening to the shouted exchange between Lightborn outside and Darkborn inside. Balthasar would be heartened by the vulgar ease of it.

Unlike Strumheller, Stranhorne Crosstracks had an enclosed platform with doors that could be operated from safety. Vladimer, of all people, was the one to pause to help her down—only to lean close and say, "What do you sense?"

What she sensed was...overwhelming. People—Darkborn—closely packed on the platform, beneath the platform, outside, across the tracks. Thousands of them in the near vicinity, hurt, grieving, fierce, resolute, afraid, uncomprehending. She staggered, and he had to steady her. *"Shadowborn?"* he hissed.

"No, not that." In all that shocking miasma of Darkborn

emotion and suffering, there was no taint of Shadowborn. "Just Darkborn. Many, many people."

"Come with me, then. And tell the Broomes' party to follow."

Tentatively she did, knowing that Phoebe Broome definitely did not approve of either her presence there or her use of magic, but she drew no rebuke. Vladimer set out confidently across the warped and pitching boards of the platform, toward what proved to be a stair, metal steps laid over crumbling stone. He had been there before. He threw back over his shoulder, "One of the first settlements to reestablish itself after the Sundering. It has a number of underground warehouses and cellars, mainly used for storage and protection against raids before, that sheltered Darkborn immediately after."

She remembered his guided tour of the archducal palace in Minhorne, as they went together to interview Floria White Hand. She did not wish to be ungrateful, but she hoped this was not more of the same; Vladimer's choice of anecdote tended toward the macabre. "Did Ishmael tell you about these?"

"Maxim di Gautier, while raiding the palace's private libraries . . . After the Sundering, the Stranhornes extended the tunnels between the chambers and opened up more. It's quite extensive. If Stranhorne had to retreat, there'd be no better place to retreat to."

Telmaine, remembering Shadowborn fires, said nothing to that. She could sense the mages coming down quickly behind them. "Where are we going?"

"Where I expect we'll find whoever's in charge."

Planking and matting marked out a thoroughfare through the crowded underground space beneath the platform. Planks and stone blocks had been assembled into rough dividers and furnishings, allowing adults to sit and sick and tired people to lie, while children weaved and scrambled between the groups in a running game of troopers and Shadowborn. The clear thoroughfare was, of course, irresistible. Three urchins pelting along it would have plowed into Vladimer and Telmaine but for Farquhar

Broome's intervention. Deflected, they tumbled into the laps of a group of men playing cards, who reared up with roars and cuffs. In a belated flurry, sisters and mothers rushed to the rescue. Vladimer shamelessly left the altercation to evolve, and led them through a tunnel under the railway tracks.

Perhaps I do not need to worry about fire, Telmaine thought, smelling the damp.

They surfaced in a circular concourse like a smaller version of Bolingbroke Station in Minhorne, but Bolingbroke Station had been built in the last century, and this, by the rough stone and thick walls, much earlier. Most of the stalls along the outer and inner ring of the concourse were closed and boarded against the press of refugees, but some had had their boards and even their counters pried loose and carried away.

"Dear boy," Farquhar Broome hailed from behind. "Where are we going?"

Vladimer pointed. "Up." Overhead, Telmaine's sonn could pick out the edge of a balcony and the hard echo of iron railings.

They made their way around the perimeter to the ascending staircase with some difficulty, since not everyone respected the corridor. They did Vladimer, though, when he put into effect his declared intention to press into service anyone he found sprawled across his path, with no respect for excuses. After the first three, a wave of warning ran around the perimeter and trespassers scrambled clear.

On the balcony, they found the defenders, some of whom were already asleep, sprawled on mats and bags and bundles, weapons close at hand. Those who were awake were cleaning and repairing weapons and armor, playing cards, gossiping, sharing rations and flasks and pipes, and otherwise taking their ease. After the underground shelter and the concourse, pipe smoke was fragrant. As they climbed the next flight of stairs, onto the floor under the cupola, the officers stayed behind to arrange for places for their own men.

Under the domed ceiling of the cupola, they found fifteen

or twenty men around a round table where, in wet sand, someone had sculpted what Telmaine presumed was a relief of the land around Stranhorne, marked with a mixture of fine game pieces and roughly carved pegs. Lord Ferdenzil—no, Duke Ferdenzil Mycene—was leaning on the table with his elbows, and was short enough that it resembled a casual pose rather than a droop. He was haggard with exhaustion, something she could never have imagined possible. The tall young woman next to him, Baronette Laurel's twin, was frankly propped against the table and arguing with him in a voice that croaked with overuse. Both turned to sonn the arrivals with open relief, though Mycene's rapidly changed to sour amusement.

"Mycene," Vladimer acknowledged. "Baronette Stranhorne."

"Vladimer Plantageter," Mycene said. "This is a surprise."

"Indeed. A word, Mycene, if I may." He drew the other man off to the side. Telmaine felt a moment's sympathy for Mycene: Vladimer would not have been her choice to tell a man his father was dead, especially given the rumors about Vladimer's paternity and the enmity between Mycene and Vladimer. Her sonn caught Mycene's motion as he lowered his head into a gloved hand and turned away. Since he had been her suitor, and one her family heartily approved of, she had used her touch-sense to tell whether she could love him. So she knew the resentment he harbored toward his vigorous, intensely competitive father. But it is the people of great greedy vitality, who consume so much of those around them, who leave the greatest hollowness behind.

The baronette said, "What's happened?" To Telmaine's surprise, given the way they had been arguing, there was concern on her face.

"Vladimer is telling him that the duke, his father, is dead."

"Sachevar Mycene?" Lavender croaked. "How?

"Shadowborn," Telmaine said. At least here there would be no contesting their existence.

"In th'city?" one of the men said.

Vladimer, returning, saved her from questioning. Ferdenzil Mycene followed a step behind, though Telmaine wondered how much he would be hearing now. His expression was taut, dazed. She herself heard little of Vladimer's report to the Stranhornes, and only slightly more of the Stranhornes' report to Vladimer—given by a well-spoken man with a rogue's face, introduced as the Stranhorne lawyer—once she heard they had had no word of Ishmael. The Stranhornes and their reinforcements had spent most of the night sweeping the area, collecting survivors, and killing roaming Shadowborn. There were rumors that the main force had established a redoubt east of Stranhorne. *I might,* she thought, *have told them that.* And if they thought to ask the mages, Farquhar Broome certainly could. So there was no need for her to stay. Quietly, and, she hoped, unnoticed, she eased back from between Vladimer and Mycene, holding her skirts out to stop them from whispering. A light cast of sonn sketched in the space under the cupola. Two heavy, barred outer doors, flush with the curve of the cupola, must lead outside, but four seemed to lead into interior rooms. She tried a door and found it locked. She was well able to deal with locks, having freed herself from the execution room before Vladimer found her, but that would entail magic and draw attention. The next door was unlocked. She opened it and slipped inside, promptly stumbling on a heap of blankets on the floor, perhaps set aside from the baronette or the duke. The air was stifling; the wall hot. *With the sun,* she realized, shuddering slightly.

But it would do. The door was reasonably solid and she had to assume it was light-tight. In case. She sat down at the high writing stool before the desk, pushing the flammable papers on it aside with a grimace of unease. Quickly, before she could think better of this, she recalled the sense of her dream, the sense of Ishmael in it. She opened her senses and reached out with her magic, trusting the affinity between them to make the connection, as it had between her in the city, him on the train.

<Ishmael?>

The blast of heat brutally broke her from the trance. Groping and wild sonn found nothing alight, nothing smoldering, no smell of smoke. Panting, hands to her bodice, she fought to calm herself. The heat had been on Ishmael's end. Where his magic, and the vitality that fed it, had seemed like banked coals, now it seemed a furnace. It took all the love she had for him to open her thoughts once more. <Ishmael di Studier. Ishmael.>

Something stirred in the furnace, something familiar. She sensed it trying to articulate.

<Ishmael? What's happened to you?>

A cascade of impressions, and the heat of a monstrous magic, raging amongst those embers. <Ishmael,> she pleaded. <You're hurting me.>

The heat was instantly snuffed. She thought, for an instant of dread, that he had exerted himself magically and died. Yet she had felt none of the terrifying draining and pain that had ended their previous conversation.

<What are you doing?> Phoebe Broome, inevitably.

Her jaw set. How dared the woman, her social inferior, intrude.

<I may be your social inferior, *Lady Telmaine*—>

<I was speaking to *Ishmael*.>

<Ishmael? *That* was Ishmael?> She, too, broke the connection—mages, no manners. Then Telmaine felt the delicate touch of Farquhar Broome's magic, and a breath later, the man himself was standing in front of her, stooping beneath the curve of the cupola. "That was brave of you, dear girl, but not at all wise."

"What has *happened* to him? It *is* him, isn't it?"

"Of course; his presence is quite distinctive. But he must have undergone a remarkable transformation—"

<Telmaine.> Raw need reaching out from the furnace. She heard herself whimper with pain, despite her best resolution.

Farquhar Broome's hand descended lightly on her head; his magic veiled her, and the sense of heat and pressure lessened. <Dear boy,> he said, <be gentler to the lady, if you would.>

<Magister Broome?> That molten stream of impressions turned on the seventh-rank mage. Farquhar Broome

grunted, staggered back, and slid slowly down against the wall. Then Ishmael's presence was gone as abruptly as it came. "Oh, dear," the archmage of the Darkborn said, breathlessly. "That does present a problem."

She slid off the stool and onto her knees beside him. "Did he tell you what had happened to him?" she said urgently. "Can we help him?"

"Dear lady," Farquhar Broome said. She felt a twitch in her pocket, and the handkerchief she had borrowed jumped to his hand. He wiped his forehead with it and handed it back with his daft smile. All she could find to say was, "It's not clean."

The door flew open, and Phoebe Broome's sonn caught them. A moment of suffused silence, and then the mage said, in a controlled voice, "Father, what exactly was that?"

Farquhar's smile was suddenly much less daft and very unhappy. "That was our friend Ishmael, dear girl. As best I understand his situation, he is captive of one of two surviving mages from the time of the laying of the Curse—"

"That's—" The speaker thought better of "impossible."

". . . Who seems to have attempted, and succeeded, in augmenting Ishmael's strength." He reached up. "Help me up."

Phoebe, and the Borders-born mage who had argued with the coachman, lifted him between them. He said, shakily, "It was a rather brutal process, and would not have succeeded in someone less robust. And as you sensed, he has very little control."

"He studied wi'us," the Borders mage objected.

"Dear boy, all his efforts went toward *increasing* the effect of the little magic he had. Even under the best of all possible circumstances, it would take him time to adjust."

"Is he ensorcelled?" Phoebe said, horrified.

Her father turned to her. "I could not tell." Briefly, he supported himself on the lintel, and then handed himself through. Vladimer was waiting outside, Mycene and the baronette flanking him. "I think, Lord Vladimer," Farquhar said to Vladimer, "I will ask you to go downstairs, smartly now, and close off the space between the floors."

"What is it?"

"By your leave," the mage said, "it will be quicker if I simply show you."

Vladimer sonned him, taking in his manner, quite bereft of all eccentricity and whimsy. His shoulders tightened, and then he thrust his fisted hand at Farquhar. Farquhar's hand closed lightly around it. Vladimer's face registered his shock. *"Ishmael?"*

Farquhar squeezed his hand and released it. "I am afraid so, dear boy. Explain it to the others."

"Do you think you can—"

"Me? I think not. But I might be able to give Ishmael what he needs, with the help of my dear people here, and, perhaps, if they will permit me to speak to them, the Light-born. It is probably safer for bystanders not to be too close. You do understand?"

Of course Vladimer understood, having been at the archduke's breakfast. "If you don't have the strength," Vladimer said, intensely, "then I order you to wait on making any move. There is no purpose to your risking yourselves. Fejelis will be in the palace by now. Give him a chance to get through to the high masters."

Farquhar gave him his wide smile. "I shall most certainly try. Now *please*, go downstairs."

"But—," began Lavender di Gautier, hoarsely.

"Shoo!" said Farquhar, with matching gestures.

Vladimer hesitated, his expression an odd mix of annoyance and helplessness. Then he said over his shoulder to the others, "Downstairs. I will explain." His sonn brushed Telmaine. "Lady Telmaine?"

Telmaine shook her head firmly, not trusting her voice. Ishmael needed her, and needed her all the more because the mages, whom he regarded as his own, seemed to have marked him as a danger, if not an enemy. He did not deserve that from them, too. She stood tensely, poised for argument, as Vladimer herded Mycene, the baronette, and their men down the stairs.

"My dear ones," Farquhar Broome began, and then stopped and spread his hands helplessly.

Shadowborn 313

"It's all right, Father."

"It is *not* all right." Telmaine sensed the interplay of magic between them, swift and cryptic, excluding her again. But this time, she found herself measuring them, measuring their magic against that inferno she had felt from Ishmael. They could not match him—Farquhar Broome's manner told him that. But if he destroyed them, it might destroy him. She remembered that dream. A warning?

<Let us sit down,> Farquhar Broome said, and, with no deference to rank, they spread around the room, found chairs and stools and trunks, and sat, leaving her to perch on a stool with her skirts spread around her.

<I shall try one last time to reach Kadar,> he said, <but I shall not exhaust myself in the effort. If they have made their choice, so be it.> He was, she realized, speaking of the Lightborn temple. Was Kadar the archmage? <A moment, my dears.> So close to him, she could sense him gathering and shaping his magic, transforming vitality into energy, into a reach across distance, with an assured, delicate touch that wasted not a wisp of vitality. *How old is he?* she wondered. *A hundred years? Two hundred? More?*

He let out a breath and shook his head. <No, no use. One can only trust that they are also able to shield against the Shadowborn, or the effort would go for naught. Let us compose ourselves. And then, dear girl,> he said to Telmaine, <I will ask you to reach Ishmael once again. Of us all, I think he is least likely to harm you. Though that does not mean you will be safe.>

No one feeling that furnace of magic could make that mistake.

The thought leaked; Farquhar Broome's wizened-apple face creased in a smile.

Telmaine drew a deep breath to settle herself and then whispered, <Ishmael.>

The heat. The overwhelming heat. That she knew it was not physical made no difference to what she *felt*. But within the heat, she could sense his alertness, his listening presence. She concentrated on that. <Ishmael, it's Telmaine. What can we do to help you?>

No words, no attempt at conversation. Was he shying from injuring her? If only she could have pretended to be unaffected by his magic. <Ishmael, Magister Broome and your friends are here with me.> She hesitated, but this was Ishmael. He *could not* be their enemy. <We're in Stranhorne Crosstracks—we just arrived. Balthasar's still alive, but he was captured by one of the Shadowborn and taken up to Minhorne. He's gone to the Lightborn court as envoy. The telegram said he had an ensorcellment on him to protect him from the light.> He would surely sense how frightened she was for Balthasar, how desperately she wanted this over and him safe—them all safe. <Ishmael, this is important: the Lightborn Temple has sent a representative, Magister Tammorn, a strong sport mage.... Do you know lineage mages can't sense Shadowborn magic? They've sent Magister Tammorn to the Shadowborn. We think they're looking for an alliance.>

<What was that?>

That was not Ishmael. She recoiled quickly, but not quickly enough. Magic split her mind like the husk of a seed, spilling and raking through the kernels within: her encounters with the Shadowborn, with Tammorn, with Vladimer, Fejelis, the archduke, Ishmael. Vaguely she sensed the blaze of Ishmael's outrage, and even more vaguely, Farquhar Broome's efforts to reach her. The Shadowborn—it was a woman—said thoughtfully, <So he'll fight for you, will he? I can use that.>

And she felt Shadowborn magic drop over her like a great sheet, and *lift*.

Ten

Fejelis

I need you to stay here, help the Darkborn...." Fejelis glanced up from folding the princely mourning jacket around the caul, and found his brother staring at him in dismay. He measured the angle and color of the early-morning light, and stuffed the bundle into his borrowed bag with more urgency and less respect than it deserved. "You know the railway. You can talk to the railway people, get them what they need. You've my authority to overturn the day-night orders...." Which he had remembered to scrawl. Celeste was translating it into Darkborn script on one of the clever Darkborn punch machines, still chortling at her own perversity in refusing to believe Fejelis's claim.

"But what are you going to do?" Orlanjis said. "And can't I come with you?"

Fejelis forgave him the plaintive tone. "Take my city back.... Find a way to get the Temple to see sense and work with the Darkborn mages.... Calm things down between Lightborn and Darkborn so the archduke of the Darkborn can see his way to reinforcing Strumheller and Stranhorne, and make sure he understands the need to . . . decide what to do *after* lunch." His brother did not react to the weak jest. "We simply can't take you with us, Jis. I need Jovance on her feet at the end of the *lift*, and I need you to hold together the alliance here."

"Why are you trusting me? I've only ever been your rival."

This was the heart of it, and no less than expected, since they'd been set up as rivals all their lives. Fejelis straightened to face his brother. He hated being hurried in a conversation of this importance, hated having to strip it down to its essence. ". . . Orlanjis, we are fighting for our lives against an enemy that few of us even recognize. I'm *trusting* you because you've seen exactly the same thing as I have, and come to the same conclusions. I'm trusting you because I watched you fight, come under attack, and not break. When we go back to the palace and all the usual problems and politics of a new reign, if I can keep you, I will. . . . You're not the boy you were even a few days ago." *Nor,* he thought, *am I.* He put his hands on his brother's shoulders and looked down into his eyes. "If I die doing this, all I ask is that you rule as you believe, not as anyone else tells you. Father didn't think that a prince's policy should survive the prince, and I agree. But try to be a good prince, and watch your back. I'll do my best to avoid leaving you quite as ghastly a mess as we have now, but if I fail, we will need as strong a relationship with the Darkborn—" He caught himself; shook his head. ". . . And here I said I wasn't going to try to influence you."

"That's not influence," Jovance interrupted from the door. "That's the verbal equivalent of sitting in a lather, tearing a piece of paper to bits. You're not telling him anything he doesn't already know. He's your father's son as well."

He gave her a grateful glance at that, then hugged Orlanjis quickly, thankful that when the Darkborn train had left with Lord Vladimer and his mages aboard, no one had suggested that Orlanjis travel with it. But the Lightborn railway workers were bringing in a day train with plans to press on to Stranhorne before sunset, and if Fejelis could not end this today, in the city, Orlanjis would go with them. "I'll give your regards to Mother, though I'd appreciate it if you sent a message to reassure her I didn't abandon you in the wilds."

Orlanjis watched from the doorway as they went down the steps of the small house and into the carefully tended garden. The perfume of the night-blooming flowers on the trellises lingered in the still morning air, though the flowers themselves were furled. A baffled bee was bumping gently against one as though trying to wake it. With the stillness and the early sunshine, and they being the only people moving in it, the world seemed new-made, free of Curse and Shadowborn.

"Nice pep talk," Jovance said in a low voice.

"I'm terrified for him," Fejelis admitted, "He's only fourteen."

"One thing reassures me," Jovance said. "I see no sign that he needs to do stupid things to prove his courage." She looked up at him, her skin warmed by the sunlight. "Nor do you; I don't think it *occurs* to you to be afraid." If she could feel his pulse, if she could touch him, she would know that was wrong. "Where do you want me to put us down? It needs to be somewhere I know, and it's best to be somewhere outside. I can sense and avoid living things more easily than inanimate objects."

". . . What do you say to the palace gardens, on the plinth of the sundial garden?"

Where, on certain ceremonial occasions, the prince would stand, his shadow marking a significant time. She stared at him, her lips parting, and then he remembered that one of those ceremonies was the public announcement of the contract between the prince and his chosen consort, and another, the sealing of the contract itself. His color mounted. "Jovance, I, um . . ."

She was still laughing when she landed them on the plinth above the sundial garden. The hour was a most unceremonial one, and their shadows tracked across the blue and silver border, outside time. She gasped as the effort of the magic caught up with her, and he got a hand around her back and guided her down to sit on the edge of the platform, all thought of his misstep slipping from his mind. "Sorry," she said, wanly. "Needed quite a punch to get through the Temple interference. It's a safe bet they know I've arrived."

"If they don't, tell them," Fejelis said. "I want to get their attention." He stepped from the platform down onto the ground. "Can you walk? I don't like us being exposed like this." He'd had one crossbow bolt through him already in his young reign. No sense inviting another.

"I'd like to say no," she remarked, gazing up under her lashes, "just to make you carry me." She slipped off the plinth onto her feet, and steadied herself with a grip on his arm, delighting him with the casual ease of the gesture. Of all the people he knew, only Tam and his father had ever touched him so easily. "No," she murmured, and he realized she was aware of his distracted thoughts. "Maybe not a good idea." Then she lifted her head. "Company, Prince."

Good company, he found, turning: Captain Lapaxo at the head of a flying wedge of palace vigilants, with a look on his face that promised a locked safe room for a feckless prince, and a fate worse than death for anyone who would think to harm him. Fejelis towed Jovance several yards down the path to get the flower beds off the line of the charge. He had enough civil wars on his hands without adding one between vigilants and gardeners.

Lapaxo halted in front of him, scowling. "Well, *curse it*, your brightness." Then the captain outraged protocol and endeared himself to Fejelis forever by clapping hands to his prince's arms and giving him a sharp shake. "Where'd you get to?"

"The Borders," Fejelis said. And could not resist adding, ". . . I'm glad to see you, too, Captain." He was; he had feared Lapaxo had been murdered to clear the way for Rupertis. He waved away Lapaxo's apology. "This is Magistra Jovance, who has been good enough to bring me back, and is under verbal contract to me." Fortunately for princely decorum, she did not respond to any double entendre. She still looked very pale.

"And Magister Tammorn?"

He started along the path, and when Lapaxo did not remonstrate, strode out. Jovance dealt stoically with the pace, following a few steps behind and stumbling only a little. "Whereabouts unknown at present, *not* by his own volition. What's been happening here?"

Lapaxo gave him a terse summary of events: the ultimatum to the Darkborn, the first signs of Darkborn retaliation, and then the arrival of the Darkborn envoy. "I knew about him," Fejelis said—it had been part of Vladimer's briefing. "What's he ... Never mind. I want to meet him." Quite aside from the envoy's political importance, he was curious to meet anyone with that much crazy courage.

He felt Jovance's fingertips graze his wrist, as though by chance. <You realize that's how the Temple learned to send Tam to the Shadowborn at night?>

He managed not to gawk at her. Even Tam had never mind-touched him like that.

"He reacts well in a crisis," Lapaxo said, which was high praise from the vigilant. Explaining how the Darkborn emissary had already survived one assassination attempt carried them up the steps and into the vestibule. Servants and staff stared. A couple skittered through various doorways, while others sidled casually out, no doubt to scurry every bit as quickly to various masters. He found himself fighting a manic grin: he was home.

"Where are they?" he said.

He didn't need to explain who, not to Lapaxo. "Up in the archmage's suite."

"All of them?" Fejelis said. Either that indicated a shift in the balance of power or a refusal on the part of either his mother or Prasav to award the other the territorial advantage. "Tell them I want them down in the main receiving room, five minutes or sooner: the archmage, the high masters, Prasav, Helenja. The Darkborn envoy, too. Tell the high masters I know where they've sent Tammorn"—Jovance's golden eyes flashed alarm—"and tell Prasav I am not pleased with his suborning Captain Rupertis."

"It wasn't Prasav alone," Lapaxo said. "It was Shadowborn—I hadn't come to that yet. And Rupertis is dead."

Fejelis swallowed. His headlong pace was making him dizzy, yet he sensed that the only way to prevail here was to move fast. He'd worked hard at training speed and timing into himself on the piste; it was time to apply these lessons outside. "*Ten* minutes, then. I need a change of clothing."

He needed a bath, too, and several hours' more sleep, but he could whistle for those, prince or no.

Jovance touched his arm again, more deliberately, and mind-whispered, <Steady.>

Lapaxo gave orders; they collected and shed vigilants and servants and staff as they rolled down the corridors. He scanned faces, gauging mood. Jovance's touch said, <They seem pleased to see you.> He sensed pleasure and pride behind the words, and wished the touch had lingered.

His chief dresser and two assistants were already waiting in the main receiving room, one assistant with an armful of red fabric and the second with a steaming bowl, a razor, cloths, a towel. A mage vigilant nodded to Lapaxo from behind them: the bowl, towels, and dressers were safe. As the vigilants deployed to their posts at the doors and on the balcony, he dropped the shoulder bag on the dais with a quick "No, I'll need that" to the servant who would have swept it away, and let the dresser strip him to his underwear and swab him down with the brisk efficiency of a mother cat washing her kitten. He was glad he'd had the chance to shave in the railway house, because having a razor plied at that speed would have tried his nerves. He stepped into trousers and shoes, and stooped for a blouse and to receive a comb through his hair. No time for the ornate styling fashionable at court. Lapaxo stayed at his right shoulder, continuing his report in an increasingly distracted fashion as servants streamed into the hall, inspecting mirrors, dusting lights, straightening pictures, carrying more lights on stands, carrying flowers in transparent bowls, trying to do in five minutes what had taken them several days before his ill-omened coming of age. Fejelis was sure his orders had not included all this, yet it took very little reflection to decide that if he had thought to give these orders, he would have. Lapaxo, finally pressed beyond endurance, said, "What *is* this?"

Letting his intuition speak for him, Fejelis said, "Defiance."

Lapaxo's look demanded he make sense. ". . . Defiance of disorder," Fejelis said. "Defiance of change. Defiance of illegitimate authority." He pulled the wrapped caul from the Darkborn bag, giving the wincing dresser a penitent glance, and unwrapped it with more care and respect than he had rolled it up. He handed the red mourning jacket to the dresser for shaking out and brushing down, and cradled the caul briefly in his hands. A few strands of pale hair were snagged in the wire. His father's, or his own? The caul was still shaped to his father's head, but its fit was close enough. By sleight of hand, the dresser produced a mirror and held it at just the right angle with the precision of long practice. Fejelis was braced for the shock of his father's cauled face looking back at him, as it had the first time he donned the caul, but with a greater shock, he saw only his own. He felt Lapaxo's hand on his elbow; his eyes must have lost focus for a moment. "When did you last eat?" muttered the captain.

"Not that long ago." Bannocks and cheese before speaking with Vladimer, though he was having difficulty remembering when he'd last eaten a full meal. "Later," he said, as the door of lesser privilege suddenly opened on a phalanx of vigilants judiciar around a familiar fair woman in red, and a black-haired stranger whose eyes were masked by smoked lenses. "That's the Darkborn," Lapaxo said in a low voice. "Name's Hearne."

"Floria's friend?" Fejelis said, finally remembering where he'd heard the name.

He tried not to stare, but the Darkborn's very ordinariness made it difficult. That slim body and narrow, intense face could have belonged to one of the palace's archivists or librarians, except for the dark glasses and the heavy, unsightly clothing. The Darkborn seemed to be perspiring a little, which Fejelis would have taken for nervousness, except that his posture suggested determination more than nerves. Those thick clothes must be hot—of course, the Darkborn were used to the chill of night. As they approached, he noticed Floria's gliding step and ceaselessly moving eyes: Floria at her most dangerous. But when her eyes lighted on him, confirming the truth of rumor, they narrowed with glittering satisfaction, and she smiled.

At his side, Jovance was staring at the Darkborn, squinting slightly. He could see her hand working. Lapaxo had said the ensorcellment on Hearne was Shadowborn, and she was lineage. . . . "Magistra?" he prompted in a murmur.

Recalled to herself, she put her mouth to his ear. "He's got the archmage's touch on him. One *mother* of an ensorcellment. That's *exactly* what they did to Tam." She sounded angry. He felt angry. But he said, low voiced, "It's not his fault."

"If he hadn't come—" The party was nearly within earshot, and she bit back the rest of the statement. He waited, but she did not finish it, even silently.

Lapaxo muttered something at his other side, and Fejelis angled his head toward the vigilant. "Forgot to tell you," the captain said, sounding annoyed at himself. "Temple claimed them as one of theirs. Say's he's mageborn."

Says, Fejelis thought. *Mages don't need the Temple to say they're mageborn.* He exchanged glances with Jovance; she shook her head slightly. *Now what are they up to?* He gestured the new arrivals to wait a moment, and beckoned the dresser with the brushed-down mourning jacket to him, slipped his arms into the sleeves, was briskly tweaked and tugged. Nodded his thanks, and, with a deep breath, turned. With the party's entrance, the hall had begun to drain of servants, and now was almost empty of them, its hasty grooming and staging, like his, as complete as it was going to be.

He realized he didn't know the Darkborn's title, only that he was a physician and—no, he had met the man's wife already; he was untitled. "Dr. Hearne, I am Fejelis Grey Rapids, styled prince." He might as well test the man's mettle. ". . . I understand you have already received a traditional court welcome."

"Was *that* what it was?" Hearne's voice was a steady tenor.

That boded well. And because this was a Darkborn and Fejelis understood such courtesies were important, he said, ". . . I just recently—a few hours ago, in fact—spoke to your wife."

He had not realized that a man already so pale could go that much whiter. Floria instantly closed the step between them, but the Darkborn, holding on to his composure, said, "No, I'm all— Excuse me, Prince Fejelis, but when I came here, it was under the impression my wife was dead. Floria told me otherwise, but to hear that you have spoken to her . . . What did she say?"

"Strictly speaking, though I spoke to her, she did not get a chance to speak to me. But we were introduced, and Magistra Jovance"— he indicated her —"sensed both her presence and her magic. She was in good health."

"Thank you," the Darkborn breathed. Poise restored, he said a little hurriedly, "Prince Fejelis, the archduke will be delighted to know you are back. He has high expectations of your help in resolving the difficulties between our peoples."

Not a professional diplomat, Fejelis thought, *but in earnest.* And he had the delicacy of phrasing mastered already. *Difficulties, indeed.* He said, "I have equal hopes of his—"

Floria's head turned like a cat's. He hadn't been aware of the noise from outside, but that was surely his mother's voice. And then the door of greater privilege burst open before a roil of mages and vigilants. He caught sight of several he recognized as Prasav's, plus men and women in the dun and ochre of the southern contingent, plus the bright glitter of chains of rank around several throats. He realized he was on the brink of entertaining an unrighteous brawl for precedence.

"Excuse me," he said to the Darkborn envoy, and started to draw a breath, but stopped as he caught Lapaxo's head-shake. He was glad of that a moment later, and gladder still that Lapaxo had the courtesy to take a step away before he thundered, "Order in the presence of the prince!"

He could have sworn he could hear the chime of shuddering glass in the silence that followed. The contested doorway cleared. Fejelis sprang onto the dais, which earned him a glower from Lapaxo as the vigilants scrambled to cover him. At his glance of appeal, Jovance tripped up the steps to stand where a contracted mage would be expected to stand.

There was a pause, then Perrin entered, flanked by mages and Temple vigilants, the archmage, Magistra Valetta, and the high masters—seven of them—following so closely on her heels that they seemed to be herding her. The change in his sister, since their meeting in the ruins of the tower, was appalling. No twenty-year-old should be that haggard. A sideways glance at Jovance, no partisan of Perrin's, showed her as disconcerted as he was. She wasn't close enough to tell him whether this was magical overreach, the burden of her awareness of Shadowborn magic, or the burden of being a usurper princess. At Perrin's first sight of him, her expression showed only relief, then guilt, and finally unease. He waited for her to draw closer, keeping a slight smile on his face all the time. "Hello, sister," he said. "Had enough of this job yet?"

Her breasts rose and fell beneath the thin, red vest and mourning jacket, reminding him how that first time they met after ten years, before he recognized her, she had demanded he mind his eyes. "Mother, *yes*," she said, strongly. "You want it back?"

The depth of his relief told him that he had not been sure that she would yield, or that the Temple would let her. She slipped through her honor guard and swiftly mounted the stairs. She turned toward their gathering brightnesses—Prasav and Helenja's retinues were in the room, and the rear was filling fast—and paused, and then pulled the blue pins from her hair that held it in its caul-like style, shaking out the braids with a vigor that was near violence. "I renounce all claim on my brother's title!" She turned to him, and Fejelis did not miss the tensing of the vigilants around him. With a silent apology to them, he held out his hand to her. And Jovance tensed in her turn, until she realized, as he had, that Perrin's hands were gloved, her touch safe.

"Fejelis, I'm so sorry," she said, so quickly her words slurred. "It happened so fast, and you were barely gone when I realized you'd been *right*, and the *Temple* was hiding from the truth—" He squeezed her hand, quieting her. Now to find out the price the Temple would extract for ceding his title back to him . . .

"Where is Orlanjis?" shouted Sharel from Helenja's side, and no doubt with Helenja's leave. His mother, true to nature, looked as disgusted at Perrin's ready surrender of her pretendership as she had at her assumption of it.

"He's in the Borders, helping the Darkborn defend themselves," Fejelis said. "And doing well at it, thanks to your teaching." She started to shout something else, but he was ready for her. He might not have Lapaxo's seasoning, but he had healthy lungs and a voice solidly past adolescence, and whether he liked it or not, the blood of generations of southern clan chiefs.

"This ends here!"

No shivering glass, but a gratifying silence. "This internecine warfare *ends here*," he said, less loudly but no less emphatically. "I pardon my sister for her offense against me. I left Orlanjis in the Borders with my full trust, knowing that he *would* fulfill that trust. I left him with instructions to support the Darkborn in every way he could—because having seen them fight, having spoken to them and heard their preparations, I'd much rather have them as friends than enemies. I *know and acknowledge* the outrage of the attack on the tower, but until we establish what part magical influence played in the decisions made by Duke Mycene, whom I am told died under magical attack by a Shadowborn"—Hearne, he saw, was surprised he knew that already—"and Kalamay, then by our own law, we cannot retaliate."

"And the Darkborn leaflets?" Prasav slipped in.

Darkborn leaflets? Ten minutes was not enough. But this was his court, not Prasav's. "I will *not* sign an order of eviction for the Darkborn from Minhorne. This city is theirs as much as it is ours. . . . But all of that is *irrelevant*. Your brightnesses, mages of the Temple: how much time have you wasted while the enemy—who murdered my father, who threatens all of us—advances? I tried to warn you not a day ago"—truly, was it only that?—"and got deposed for my pains, and nearly shot at the command of a captain of vigilants who had been suborned by the Shadowborn."

Prasav's expression was sweet revenge for those twisted

half-truths about Tam and the artisans; he didn't expect Fejelis already to know.

"But for the actions of Magister Tammorn, my mentor and my friend. Who is not here because he was sent, by his own superiors, the masters of the Temple, to the camps of the enemy. *Tell me,*" Fejelis fired at the high masters, "*that you did not send my friend to treat with the enemy!*"

In his peripheral vision, he glimpsed his sister's horrified face, Jovance's frozen stance, Lapaxo crouching to lunge, before it came to the captain that the one threat he could not protect his prince from was the prince's own madness.

"No," said a voice he had never heard before. "I did not send him to treat with the enemy."

It was the archmage, who had not been known to speak aloud in the hearing of earthborn—even Temple servants— in living memory. The small man clasped his hands and bowed over them to Fejelis, a gesture of respect from two centuries past.

Several heartbeats went by before Fejelis realized that the archmage was not going to elaborate on that statement. By then he had waited too long and lost the initiative for the obvious question. Then Jovance said from beside him, in a voice that sounded girlish but determined, "Magister Archmage, Tam explained to me before he left what you had asked him to do."

Magistra Valetta said, "That was what we had asked him to do." Hitherto the confident mouthpiece of the archmage, the one he spoke through, she suddenly had the air of a woman who no longer knew what would drop out of her mouth.

"Please do us the courtesy of explaining," Fejelis said, quietly.

"By their deeds," said the archmage, "we shall know them."

"You set Tam out," Fejelis said slowly, "as bait."

"With Lukfer dead, Tam is the strongest living sport," said Magistra Valetta, still with that expression of one about to go cross-eyed from watching her own lips. "We had no one better suited. But we could not tell him because we wanted to know . . . what they were."

They didn't tell you, either, Fejelis inferred. Plans within plans—he could almost feel sorry for her. He met the archmage's eyes, experience centuries deep in them. More than three hundred years old, he knew the man was. And the archmage's father—how old was he? How close was the archmage to a living memory of those who had laid the Curse?

He weighed what he should say next. He had been lucky and inspired to have come this far, but he had done so by outrunning the opposition. Now they were all standing still, listening.

Friendship demanded that he argue that Tam be spared, as he had done not a day ago, without a moment's thought—charging in to challenge the high masters, throwing himself into Prasav's trap. He had been lucky to keep his life, lucky to keep his brother, lucky to keep his sister, lucky to regain his caul. Lucky to have remained alive, so far. More than half that luck accrued from the luck of meeting Tam.

He remembered sharing breakfast with his father in the prince's private chambers, having one of their rare conversations about the costs and burdens of being prince. They rarely dwelt on it, as there seemed no purpose: as night followed day, as summer followed spring, Fejelis would be prince. But he remembered his father saying, eyes half closed against the early sun, *"And then there will be the first time you must sacrifice a friend. . . ."*

He could feel the quiet in the room, the expectation. He wondered what Jovance would think of him—but if she chose to remain with him, she would see him do worse than this, to try to make something of his reign, salvage earthborn and mage.

"And do you know yet?" Fejelis said, quietly.

The archmage said, "Not yet."

Telmaine

She heard Ishmael's growled *"No,"* and felt magic grapple with magic, his great, unformed seething rising against the woman's. The *lift* suddenly released her and she swayed on her stool, and then reached down to grip it with both hands through the folds of her skirts. Sonn and magic intersected on her from her companions. The young Borders mage, Bryse, had come to his feet, inspired by an impulse of chivalry.

"Should I—?" she gasped to Farquhar Broome, though did not know what she wanted to ask. In the end, it was not for him or for anyone else to say. *I walked through the fire to rescue my daughter, and Ishmael went with me.* And when in distraction and weariness her concentration failed her, he had held back the inferno, though it had cost him his magic and nearly his life.

Now Ishmael was the one standing in the inferno, and she the one who must hold it back.

She felt their surprise, Ishmael's and the woman's, at her touch, and from him the same emotions he had felt as she went to rescue Florilinde: admiration and dismay and protectiveness. Whatever the Shadowborn had done to him, he was still Ishmael. They had no chance for any further exchange. Through him, she heard the woman say, <*Now,*> and felt her magic fasten on to Ishmael, spinning strength and vitality from him. He did not resist. Telmaine's resistance on his behalf had no more effect than a sparrow's pecks and fluttering wings on a boy stealing her eggs.

<Don't distract him,> ordered a woman whose presence she had not registered until then, distracted by Ishmael and the sorceress who held him. Ishmael braced himself at that voice. Not a flinch or a cringe, because Ishmael would never cringe, but he remembered what she had just done to him in making him a monster.

No matter her power, Telmaine would *not* cower before her. <Why *not*?>

<Because of this,> said the woman. Fleetingly, she thought that they were trying to *lift* her again, trying to carry her bodily away, and then she knew where she had felt this sensation before—fighting the Shadowborn beside Vladimer's bed, as he seized on her magic and vitality both and began to drag them from her flesh. <*Ishmael!*>

<Idiot,> said the woman, and *did* something to release

her. Magic reunited dramatically with flesh as she struck hard floor and sprawled, gasping, on it. She rose, dazed, smelling the smoky, sun-warmed air of the railway-station cupola. Her hip and shoulder and the side of her head hurt. Her companions were silent, motionless, their heads turned toward Farquhar Broome. She sensed the magic that knotted them together and excluded her.

She rose to elbows and knees, then hands and knees, in the billows of her skirts. A lady did not fight; that was one of the earliest lessons of the nursery. Any instinct for it she had as a small, unruly girl was whipped and shamed out of her. Denied the means to protect herself—physically, legally, or magically—she shied from dominant or cruel men, and so never learned how to fight as she had learned other things secondhand. She would have lost against the Shadowborn—lost magic, mind, and life—were it not for Ishmael. She would *not* abandon him.

But she could not fight his warder, and could not last against that terrible draining of vitality. She reached instead but for Ishmael's adversaries, the ones she had sensed beyond the ruined manor of Stranhorne. One, as monstrous as the ones preying on Ishmael, two, three; the third the boy she had met—and bested—in Minhorne. Let that give her hope. She could sense the weaker presence—weaker in comparison to *them*—of the Lightborn Tammorn, and sense his despair. What price the Temple's solicitations now?

None of them were paying attention to lesser beings. She knew about *that* as a great lady among servants. Crouching, grinning savagely, she gathered her will, gathered her magic, and aimed it at the distant trio.

Burn, Telmaine willed. *BURN.*

She poured her magic across the miles between them, poured it into the place where he and his mistress were, igniting mats and drapes and clothing. The boy screamed in terror. She sensed the woman's magic welling up inexorably to quench the fires, stoke them though Telmaine might with vitality and will. In doing so, the woman was killing Tammorn. Strong as he was by himself, in this company, he was the weakest of them all. She must not waver, for Ishmael's sake.

Then the Lightborn mages stooped upon them, seizing Isolde, Ishmael, Ariadne, and Telmaine. Her skirts ignited and flame leaped up her bodice; she threw out arms and magic, trying to push away the flames from her shriveling flesh. Across her awareness came a great gust of magic— Ishmael's magic—snuffing them out and sending her to the floor again. She curled up there, clad only in rags and cobwebs of burned lace, and choking on smoke and ash.

Phoebe Broome screamed, <*Kadar, listen to me!*> The mesh of magic between the commune mages hummed and pulsed. She lifted her head and sonned Farquhar Broome's wizened face working with effort as he exerted himself, a seventh-rank mage, to the fullest.

It would not be enough. She pushed herself up on shaking arms and dragged a rag of skirt around her body, a scant but necessary gesture toward decency. Sweet Imogene, but it *hurt* to reach outward, hurt as much as it had bearing her children, hurt as much as it had those last dozen steps carrying Florilinde out of the inferno. Yet she pushed away the storm of magic around her, moved in a self-created void through it, toward the inferno that had Ishmael in the heart of it. This time she would not falter; this time there could be no lapse. She reached out her hand and touched not the chilled metal of a doorknob, but a broad, fever-hot hand.

Had this been the living world, clothes and skin and their own solidity would have constrained their embrace, but this was some domain of magic alone. She passed through and into him like vapor mingling with vapor. She could feel the beat of his heart behind her own ribs, the heave of his breathing in her own chest, the ache of his effort behind her own forehead. She—he—*they* were sitting in a small room, the warm wind from the open doors to a balcony on Ishmael's sweating face. Seated to their left was a small old woman whose magic was one of sickly, draining cold. Behind them she could sense another woman, his warder, Ariadne, leaning with her hands on Ishmael's shoulders, her magic caging him. The magic of the Lightborn wheeled around them, swift striking and merciless—still air turned suddenly to gales, bare tile raged with flame, bone cracked, scars split, flesh turned to rot.... She found herself suddenly, urgently, called to heal as Ishmael's lungs began to bleed.

<Kadar,> Farquhar Broome cried out. *<They are not the enemy.>*

All the bones in Ishmael's right hand shattered. Reeling with his agony, Telmaine wrapped them with her magic, started to mold them whole. Ishmael said, *<That'll not kill me. Ignore it. Save yourself for what will.>* The woman's hands tightened spasmodically on his shoulders, and Telmaine could hear her choking. A man's voice—Balthasar's? No, not possible—cried, "Ariadne—"

<Ishmael. What's happening?>

<Usual muddle when a skirmish goes sour,> Ishmael said, but she could sense his struggle for breath. *<They take us for th'enemy. The strength's on this side, but the Lightborn have the knowledge—and they're cursed inventive.>* A vertebra in his spine split like a rotten log; he groaned aloud and braced himself against falling as his legs lost all strength. In his memory two revolvers cracked together and he slid limply down a wall into the mud and surrendered himself to death. Frantically, Telmaine poured her magic over the damage, repairing bones, nerves ... *<Can't fight the magic,>* Ishmael explained. *<Can* hurt *the bodies ... Steady; you'll overreach.>*

<What does that matter if we lose?> This. *You.*

<No ...> The Lightborn assault abruptly ceased. Ishmael coughed to clear his windpipe, leaned over to spit blood, coughed again, and swiped his sleeve across his mouth. He sonned right and left, checking around him by ingrained habit—checking *on* those around him by ingrained habit. Fleetingly, he noted the humor of it, those reflexes expressing themselves in these circumstances. It was an amusement she did not share. From the floor, from where he crouched cradling the fallen woman, another man sonned back. He had Balthasar's narrow face and fine features, but, as he wiped froth from the woman's lips, there was a helpless ferocity in his expression that was quite alien to Balthasar's face. This had to be Lysander Hearne. But the

woman, though she was dressed in Darkborn fashion, was pure Shadowborn.

On the other side, the older woman's head turned toward Ishmael. Telmaine's perception of her was overlaid with Ishmael's knowledge. Isolde, daughter of Imogene herself, last but one survivor of that cursed generation, who had killed most of her descendants in trying to create another mage as powerful as she, and had finally succeeded in Ishmael.

<Best go back,> he said.

<And leave you alone here? Never.>

She could sense his struggle with himself, conveyed in impressions rather than words, and it was all the stronger for that. He had no hope for himself: his strength was beyond his control and barely in Isolde's. He was no more than a reservoir for Isolde to tap, a weapon for her to aim. Before Telmaine touched him, he had not even been a thinking weapon. <You *need* me, Ishmael.>

<It's likely t'kill you, Telmaine.> She might overextend herself, she might be killed by the Lightborn or the other Shadowborn, or drained to death by Isolde or Ariadne . . . or by Ishmael himself.

But all the love he had never declared had been in her name. She might tell herself that she was staying for Balthasar, for her children, for Sylvide's widower and son, for Vladimer and the archduke, even. That was all true enough; if they did not, somehow, turn this battle, then all of them would suffer. But even if there had been no one else, she would have stayed for him.

<Ishmael?> Farquhar Broome said. <Dear boy, can you hear me?>

Telmaine felt him hesitate, and answered for him. <We can hear you.>

<Dear lady . . . this is admirable, but not at all wise; you do not know what you are doing.> Fortunately for decorum, he did not give her an opening to rejoinder. <We have an understanding with the Lightborn now, though I do wish that had come sooner. But whatever you do, you will have all the help we can give.>

<Pass my thanks,> Ishmael said. <Though I doubt there's much for them t'do.>

<There *must* be something,> Telmaine said. Involuntarily, she remembered her dream, his double-ended gun, and sensed his stillness, the forming of a plan. <*No*,> she insisted, appalled. <Ishmael, there has to be a better way.>

An eerie sense of touch, like a warm hand brushing her face. <Not that, but—>

Isolde spoke: "Again."

From the floor, Lysander Hearne said, "No," as the woman struggled free of his embrace, rising on her knees.

Isolde disregarded him, and Ishmael did not react, did not resist, as her magic fastened upon his magic, his vitality, once more. Telmaine reared up, raging, but Ishmael said, <Wait.>

<You can't just—>

<*Wait*.> That was Ishmael the Shadowhunter, Ishmael the veteran, alarming and reassuring both. She had trusted him then; she had to trust him now, even though the last thing she wished was to sit passively while Isolde bled him cold of magic and vitality. He said, <It has t'be between them.>

<What has to?> But he did not answer, not directly. Instead he fed her what he had taken from Isolde's mind when he set his hand to hers: Imogene, monstrous in power if not in character; Ismene, monstrous in power and character; Isolde, the denigrated younger child pinned between worship and resentment. Child enough to be bewildered and terrified when Ismene died—mages were not supposed to *die*. Child enough to be flattered when Imogene proposed making her part of her vengeance, making her a keystone of the Curse. Child enough to believe that if she did this for Imogene, Imogene would come to care for her as she had for Ismene. <How could a mother?> Telmaine demanded, but the demand went unanswered. And she had known mothers as cruel on the earthborn scale...Too young to endure the horror of the aftermath of the Curse, watching the mages around her warring and dying, the earthborn who had served or befriended them burning at

sunrise or melting away at sunset. Too young to endure the isolation and hatred of the others for being Imogene's daughter.

I might pity her, Telmaine thought, *but for what she has done to Ishmael.*

She could feel the strain on him as the vessels in his lungs began to ooze again, his legs went numb, his hand ached with crumbling bones, and magic drained him. She pinched off those vessels, eased pressure on those nerves once more, but it was a shocking effort now. <*Ishmael,*> she whispered. <I can't—>

<Hold a little longer. They have to exhaust each other before—>

<Before?>

<Shh.> A whisper in her mind, shockingly weak. He let her feel Isolde as he felt her, the great, thrumming rope of magic stretching out between the Shadowborn, dragging on Emeya's vitality and magic as Emeya dragged on hers. She remembered how the Shadowborn at Vladimer's bedside had sought to uproot her own magic and her life. <All I can think t'do—> Ishmael's heart suddenly stuttered.

<*Ishmael!*>

He took a terrifying moment to answer her. <Aye, I'm out of time. Tell Magister Broome I mean t'try to bind them both together. Cage them, so they finish each other. It may not go well—>

She pummeled his stalling heart, frantic. <We don't have time to think about that! Magister Broome!>

<Yes, dear girl.>

<Help us!> She threw open her mind, let him have Ishmael's intention, Ishmael's knowledge, her determination to stay, her reasons for staying—little caring anymore about propriety.

<*Kadar,*> Broome said. <Let us try young Lord Vladimer's idea, shall we?> And the harsh, sharp-edged Lightborn magic, expertly shaped and deftly wielded, severed the magic binding and drawing on Ishmael. Farquhar Broome said, with an incongruous, childlike glee, <It worked!>

Ishmael's heart steadied to its powerful beat. <Aye, it

did.> He pulled himself forward in the chair, oblivious to his damaged hand, and sonned Isolde, whose face was strained with hatred, oblivious now to anyone but her nemesis. <Don't know how long that'll pertain.> Swiftly, he sonned the two on the floor. Hearne was alert; the woman in his arms staring. Ishmael ground out, "Are y'with us, or not?"

Lysander Hearne said, quickly, "With you. Don't hurt her. Ariadne." He turned her face to him, kissing her forehead gently. "Ariadne, it's over."

A grim smile pulled Ishmael's scar at such a presumptuous promise. <Telmaine, mind them. I trust them far as I could throw them—yesterday, not today. Magister Broome . . . >

<*Tammorn now*,> said the Lightborn archmage. Far to the northeast, on the summit of an earthworks, the Lightborn mage slumped to the ground, semiconscious but free. There was a brief, forceful interchange between the archmage and the other Shadowborn mage present, his mind as half tamed as his magic, his thoughts evasive and wary.

The boy cried out, <Emeya, they're trying to—> Suddenly decisive, the stronger mage smothered his warning.

Isolde's head turned toward Ishmael. Ariadne sat up suddenly, her mouth gaping in shock or on a cry.

<*Mine*,> Ishmael said. His power suddenly surged around them, a wall of furnace flame. On the far side of it, Farquhar Broome's magic played around it like a flute around thunder, coaxing, guiding, swift and deft in its touch. The Lightborn mages were there—several of them—lending their guidance to Farquhar's. She could sense the structure of the binding, like the one Tammorn had worked on her, but that seemed no more than a cobweb in comparison to this. She could feel Isolde begin to struggle, heard her cry out to Emeya to cease and join with her. If Emeya heeded her, Telmaine was not aware of it; her attention was fully on Ishmael, on the heart and lungs and bones and muscles striving to sustain such massive, magical effort, despite their burden of a lifetime's injury and hard use. He could not last . . .

Isolde, her energies divided, died first. Briefly, furiously, Emeya's ferocious energies turned on Ishmael's. Telmaine wrapped her magic around Ishmael's faltering heart, wrapped her will around Ishmael's life. And then, suddenly, Emeya fell away, her last scream—that of a young child—reverberating through the link between them.

Ishmael went limp in his chair, drawing huge, gasping breaths. She thought for a moment he was going to black out, but he stayed her efforts to lend him strength. <Thank you,> he said at last. <Now you'd best get back. You're about spent yourself.>

At first she could not remember where she might get back to, that she had existence herself, a body, magic, separate from his. She could feel him pushing at her, untangling her like a twining vine. <I don't want to,> she pleaded.

<Telmaine, I've more left now than you.>

<What are you going to do?> she demanded, clutching.

He sighed. <The first thing is t'get control, if I can. I've wished all my life t'be stronger, but there should be limits t'wishing.>

<That was clever of you, dear boy,> Farquhar Broome said, a gentle imposition.

Ishmael sonned Isolde, who had slumped sideways in her chair, one arm trailing, with no sense of life or magic about her whatsoever. Sonned Lysander Hearne, who sat supporting—indeed wrapped around—his Shadowborn lady.

Lysander breathed, "You did it." Then, his face hardening, said, "Leave her alone. Do you understand? You'd not have done that without her."

He does not understand at all. Ishmael and Telmaine shared the same thought, his one of weary amusement, hers of exhausted outrage. <Nothing else t'do,> Ishmael said—answering Farquhar Broome more than Lysander. <A sad thing, though. They'd this done t'them as children, and no choice t'be other than they were.>

<There's much about magic that's sad, Ishmael,> said the strongest living Darkborn mage.

<Lucky to bring it off, we were. . . . I'm going t'need your help. I'm no child, but—>

<*Sebastien*, don't!>

Raw strength of magic and rage of defeat, transmuted to fire and death, hurtled across the distance between the Shadowborn redoubt and Ishmael. Sebastien held back nothing of his magic or his furious young vitality. Ishmael was exhausted and unguarded, against them and against his own strength. Telmaine felt Sebastien's fires roar up around him, the death magic batten onto him.

She responded without thought, tendering her vitality to sustain his once more. Magic seized on hers, as the Shadowborn's had, but this time it was his—all his. She began to struggle, as she had struggled then, but she was completely overmatched. She felt his vitality resurge against the death magic, and felt the heat of his power mount, but there no longer seemed to be anything familiar about it, any part of the man she loved. She remembered again his face in her dream, with its terrible regret.

Tammorn

Neill closed Emeya's staring eyes and smoothed her dress down over her thin, childish knees. Her circlet of flowers had tumbled from her head and made a pale smudge in the shadows. Neill scooped it up, hesitated, and then bent his head to kiss it. He glanced toward Sebastien, who lay on his side, head propped on outstretched arm, eyes half closed, tears seeping from them, lips trembling. Neill's face was almost devoid of expression, his eyes dark. He sighed, spilled his handful of wilting flowers onto Emeya's chest, stood, and came back to Tam, who sat in the entrance, clinging to the sunlight.

"I'll be going now, I think," Neill said, conversationally. "I'd rather not wait for that"—he gestured south with a thumb—"to get organized and come looking for me." A wry, humorless smile. "Emeya wanted him dead from the start, but I could never see bothering about a first-rank mage, even one so adept at killing my creatures. We had bigger threats to worry about." He glanced over his shoulder at the dead, eight-hundred-year-old child. "She couldn't have known, any more than I. It was just that she liked my beasts."

Tam said nothing. He felt hollowed out, too numbed by horrors to feel glad or grateful for his life. He didn't have the strength to hold Neill, even if he could have found the resolution.

"I won't take the boy," Neill said. "If either of his parents survived this, they'll be looking for him. And if they didn't, there's still the uncle. I'd rather not give anyone more reason to come after me. Try to see he's treated decently, would you?"

"Where will you go?" Tam said. "The Temple—"

"Will . . . ?" prompted Neill, with a lift of an eyebrow, as Tam paused to muster his weary thoughts.

"There are provisions in our laws—"

"The ones that dealt so fairly with you?" said Neill, ironically. "Thank you, but no. I cannot claim to be only a boy. I'll just be going—my creatures here will follow me. I'll make no trouble if I'm left alone. I'm no Emeya. Maybe I'll drop by for a beer, in a century or two."

"Traitor," whispered Sebastien.

Both men looked at him. He levered himself up on his elbow and spat in Neill's direction. "Traitor," he said, louder.

"Yes, I am," Neill said. "And because of that, we're all still alive. Do you want to come with me?"

The boy did not answer. He was staring at Emeya's body, his thin chest rising and falling erratically. Neill said, "They'll be looking for you soon, Ariadne and Lysander. Or you could go to them. I'd suggest, though—"

Sebastien's head swung like a lodestone findings its pole. His face twisted with hatred.

Neill's *"Sebastien,* don't!" was late—how late, Tammorn would never know. The boy's magic blazed out. Tam recognized in it the annulment of life that he had almost lost Fejelis to, and that his master Lukfer had died while undoing in the ruined tower, driven not at Neill, but into the vortex of unstable strength far removed from them. Tam had known magic that unstable. He had loved the man who possessed it, but he had always known that, were he not himself a mage of considerable potential, he could not have been Lukfer's friend. Had he ever achieved control, Lukfer would have been eighth rank. Tam had no idea how the tower might rank Ishmael di Studier.

He had time to recognize disaster, time to extend a hand toward Neill, time to draw breath to speak a useless warning, before Ishmael di Studier's unwilled retribution reached them, his inchoate power finding shape in the form that Sebastien had thrown at him. Neill threw his own strength between it and Sebastien. Tam felt him reaping vitality from the creatures around him. Mayfly lunged past Tam, snarling at a threat he could not see. Neill caught the brindled pelt as he slid to his knees. "Get out," he gasped to Tam.

It was already too late. Di Studier's raging magic engulfed him, too.

Balthasar

"It's over," Perrin breathed.

Balthasar, leaning against Floria, turned his head to sonn in the direction of the voice. He was still off balance from the flux of magic around him. Perrin was speaking to her brother; the young Lightborn prince was crouched on the platform at Jovance's side, one hand spread on the floor to steady himself, the other gripping his knee in painful self-containment. Jovance sat cross-legged and unresponsive, her expression one of intense, pained concentration. Despite his obvious concern for her, Fejelis's face was turned toward the circle of high-ranked mages in the middle of the room. Like Jovance, they were sitting on the floor. Unlike Jovance, they were ringed by a guarding circle of mid-ranked mages and vigilants contracted to the Temple, and who held back any threat from the earthborn around them.

The prince said, quietly, "What's over? Can you tell me what happened?"

Perrin's face turned briefly toward the high masters, but no guidance came from there. "There were two very strong—very, very strong—mages. Shadowborn," she said with an undertone of defiance. Fejelis nodded impatiently. "And a third, Darkborn, almost as strong, and unstable. The two fought each other. And the third—the Darkborn—

bound them together until they died. With the help of the Darkborn and the high masters."

"The Darkborn was Magister Broome?" said Fejelis, frowning.

"No. One by the name of Ishmael di Studier."

"Ishmael?" said Balthasar, involuntarily.

"You know this man?" Fejelis said, head turning swiftly.

"I mentioned him in the account I gave the judiciary." Which Fejelis would not have had time to read. What were the essentials? "He's—was; I'll explain later—Baron Strumheller of the Borders."

"They told me in Strumheller Crosstracks he had been lost during the retreat. They told me he was a mage, but not that he was high ranked." His voice was edged with strain and suspicion.

"He's not. He's first rank, and he'd taken an injury that left even that unusable. Something must have happened to him. He trained with the Broomes—follows their codes."

Jovance lifted her head. "We must bind him," she said in that strangely hollow, uninflected voice that told them the archmage and high masters were speaking through her. Fejelis's shoulders tensed. He stood up to his full height, looking down at her. "Why?"

"His magic is unstable; he's a danger to us all." Jovance's voice shifted to a normal, young woman's alto. "Fejelis," she said, urgently, "this man is even stronger than my grandfather was, and has no more control. It's not punitive; it's for all our safety."

The Lightborn prince was young; he could not entirely hide his thoughts, though Balthasar did not know him well enough to guess what they were. But if the Temple's handling of Balthasar himself were any measure, there would be layer upon layer of motivation for this, and one of the layers would be power.

Jovance tendered, softly, "Fejelis, Tam's still alive."

Fejelis blinked a couple of times, facing over their heads, but chose not to answer her. To Balthasar, he said, ". . . How will the Darkborn react to this?"

"Farquhar Broome will understand the necessity," Magistra Valetta said. "The rest ... are not strong enough to trouble us."

Balthasar only half understood this, but what he understood did not sound good. "Baron Strumheller is a nobleman of the Darkborn realm. Please don't underestimate the reaction of the archduke and the aristocracy." Which was stretching it, considerably, in one direction, and not at all in another. The aristocracy might not care what became of Ishmael, but they would care intensely about the principle, the trespass against the boundary of sunset.

"Envoy Hearne," Magistra Valetta said. "This is a matter of magic."

Floria's hand closed firmly on his arm. He knew a warning grip when he felt one. Nevertheless, he said, "Knowing the man as I do, if he truly is a danger to you all, he would willingly let you bind him until he achieves control. He is highly principled, deeply loyal, and has used his magic solely to heal and protect."

"It is not a matter of the man's intent—" She broke off suddenly.

Jovance gave an urgent shout of, *"Tejelis!"* The prince whirled and dropped down beside her and caught her as she pitched backward. Balthasar felt magic surge around him, roiling and chaotic, and redolent of the death that Sebastien had carried in his touch.

"Come with me," said Floria, harshly, to him. On the far side of the prince, Lapaxo raised his head; Floria, ever alert, answered his stare. "If that ensorcellment comes off him, he's a dead man." She didn't wait for leave, but three vigilants caught up with her in the doorway. Floria said, "Carry him," and he felt himself caught up and lifted off his feet by two taller vigilants.

"Where?" one said.

"The training room."

Hallways, stairs, at a sprint, Balthasar pinned between them, his sonn making scant sense of anything he passed. Smells of fresh bread, laundry, old socks. They skidded to a halt in front of a door; Floria wrenched it open, and they threw him in. He landed badly, painfully hard, on bare floor. The door slammed on him. He heard her shouting his name, but all he was aware of was the magic, deathly and incoherent, as it tore at the life of every magical entity within the city, from the strongest to the least significant. His last conscious thought was, *Telmaine* . . .

Eleven

Telmaine

Well" was the first thing Telmaine heard. "Words quite fail me."

The voice was that of Telmaine's imperious elder sister, Merivan. But Merivan was in the city, where Telmaine had left her. Merivan could not be here.

"That'd be a first," whispered Balthasar, breath stirring Telmaine's hair.

She turned her head toward his voice, sensing even as she did the presence of magic encasing that familiar vitality. What was Balthasar? "Bal?"

His answer was to draw her to him, bedcovers and all, tucking her head against his neck, mind open to her in utter abandonment and an incontinence of thought uncharacteristic of him. She mumbled protest, both at that and the force of his embrace.

"I shall tell Mother that she appears to be awake," Merivan said over their heads. "Assuming," she added, "you do not smother her in the meantime, and add to the scandal the two of you have visited on our family."

She left in haste. Merivan never liked to be around people when she cried.

"Bal," Telmaine mumbled, "I have to breathe."

His grip eased, and she abruptly changed her mind and put her arms around him. "I thought you were gone," he whispered against her neck. Through her touch-sense, like a spill of gaming chips, came the memories: that ghastly boy insisting she was dead, the archduke failing to contradict it, crossing to the other side of sunrise, Floria . . . She caught her breath in jealous shock. "Why didn't the archduke *tell* you?" she demanded. "Vladimer said he was acting on *his* orders. Wasn't he?"

"He was. He simply did too thorough a job of making it appear you had died, using the ash, having you leave your jewelry—"

"Oh, do you have it?" It seemed of paramount importance that his silver love knot once more be resting in the hollow of her throat, that his rings be circling her fingers, all recovered from the ash of her false death. He produced all from his breast pocket and silently fastened the chain around her neck, and slid the rings onto her fingers. She remembered how cold his hands had been during their wedding ceremony, the high-society wedding an ordeal for the shy, young physician. They seemed little warmer now. They also reeked of Lightborn inks. His thoughts were troubled and complex and scarcely coherent—but she did sense his joy and profound relief at having her *back*. "What have you been *doing*, Balthasar, and why do you have that ensorcellment on you?"

"Acting as the archduke's personal envoy to the Lightborn court. It's likely to become a long-term position—"

Before she could question the thoughts behind his words, the doors swung open on a chorus of "Mama, mama, mama!" Balthasar intercepted their daughters' charge long enough to rescue Amerdale's kitten before Florilinde, with Amerdale two hands and a knee behind, threw herself on Telmaine.

Amerdale got the first words in. "Mama, you slept through my *birthday*!"

Florilinde corrected, with all the authority of her year's seniority, "She wasn't sleeping; she was *very ill*."

"Did you have a baby?"

"Amerdale!" That was Merivan, shocked.

Telmaine abandoned her maternal responsibility to correct and guide, and forgot her concerns about her husband,

and simply shook with laughter. Balthasar remained straight-faced, cradling the kitten in one hand and stroking it with the other. Its tiny mouth opened and closed, mewling unheard over the rumpus. The room filled: Merivan; the dowager Duchess Stott, who had last sonned her daughter being led to her execution; her stodgy elder brother, the current Duke Stott; her flighty younger sister, Anarysinde; her other brothers . . .

"I haven't the stamina to be an invalid," Telmaine complained, after the dowager had finally shooed them all out—knowing her family, just before celebration turned to recrimination. "I couldn't entertain all these *visitors*." Getting out of bed was easier announced than achieved; she was shocked to find how much support she needed simply to reach the armchair. Balthasar succeeded in tucking in the corners of his smile at her affront, but not the smile itself.

"And how *many* kittens did Amerdale cozen you into allowing into the household?" she said, once settled.

"Only three. One for her, one for Flori, and one for me." The rhythm was that of a six-year-old piously enumerating fair-shares. "There'll be one for you, if you want it. Of course, if we take that one, we'll not be able to leave the last of the litter behind."

"Mother of All, we'll be overrun with cats." She put her hands out, decently gloved again, and he took them tightly in his. "There were times I never thought we'd . . . Bal, what happened? After I . . . after—"

He released a hand to touch her lips, gently; behind the touch was the memory of retrieving her from the Borders and bringing her home. "You've been unconscious for nearly three weeks; that's why you're so weak, in part. Olivede thinks your magical strength will come back, given time. I must let her know. You mustn't try to use it yet, and you shouldn't try at all unless there are one or more other mages around."

"I would be happy never to use it again," she said, with feeling. "Oh, Balthasar, *who*?"

She hated that guarded professional expression that told

her he was weighing how much to tell her. "Balthasar, please. I *know* people died. Just tell me who." *Ishmael* . . .

He sighed. "We lost Farquhar Broome. The Lightborn archmage and two of the high masters. Magister Tammorn. Neill of the Shadowborn. Between the six of them, they managed to shield the rest of you, to some extent. Magistra Phoebe is still unconscious—she was most closely linked to her father. I'd have been dead, too, but for Floria. She realized what would happen to the ensorcellment on me if anything happened to the high masters. She got me into a dark room just in time."

"I will thank her for that." She breathed into her hands. "But Ishmael. Is he . . . ? Where is he?"

"My brother, who turned up in Isolde's service, told me that Ishmael simply disappeared. *Lifted*, to where, we don't know. Olivede tells me that she thinks both Magister Broome and the archmage of the Darkborn *gifted* him—as Ishmael did you—with as much of their knowledge of magic as they could. This was in the last moments of their lives, and quite possibly a sacrificial move. It may have helped him regain control. In any case, none of the surviving mages have been able to sense him. As far as I know— and I think I am close enough to both the archduke and the prince now that I would be told—no one else knows where he is, either."

"He could be dead," she whispered.

"I don't think so. If he were, and assuming we understand the situation correctly, the Curse would have failed. We are still Lightborn and Darkborn, and still alive."

"Still . . . alive?"

"A rather chilling speculation that came up in the aftermath: given Imogene's nature, would she permit release of her curse without consequences?"

"You've been spending *far* too much time around Vladimer."

He gave a rueful smile and a slight headshake. "Not Vladimer; Lysander. He was captured outside Stranhorne, searching for his son."

"And the boy?" she said, tight-lipped.

"He lived," Balthasar said. "In poor shape, but expected to recover eventually. He's with the Temple. They'll be able to train and discipline him; they've still got enough mages of sufficient strength to control him. And he's safer under Lightborn law. His twins are with the Broomes still, which is where I'd sooner they stay."

She sat straighter in her chair, the better to give force to her assertion. "If either that boy or your brother does the least thing to hurt you—"

"Lysander went south—to Isolde's stronghold—as soon as he was certain the Temple would look after the boy. I think his Shadowborn lady—Ariadne, the boy's mother— came through, but I don't know how well. I offered to help, if he needed it, but I don't believe he will take me up on that. It was a strange meeting. I suspect he might try to come to an arrangement with Vladimer. I think they might understand each other quite well."

"Vladimer," Telmaine said, suspiciously. "Why Vladimer?"

"The archduke signed an order of exile on Lord Vladimer four days ago."

"That's not fair!"

Balthasar smiled at her swift reversal. "Political necessity, given the mood in the Lightborn court. And Sylvide's death." She chewed her fingertip. How could she have neglected Sylvide? Yet Vladimer's public trial and punishment—possibly even execution—would achieve . . . what?

Politics, she thought. When had affairs she disdained as not seemly for a lady's attention come to define the fates of people she cared for? *Despite* herself, in some cases.

Balthasar continued, thoughtfully. "I also suspect that Sejanus is using this to place Vladimer in Atholaya. Ferdenzil Mycene will surely take an interest in the choice parts, though the archduke may regard that as preferable to his interest in the Islands. Though I think his relationship with the Stranhornes will not be the same as before, which is all to the good."

"Might Mycene marry Lavender? They seemed to be getting . . . on in Stranhorne Crosstracks." He'd laugh at her

if she had to admit that she'd concluded it from an argument and Lavender's concern for Mycene's bereavement.
At least, she hoped he would laugh at her. She hoped he
was still capable of laughter.

"Too early to say," Balthasar said. "Mycene came back
to the city only a week ago to settle his father's affairs; he'd
been helping the Stranhornes deal with the survivors of the
Shadowborn's army." His expression was suddenly stark,
haunted—remembering what? She thought of what she had
sensed from him when he said he had gone to the Borders
to find her. Find her amongst the dead and senseless, the
dead and the hideously mutated.

She swallowed. "I . . . Could they be changed back?"

"Not and live," Balthasar said bleakly.

He drew a breath and resumed, with a self-possession
she was beginning to find eerie. "The mages are interested
in those territories as well, though Prince Fejelis is working
hard to try to prevent the Temple from moving out of Minhorne. They're feeling vulnerable, I think, and—" He
checked himself and left that thought unspoken—*for the
moment,* she resolved. "Long-term, I think Sejanus would
rather like Vladimer for governor of the Darkborn aspect
of the territory."

"You're very free with the archduke's name, all of a sudden," she observed.

"I've got to know him better. He's a good man. He asked
me to offer you his apology for what he put you through,
and his thanks for everything you have done. He will, of
course, offer you his thanks in person and in public, when
you are fit."

"I'll forgive him what he did to me, but not what he did
to you. He should have *told* you *immediately* that he hadn't
had me executed."

"In the circumstances, he didn't know that Vladimer had,
in fact, carried out his orders. So what could he say—that
he'd tried to save you, and failed?"

There was obviously no use arguing, but she would have
the matter out with Sejanus Plantageter. "This envoy post,"

she prompted. "That's why you have *that* ensorcellment on you."

"Yes," he said. "By contract with the Lightborn Temple, the first ever arranged between Darkborn and Lightborn. How much do you know about what happened in Stranhorne, about Sebastien—"

"I know you *beat* him," she said, fiercely. "I know you freed yourself and saved the archduke. That's *all* I need to know." Which was ridiculous of her, she knew, because as they shared a bed, she would have no choice but to know everything, but she would not let him condemn himself for weakness. "And then you went over to the Lightborn side, to prove—" A sudden, frightening thought came to her. "Are you *staying* there? Is that what you're trying to tell me?"

"No," Balthasar said, emphatically. He took her hand, turned it up, cradled it between his hands. "I did not want to get to this until you were stronger, but I suppose it is inevitable ... given that you can't help knowing what I think. Telmaine, we—Darkborn and Lightborn, earthborn and mage—came closer to disaster over this than I ever want us to come again. Without Ishmael and you and Vladimer and the Stranhornes, the Shadowborn would have overrun us all."

And without you as well, she thought.

"Without the mages, Ishmael's magic might have destroyed dozens, if not hundreds, more, and perhaps even himself. If Ishmael had died, the Curse would have failed, and we have no idea what the consequences would have been. The best outcome may have been for us to survive, but in a state of civil war."

"What has *Ishmael* to do with the Curse?"

"As best I understand it, from Olivede and others, Ishmael has inherited the sustaining of the Curse. Which means it lives as long as he does, if he cannot find a means of either sharing or releasing it. I believe we must work to bring our people to a point at which we can release the Curse. Which won't happen overnight; I don't expect it to happen in my own lifetime, but it is what I will be working toward."

"But you're not a diplomat, Balthasar. You're a physician."

He started to say something; stopped. The animation left his face. "Gil di Maurier died."

Who? The young Borders nobleman whom Balthasar had been treating for his addictions, and whom Ishmael had set to finding out where the kidnappers had taken Florilinde. He had succeeded, too, but in doing so had been badly wounded. She had done what she could to tip his chances toward survival, but covertly and timidly, still trying to protect her social position. Which she had probably lost. And Gil di Maurier was dead. "Balthasar, I'm so sorry. If I had done more—"

"I'm told he just gave up," Balthasar said, his voice clear with pain. "A version of recent events made its way into the broadsheets, of course, and no one would have thought to restrain their tongues around him. I'm sure he heard his survival being called a miracle. He wasn't a stupid man. He might have thought it was you; equally, he might have thought it was me. I'd been having some success, after all, when others had given up on him. He had a pathological aversion to magic and mages. In his weakened condition, it was too much for him to suspect that magic had kept him alive."

Telmaine began to cry. "I meant to help him."

He drew her against him, tucking her head against his cheek. "I know. So did I. But the wound and the cure were equally mortal." She could feel his grief, read his memories of the laying-out service. When everyone else had taken shelter at the tolling of the sun bell, he had waited outside by the bier as the sun came up and turned the body of Gil di Maurier to ash.

He seemed to have momentarily forgotten she knew what lay behind his words as he said, "Unfortunately, others feel and will feel as he did. I have already had letters declining my services. So I will think of this envoy post as an extension of my work with the Intercalatory Council—which it is—and know it is something that desperately needs doing. . . . And, Telmaine." He rested his forehead against hers. "Others lost far more."

She wanted to cry out the protest that he would not give up so readily, but she sensed, too clearly, that he did not want that. He had changed. He had always been dutiful and intensely civic-minded, but there was a new hardness and purpose to him.

"What will they do to Ishmael if they find him?" she whispered. "Try him for murder and sorcery?" She heard the edge to her voice as she named the charges, false when they had been laid, but now, in a cruel, twisted way, *true*.

"*Shh*," Balthasar said. "We'll find a way. The archduke signed a formal pardon for the original charges, and we're working on preventing any more from being laid. When it's safe, we'll find him. Vladimer's started working on it already." He kissed her, a light brush of the lips, and she was not displeased to sense the claim in it. "I could use your help with the Lightborn Temple. You've at least had some contact with them, and your being a mage is more than a convenient fiction. They regard women differently on the Lightborn side."

And he had been spending entirely too much time in their company. "I am *not* a Lightborn woman," she reminded him, dangerously.

"I know that. But you're also one of the strongest surviving Darkborn mages. If the Darkborn mages had a representative in the courts—"

"I'd rather have a baby," she muttered. *I'd rather have my ordinary life back*. Unlike Merivan, she enjoyed the months in confinement, when it was not proper to be in society—assuming, of course, that society would ever admit her again. It was cowardice—she knew it was cowardice—but she could long.... Abruptly, through the touch of his skin on hers, she read his thought and reared back. *"Floria?"*

His expression was far less penitent than it ought to have been. Alas, surging to her feet and stalking out of the room needed more energy and muscle tone than she had. She started to rise and fell back. "Balthasar," she protested, detesting the waver in her voice.

"I did hope to wait until later, but yes. Floria has made a

request of me, which I am considering honoring." She snatched her hands pointedly away from his touch; he was lucky her magic was spent. "I love you, Telmaine," he said. "It tore the heart out of me finding you in Stranhorne, and hearing what you and Ishmael had done. I don't want you ever to go through that again."

She pushed down the thought of her and Ishmael's intimacy. Nagging conscience refuted her argument that it was *not* the same. "What does your being unfaithful to me have to do with that?"

That made him flinch, as he deserved. "Perhaps it doesn't, but a child born across sunrise will be one more tie between Darkborn and Lightborn. I owe her my life, three times over, already. I . . . We'll have to talk about this. . . . I don't love Floria, not as I love you; I am sure of that now, but I am, and probably always will be, her friend." He paused. "You'll know that I'm telling the truth."

And you're still *a rat bastard, Balthasar Hearne,* she thought. "And what about when we find Ishmael?" she flung back at him. "What if *he* still loves me?"

"Telmaine," he began, and stopped, and for the first time since she had awakened, that composure of his wavered and she realized how tired he was. How much rest had he had, as envoy between Darkborn and Lightborn courts, and then worrying about her? "You *know* how I feel about you," he said in a low voice.

Which was true, *curse* him.

"I will take you on *any* terms," he said, softly. "Because, even without magic, I know you. I know that, angry as you are, you wouldn't do anything that would truly break my heart."

"But you would break mine." She growled.

"No . . ."

There was a long silence. "Do you realize," he said, slowly, "that as a sixth-rank mage you might outlive me by one or two centuries? And Ishmael by even more. Isolde and Emeya were eight hundred years old when they died."

"I don't *care* about centuries." What mattered was the here and now. If she could learn how to turn him into a—a *cat*, then she need never worry about Floria White Hand again. But what use would he be as a husband then? If she could turn *Floria* into a lizard, now . . . Poor Farquhar Broome would have been appalled. Or maybe not, if he had all the experience he claimed.

"Telmaine?" he said, sounding uncertain.

She didn't have to explain what she was thinking, or what she felt, or why she had stifled a giggle, or why she was now starting to cry. She did not want to think about living without Balthasar. When he gathered her against him, she let him.

Eventually he said, "That young man who was working for you and Vladimer, Kip—"

"Kingsley," she muttered, rubbing her cheek against his collar. She would not permit the ex–prison apothecary to flaunt his dubious birth in her service.

"I think I can use him as a secretary. He's very sharp."

He was that. And impertinent, telling her that the River-march would receive her, if society turned her out. "He's not trained as a secretary."

"I'm not trained as an envoy," Balthasar pointed out. "And I do need someone who is, even if they won't take the ensorcellment. I thought about speaking to Daniver di Reuther—I know he has been looking for a post—but given the circumstances of Sylvide's death, I don't know."

She would have to visit Sylvide's widower, express her regrets, try to explain if she could, let him hate her if he must. She remembered Sylvide at the archduke's breakfast, talking about visiting an aviary with her young son, spending the day there, to the horror of Daniver's dictatorial mother. She remembered Sylvide throwing her arms around her, understanding nothing except that Vladimer was threatening her dearest friend.

Others had lost more, Balthasar said. Sylvide, Gil di Maurier, Farquhar Broome, Tammorn, the Lightborn high masters she had never met, Tercelle Amberley . . . Ishmael. She had her life and her magic, and the loss of her reputation was a much smaller thing than she had ever imagined it would be, when she was desperately trying to protect it.

She had her children and her husband. As he said, she could be sure of that, even if he was no longer as entirely hers as he had been. She would learn how to maintain that ensorcellment on him herself; she was not leaving it to the Lightborn. She would help him with the Lightborn mages. And she probably wouldn't turn Floria White Hand into a lizard, no matter the temptation.

But she wouldn't tell Balthasar that quite yet.

Epilogue

Ishmael

*N*o relief map carried the island, or none that he had never laid hand or sonn on. It was a crumb of rock dropped from the land's table and forgotten, far to the southeast of the mainland. He supposed, when he regained enough of his reason to do so, that Isolde must once have visited here. Or perhaps one of the others. He must have taken the knowledge from someone.

He did not remember how he found the cave. It was deep enough to escape the sun, had he needed to. From an unknown predecessor he inherited a battered cooking pot and a bent ladle, a small poke of coin, and a blanket gone mildewed and rotten in the damp. The coin suggested that the previous tenant had not simply moved on. He turned it over in his fingers, trying to remember why he would think it at once insignificant and of great importance.

He had not much time for wondering, that first year. He had to survive, which he did by foraging, hunting for anything edible on the scrubby hillsides, under the rocks, and amongst the tide pools. He improvised a hook and a line and he fished, with admittedly mixed success. With a strip torn from his increasingly ragged clothes, he fashioned a slingshot and taught the greedy seagulls to be wary of him.

He knew from the first that there were Darkborn on the island, a village saved from dire inbreeding by the sea and its well-traveled pathways. When the wind was right, he could hear the bells on the buoys rocking in the swell outside the bay, and in the stillness around sunset and dawn, he could hear the sour note of their cracked warning bell. Sometimes he heard their voices as they emerged for their night's fishing. He did not realize they knew about him until, returning from the rocky beach with his thin pickings, he found a wrapped parcel laid across his threshold: a new-caught fish. Subsequent gifts contained more fish, potatoes, better fishhooks and twine, a knife, a rusty ax, a length of cloth, and even an unsigned note telling him where he could find a derelict dory, his for the mending. The kindness, the knowledge that he was not completely outcast, was the greatest gift of all. There was nothing he could give his benefactors in return but his thanks, not even a name.

Until early in the second year, when he heard the village bell ringing an alarm. He was running down the path toward the village before he knew it, knife on belt and ax in hand. The villagers gathered on the beach were too distraught to notice his sudden arrival among them, a gaunt figure with knife-barbered hair and beard, and ragged clothes covered by a length of plaid. Something had come from the sea and seized two of the children collecting crabs and clams on the water's edge. Something . . .

He strode to the edge of the sea, hand coming across to unsling his rifle, sonn hammering the water . . . but only the waves moved, and he had no rifle. . . . He felt some new force spread out from him, vastly more powerful than sonn, thrusting across the waves, down through the water, along the bed of the bay, finding the fading vitality of a child, and beside it, something hungry. Not all Shadowborn were sustained by magic and had died with their makers. He raised his ax and brought it down to cleave sand, and felt the magic cleave water and bone. The smell of brine and blood rolled in with the wind, and with a heave of its skin, like an obedient dog, the sea laid two small bodies onto the packed sand at his feet.

After a few weeks, the rumors died down, the village sages agreeing that the children's lives were a gift of the Mother. But now when the children foraged, one or more of the women or old men stood guard; they knew not to presume on the Mother's generosity. It was a pitifully weak guard, had there been anything dangerous in the bay— which he knew there was not—but he did not interfere. He was too busy. The islanders might give charity to a hapless madman washed up on their shores, but a grown man with some of his wits come home must make shift to feed himself. So he was busy learning how to make his dory watertight, how to braid a line that would not break, how to choose bait, how to weave and repair a net, and how to cast the net from a boat without following it into the water. And how to put up with being teased for getting seasick on waves gentle enough—so they said—to soothe a baby in its cradle. He found their mockery as welcome as their kindness. He also found a name to give them: Ish.

He did not leave his cave to move into the village. He trusted himself to work around them, but not to sleep, not to dream. He took to storing his supplies and provisions outside after once too often finding them strewn around him when he woke. He had too little to break it carelessly. He refused all offers to help him make the cave more livable, to enclose it, for instance, or build furniture. He would not be able to explain a splintered wall, shattered furniture—or, rather, he would not have wanted to find an explanation for such violence. And he needed time alone for the exercises that, years ago, he had learned to focus his small strength, and now had to find a way to apply to the mastery of more power than any sane man could want. The magic seemed bent on emerging, no matter how firmly he tried to sit on it.

Though he supposed he would not be considered sane by most measures, while scratching out an existence on a crumb of rock on the borders of the known world, learning to fish and taking lessons in magic from dead men, bringing to mind everything that the archmages of Darkborn and Lightborn had tried to *gift* him as they died. If he did not master this strength of his, he would be the one breeding monsters and sending out his Call.

In the third year, during the quiet seas of midsummer, he let himself be talked into crewing for a visit to the mainland.

By then he rarely woke in a shambles, and he had been able to equip his cave with a bed and a table and a chair, build a fireplace and chimney, and start on a curved stone wall to enclose the mouth of his cave before winter. He thought he dared risk leaving the island. He needed to risk leaving the island. He was half delirious with island fever. Since his sixteenth year, he had been constantly on the move, and now his world was circumscribed by the shores of one small island and the unfriendly sea. He needed off the island, whose every crack and crevice he knew, and he needed to taste and smell something other than fish. He needed news from the north, needed to know that those who had fought and lived had won what they deserved. He wanted to buy spice seeds, remembering how far to the north and long ago, he had sat in a prison cell and told Lady Telmaine that he wished to retire and grow spices on a remote island.

He needed to know that he had not killed her, too.

So he took ship to the mainland. The port was a third the size of Stranhorne Seaport, but still seemed so crowded to senses and magic after the island that he spent the first day in the fisherman's inn, sleepless, afraid he had made a serious mistake. The second night he forced himself into the market to bargain for seeds, and for the herbs for a recipe against seasickness he'd learned years ago. No surplus of magical strength seemed to suppress his body's conviction that it did not belong on water. After that, he found his way to a sailors' bar and used some of the small stash of coin to order a plate of lamb stew and start a round of drinks and gossip. The north was at peace, he learned as he nursed his beer. The mages had gone south into exile, like the archduke's half brother. Always trouble when two brothers shared the same dam but not the same sire . . . Heads nodded complacently—as if all the men in the room were the sons of the fathers they claimed. There was talk of a railway line running all the way from north to south, crossing the Shadowlands, to terminate a mere two hundred miles along the coast. A new type of steam-driven ship was being built in Minhorne. Ishmael sighed, regretting the want of sailors' wives. The one accomplishment Vladimer had ever conceded women as a sex was their effectiveness as gossips. If Ishmael wanted to know more, know about the people, he would have to go north.

He was not ready. He went back to the island instead, to fish and plant spices in the salt-soaked, barren earth, and then to learn to read the soil and change it. That autumn, the island had its best-ever potato crop, and Ishmael his first meal of seasoned sole. He wondered if he could grow lemons.

The following year, he went again to the mainland, though his purse could not produce lemon trees, and he had greater concerns than farming. The coast had suffered a summer of raids by a lawless band that had established itself in a village to the west. Ishmael, listening with a veteran's ear to the accounts of their atrocities, agreed that the raiders needed to be cleaned out before their numbers and ambition swelled further, but was appalled at the proposed tactics. With considerable bellowing and a show of his marksmanship, rusty as it was, he gained a hearing, and more roaring and storming got him time to start training the scratch troop they mustered. Not to mention to recover some of his old form. But if he could win arguments with men, he could not win them with the seasons; the onset of winter forced their attack long before he felt prepared. Fighting men was grisly, sickening work, and they took far too many casualties for him to call their success a victory. The worst was that he could neither help the wounded nor escape their pain. He stayed awake three days and nights straight, until he was staggering with exhaustion and could sleep like the dead.

The next summer he kept to the island, fished, planted spices and potatoes, guarded the bay, and built the wall that might eventually enclose an orchard. He told himself he might be wise to be circumspect, in case a report had traveled up the coast. He remembered Vladimer saying, "If a man truly intends to disappear, he must give up his old habits." He healed a seagull's broken wing, and then the gashes to his hands from the bird's beak, and stroked away a cancer that was slowly killing the village-hall cat. *Sheep,* he thought. He should keep sheep. If the shepherds in Strumheller were to be believed, sheep were susceptible to every ailment known. Sheep would give him practice.

He was sitting on a barrel outside his cave one night in late summer, mending a net. Though the night was still clear, a gale was rising in the west, and only the hardy and hungry had gone far beyond the bay. He was neither, but he was keeping vigil over those flecks of vitality in the cold sea. So it was that he sensed the ship running before the wind, even before he heard its passing bell. Sensed the ship, its living crew, and its two passengers, and that familiar, magical touch, gloriously matured and refined.

He stood up, the net sliding unnoticed from his hands. He drew a deep breath of the storm-heavy wind, aware of the sudden cessation of pain from a wound that had not closed until now.

<Lady Telmaine. How good it is t'speak to you again.>

About the Author

Alison Sinclair is the author of *Legacies, Blueheart*, and *Cavalcade* (which was nominated for the Arthur C. Clark Award), as well as *Darkborn* and *Lightborn*. She lives in Montreal.

Connect Online

www.alisonsinclair.com

twitter.com/alixinc

ALSO AVAILABLE

FROM

ALISON SINCLAIR

Lightborn

The Darkborn aristocracy has rejected magic, viewing the pursuit of science as the only worthy goal. But Lady Telmaine Hearne does not have that luxury. She has kept her own powers secret, fearful of being ruined in society—until her husband Balthasar draws her into a conspiracy to protect the archduke and his brother against a magical enemy. But who will protect them from her?

On the other side of sunrise, the Lightborn not only embrace magic, but depend on it for their survival. In the courts of the Lightborn, the assassin Floria White Hand is one of the prince's most trusted guards, as well as Balthasar Hearne's oldest friend. When the prince dies in darkness, Floria is suspected and must flee to the Darkborn for her life…

"Alison Sinclair's writing is addictive and elegant."
—Lane Robins, author of *Maledicte*

Available wherever books are sold or at
penguin.com